ARLEN'S GUN

A NOVEL *of* MEN AT WAR

EDGAR DOLEMAN

authorHOUSE®

AuthorHouse™
1663 Liberty Drive
Bloomington, IN 47403
www.authorhouse.com
Phone: 833-262-8899

Published by AuthorHouse 11/18/2020

ISBN: 978-1-6655-0860-5 (sc)
ISBN: 978-1-6655-0858-2 (hc)
ISBN: 978-1-6655-0859-9 (e)

Library of Congress Control Number: 2020923361

Print information available on the last page.

Any people depicted in stock imagery provided by Getty Images are models, and such images are being used for illustrative purposes only. Certain stock imagery © Getty Images.

This book is printed on acid-free paper.

CONTENTS

To those men whom fate took from the cities,
towns, and farms of America
and put on the ground in the forests and fields of Vietnam
to fight a war they hardly understood;
trained in arms, but not particularly for what they would actually face;
led by young men only a little older;
and directed by leaders with little more
experience in that war than they;
but who,
in the crucible of the fog of war,
far, far more often than not
revealed a nobility of courage and compassion
perhaps unique to the American ethos;
to be remembered and not forgotten

ACKNOWLEDGMENTS

I owe an unpayable debt of gratitude to my late wife, Donna, who encouraged me to write in every way. Likewise, I am indebted to my dear friend Pauli Dillard, who got me living again and pushed me to finish this book. I especially thank Gene Underwood and Bill Johnson, Vietnam combat veterans who, on reading my first drafts, greatly encouraged me.

PREFACE

One night in the forests of South Vietnam, I had cause to make use of the fire support from an AC-47 gunship, at which point this story begins. Of all the forms of fire support the American military could offer, nothing struck me as so almost supernatural as the fire from an AC-47, which seemed to come down like the fiery sword of an avenging angel in the darkest hour of the night. Yet that fearful image is linked in memory to others—instances of fear and courage, anger and compassion, dumb luck and clever thinking, love and hate, and strength and weakness. It is perhaps this juxtaposition of the great power of weapons and the weaknesses and strengths of flesh that gradually prompted this story.

Although this story is fiction and the names, places, and story lines are fictitious, many of the acts of individuals that make up the story are drawn from actual events, pulled from their historical context in order to better ground this story in reality.

Experiencing such an event is like experiencing a tornado. The air is filled with mind-numbing sounds and deadly debris, and every instinct screams, "Run! Hide! Find a hole!" Yet for either defenders or attackers to obey these instincts is to fail. Sometimes it is rage at the circumstance that lifts the head and aims the weapon; most often it is a blend of fear for one's own safety amplified by fear for the safety of one's comrades who count on him, and he on them, guided by training

The numbered military units named are fictional. However, it is not possible to assign a realistic designation that did not actually exist somewhere at some time in the US Army. So the named units do exist or existed at some time, but they have no particular relationship to the war in Vietnam, and in that sense they are also fictional. I also took the liberty of reducing the number of members of the crew of the AC-47 in the story to better focus on the characters.

The story includes military slang and terms from the Vietnam War. There is a glossary at the back of the book. Readers not familiar with the military in that era might find it helpful.

CHAPTER 1

SPOOKY 45

Arlen Washington stared out the window of the hooch into the night. The hooch was a prefab one-story barrack sitting on the air base at the coastal city of Nha Trang, Republic of Vietnam. It was dark inside the hooch. The air conditioner had rattled off into silence, and now Arlen could hear the sounds of the air base, of whining turbines and muttering pistons. The darkness outside was emphasized by pricks and threads of light reaching through the rain, distorted by the rivulets running down the glass.

A voice came to him out of the darkness in the hooch. "Hey, man, you okay?"

Arlen Washington's body jerked. "What?"

"You okay? You was shouting."

"What you talking about?" Washington replied sharply.

"You was shouting. Woke me up."

"Shouting?" he said in disbelief. "What you mean?"

1

"You wanna know? You was shouting 'Fuck you, Big Ma, fuck everybody!'"

Arlen balled his fists, realizing Jack was right. He must have been shouting aloud. It had just felt like it was all in his head. "Bullshit, Jack!"

"That's a fact, man."

"Fuck off. Leave me alone."

"I did. Till your shoutin' woke me up." After a brief pause, Jack's voice came again. "Aren't you on a mission tonight? I heard Timmy come in and call you. That was before I fell asleep. How long you been standing there, man?"

Arlen looked at the faintly glowing hands of his watch. He was close to missing his flight. "Not fair," he blurted. "Nothin's fucking fair." He flipped the light on, ran past Jack's bunk to his own locker, threw on his poncho and his boonie hat, grabbed an M16 rifle and two loaded magazines, and ran out into the rain.

He had missed the crew truck, and it was a half-mile trek to the waiting AC-47 that would give him another uncomfortable ride through the night. About halfway, the rain let up, leaving behind a fine drizzle that was little more than a falling mist, and Arlen stopped, panting, partly from running but mostly from a sudden, sharp pain in his mind.

The rain had let up, but the night seemed darker than ever. There on the tarmac, the night was pierced by countless tiny shards of light—stray beams from windows, headlights, runway lights, and beacons—ricocheting off the rain-polished tarmac, windshields, propeller blades, and even the black rubber tires, rendering objects into fragments of things etched on the night, emphasizing its darkness like sequins on an ebony shroud.

As he had run, Arlen had been thinking about how much trouble he might or might not get into for being late, but the pain of the new, unbidden thought pushed worry aside so violently it almost made him stumble. Earlier that day, a friend, maybe his only real friend, had remarked in passing, "Sorry to hear about Big Ma, bro." He had had no idea what Jason was talking about and had just shrugged and walked off, but the reference to Big Ma made him turn back and ask Jason what he had heard. There never were letters from home for him, although Jason regularly got letters from his mother and sister. Big Ma had dropped dead of a massive heart attack while walking home with a bag of groceries. Arlen had barely responded before locking the news away in a mental closet with a key of indifference, as he did with every bad thing in life.

Now, there on the tarmac, Arlen imagined the cans rolling away, the eggs breaking, pills scattering from a broken bottle. He saw her again: thighs like tree trunks, ass like a pair of beach balls, boobs like watermelons, her black hair shot with gray, rigidly styled and curled, framing the big, round face. But driving the imagery were echoes of an enveloping, comforting warmth—a balm for a child's fears and pains found nowhere else. Now the old woman was gone. Just fucking gone. And no one had told him.

Arlen shook his head, gritting his teeth. Now *he'd* better be gone too, into the shit of a long night of noisy, cold, damp winds. It was not fair. Nothing was. Jason was now in his warm dry rack, not like Arlen about to be late for another pointless night boring holes in the dark.

The jeep had its canvas top on, but the canvas doors and sides were missing. As a consequence, the right leg of air force captain Eddie McLaughlin's flight suit was soaked by the time the jeep pulled to a stop and he got out—just as the rain eased to a thin, fine mist hardly distinguishable from the air's normal heavy humidity. The jeep took off. Captain McLaughlin hefted his flight bag and smiled. He couldn't help but yield to an anticipatory smile every time he saw the plane that seemed so tangibly his. After all, stenciled on the nose several feet above his head in bold, flowing script was the name *MaryAnn*—his wife, who regularly claimed, in spite of his protests, that she was only his second love. The name was invisible in the dark, but the small, somewhat rectangular window above and behind it was evident, as was the classic outline of the nose that had rolled out of the factory around the year Captain McLaughlin was born.

As always, the plane seemed to be looking to the sky as if eager to fly, reminding him of his setter sitting on his tail and staring out the sidelight by the front door, quiveringly eager to race outside. The AC-47 did sit on its tail. In World War II, the Douglas DC-3—perhaps the world's first truly successful airliner in the 1930s—was modified for the military as the C-47 to haul cargo, passengers, and paratroops around the world. Still in service in Vietnam, some had been modified again into combat aircraft, the A in AC-47 standing for "armed."

"Hola, Capitan!" The voice came from the open cargo door and belonged to Technical Sergeant Hector Pastor-Villanueva, the loadmaster, who was usually addressed as Chief.

Captain Eddie McLaughlin glanced up at the short, stocky figure and blunt features that echoed a lineage seemingly unchanged from the days of the Inca empire in the high mountains of Peru. "Yo, mi pastor!" Eddie shouted back. We good to go?"

"Mas o menos, mi lider maximo! Ammo and flares on board. Otis is about done racking and stacking it. Fueling's complete. *Menos part*, missing Washington. Again."

"I think he's on his way, sir!" the higher, almost prepubescent, voice of Airman Timmy Otis called out. "I hollered at him, and he was dressed and vertical."

"Well, he missed his ride," Chief added.

"What the hell, Chief!" Irritation etched Captain McLaughlin's voice. "Much as I'd like to do without him, with Mitchell still in hospital with that damn FUO, we need him!" McLaughlin's jaw clamped for a moment before he added, "What the hell's wrong with him?"

Just then the jeep reappeared, and Captain McLaughlin's copilot, Lieutenant Tom Blagget unfolded his long, lanky frame from under the canvas top and joined him under the shelter of the wing. "Got the weather. Just as you suspected, dark, rainy, overcast on top of overcast, and no change in the next twelve hours except from black of night to gray of day."

"Of course," Eddie said. He looked at his watch. "We're supposed to be wheels up at twenty-three hundred! And Washington's maybe AWOL!" he said loudly for the crew's benefit. Then, in a normal tone, he stated, "Let's check our little lady out."

"Washington again?"

"Yeah, yeah. And Mitchell's still out with FUO. Again."

"Fever of unknown origin. Ain't medical science great? FUO. As an acronym, it at least sounds curable. Like somebody knows what it is."

"Lucky we have mechanics for our little lady here and don't need doctors."

Moments later, Tom and Eddie were walking slowly around the outside of the aircraft, Eddie with a flashlight and Tom with a checklist. Tom was calling out each item and then muttering to himself.

"You doing your rosary thing again, Tom? Think that helps?"

"Like this checklist, Cap. A form of communication." Tom gave the clipboard holding the checklist a brief wave. "This baby talks with the builders of a beautiful, complex machine, sort of bringing us in tune with their vision of how it should work. Guess I feel the rosary's like that, only it talks with the Creator of all, you know, maybe bringing me more in tune with His vision." He shrugged, giving out a slightly sheepish chuckle. "Maybe," he added, and he then called out the next item on the plane's checklist.

"Could be, could be, Tom. But right now, we have one thing to focus on. One thing—our little lady here."

"One reason I like flying with you. You really focus."

"Drifting minds can soon be dead minds, my friend. We can bullshit upstairs when we've got nothing better to do than wait for a call."

Arlen Washington slogged into view, glistening in his poncho, his lower legs soaked. Chief announced his arrival by shouting, "Washington! About time! Get your ass in here! We've got work to do, and we're running late!"

The "running late" part wasn't true, but it served Washington right. Eddie muttered, "Don't know how Chief puts up with him."

"Can't you get him replaced?" Tom asked.

"Chief hasn't asked. Washington's his responsibility; I know." Eddie waved his flashlight at the night. "Mine too, overall, but hell, maybe Chief sees something we don't. Or he's got more patience." Then Eddie put thoughts about Washington aside. Glancing at Tom's clipboard, he asked, "Next item?" and gave all his attention back to the plane.

Spooky 45 was the radio call sign of Eddie's AC-47 gunship. A few minutes before 2300 hours, Spooky 45 was given clearance to taxi. The old plane gracefully pirouetted and taxied onto the runway. Tom called out the pre-takeoff checklist. Engines and controls were given a final check, and Eddie called for takeoff clearance. After receiving it, he pushed the throttles forward while standing on the brakes. The plane shuddered as the engines strained to pull her forward. He released the brakes, and Spooky 45 began to roll, smoothly accelerating until the tail lifted and the crew in back felt the floor come horizontal and the wind noise in the open cargo door and windows grew almost to a shriek. Then they were airborne, climbing and banking sedately away from the airfield.

The US Air Force was constantly experimenting with motley collections of unconventional weapons. Originally, Spooky 45 had been fitted with ten .30-caliber machine guns of World War II vintage, but these had soon been replaced with three General Electric GAU-2/M134 miniguns. Each of these new guns could pour out up to six thousand rounds a minute, compared to the six hundred rounds of the old machine guns. They could do this because each gun had a cluster of six barrels. When a machine gun is fired, it automatically ejects the spent cartridge case and then loads and fires the next cartridge. As long as the trigger is depressed, it repeats the cycle at a rate, depending on the design, of five hundred to over one thousand rounds a minute. With its six barrels, a minigun was the equivalent of six regular machine guns. This firepower gave the AC-47 a nickname from a popular song of the time—"Puff the Magic Dragon."

On Spooky 45, one of the new miniguns had been damaged and had been replaced with a slightly different model, a Dillon Aero M134D-H. It had the same capability as the General Electrics, but this model had handles, for it was designed to be used both on fixed-aim mounts, like the General Electrics, or on flexible mounts to be manually aimed and controlled. This was the gun mounted in the cargo door.

Arlen Washington was the first to unstrap from his seat. He rose and stepped to the gun mounted in the cargo door. It was his favorite of the three because it had handles.

Arlen gripped the handles as if it in fact were on a flexible mount, his shoulders jerking left and right as if he were trying to make it swivel. "You in love with that gun, Washington?" Chief shouted. Washington didn't react, and Chief shouted again.

"Ought to put this one on a better mount, Chief!" Arlen shouted back over the roar of the engines and wind whipping across the open cargo doorway. "What'll let you aim it, man!"

"The captain aims it with the plane!"

"So let him aim them two GEs. Then I could use this one on a different target, see? Get two targets at the same time, Chief, right?" Chief didn't respond except with a short bark of a laugh almost lost in the noise. Washington pressed on. "Why not, Chief? This one's got a simpler mount. Easy to change. And the power cables and ammunition feed chutes. Simpler. Easy to, you know, get to shift."

"Thought it all out, hey?" Chief shouted.

Washington looked back at Chief and grinned. "Sure, sure, Chief. It's an idea, you know. Just an idea. But why not, Chief?"

Washington and Airman Timmy Otis were gunners, but they had nothing to do with actually aiming and firing the guns. Their job was to keep them working and fed with ammunition. The pilot was the real gunner. He handled aiming and firing.

When Chief did not comment, Washington turned his gaze to the coal-black night outside, his mind on a vision. It began with a black four-door 1968 Lincoln Town Car, one with a leather-covered roof over the rear half of the passenger compartment and a huge trunk. The trunk was filled with ammunition, and a large hole was cut out of the roof with a sliding cover like a sunroof. The windows were tinted so one could not see in from the outside. The gun, by some as yet vague mechanical means, could telescope up through the roof and swing in any direction. Sometimes he was cruising the streets, clearing his hood of gangs and their cars, and sometimes he was penetrating into gang territory, blasting their hideouts. He'd heard one could actually get Lincolns with bulletproof glass and armored doors and such. Invincible. That's what he would be.

Adrift in his fantasy, Arlen was pulled back into the reality of the night in Vietnam by the odd sense he was being stared at. He looked back. Chief was looking at a manifest, but Otis's eyes were shifting as if

7

he had indeed been staring. Arlen thought back to a conversation in the mess a couple of weeks earlier. He, Timmy Otis, and Lemuel Mitchell had come in late, and the mess, while still open, was mostly empty. They went down the serving line together, but when Timmy started to sit with them, Arlen told him he and Lem needed to talk privately, so Timmy took his tray to an empty behind them.

Arlen and Lemuel began talking in low, secretive voices, but soon Lem's, and then Arlen's, volume rose with excitement and laughter. By that point they'd been imagining how to mount the minigun in a big Lincoln and how much ammo the big trunk might hold. Their voices dropped again as the discussion shifted to actually getting the gun home. Arlen knew there was traffic in getting souvenir guns out of country, but when it came to one as big as a minigun, Lem had laughed, saying it was impossible and asking what kind of place home was to think it needed *cleaning up* with a minigun. Arlen laughed back, hiding a sudden hurt and doubt, claiming there was always a way, as if he already had a plan.

As Spooky 45 droned on, Arlen's thoughts about the gun picked up where he'd left off on the last mission. This was the problem of not being caught. Jason had assured him he would be, especially as Arlen himself had confessed no one on the crew liked him. He'd automatically be suspect *numero uno*. He would have to figure out a way to steal it so that it looked as if he couldn't have done it. No bright ideas had come to him, but he didn't worry too much about it. There was plenty of time, as his one-year tour was nowhere near over, and who knew what opportunities could come up. Anything could happen. His last thought about this was immediately followed by an inner response: *Yeah, anything can happen, but what usually does happen sucks.*

He let his mind drift to the easier parts, such as dismounting and disassembling it and figuring out how to get it home. This last part he thought he had solved, or at least he had an approach—or, rather, two approaches. He'd learned that one could ship souvenirs home. Jason had bought a big ceramic elephant that was supposed to be some kind of side table or maybe sit in a yard—if one had a yard. The cool thing was it was hollow. He'd just have to figure out a way to cut a hole in the bottom and seal it up again, invisibly. But there was one problem. Something like Jason's elephant could hold some of the gun's components but was not big enough to hold the barrel assembly. He'd have to find something else. A second possibility was to somehow get involved in the drug smuggling he'd heard about. If they could smuggle drugs, well, hell, they could surely smuggle his gun, once he figured out how to steal it. This second option had a drawback, though. There was a big risk down that path; whoever ran the operation would likely want to keep the gun and stiff Arlen—or maybe something worse.

Arlen lost his threads of thought and shivered. At several thousand feet, the sodden night wind was chilling, especially through wet clothing. It was as if nothing, absolutely nothing, was out there except wind crying in misery and, somewhere below, unseen, invisible bad guys and good guys, hiding in the jungle, cursing the rain. That's the way it was. He snorted and turned his mind from the dark to the light within, riding high down the street, laughing at the neighborhood rats as they turned and ran.

They reached altitude and began to cruise around their planned loiter box, waiting for a call for fire support. In the cockpit, Captain Eddie McLaughlin peered through the gunsight by his seat that was aimed out the left side window, and he delicately fingered the controls for the guns. There was nothing to see, much less to shoot at. He was just awakening muscle memory like a batter taking practice swings by the dugout. After a minute, he leaned back in his seat, scanned the instrument panel, and enjoyed the pleasures of the plane performing its wonderful magic of not falling. The cockpit was much quieter than the cargo bay; it was insulated, and the door leading back to the cargo bay was closed.

Eddie turned to his copilot, Lieutenant Tom Blagget. "You know, Tom, being shorthanded, it just occurred to me, being short two crew is equivalent to what, four hundred pounds? We could have four hundred pounds more ammo loaded. That's what, like, six, seven thousand rounds?"

"Whoopee," Tom replied. "A little over two minutes' worth with all guns at low speed."

"Two minutes could count. Could be decisive."

"Yeah, I guess sometimes a minute can make all the difference in the world." Tom shrugged and looked backward. He could dimly see the empty seat for the flight engineer and the navigator's table in the small compartment just beyond the open cockpit door and past the open door to the cargo bay, he could make out the blunt shapes of the gun housings, but not much more. They blocked any view of the crew.

Shaking his head, he looked over at Eddie. "I wasn't thinking about being shorthanded. We're not really suffering from missing a navigator and flight engineer. It's not like we're crossing an ocean and navigating by the stars. I was thinking more about, oh, missing the wrong hands. Like why couldn't it have been Washington out with the FUO instead of Mitchell?"

"Technically, Mitchell's excess. Gunner in training. But yeah, life'd be smoother for Chief back in the cargo bay with Airman Mitchell instead of Airman Kind of General Pain in the Ass."

"Sort of surprised he wasn't just drafted into the army."

Eddie chuckled. "We're special, but not that special. Chief told me Washington's got a buddy here. Grew up together, enlisted together, came here together. Jason something—a clerk in headquarters, apparently well thought of. Anyway, this kid apparently had planned to go air force and pushed Washington to get good enough grades in high school to enable them to enlist in the air force before they got drafted. Washington was at least smart enough to go along, and here he is."

"Great. Kid has buddies: Mitchell, who's laid back, easygoing, smiles at most everything, pitches in with a will, and who everyone likes; and Jason, who's well thought of. Yet no one seems to think well of or like Washington? How's that happen?"

"No idea," Eddie said, and he nudged Tom. "Turn coming up; want to take it?"

"I'll have the aircraft." Tom made a gesture of gripping the wheel.

"Roger," Eddie acknowledged.

Spooky 45 began to bank in a gentle turn to plow the night in a different direction. "Different backgrounds? Maybe Mitchell." Tom shrugged. "I don't know."

"Chief says Washington grew up in some crummy side of Baltimore, and Mitchell in a dirt-poor part of Annapolis. Sound similar."

"I know some great guys from crappy backgrounds and some real shits born to privilege. Guess the Lord works in mysterious ways." Tom reached over the center console between them and fiddled with the trim. Eddie closed his eyes and concentrated on the subtle sensation he felt as the plane became a tiny fraction more aerodynamically efficient.

Eddie scanned the instruments again and then looked at his map. "More like poker to me," he said. "You don't control the cards you're dealt. It's all in how you play the hand. Take a guy like Chief. Born in some barrio in Peru. Lousy hand, good player."

Tom grunted. "Must have had some help. Someone got him here."

"Interesting story, actually. His mother died when he was still young. His dad met a woman whose parents had immigrated to the States. Apparently her dad was some kind of staffer in the Peruvian embassy—made him sort of upper class. So upper-class daughter visits the old country to see extended family, falls in love with the gardener, Chief's dad. Rest is romantic history."

Tom laughed. "So Chief got to trade in some bad cards and lucked out on the draw. See? The Lord works in mysterious ways."

Both scanned the instruments and noted the next turn coming up, and after making it, Eddie said, "Speaking of how to play your hand, you planning to stay in the air force after your commitment?"

"Well, I thought I was, probably, but now I think probably maybe not." Eddie said nothing, prompting Tom to go on. "I mean, I love being a pilot—well, a copilot now—but you know, flying in general. And what's more exciting than flying in the air force? Except maybe being a bush pilot or something like that?"

"Yup."

"I mean, you know, but air force flying comes with guns, missiles, and bombs, and bush pilots don't have to sweat that. Okay in my mind in, like, noble, righteous wars, but frankly, I can't figure this one out. Something vague and dingy about it. Shit, we can't say we're winning, but we've apparently already decided to start kind of withdrawing … so what's the point? It's kind of confusing, and that's a problem with me."

"True enough. But we gotta have a little faith, right? We go to the doctor, he says I'm healthy or he says I'm sick, I believe him. Put my car in for service, mechanic says I need an alignment, I believe him. So are generals that different?"

Tom snorted. "Live by faith. Parents taught me that, priests say it, the Bible says it. Faith in God, sure, but faith in a war? Or the politicians who make it?"

"Yup. Hey, Tom, I'm afraid the four-stars don't keep me in the loop. And these are four-star questions, and you and I—we're not even close to having access to one star's worth of facts. 'Ours is not to reason why.'"

"Yeah, yeah, 'Ours is but to do and die.'"

"'Charge of the Light Brigade.'" Eddie, like Tom, had been gazing at the instruments. "Next turn coming up. My turn. I've got the aircraft."

"Roger." The plane banked smoothly to left. "My sister's a sophomore at UCLA. She thinks I'm a baby killer."

"Well, my friend, she hasn't got access to any more facts than we do; most likely a lot less. But she does have access to a lot of pressure. Cut her some slack."

"Oh, I do; I do. My wife's kind of on her side too."

"Love conquers all."

"True enough, boss. So far, so good. Still, it bothers me, you know. And gets in the way of making career choices."

Another turn came up and was taken in silence. Eddie then said, "Radio altimeter says we're only at five hundred feet."

"Hills are higher at this end of our box."

"Can we go up another five hundred? Charlie's guns can be on top of the hills too."

Tom peered at the map and got on a radio. A minute later, Eddie put the plane into a gentle climb.

"You know, Tom, if this war's fucked up ... hell, all wars are fucked up. I mean, like, in the fundamentals, whatever they are, then those fuckups are on the backs of the generals and politicians. For me, it's all and only about us being up here, making it more likely they down there get home in one piece."

"I know, I know. Same here. I like—still, I think ... I think I'd rather be a bush pilot."

"Grab the fun and don't get shot at?"

"Something like that."

"So where?" Eddie realized that his own fantasy was not far from just that—man and flying machine at their most elemental: rugged, rugged, rugged; man, machine, environment. Yahoo. "Africa? Alaska? Canada? South America? Antarctica?"

Tom chuckled. "That's the problem. All sound like fun, but can't think of any of them being good for family life."

"My problem too. Fall in love, get married, get a family, and suddenly one day you realize you've got to grow up. It's not just me, the boy with his toys, anymore. Closest thing is airlines or stay in the air force, I guess."

"So which is it for you?"

"Leaning air force."

"Airlines pay a lot more money."

"Yeah, but the biggest benefit I see is air force bases—good hospitals, commissaries, family housing, security, good schools. Wherever you get based or move to, you're still part of a community. Got to balance that with the ton of money. And the flying's more fun, most likely."

"Like tonight?" Tom chuckled as he shivered. Even in the cockpit, at several thousand feet and with rain-soaked trouser legs, they felt the chill.

"Hey, day or night, any time with an airplane is a good time."

Captain McLaughlin switched to the intercom. "No missions in our queue, gentlemen. Looks like we'll be boring holes in the night, least for a while,"

"Okay, Captain," Chief replied. "We're locked and loaded back here. All cool."

"Roger that, Chief. You guys enjoy the ride. Out."

Sergeant Hector Pastor-Villanueva stood up, taking a wide stance on his slightly bowed legs, and strode slowly up and down the length of the cargo bay, examining the guns, ammunition feed chutes, and ammo boxes. He walked like some old seaman after a life on a rolling deck, but his walk came from the steep trails in the rugged mountains around Cuzco he had grown up on. He had inspected it all while still on the ground, but now he did it again, just in case something had shifted from the motions of the plane. To this point, the flight had been perfectly smooth—no turbulence at all. Still, he took no chances.

Satisfied, Hector paused to look at his two gunners: Otis, sitting on a bench seat, looking alert and almost eager; and Arlen, his back turned, hanging onto the gun, staring out at the night. *What a pair*, he thought. Both were about the same height, a little shorter than average for young men, barely taller than himself. Arlen was lean but had beautifully proportioned broad shoulders and narrow hips; a narrow head with a dramatic, almost aristocratic nose; and a wide mouth showing, on the very rare occasions he smiled, beautiful white teeth—all, Hector thought, a result of great genes and inadequate nutrition as a boy. Otis was kind of the opposite. His rounder face was not striking—not really handsome but what girls might call sweet. His body shape was not striking either, with shoulders and chest a tad too narrow, and hips a tad too wide. With a sigh, Hector sat down beside Otis and shouted, "Hey, Washington! Come here and have a seat, man!"

Washington shifted his feet but made no move to join Chief. Hector shouted again. "Nothing to see out there, man! Looks like a quiet night! Come on and have a seat!"

After a moment, Arlen Washington decided that was probably an order. Reluctantly, he left his gun and sidled across the cargo bay to sit next to Chief. "What's up, boss?"

"Chief," Chief corrected. "Hey, I guess you got your problems, man," he shouted loudly enough to be heard, "but whatever; you're part of this team, you know? An' we want you as part of this team. Make it a lot easier for you and the rest of us we be a team, you know?"

"Yeah, suppose."

"So what's going' on?"

"Nothin', Chief. Just makin' circles in the night over the fuckin' jungle is what."

"Don't mean that. Mean with you. Like, heard you lost a relative, like, someone close? That so?" Washington didn't respond. Chief waited. Getting no response, he said, "Okay, sorry. Don't mean to pry where it hurts. How about happy stuff. You got a girl at home?"

"Shit, got me a girl for every night of the week!" He straightened and shrugged sharply.

"No shit? Hey, Otis! You got a girl?"

"Well, yeah, Chief. You know. Told you about Merry!"

"Jus' one, man? Only one?" Washington laughed.

"All I need!" Otis snapped.

Chief rubbed his eyes. "So! Washington! Your girlfriends got names?"

"Sure! Let's see; there's Tanya, Della, and ... and Ida—Ida Mae, I mean." Washington dragged the names out slowly.

"You making those names up!" Hector joked. Arlen snorted derisively and looked away. Chief changed the subject. "So what you guys wanna do when your tours are up? Re-up?" Chief gave the last word a joking inflection.

"Maybe!" Otis said quickly. He then added, "I really want to go to college!"

"Washington?" Chief asked.

"Not like Timmy Kiss-Ass! Get the fuck outta here an' outta uniforms!"

"Hey! No call for names like that! So you'll be getting out and do what? College?"

"What good's that gonna do a guy like me?" Chief started to say something, but Washington cut him off. "Yeah, it's benefits! Free money, I know! I'll find a way to use 'em too. Might go to a technical school. Recruiter said I could learn some high-payin' shit! Maybe!"

Hector turned to Otis, tapping him on the shoulder. "Might re-up, eh?"

"I don't know. Maybe. I got time. But I sure won't do it to kiss ass!"

"I know that. What you want out of college? You, like, got an interest?"

"I don't know! One reason I might re-up—have more time to figure it out!"

"That can be a plan. You, like, engaged?"

"To Merry? Sort of. She said okay, but she didn't want to make it formal until I got back." Otis rubbed his chin for a moment. "That kind of hurt my feelings! But she's probably right. I think girls are more practical than boys!"

"You got that right! They seem all romantic, but the good ones? Underneath they're practical! Always practical! Good thing too!"

The need to shout over the roar of engines and wind made it hard to just chat, and after a while they fell silent. When the silence had dragged on for a while, Washington took it as permission to leave.

Back at the minigun with handles, Washington stared into the night through the barely visible cargo door, killing minutes, thinking nothing, feeling nothing. Then a sharp pain seemed to grab his chest—a ghostly pain touching no muscle, bone, or nerve, yet as real as a punch or the cut of a knife. The image of Big Ma burst into his mind, and for a few moments, he could not get rid of it. The pain came in spasms of loss, longing, grief, and anger welling up one after another like surf on a beach. He felt anger at fate, at those who could have sent word but didn't, at those who'd given Big Ma hard times, at Big Ma for letting herself die, and at time for making him outgrow her embrace, turning her into a memory, something gone and lost already.

He became aware that his hands hurt. It took a moment to realize he was holding the handles of the gun in a death grip, his emotions seeming to surge through them and out the gun like a stream of silent, invisible bullets sweeping away a past that wouldn't quite die. His body slumped a little, and he let go of the gun, spreading his hands apart and wriggling his fingers to ease the cramps.

Hector Pastor-Villanueva had watched Washington go, wondering why he liked to stand at the stupid gun. It was sure as hell not the most comfortable place, close to the chilly, wet eddies of the keening wind. Yet on almost every mission, that is exactly where he preferred to be. After a moment, Hector noticed a difference. Washington's shoulders were not twitching from his fantasies of aiming and firing the gun. He was as rigid as a statue. He thought of a pool toy he'd bought his son for playing in the inflatable backyard pool not long before he'd had to ship out. He'd used a tire pump and overfilled it, making it as rigid as Washington now looked—too rigid for his boy's little hands to easily grasp. That's what Arlen seemed like—filled to near-busting, but not with air—with something toxic. Grief over the relative that died? Anger, for sure, but at what only God knew. But it was trapped inside, cutting him off from everyone else, except maybe Mitchell.

That is a puzzle, Hector thought, *those two boys being so different.* Mitchell was friendly with everyone—always smiling, it seemed, and always eager to please. Hector knew it could be some defense or coping thing, maybe from being bullied a lot or, as he hoped, maybe from Mitchell's true nature. Maybe he was just one of God's true innocents.

Hector sighed. In his years in the service, he'd learned two things. The first was that the service was made up of people from all cultural and economic backgrounds, though damn few from the upper crust, and that one can never fully penetrate a different background; it's hard enough to put one's own background in perspective. The other was that all that diversity was equally human, and building human-level connections bridged gulfs of culture and background to build teams. Arlen Washington wasn't open to any connections. Maybe a guy like Mitchell could get through, but Lemuel Mitchell was sick—again. He was a great kid but had a weak constitution. And Washington? He was a healthy kid, and a smart one, but was locked in his own closet. Hector wondered sadly if there was anyone or anything that could unlock that door.

CHAPTER 2

DARK NIGHT

The voice in the headphones finally said, "Out." Eddie switched to the intercom to address the crew. "Gentlemen, looks like we have a mission. Got some grunts under heavy attack. Now we just have to find them." The corners of his mouth twitched—not down with anger or up in irony, but with a grimace as if from a sharp pain, caused by fear for men dying just because he was fucking lost. He tried to imagine being down there, a soldier in the jungle—a cauldron of chaos—while he, in the clean air above the mud and bugs, enjoyed order and control, an integration of man, machine, and the laws of physics. Someone had to be down there in the mud because, in the jargon of the day, they were the "point of the spear." Puffery, maybe, but while the point is the smallest part of a spear, it is the whole purpose of the spear. To Eddie, that fact made it vital that he be where he was needed and not be a lost fuckup. "So Tom, where are they from here?"

"I've marked the coordinates. They're higher in the hills. We should still have five hundred feet to spare over the highest peak in that area, and as to a heading, hold on."

"'Should.' You know I don't like that word. Don't forget the artillery fans. Don't want to fly into a cannon shell."

"Right. RDF says we're about ten klicks out. Take a heading two niner five."

"Okay, turning two niner five now."

Tom peered at the needles of two radio direction finders, tapping one and then the other. He double-checked the map and the artillery fans marked on it. These fans were the zones of fire support reported by artillery units. Anywhere within the fan, it was possible, if one were unlucky enough, to run into a shell on its way to a target. Satisfied, Tom set a radio frequency. "We're on the ground unit's channel. Coordinates they sent are in the fan of a one-five-five battery near their max range." He turned his eyes back to the blackness outside. After a moment, his lips moved, but no sound came out. A moment later, he said, "Wait. Flashes one o'clock, maybe three, four klicks? Could be them."

Eddie called, "Queen of Hearts, Queen of Hearts, this is Spooky Four-Five, over."

"Off with their heads," Tom said. "We're approaching the fan. Turn two four five."

"Roger, two four five, coming up." Eddie called again, "Queen of Hearts, Queen of Hearts, this is Spooky Four-Five. Over."

The radio erupted in a static-blurred reply. "Hearts Six. Over." The words were fast and clipped; the speaker sounded breathless. "Roger, Queen of Hearts. Understand you could use some fire support. We're maybe two klicks southeast of you if you are currently under fire. We got a glimpse of some flashes—tracers. Over."

"This is Hearts Six. Yeah, that's us. I hear you, I think. What are you? Over."

Eddie thumbed the radio transmit button. "Spooky Four-Five. We are Puff the Magic Dragon, otherwise known as an AC-47 gunship. We are old and slow, but we can fly all night and put up to eighteen thousand rounds a minute where you want. Over."

"Holy shit! How do we mark for you? Over!"

"Four Five. Mark your center, give us a radius from the mark, and we'll hose a circle of hell around you. Or give me a radius and direction to the hot part of the circle, and we'll send that part to hell and stay around longer. Over."

"Hearts Six. I can make a fire, put down an orange panel. That do?"

"Long as we can see it. You have artillery firing for you?"

"I did. All that can reach us is a One-five-five battery. We're pretty much at their max range, and to get into us, they have to fire high angle, which means a shell will land anywhere within two hundred meters of the aim point. So, shit, I can't … can't use them for close support. Over."

"Okay. Can you still hear us? Over."

"Hearts Six. Yeah, but you sound like you're heading away. Over."

"We're circling. Let me know when you hear us approaching, and give me a bearing on the sound. Soon as you do that, make sure no artillery is incoming. We'll make a pass over you, drop a flare, and identify your marker. Then we'll swing around ready to put fire where you need it. Over."

A minute later, Queen of Hearts gave Spooky 45 a direction and shortly after changed it by a few degrees. Spooky 45 dropped as low as seemed safe and passed over the position of Queen of Hearts. The lowest clouds had broken up enough for them to see the ground unit's marker. Eddie put the plane in a gentle, timed turn. As he did, the cockpit door opened and the loadmaster, Sergeant Pastor-Villanueva informed them, "Ground fire, boss. Sounded like a hit in the tail section. Small arms."

"Small arms. Always a sign of clearing skies," Tom said brightly.

"You'd find a silver lining in a toilet," Eddie replied. Then a call from Hearts Six interrupted.

The loadmaster slipped back to the cargo bay, leaving the cockpit door open.

"Spooky Four-Five, you asked for a radius. Things are getting hot. My outposts have been pushed back. Make radius one hundred meters, Four-Five. No, make it a ninety-degree arc centered on, uh … due east. Ninety degrees. Over"

"Roger that, Hearts," Eddie replied. "Got visual on your marker. Circle of half a dozen small fires. Dayglo panel on the east side. Copy radius one hundred meters, ninety-degree arc, centered due east. Stand by." Eddie got on the intercom. "Hey, Technical Sergeant Hector Pastor-Villanueva! Ace loadmaster, crew chief, and flight engineer. Time to earn your big bucks! Ready a flare!"

Behind the cockpit of the old plane, the interior was stripped down to the ribs and the aluminum skin of the fuselage. On the left side, the two six-barreled General Electric SUU-IIA/A gatling guns poked their muzzles through what had once been the small, rectangular passenger windows. The Dillon Aero M134D-H stood in the opening for the cargo door that had been removed. The 120-knot wind alternately keened and moaned in these openings and carried in the growl of the engines. The cargo bay was neither quiet nor comfy.

The guns were on rigid mounts and were aligned with the axis of the wing. Whatever the line from wing tip to wing tip pointed at, the guns would hit it. A new sound was added to the noise in the cargo bay as electric motors spun up the miniguns' barrels in a final check. Each gun was powered by a two-speed motor which could spin the cluster of six barrels to a firing rate of 3,000 or 6,000 rounds per minute. Captain McLaughlin had selected the slower rate. With all three guns firing, he would be pouring 150 rounds per second into the jungle. A web of flexible metal channels ran like tentacles from the guns to large metal ammunition boxes.

Tom looked back through the cockpit door into the cargo bay. The loadmaster was kneeling, setting the ejection and ignition controls of a Mark-24 magnesium flare. Once the controls were set, he stood, hefted the three-foot-long, twenty-seven-pound metal tube, now armed and very dangerous, and passed it to Washington, who was standing in the cargo door. Arlen hooked a finger through the ring of the arming trigger safety, and all heard him say, "Ready, Chief!"

When dropping a flare, Arlen Washington's job was to stand in the cargo door, receive the armed flare canister from Chief or Otis on command from the cockpit, pull the safety pin, and toss it out the cargo door. With safety straps, Arlen felt perfectly safe standing in the door, and it was the one in-flight duty he enjoyed. He couldn't personally fire the guns, but this was at least throwing something at the enemy. Outside air whipped around the door edges and eddied turbulently around him, bringing in the misty rain, the smells of the engines, and the loamy rankness of the jungle below. At the door, he caught hints of treetops and, in a clearing, a glimpse of Queen of Hearts making fires. "Man, I wouldn't be one of them suckers. Fuckin' desert first," he said to himself, forgetting his mike was hot and he was talking to the whole crew.

"Cut the mouth, man, it's showtime! Flare armed and ready!" Hector announced.

Washington snorted, slipped a finger into the ring holding the safety pin, and, staring into the blackness beyond the cargo door, waited for the command to toss the flare.

The circling plane was approaching a point where the wind would carry the flare across the position of Queen of Hearts and not away from it. Washington's head suddenly jerked sharply to the side, and he staggered backward. The flare fell to the deck and rolled toward the tail. Washington's mouth fell slack, his head lolled, and his hands fluttered aimlessly.

McLaughlin called out, "Drop!"

Chief saw the flare canister roll free and lunged for it, screaming, "Oh, shit!" for he'd also seen the safety pin still dangling from Washington's limp hand.

Tom and Eddie had heard Hector's cry, and when Tom looked back, he saw an empty-handed Washington at the cargo door. "Flare away," he said, and he turned his attention back to the instruments.

Hector threw himself over the canister as if his body could shield the plane from its four-thousand-degree sun-like fire. Hugging it, he got to his feet and ran for the door. Washington's dazed eyes focused on the safety pin dangling from his finger. The flare had not gone out the door. He looked back into the bay, where he saw Hector sprint toward him and slip, the canister flying from his hands and rolling toward him. Otis scrambled after it but was too far away.

Washington lunged but was brought up short by his safety strap. A blinding pain stabbed his head. He lashed out with his foot and managed to kick it. The canister spun, but not toward the door.

Hector, still on all fours, reached out and managed to shove it toward the door, but it hit the gun mount and stopped. Washington kicked again, hard.

The top of his boot toe caught the end of the canister at an angle. His long second toe broke, and the canister, instead of being kicked toward the door, was kicked straight back at Hector. Hector threw his body at it, taking a slap shot at it with his shoulder and upper arm. The canister rolled out the door just as the parachute release charge exploded. Something whined and clattered into the cargo bay, followed by a strong whiff of smoke. Hector's arm and shoulder followed the canister out the door and were caught in the airstream, which jerked his torso painfully against the doorframe. A moment later, he managed to drag his numb arm back inside.

Arlen Washington looked again at the safety pin still dangling from his finger. He couldn't understand how he had managed to drop the canister. Shaking his head, he wondered how he could fuck up the one job he actually liked. The shaking sparked new pain. Putting a hand to his head, Arlen felt a ragged tear in his helmet. "I've been shot!" No one heard him, for the bullet that had plowed a deep furrow in his helmet had also knocked out his headset. The combination of pain and frustration from the task he'd failed at almost brought tears, but they were cut short by a new sound. The guns were spinning up. Washington freed the strap at the door and stumbled to the other side of the compartment to sit heavily on a bench beside Otis.

"Now we rock and roll, gang!" McLaughlin cried ten seconds later, when two million candlepower lit up the forest. Under the light of the flare, the jungle canopy around the clearing wasn't as solid as it had seemed. Through the gaps revealed stroboscopically by the swaying light from the drifting flare, he could see dozens of ant-like figures

"Four-Five! Four-Five! Hearts Six!" The voice was almost frantic. "They're coming! Shit! They're making their assault! All over! If you can do something, do it now!" The assault had come in the lull in artillery fire forced by Eddie's overflight.

Eddie oriented the plane so he could see the panel and the marker fires placed by Queen of Hearts out his side window. As the flare lit up the battlefield, Eddie banked the plane into a pylon turn such that the wingtip seemed to point at one spot on the ground—in this case, the marker fires. Peering through the simple Skyraider gun sight bolted to the side window, he delicately adjusted the bank angle and rate of turn so the wing tip seemed to move away from the marker fires to trace a circle a hundred meters out from the marker fires. There were no electronics. Eddie had to eyeball the distance from the guns to the target, estimate the Kentucky windage—or aim offset—to compensate for the plane's speed, and take into account the ground wind and the slewing that the recoil of the guns would cause, all while flying by the seat of his pants. He loved it.

"We see 'em, Hearts! Hang tight!" He keyed the intercom. "Showtime, Chief! Ten seconds!" Eddie fingered the trigger button, selecting all three guns, and deftly nudged the wheel. The wingtip began to trace an arc stealthily through the jungle.

Hearts Six could not hear the drone of the old Pratt and Whitney radial piston engines over the explosions of hand grenades and the rifle and machine gun fire around him. It was hard to see anything clearly. The harsh light of the flare exposed and hid things almost before he could tell what it was revealing. Figures flashed strobe-like between glare and black shadow. Then he heard a strange, mournful hoot that sounded something like an owl, something like a foghorn, something like the roar of a distant, large, and angry beast, made more dreadful and penetrating because the cargo bay of the gunship acted as a resonating chamber.

A bright, hot-pink neon ribbon of light lanced down out of the clouds and swept through the forest. Abruptly, mostly from surprise and shock, the firing on both sides stopped. Again the terrible, mournful hoot sounded, and he could see leaves, branches, mud, and sparks flying in the wake of the ribbon of fire. It looked like a solid spear of light, and after the sound cut off, the spear seemed to drive itself into the earth and disappear. For a moment, the plane's engines were the loudest sound in the shocked silence.

Captain McLaughlin began climbing in a wide circle, preparing to drop his own, much brighter, flare. Firing on the ground picked up, but not to the same intensity as before, and Tom sang loudly in a good baritone,
"Puff the Magic Dragon,
A bird of days long gone,
Came to fly the evening sky,
In a land called Vietnam"
"Fantastic! God! You broke it! You broke 'em!" Hearts Six shouted into his radio.

The dreadful sound and light erupted from the sky again. The hot-pink light was the color of the tracer rounds being fired. Although only one round in five had the small bit of burning phosphor that enabled one to see the flight of the bullet, the firing of so many so fast created the illusion of a solid beam. From the enemy's perspective, everything—earth, vegetation, and the unlucky men in the broad swath of the terrible light—seemed simply to explode, and it swept the earth far faster than a man could run. When the guns stopped, the silence seemed total, except for the soft rustle of thousands of leaves falling as though autumn had come to the jungle.

Terrified survivors of the attacking force fell back in disarray.

But not all the enemy were terrified.

Not far from the battle scene, on the side of a hill almost overlooking it, a squad of the enemy force had prepared a position and mounted in it a 12.7 mm heavy machine gun. It weighed over a hundred pounds and was mounted on a carriage equipped with a pair of spoked wheels with hard rubber rims so it could be towed rather than carried. The carriage allowed a gunner to crouch behind the gun and aim and fire it at targets at ground level, but the carriage could also be opened to form a tall tripod that allowed a the gunner to almost get under it and sweep nearly the full arc of the sky, turning it into an antiaircraft gun.

Here the soldiers had mounted it to be used in its antiaircraft role. Jet fighters, the usual attack aircraft that supported American or Vietnamese ground troops, were fast and hard to hit. Pilots could easily spot the distinctive greenish tint of the 12.7's tracer rounds and had great dislike for the thumb-sized projectiles that could shatter an engine or tear a hole in a fuel cell or an arm off a pilot. The usually ineffective effort of shooting at jets was frequently rewarded with a barrage of rockets, bombs, or, worse, napalm. Helicopters, used to bring reinforcements and resupply or evacuate casualties, flew slow and low and were much easier to hit. They also did not have as much firepower to hit back with. Even helicopter gunships, with their rockets and grenade launchers, were still low, slow, and vulnerable when they attacked. If jet fighter pilots did not like the 12.7 mm heavy machine gun, helicopter pilots loathed it.

The 12.7 would be just as dangerous to Spooky 45 if the gunners could get a bead on her. But screened by the clouds and the night, the gunners could not see the thing that was raining death—until the flare solved the problem for them.

Captain McLaughlin widened the circle by roughly a hundred meters, as the action had dramatically slackened near the perimeter Queen of Hearts had marked. The flare that had nearly destroyed the plane was still burning when it hit the trees and hung up on a high branch. Gaps in the forest canopy let the light through like searchlight beams that diffused in the thin mists still drifting by and silhouetted the distinctive shape of what, over thirty years before, had been the world's first truly successful airliner.

The aircraft vanished again, but now the gunners knew where the plane was relative to the stream of fire it sent out. They adjusted and opened fire.

Slugs that did no real harm made a distinctive double pop as they punched in the bottom of the plane and out the top. Those that found something made only one pop. Both McLaughlin and Blagget heard the hits. "Chief, anything hit? Y'all okay back there? Chief? Chief?"

Otis's voice came, high pitched with shock. "Shit, sir! Chief's hit! Oh, fuck, man, PV's hit bad!"

"Tom."

"On my way." As he unstrapped, Tom took a final scan of the instruments and stopped halfway out of the copilot's seat. "Shit! Fire light on number two!" He sat down, reaching for the fire extinguisher switch. The plane yawed right as the number-two engine began to lose power. McLaughlin increased power to the good engine, leveled the wings to gain better control and more lift, shoved the rudder pedal to slew the plane left to counter the yawing, and tried to climb. "Otis! We have an engine hit. See what you can do for Chief! Good man! Tom, any flames?"

The copilot could see nothing at first, and then bright tongues of flame flickered in black smoke streaming from a ragged palm-sized hole blown in the nacelle. Almost immediately, what looked like thick white smoke streamed out of the hole and from between the nacelle and the engine cowling. "Yeah, but I think we got it." He shone a flashlight onto the wing. Much of the engine nacelle and part of the wing glistened with black oil.

"Oil pressure's dropping."

"Great. We'd better get out of these mountains."

McLaughlin quit looking outside and turned his attention to the instruments. He thumbed his mike. "Queen of Hearts, Spooky Four-Five. We got some 12.7 ground fire. One engine hit. Afraid we can't hang around. Hope we were able to help. Over."

"Saved our ass, Four-Five. Believe me!"

"Good. Looks like we have to head for the barn, Hearts. We'll call in a replacement. Hang in there."

"Wilco. You too, Four-Five."

"Spooky Four-Five out."

Below, the firing around the perimeter continued, but it was now sporadic enough for soldiers and medics to risk crawling to cries for help, moans, and too-silent foxholes. Away behind their hill, surviving leaders made a decision. By the time another charge could be organized, they would risk being caught by sunrise. Their losses had already been heavy, and daylight would risk exposure to the full spectrum of American air power. The battle was over.

Having signed off from Queen of Hearts, whoever that was, McLaughlin switched to intercom. "Otis? How're we doing? … Otis?" He could hear heavy breathing as someone keyed his mike but couldn't speak.

Then Airman Timmy Otis cleared his throat twice. "Tore Chief's leg open! God! It's one big-ass hole! We got a tourniquet on and … and can't put a pressure bandage on. Too big. I'm sittin' here; I'm sittin'." His voice faded into raspy rapid breathing.

"It's okay, son. Hang in there. Washington? You on?" Washington couldn't hear.

The raspy hyperventilating slowed. "Sittin' here holding his leg artery shut with … with my fingers. Arlen's helmet got whacked. He can't hear, sir."

"Jesus, Otis! Hang in there!" Mike off, he said, "You hear that, Tom?"

Otis's voice came back. "Chief feels cold and he's shaking, sir. I don't know what else to do."

"Let me go back, Eddie."

"Go. We're flying. What more could you ask for on a cool tropical night?"

CHAPTER 3

DRAGON DOWN

No sooner had Tom gone back than Eddie swore. Oil pressure was now dropping in the number-one engine. The lower clouds were clearing, and he could make out more distant land features. He had been climbing at two hundred feet per minute, but now he couldn't do better than fifty to a hundred feet a minute. The plane was crabbing sloppily through the air with the asymmetric thrust of the one good but now dying engine. *It would be nice if it were crabbed the other way; it would be easier to see where we were headed.* He called out for Tom but got no answer. Ahead, the faint ash-toned line of a road took sharp meanders as it climbed into more rugged terrain, where it disappeared into cloud, rain, forest, mountain—he didn't know.

"Tom!" He hated to call. *I'm killing Chief,* he thought. He found the flashlight, shone it on the number-one engine, and saw no smoke and no new oil smears, just a small hole in the wing about midway between the engine nacelle and the fuselage. The hole was oblong and ragged, too small for a rifle bullet. A 12.7 had obviously hit something and tumbled to make the hole he saw, so it had hit something more than just the aluminum skin as it passed through the wing, and that was not good news.

They weren't climbing any more. The radar image ahead wasn't clear. The radio altimeter was. Something was less than five hundred feet below. When they had gotten the mission to support Queen of Hearts and marked their location, Eddie had automatically looked at the map hard enough to imprint in his mind a general picture of the nature and flow of the surrounding terrain. Based on that memory, Eddie turned toward lower ground.

Tom reappeared. "I got an IV in him. Looks like he's lost half his blood."

"An Khe is closest if we can make the pass."

"We need a hospital, pronto," Tom said, scanning the instruments as he sat. "Shit! Oil pressure dropping in—"

"I know. Terrain. Navigation. Are we about to hit a mountain? Don't say 'should' or 'shouldn't.'"

The rate-of-climb indicator was flat, the altimeter steady, but not high enough, and the height-above-ground indicator was falling. "We need two hundred feet a minute now!" Tom shouted.

Instantly, McLaughlin began to bank. There was no choice. The plane shuddered on the edge of a stall, and the rate of climb indicator briefly showed a thousand feet a minute drop. Then, over the following long seconds, it returned to a fifty-foot-per-minute drop. "We're not gonna sleep in a bed tonight."

McLaughlin changed frequency. "This is Air Force Spooky Four-Five. Mayday. Mayday." McLaughlin made contact and described the problem, intentions, and general location. He'd be more specific later or use the crash beacon.

Tom got on the intercom. "Otis! You there?"

"Yes sir!"

"Otis, we're going down. You guys brace yourselves."

"Sir, I can't let go of Chief!"

"There clamps in the medical kit, Tom?" McLaughlin shouted.

"Was, maybe," Tom said. "Kit got hit. Half the shit's missing. Lucky there was an IV bag. I ... wait." He stared at a clipboard with flight charts on it. A small notepad was attached to the charts by a paper clamp. He pulled it off. The clamp was way too strong. He fumbled in the chart bag and pulled out a wad of charts secured with rubber bands. He wound one around the handles of the clamp so that it closed with very little force. "Give me a minute." Tom left and returned quickly, minus his flight suit, wiping bloody hands on his shirt. "Not much blood pressure left. He feels cold, losing body temperature. Wrapped him up in what I could. Clip helped with the artery, but Otis has still got his fingers in there. He's gonna have to hold Hector. They're semi-secure with some cargo straps."

"Guns, ammo, gear secured? We only have Washington to see to it."

"He's come around. He's doing that now. Bullet hit his helmet—tore a furrow in it and killed his intercom. Also rang the hell out of his bell and gave him a good headache. From the look of his helmet, another half inch and he'd be answering to Saint Peter."

"But he's functional?"

"Yeah, he's serious."

McLaughlin nodded. "Not much air time left."

Tom grabbed the charts, turned on a small map light and found the red grease pencil X, under which had been scrawled "Queen of Hearts" and a frequency.

In number two, the oil pressure fell to zero. McLaughlin killed the engine and feathered the prop, turning the blades to slice straight into the wind for the least air drag. He crabbed the aircraft more and continued to sink, unable to get enough power from the number-one engine. "Find a spot?"

"Six miles ahead is a small valley running north–south. Mostly rice paddies with a road more or less paralleling a stream. It's our only shot. The road bends right, then is straight heading pretty much north. Take a heading of 110 from here to there, then left to 355, which should—is going to be—straight into the wind. Are we lucky or what? A straight stretch of a half mile or so. Ends at a bridge. Try to touch down where the road straightens toward the bridge. That gives us a good three thousand feet."

Eddie nodded. Six miles. They would be crash-landing as close to the enemy as to any friendlies, and if the stream was fordable and the enemy near, the friendlies might as well be on the moon.

Airman Washington, dried blood caking the left side of his face, shoved his helmetless head into the cockpit. "All secure, Captain!"

"Good!" Blagget said. "Hey! Take these headphones. Plug in at the bulkhead. We got about three minutes. I'll holler."

"Roger, sir!" He didn't move but stood staring into the blackness ahead.

"Piece of cake! Pilots can see in the dark." Tom thumbed the radio and gave the map coordinates of where they hoped to land.

Washington didn't move. Lieutenant Blagget shouted, "Earphones, Washington! Bulkhead! Strap down!"

"Okay, sir!" Washington seemed to come out of a trance and staggered out of the cockpit.

A moment later, Washington's voice came over the intercom. "Read me, sir?"

"Roger. Two minutes, Tom. I'm getting some visual of the ground now. Hey. This is real flying."

Tom jerked his head toward Eddie, shook it, then started through the emergency landing checklist. As Eddie called the items out, he added flaps and lowered the landing gear, which lowered, but only one of the lights indicating that the gear was down and locked came on.

They reached the beginning of the straight stretch of road that ended at the bridge. Tom helped Eddie line up, as the crabbed path of the plane gave him the better view. But he had a lot of other things to do as well. "Thirty seconds! Everyone brace!"

"I'm going to touch down on the right gear and then see if the left is there. If it isn't …"

"Up gear. One hundred. Come right … more right … dead on … fifty. We're eating up our straightaway."

The fat single wheel of the right landing gear kissed the road, bounced, touched, and began to take the weight of the aircraft. The engine was no longer adding thrust, and McLaughlin straightened and eased the left side down. The left gear proved to be down and locked. "Flaps up." Tom moved. The tail eased down, and the tail wheel bounced lightly. They had just greased in. McLaughlin grinned but didn't relax.

Tom voiced a sudden thought. "Hope it's not mined."

"Shut up."

Something lay ahead. McLaughlin, with a sudden unease, impulsively turned on the landing lights. The vague, dark ash-gray ribbon of road flashed into red ocher clay hardpan glistening from the rain. The glistening hardpan was not the immediate problem. The problem was a short distance ahead. They had touched down much closer than intended to the bridge, which was just a black gulf between broken abutments. "Shit!" As one, both men stamped on the brakes. The wheels shuddered and locked, skidding down the road with little friction or slowing of the plane. Now the glistening clay became the problem. "Gear up!" McLaughlin shouted.

The old warhorse plopped heavily onto its belly, and instantly the plane was filled with shrieks of metal against earth and a cacophony of snapping and cracking as bits and pieces of the airplane were torn off. But the rain had soaked the road, and the top layer of the hard-packed clay was like grease.

They were still not going to stop in time. McLaughlin kicked hard left rudder. The small tail wheel skipped and clawed at the road as the diminishing airstream pulled weakly at the rudder. For a short eternity, nothing happened. Then the tail bumped right slightly, nudging the nose left. The left wing dipped and touched earth, turning the plane further and dragging it toward the edge of the road, where a ditch caught and channeled the engine nacelle. But the ditch angled off to drain the road away from the abutments, pulling the fuselage toward the edge of the roadbed just before it rose toward the bridge footings. The main spar of the left wing bent, and the engine bounced out of the ditch, the engine cowling flying off in pieces.

The right wing dragged along the rising roadbed, and finally wing and right engine struck the edge of the abutment and bridge footings. The engine collapsed backward through the wing. The outer section of the wing crumbled and folded upward. The weakened concrete abutment wall collapsed into the river. All these events, happening more or less sequentially, acted like a one-time-use arresting gear. With a final screech, the fuselage tipped down the short bank. There was a splash, and everything surged to a stop as the nose buried into the river mud.

McLaughlin and Blagget let out a collective breath, as if they had shared a lung. Neither of them moved for what felt like minutes but was actually seconds. Eddie finally spoke. "I've never crashed before. You?"

Tom shook his head and then asked abruptly, "Fire?" Both peered and sniffed around and outside for signs of fire. There were no flames, just darkness, occasional creaks and pops, and the sound of water lapping against the nose. The landing light in the left wing, still alight, illuminated the muddy water, which seemed to have been painted the same olive drab as Spooky 45. For a moment, it seemed to Eddie his plane was dissolving in the water. Both men stared calmly ahead. Tom crossed himself and said, "Actually, I thought it was a nice landing."

"A last landing. Well, a landing with no fire is a good one. Check the boys out, Tom."

"After you, sir." He was flipping circuit breakers.

"Leave the radios on. Go on."

"Use the survival radio, Cap. It's time to get out."

"So get the men out. Move, Tom!"

"Yes sir! Don't cry to me if you're toasted."

"No smoking. Move."

The fuselage was angled nose-down about ten degrees, so it was a hard walk back. Eddie McLaughlin fiddled with the radios, trying to get a response. Tom was right; he was being stupid. The fact was, his foot hurt, he didn't want to think about what that might mean, and the water seeping around it felt good. He checked his official air force–issue .38-caliber revolver, with which he could hit a barn if he happened to be inside it.

Tom pushed himself into the main bay where the crew was and turned on his flashlight. "Washington? Otis? You guys okay?" Both men mumbled incoherent replies.

"Well, welcome to Bumfuck, Vietnam, gentlemen; hope you enjoyed your flight." His cheery little litany wound down to a mechanical drone as he shone the light on the crew chief. He was pasty and sweaty. Miraculously, the IV had not pulled loose. Tom set to work double-checking the IV, Chief's breathing and pulse, and the wound.

"Good landing, sir, I guess," Washington said, getting survival kits together.

"Real greaser. Couldn't have done better myself."

"Yes sir. What happened? We touched real smooth. Then it turned to shit."

"Hit a bridge. We didn't have a quarter for the toll booth."

Washington looked away, shaking his head, and then stepped out of the way, leaning against a bulkhead. He tried to look calm, but his hands were trembling.

In Chief's gaping wound, the paper clamp had slipped off. Otis had held the artery closed with his fingers through the entire episode and was in shock himself. Tom's flashlight was on Hector, but in the reflected light, he could see that much of Otis's uniform looked black, soaked with Hector's blood. The whites of his eyes were visible all around his dark irises; his left cheek was streaked by a tear, his right smeared with blood from unconsciously wiping with his bloodied hands.

Tom looked at Otis. "He's breathing good and has a pulse. You and God made a good team." Tom glanced past the gun mount out the cargo door, barely distinguishable from the night beyond, and thought of standard operating procedures. *Stay with the aircraft unless forced away by approaching enemy or there is no possibility of rescue before the enemy finds the crash site. If they know an aircraft has gone down, they will look for it.* "Fine," Tom muttered to himself. "And no clue whatsoever about the enemy. Who, what, when, where, how? Nada. Rescue? When? How? Christ." He blew out a gust of breath that was half fear, half disgust. To Tom, the possibility of rescue in this weather seemed about equal to the probability of winning a lottery. *Time to escape and evade*, he thought. *Except we can't.*

It was time to do something—anything. He called Washington to follow him. The wings had been torn up, which certainly meant fuel spills. *A miracle we're not on fire*, he thought. *Both engines out, cooling off, the ground soaked, no sparks. What screwed us might just also have saved us.* He still needed to check the risk of frying if they stayed with the aircraft. The deck was canted, but not too badly, and it was at least dry inside. But if there was any risk of fire, they'd have to get Chief out now no matter how crappy it was outside.

Washington heard Lieutenant Blagget but didn't move. His head hurt like hell, and so did his foot when he pushed on it. He had brought

35

his M16, but now it wasn't where he had stowed it. He cried out in a low, hoarse voice. "Fuck, I'm hit, man! My fuckin' head's killing me. My foot too! Where's the fuckin' gun? Gotta get out. Where's the fuckin' gun?" All he could think of was to find the damn thing, as if it were his only hope for survival. He needed out—needed to move. But his mind raced in circles. "Got to book! Where's the fuckin' gun? Gotta get out. Where's the fuckin' gun?"

His mutters were interrupted by his name. "Washington! You coming?"

"Lookin' for my M16, sir. Gonna need it out there!"

"Find it later or be a crispy critter, damn it! Bring your flashlight." Washington had no idea where it was and scrambled out the cargo door toward the sound of Lieutenant Blagget's voice. As gingerly as he tried to ease to the ground, he cried out in pain when his injured foot struck the dirt.

In the cockpit, Eddie looked over at Tom's vacated seat. Tom had opened a window on his side, and through it Eddie could smell aviation fuel. He quickly unbuckled, tried the radio again, eased his painful foot into the aisle, and forced himself to stand. It was, he guessed, just a sprain, and he wondered how the hell that could happen. He limped carefully up the sloping floor.

Otis and Hector were motionless on the deck. Eddie stepped in Hector's blood, slipped, and fell. A white-hot pain shot through his ankle. He swore. When the pain subsided enough to let him speak, he called out, "Tom! I smelled fuel out the right side!"

"Roger. I can smell it too. You okay?"

"Sure. Shit. Sure as shit. Uh huh. Otis! You and Hector okay?"

"He's hanging in there, sir. Can they … can they get to us soon?"

Eddie rolled over and sat up. He slid over until he could grab a gun mount and haul himself upward toward the door.

Tom's voice came in through the cargo door. "You okay, Captain?"

"Swell, just swell. Check that smell, though."

"We're on it. You okay?"

"Twisted ankle. Be out in a sec."

"Let me help."

"Nah. Oh. Got the fire extinguisher?"

"No."

"I'll get it."

"Right."

Eddie decided he wasn't being stupid. He was being *really* stupid. The trouble was, he didn't want to leave the aircraft. Ridiculously, he felt safer in it, more in control, as if while inside his plane he was still master and commander of the air and the night. There was an extinguisher secured to the bulkhead separating the cockpit from the cargo bay. He pulled himself to his feet—to his good foot, rather—and eased back until he felt the bulkhead. Then he felt for the extinguisher and unfastened it. His ankle still seemed on fire, but holding on to the gun mounts with one hand and shuffling, he made it to the door and sat on the edge, his feet dangling above the road.

"Tom?"

"Yeah?"

"Here's the extinguisher. I may need a little help getting down."

"Ankle?"

"Yeah."

Tom took the extinguisher and then brought Washington back. "Let's look at the ankle first. Washington, let me have the flashlight."

"Don't have it, sir. Shit moved all over when we crashed."

"Well, go find it!" Washington made no reply but scrambled back into the plane and after several minutes returned carrying a flashlight and his M16.

Tom took out a pocket knife and, with Washington holding the flashlight, cut away part of Eddie's flight suit and sock. "Captain! You got a piece of shrapnel sticking out of your foot!"

Washington leaned closer and looked at it. "No, it ain't shrapnel. Piece of aluminum. Guess one of the slugs chipped something off. At least you didn't get the slug, sir."

Thinking a jagged piece of shrapnel would be like a fishhook buried in the flesh and might take surgery to get out, Tom muttered, "How in hell can we bandage that?"

Washington nudged him. "Lemme see, sir." He gently poked at the thin piece of metal and felt the wound, talking all the time, sort of prattling, and then he suddenly jerked the three-inch fragment out.

Eddie cried out, "Shit!" Washington held up the bloody fragment. Almost irate, eyes wide at the sight of the fragment, Eddie said, "You just jerked that out of me, *Doctor?*"

"Jus' like Big Ma pulled a big ass splinter, bigger'n this, out of my foot once, sir. Jus' running her mouth like nothin' was wrong and whack! She just pull it out before I knew anything. Worked too." He grinned.

Eddie looked at his wound, which was now bleeding freely, "Well, you got a Band-Aid for this, Doc, or a tourniquet?" As quick as the grin had come, it vanished, and Washington stepped back, looking off into the night.

Tom saw the sudden stiffness in Washington's posture. He slapped him lightly on the shoulder. "Washington, you're something. Come on; let's bandage the boss before he bleeds to death."

Moments later, Eddie was standing on the road with both feet, his bandaged ankle feeling better and, most importantly, feeling able to do its job. The first thing he did was turn on his AN/PRC-90 survival radio and call.

Tom had a report. The fuel they could smell had leaked from the right wing, puddling in the ditch. Most of the medical kit had been used up, but the survival kits were all on hand, as well as some emergency rations and five canteens of water. Weapons included the officers' two .38 revolvers with a dozen rounds each, Otis's and Villanueva's .45s with two magazines each, and Washington's unauthorized M16.

"Good. I have a report too. They're sending a Spooky to cover us. Should be on station in forty-five minutes. Too soupy for choppers, but they're trying to get a ground rescue going. ETA probably a couple of hours, minimum."

"Weather?"

"Will continue to suck for the next twelve hours or longer."

"So for the next forty-five minutes at least, we have four pistols and an M16. Anyway, we'd better get Hector out and under the tail, just to be safe," he said. Tom looked around and, of course, could see almost nothing. "Oh. Shitty thought. We've got some flares, but will our Spooky be able to see them? When we used the flashlight, I saw mist and fog all around. We've got cloud cover from the ground up."

Eddie coughed and cleared his throat. "Don't know. The prick ninety has a locator beacon. Anyway, uh, I'm told there are no reports on enemy activity in this area."

"That only means they don't have diddly squat for intel out here. Poor Queen of Hearts on the other side of the hills we skimmed had plenty of company, which I imagine he hadn't been expecting."

"Thanks for your cheery analysis, Tom." After a moment of silence, Eddie asked Otis, "He conscious?"

"Kind of, sir. Not sure. Just breathing and has a pulse is all I really know, sir."

"Well, God willing and the cavalry gets here in time, he'll keep on doing that. Thanks, Otis," he said softly. He then added loudly, "Help's on the way, Chief! Hang in there!" Eddie limped to the end of the aircraft where he could see to both sides all of ten or fifteen feet. "Keep him awake, Otis. Even if you have to slap him."

Just then Washington appeared at the cargo door. "Found my mags, sir."

"A moment ago you had a rifle. You had no magazines?" Eddie snapped.

"They kind of slid around, sir. In the crash and shit."

"Okay, good," Eddie said, rubbing his forehead. "Sorry. You're right. It was a crash and shit. Let's get everyone out on the ground."

It was not a simple task. Otis and Washington dragged out boxes to make a raised bed to keep Hector out of the mud and gathered ponchos and jackets to keep him warm and dry. Lacking a litter, they maneuvered Hector onto some cargo netting, and all four lifted him out—painful jobs for Washington and McLaughlin. The tail provided a sense of shelter; the horizontal stabilizer, an illusion of a roof.

The breeze that would have provided a headwind to help slow them down in landing died before they arrived. Now everyone except Hector was sweating, not from their exertions but from the heavy humidity of the still, warm, dead air.

Eddie settled down to listen, though for what he wasn't sure. Bogeymen? Monsters in the closet? Thoughts of E&E, escape and evasion, crept in—doing something, taking action, exercising control—until a thought struck him. *Damn! there are tigers in Vietnam! E&E into the jaws of a tiger. Great idea.* The thought of a tiger was the most frightening thought he'd had so far that night. On a daylight mission not long before, he had seen one. The unit he had been supporting reported that the enemy had withdrawn toward a ravine, and Eddie had taken a pass over it. Seeing nothing, he dropped lower and made another pass. Almost skimming the trees, he had seen no enemy but had caught a glimpse of a tiger in the wild, as lithe and graceful as a cat stalking a mouse but longer than a man was tall. Enchanting and beautiful in a zoo, the thought of walking in the same jungle with one transformed enchanting into terrifying.

He could not imagine ground troops making it to them before daylight. He was sure as hell the enemy could find them sooner. He had begun to imagine a route, just vaguely, since he couldn't look at a map in the dark. Even as he did, he realized that putting Hector on a stretcher—even if they could make one—for a one- or two-day walk through the hills was just a slower killing than shooting him. He suddenly felt a bit pissed at Hector for getting himself shot, then snorted at the cowardice in his feeling.

The very unpleasant thought crept in that they weren't going anywhere by themselves. He couldn't abandon Hector. Once upon a time in history, whoever won the battlefield took care of the wounded left behind. Not here. He couldn't put Hector out of his misery so the rest could run off, either. He couldn't even want to. They were going to live or die here with Hector. Eddie concluded that he needed to think of how the enemy might attack and how he and his crew might counter, and there his imagination and wits ground to a near halt, his mind like a car stuck in the mud, spinning its wheels.

While Eddie McLaughlin was running through the options, Washington stayed with Otis beside Hector for a few minutes, and then feelings of vulnerability and helplessness crept back. Something about Otis's intense concentration on Chief bothered him; it just didn't make much sense, and it made him feel almost angry at Otis. He grimaced as if disgusted or angry, slipped away, and crept back on board to lean on the cargo-door gun and peer into the black night, idly caressing the weapon.

Tom and Eddie took turns pointing their next-to-useless pistols and useless eyes in various directions. Eddie had mentioned his sighting of a tiger, and soon Tom's imagination had him retreating from VC into the jaws of a tiger, or the other way around, his imaginations felt as pointless as pointing his pistol at the dark. He gave it up and joined Washington on board the plane. Tom slid to the cockpit and double-checked that all the power was off. He checked his survival kit. When he returned to the gun bay, Washington asked, "LT?"

"Yeah?"

"We know where … I mean, they know where we are?"

"Sure. Cavalry's coming. Captain said so."

"In this shit?"

"Somehow." Tom had no idea how the grunts could get to them. Surely coming by road this deep into Indian country, they'd run into mines or ambushes.

"Charlie?"

Tom wondered where Washington's ears had been. "Like the captain said, no reports of enemy activity in the area. So probably no sweat. No sweat. I calculate we'll be back before the clubs close tonight." A silence followed. Tom was beginning to feel very stupid behind the bravado. And that sensation was simply a cover for the real feeling—a creeping fear born of his sense of helplessness. He broke the silence himself, asking Washington, "Got your survival kit?"

"Stowed, sir."

"Better have it. Just in case."

"Case what, sir?"

"We might have to E&E."

"Shit, sir, if we can E&E, why not do it now?"

"E&E is a kind of a last-ditch thing, Washington. I mean, like, there's things in the jungle besides Charlie you don't want to run into, like tigers. Captain has even seen one."

"Tigers?" Washington squeaked. "You shitting me, sir!"

"Afraid not. Like I said, the captain's actually seen one. We were there. He saw it, but we didn't. Just a glimpse."

"He must be shitting you, LT. I mean, the grunts are in the jungle all the time. Never heard of one being eaten by a tiger. You?"

Tom hadn't. He thought maybe Washington had a point, but it didn't make the thought of a hike in the jungle any less unappealing.

"No, have to say I haven't. Anyway, if we try to E&E, what about Chief?"

"We make a stretcher. We carry him." Washington had dismissed the thought of tigers.

"Out of what? Anyway, SOP is to stick with the plane unless, you know, things get really bad and you can't."

"Don't that make it too late then, sir?"

Tom hadn't thought of that. He made a noise. After a moment he said, "Sorry, Washington; I don't have any bright ideas. You?"

Washington didn't say anything for a long minute. "We know where our side is, sir? Don't mean the guys we was shooting for, but you know, others who ain't stepping in shit?"

Tom waved vaguely toward the tail of the plane. "Down the road that way. Mile or so down it cuts east through the hills and into, uh, sort of good guy country."

"We could just walk down the road?"

"Theoretically. We'd probably be sitting ducks, though."

Washington thought about it not as in heading down the road but as in slipping through the jungle, this way and that. Was it so different from running from the storekeeper or a cop after snitching candy? A frisson of excitement flitted through and died. It wasn't the same at all. Arlen the kid had known every alley, Dumpster, grate, and fire escape. It was his turf, not the cops'. This was Charlie's turf, not his by any stretch. "Shit," he said.

"Yep. You're right there, and there's Chief. Even if we could make a decent stretcher, think he'd survive all the bouncing and stumbling in the dark? It'd kill him for sure."

"And he ain't dead, so we got to sit here, right, sir?"

Tom sighed, wondering what the hell was wrong with this kid. *He's just human*, Tom answered himself, *and buried in me is the same selfish feeling*. "Hector's got a family, you know. Wife and kids."

"Yes sir, yes sir," Washington muttered, wondering why that was important. But somehow it was—it always was. The grief and hurt of Hector's loss would spread much wider than his own. Maybe that was it. No, there was no math to it, it was just a fact. Chief counted. Even Otis had a girl somewhere. Washington didn't—no wife, no kids, just a mama—and she didn't know up from down, so he didn't count. He bit his lip, and shook his head, bringing on a sharp pain. In a normal voice, he added, "They say how long it be to pick us up?"

"Choppers can't get here in this weather, so they're coming by road. Couple of hours, I'd guess."

"So maybe Charlie can get here first, LT? And all we got is my M16."

"The rest of us have pistols, Washington," Tom replied weakly.

Sure as shit Charlie will find us, Washington thought. *Not just one or two, but gangs, sure as shit, because if shit can happen, it does. Always. And my one M16 won't do spit to stop it.*

Minutes passed uncomfortably, and Washington found himself caressing the minigun, noting how the tilt of the aircraft aimed it uselessly at the ground. "We have a shitload of firepower here, LT. If we could maybe fix this gun so we could aim it, could blast some shit out there."

Tom snorted. "Which one of us is John Wayne?" He had been blocking fearful thoughts by silently mouthing his way through the Rosary, then the twenty-third psalm.

Washington almost snapped back at the lieutenant for being a negative smart-ass. "John Wayne!" He snorted and recalled some black-and-white war movie he'd seen on TV with Wayne, the hero, holding a big machine gun, belts of ammo over his shoulders, bullets flying, charging an enemy hill. He was jumping up from the safety of his foxhole or wherever, all pissed 'cause some other guy or guys, some buddy maybe, had been killed. Big hero. Big dumbass hero. "Seen him in a movie once—old movie, you know, no color. Chargin' some hill holdin' a big machine gun, bein' a real badass. Got wasted anyway." But then the imagery he had just conjured up caused his thoughts to shift.

He remembered seeing the same machine gun, or one sort of like it, in a chopper, just slung from a strap hooked above the door. There was no mount—nothing but a canvas strap. *Must have worked. Wouldn't have been there if it didn't.* He began visualizing the minigun he was leaning on, the Dillon Aero M134D-H, with handles hung from a strap. That old machine gun, he guessed, was maybe thirty pounds and fired maybe six hundred rounds a minute, yet some movie dude could hold it in his arms and shoot it; the baby he was holding on to, maybe 100, 150 pounds. Not even that much. And it fired three thousand rounds a minute at low speed. *Maybe three, four times the weight, five times the recoil, or something like that. Need more than a strap.* He began visualizing how it might be suspended like the gun in the chopper and still control the recoil; how the feed belts, power supply, and control circuits could be managed. It was, at least, something to keep his mind busy. Finally he said aloud, "LT! Back awhile I saw a machine gun set up in a chopper door, just slung from a strap hooked above the door. Must have worked. Wouldn't have been there if it didn't, right, sir? We could maybe mount this fucker the same way in the door so we could aim it."

"What're you talking about?" Tom asked.

Washington explained. Tom didn't think it could work. "I think we'd just end up hosing the plane." But he called to Eddie, who limped around to the cargo door, not bothering to try to get in, and Tom explained Washington's idea.

"I don't see how he could control it. Just be spraying bullets everywhere. Can't imagine holding the sucker," Eddie said. "Besides, how you going to start and stop firing?"

"You push the buttons, sir."

"Not from the cockpit. We'd be too far apart. And it's half underwater. Probably short out."

"We got battery power, sir?" Eddie nodded. "Hot wire it, then."

Eddie pondered. He couldn't imagine troops getting to him before daylight. Hell, they'd likely not even try before then, and that meant hours, maybe six to eight very long hours, before they might see a friendly face. He felt pretty sure Washington's idea wouldn't work, but it would be stupid not to try. "Okay. You really think you can control it? Shit. Go for it, then." He looked at Tom. "If we don't blow ourselves to bits with it, at least the enemy will know the sound. Maybe scare him off. Hopefully. For a while."

Tom asked, "What if the enemy comes from back there, not from out front here?"

"I think I hate you."

"Well?"

"Eddie put his hands over his eyes, rubbing them with the heels. "They shouldn't, I don't think."

"You know you hate that word, sir. Captain."

"Washington, you think it could be rigged to shoot that way *and* this way?"

"What the fuck for? Uh, sir, I mean, ain't no door there; couple windows can't even see, boss. Cap'n."

"Hell, bullets come in with no problem; ours'll go out just as easy."

"Still can't see shit. And what about ricochets, like off the ribs?"

"See bullets coming in through that side, hose that side. God, this is becoming too surreal. What the hell. I mean look; it's as dark as a closed coffin out there. We'd be shooting blind out the door, so we won't be any less blind shooting through the other side. Ricochets? Gets that bad, we have a choice. Maybe die from a ricochet or for sure die from the enemy. Can it be rigged? Yes or no?"

"I'd be hanging out the door!" Washington forgot himself and shook his head as if clearing it, bringing on another sharp pain. "Shit! Straps," he said. "Shit, boss, if I can strap the gun, guess I could strap myself too. Hang out the door, swing the gun around. Still, my ass'll be hanging way out the door." Imagining that was not at all appealing.

Eddie was carrying the survival radio, and it crackled to life on the voice channel. "Spooky Four-Five," he answered. He listened for a few seconds and calmly said, "Roger. Out. Shit."

"What?"

"Our air cover has delayed takeoff due to an engine warning light. Nothing else available that's not already supporting ground troops. They're working on rounding up another from somewhere."

Tom erupted, "They're hanging us out to dry over an engine warning light? A friggin' warning light?"

"I guess they think better one plane on the ground than two. So make this work, guys." Eddie limped back to keep a lookout on the blank walls of fog, leaving Tom to help Washington.

Map

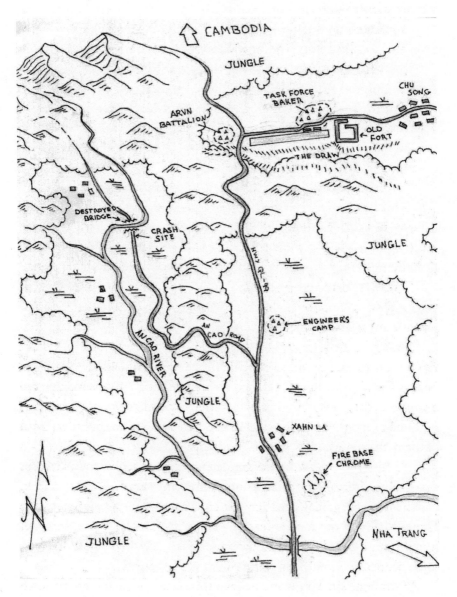

CAMBODIA

JUNGLE

TASK FORCE BAKER

CHU SONG

ARVN BATTALION

OLD FORT

THE DRAW

DESTROYED BRIDGE

CRASH SITE

JUNGLE

HWY QL-19

AN CAO RIVER

AN CAO ROAD

ENGINEERS CAMP

JUNGLE

XAHN LA

FIRE BASE CHROME

JUNGLE

NHA TRANG

CHAPTER 4

RESCUE MISSION

"**L**ieutenant! Wake up, sir!"

Second Lieutenant Randall Hanley was awake almost the instant PFC Will Frederick touched him. "Huh? What?" he asked, the confusion of transition from dreams to reality amplified by the wavering red beam of Frederick's flashlight. Then he heard a squishy sound. It was Frederick bracing himself as he leaned into his lieutenant's tent. Both of them muttered curses at the same time—Frederick for realizing he'd planted his hand in mud, and Hanley for realizing his tent's defenses against the intermittent rains of the monsoon season had sprung a leak.

Lieutenant Hanley's tent covered a shallow dugout augmented by a couple of rows of sandbags serving as his protection against shrapnel from enemy mortars. In the monsoon season, the challenge was keeping these prudent dugouts from becoming muddy bathtubs.

"Battalion, sir. You won't believe this. They're saying an air force plane went down. Want us to go get the crew, uh, ASAP."

Randy Hanley was platoon leader of Second Platoon, A Company,

134th Combat Engineer Battalion. His platoon's mission was to make usable a long unused road between the hamlet of Xanh La, several kilometers behind him, and the village of Chu Song, some fifteen kilometers ahead, measured as the crow flies. In actuality, he was in command of a motley group of forty-six men, including himself. Twenty-three were his understrength combat engineer platoon. Five were operators and mechanics for a road grader and a bulldozer with a sheep's foot roller, both attached from a construction battalion to support his mission. Fourteen were two squads of infantry attached from C Company, Second Battalion, Twenty-Second Cavalry, to provide security and scouting.

In Vietnam there were no clear front lines, so one could seldom say he was behind or in front of the enemy in any meaningful way. The country was like an old stained carpet, the stains representing areas of enemy control of enemy forces, although in this analogy, the stains were dynamic and moving. Randy's road-clearing task was taking him through what was considered a relatively clean part of the carpet. At least it had been.

Isolated small-unit missions like Randy's were tempting targets, and he needed all the firepower that could be spared. Four of his forty-six men were the crew of an M728 combat engineer vehicle, or CEV, attached to both assist with his mission and provide added firepower. A modification of the army's main battle tank of the time, it had a bulldozer blade in front and a powerful crane attached to the tank's turret. The tank's high-velocity gun had been replaced with a stubby cannon that fired bigger shells for blowing up fortifications and obstacles. It also had a .50-caliber machine gun in a small turret on top of the main turret. The remaining four men were the crew of an M42 Duster, a tank-like vehicle with a lightly armored open turret sporting a pair of 40 mm antiaircraft guns. In Vietnam, Dusters supported lightly armed units, such as transportation and engineer units like Randy's. With each of the two guns firing 120 high-explosive shells a minute, the effect on enemy infantry was not unlike that of an AC-47's mini-guns.

For this mission, his platoon had been detached from his parent company and was directly under the control of his battalion headquarters simply because it was within radio range and his company headquarters was not.

"ASAP? Now? On the road now? For Christ's sake! It's the middle of the night! Ahh!" Sitting up, Randy had also put his hand to the dirt floor and found not dirt but mud. He muttered, "Just a minute," carefully pulled off the poncho liner he'd been wrapped in and put it in his lap, and then found his boots and pulled them on. One corner of his poncho liner was wet. He shifted to make a place on his air mattress for the liner, hoping the next rain would hold off long enough to let it dry out. "You sure? Crazy!" When Frederick didn't respond, Randy sighed. "Okay, let's get to the truck and see what they really want."

"Got the radio here, sir. It's Bagger Three." Frederick had brought the backpack radio with him from where he had been sleeping with the handset next to his ear. He was one of those men who could fall asleep almost anywhere in an instant but always slept lightly, awakened by almost any disturbance, such as a radio call.

"You said it was Bagger Three."

"Yes sir. It's set up to relay through the VRC on the truck, so we've got the range."

"Right. You think of everything, Frederick." Randy took the handset and pressed the transmit button. "Bagger Three, Boiler Two-Six. Over."

"Two-six. An AC-47 gunship went down at 0015 this morning at the following coordinates. Prepared to copy?"

Randy fumbled for his pocket notebook and a flashlight. PFC Frederick was faster, and his light already had the red filter on it. When Frederick turned on the light, he saw the lieutenant's notebook and held the light on it. Randy shoved his watch into the glow of the flashlight. Five minutes before one in the morning. Already over forty minutes on the ground. "Thanks," he said to Will. "Go ahead, Bagger Three." The coordinates seemed to be no more than ten kilometers from his location, but that could mean a hard day's walk in this area of operations even without an enemy.

"Crew is alive, one badly injured. About a klick or so behind you, there's a fork to the West. It runs through some hills, then turns north up the An Cao valley, following the east bank of a stream. About six klicks up, the road crosses the stream. The plane is on the road right by the bridge. You know the weather. No way choppers can get in there. Your mission is to rescue the crew and destroy the aircraft. Over."

"They go down on this side, the south side of the bridge? Over."

"South side. Affirmative. Over."

"No friendlies in that valley? Doesn't that make it like real Indian country? Over."

Bagger Three replied that the An Cao was not an operational area for either side as far as they knew, so they expected no increased risk. He added that another gunship was being sent to provide cover and that artillery support that had the range to support him all the way to the crash site would be the heavy eight-inch and one-seven-five battery at Fire Base Chrome, about eighteen klicks south east of the objective. He concluded, saying, "I don't want heroics, Two-Six, so think it through. But if those birdmen are going to chirp another morning, it's most likely going to be up to you. Over."

Randy blew his breath out sharply and glanced at the barely visible face of his radio operator, which was completely impassive. "Any intel? Over."

"Not much. NVA battalion-size force attacked an infantry company twenty klicks southwest of where they went down. They got hit helping break up the assault. 12.7-millimeter fire. Where you find heavy machine guns, you can count on at least a battalion or a regiment. Not likely to target small fry like you. May be some VC in that area supporting the NVA, covering withdrawal and supply routes to the west. So most likely nothing near your objective. They'll have farther to go than you, and they're on foot. Over."

"Reinforcements? Friendlies? Over."

"Nearest grunts are two platoons securing Fire Base Chrome. Same bunch your two infantry squads are from. At best they could get to you in three hours. Time is critical, so they're not part of the equation."

"Part of the equation! Bullshit!" Then he collected himself, realizing he still had his radio's transmit button depressed. "Sorry, sir." Randy realized they were air cavalry, and with no choppers flying, they were strictly on foot and lightly armed. "Right. Never mind. You know what I've got. I can't break them up. I'll have to take everyone. Over."

"Your call. Speed is essential. Over."

"Then I'll have to abandon the grader and the dozer. Over."

"Roger. Disable the ignitions, but otherwise leave them alone. We can recover them later if Charlie doesn't blow them up, which he probably won't. Over."

"Roger."

"Good luck, Two-Six. Let us know when you're rolling. Out." Randy stared at the handset.

Frederick had heard both sides of the conversation. "We really gonna have to move out in this shit, sir?"

"Yeah." Private Frederick and Lieutenant Hanley stared at each other, their expressions blank, as if the crests and troughs of contrary emotions, fear, annoyance, resentment, empathy, worry, and challenge were exactly canceling each other out. Through the moment, they accepted it all.

Frederick blew out his breath sharply. "I'll get Sarge."

Randy nodded and then added, "Get everyone else up too. Have the NCOs and Vasquez meet in the office in five minutes, and we'll figure out a plan."

"Right, sir. Here's the map." Frederick stood, heaved the radio to his back, and slipped away. The mission was scary. As with most soldiers, his training had not included much in the way of night operations. The only night experience he'd had as a soldier had been in training, and consequently, tonight's mission filled him with trepidation. Even the lieutenant seemed really nervous about moving around at night. He glanced back at the dim silhouette of his lieutenant. He was not much older than Will. He had more education, for whatever that was worth in the jungle, but not much more experience. That confident statement, "We'll figure out a plan," could be bullshit, but he felt it wasn't—not because the lieutenant knew everything, but because Will knew he wasn't a bullshitter, and more importantly, he knew that his lieutenant cared about the men he was responsible for and not all that much about looking good to the brass. Somehow that kept things together. He headed off to give everyone the bad news.

As Frederick left, Randy grabbed the map, his gear, and his rifle and carried them to his office—the cargo bay of a three-quarter-ton utility truck, which basically was a no-frills four-wheel-drive pickup with a canvas top over the cab and cargo bed. Randy banged lightly on the tailgate.

A muffled voice came back, "Who goes!"

"Me, Esteveria. Rise and shine. We got to crank up. We're on a rescue mission."

"Jesus, LT, it's the middle of the night!"

"They'll never expect us. Come on; gotta hustle." Randy tossed his gear over the gate and unlatched it.

Private Ramon Esteveria, recently downgraded from private first class owing to the unforeseen consequences of a visit to an unregistered brothel some weeks before, was already up and moving as Randy levered himself into the back of the truck. Ramon slid out in jungle fatigue trousers, unlaced boots, and T-shirt, holding his rifle, web belt, and shirt in one hand.

A small World War II vintage field desk that looked like a cube-shaped footlocker had been fastened at the cab end of the truck bed. Randy lowered the rear flap of the canvas truck cover, folded down the front of the field desk to make a small table, turned on a tiny red-lensed reading lamp, and spread the map out. His current position was marked on the plastic map cover. He found the fork and where that road crossed the stream draining the An Cao, which would be pretty full now. Hearing Ramon start the truck, he—unnecessarily—checked the frequency set on the more powerful vehicular radio and turned back to the map. He used the edge of a piece of paper to quickly mark off the road distance to the wreck site. Major Bob Gridley, the battalion operations officer, call sign Bagger Three, had obviously been looking at straight-line distances. Road-wise, it was about thirteen kilometers.

"LT?" The voice came from just outside the rear flap, deep and gravelly.

"Hey, Sergeant Jarvis! Listen. We have a rescue mission. First thing, we need to disable the ignitions on the grader and the dozer. We'll come back and get them, or someone will. Can you get Olmstead on that right away?"

There was a moment of silence as Sergeant Jarvis considered this. "Rescue where, sir?"

"An Cao valley. About ten klicks up the An Cao."

"We should take the dozer, sir."

"Too slow. We have to haul ass."

"Pretty fast in reverse, sir." Randy didn't reply. The big D-7 dozer was formidable. The blade was good armor to shield infantry, and the wide, unpadded steel tracks gave it better traction and lower ground pressures than a tank. They also tore up road surfaces quickly.

"Let's think about it."

"Right, sir." Master Sergeant Floyd Jarvis, Randy's platoon sergeant and second in command left without another word.

Randy reached into a cubby in the field desk and pulled out a sheaf of large-scale photo maps. These were more current and contained more detailed landform information than the standard topographic maps, many of which dated back to the French colonial era. They were also hard to read, especially under red light. He pulled a magnifying glass from a drawer in the desk and studied the maps.

The short stretch through the hills looked to be mostly scrub and brush rather than real jungle, and the hills appeared low and gentle with no hints of steep grades or defiles. Once in the valley, it was rice paddies on both sides of the stream the rest of the way to the crash site. Consequently, good cover for an ambush was a good hundred meters from the road at the closest point. Mostly, the paddies reached a good two to five hundred meters or more from the road on both sides. The maps showed a couple of tiny hamlets along the way, one about one kilometer in from the fork and the second about four kilometers in. A third was half a klick beyond the crash site on the other side of the stream.

Randy picked up the handset and called, "Bagger Three, Bagger Two-Six. Over."

"Go ahead, Two-Six."

"Map shows two small hamlets in the An Cao along the road. Any civilians, friendlies there? Over."

"The An Cao is a free-fire zone."

"Roger; just asking. Anyone in them would be a Victor Charlie, right? Over."

"Two says the An Cao was evacuated after the battle of Canh Mah six months ago, so technically that would be an affirmative. Over."

"Technically?"

"They never get them all to come out. Over."

"Roger. Out."

"Two-Six," the radio blurted.

"Two-Six. Over."

"You okay with this?"

"No one in their right mind would be. We got a choice? Over."

"You might find it not feasible."

Randy felt the temptation. He was not anywhere near as sanguine as he had sounded to Ramon. "Shit," he said softly and tamped down the thought of his wife twelve thousand miles away. "I wouldn't want someone thinking that if it was me out there. Over."

"Roger that. Out." Just as Bagger Three cut out, Randy heard, "... anite Six-Three. Over."

"Green Granite Six-Three, this is Bagger Two-Six. Over."

"Granite Six-Three. Need anything blown up?"

"That's my line, Six-Three. No, not at the moment. I'll have some on-call targets for you to plot shortly. Over."

"Roger. Standing by. Out."

A clattering noise from outside the truck was followed immediately by the sound of the Duster's engine starting. Sergeant Jarvis poked his head in under the canvas flap. "Everyone's alerted, sir. Olmstead and Figueroa are taking care of the sabotage. We really going to go screwing around on the road in the middle of the fucking night?"

"Good. Come on in. I'll show you." A moment later, Sergeant Jarvis was sitting beside him, and Randy described the mission.

"Wish to hell we were somewhere else," Jarvis said, noting they had a long thirteen kilometers by road, visibility was lousy in the mists, and the hard clay road would be as slick as ice, even for tracked vehicles. He shook his head in disapproval and asked, "We got any intel?" Randy filled him in. "So it's a race. Us and Charlie. We can inch in there as careful as we want, but we're going to make noise."

"Thunder run?"

"Have to use headlights. Crazy. Shit, sir, besides, it's dirt road. Could be mined."

Randy put his hands over his eyes. "Time. We use mine detectors, we walk there. What, four, five, six hours? Get there just to bring out the dead?"

They fell silent for a minute, staring blindly at the map. "I guess we've got to go get 'em, sir. It's just, you know, crazy. Shit, we're being asked to put forty-odd asses on the line to get a crew of five."

Randy didn't reply. Instead he took the handset and called the eight-inch howitzer battery again and asked how fast they could shift fire and what the time of flight and the circular error probable would be. This last number was very important because it would dictate how close to the road or to his own men he could plot concentrations. The news was not all that good. The crash site was just two kilometers inside their maximum range. The closer they got to the crash site, the longer the shell flight time and the greater the circular error probable, or CEP. This meant that when one plotted a nice, exact point on the map as the target, the shell would fall somewhere in a circle drawn around the point, and that circle got larger as the distance from gun to target increased. *Well, another gunship is coming. You go with what you've got. Been true since man first threw a rock.* That settled, he sat back to think and wait for the other NCOs.

Moments later, they were all there: Sergeant Jarvis, the two infantry squad leaders, Sergeants Carter and Warrant, the CEV and Duster commanders, Specialist Higgins and Sergeant Newsome, his three engineer squad leaders, and Specialist Henrique Vasquez, the platoon medic. This made for too big a crowd for the back of the three-quarter-ton, and some had to stand outside, leaning on the tailgate with their heads and shoulders inside the back flap. Randy briefed them on the mission and the intelligence he had, and he showed them the route on the map. He let the information sink in for a moment and asked, "Ideas?"

Vasquez piped up, his eyes wide, the whites showing all around his dark irises. "The wounded one, sir—they say what kind? How bad?"

"No. They just said, 'in a bad way.' I'll try to get more on it."

Vasquez bit his lip and nodded.

Specialist Higgins rubbed his chin, his eyes shifting here and there. "Dirt road, sir. Mines? I mean, I lose a track, we're dead in the water." Sergeant Jarvis grunted and nodded.

Sergeant Carter was the senior infantryman and had the most experience in country. He cleared his throat. "They tell you the last action in that area was, like, six months ago? And it's a free-fire zone?"

"Yeah," Randy replied. "And?"

"That means hamlets there been evacuated. No one to grow rice, so it ain't useful to Charlie." Sergeant Carter tended to speak as if one should extrapolate a paragraph of meaning from an opening sentence. His chin resting on his fist, he glanced around. "So have the flyboys seen or heard anything since they went down?"

"Don't know, Sarge. Let me check." Randy made a call on the radio. "Battalion'll call back."

"What I'm thinking, sir, is that the valley is like a dead zone nobody gives a shit about unless they happen to be gathering there for some purpose. Most likely won't be. Max, a handful of local VC."

"Think they could take the plane?" Randy asked.

Sergeant Carter shrugged. "Depends on the crew. Local VC, if any, be there to keep tabs on things, but not high on combat initiative."

"What about booby traps, mines?" one of Randy's squad leaders asked, nervously waving his palm over the floor as if it were a mine detector. "Take hours to sweep that far. And in the dark."

"Or ambush?" another one asked.

"Like I said, looks like Charlie's got no reason to give a shit about the An Cao. So why mine the road? Why set up an ambush?" Sergeant Carter shrugged again. "If they did, here'd be the best place." He pointed to a sharp bend in the road about halfway through the hills to the An Cao. That set off a round of discussion hopping from worries to complaints to suggestions trying to balance the desire for caution and the need for speed, all in the face of darkness, bad weather, and ignorance of the enemy. Any meaningful speed meant a "thunder run"—travel with lights on and as fast as road conditions allowed, firing artillery blindly ahead in hopes of keeping any enemy heads down and keeping fingers crossed there were no mines. And any meaningful caution almost certainly meant a dead or captured air crew for sooner or later; the enemy would come for the plane.

Randy looked at his watch. Time was passing. He realized the discussion was allowing him to not make a decision. The radio interrupted his worrying. A few seconds later, he handed the receiver back to Frederick and rubbed his eyes. "Vasquez, they say it's a bad leg wound, lost a lot of blood. No sign of enemy activity."

Sergeant Carter cleared his throat. He'd been quiet through the discussion and now everyone turned to him. "Any serious VC that'll go for the plane are also probably outside the valley and have to walk to it. First one there wins."

Randy rubbed his eyes again and took a deep breath. "All right." He shrugged, "We've got to do this. We go down to the fork, combat lights only, turn up the road, final check. By then the gunship's on station. Final check, then pedal to the metal."

"Guess that's the best we can do, LT," Sergeant Jarvis said.

Carter nodded. Higgins muttered, "In that case, the best sucks."

Randy scanned the faces for signs of doubt or disagreement. Sergeant Jarvis broke the silence. "Okay. Dozer leads; then the Duster; then two dump trucks with the infantry; your three-quarter, sir; the other trucks; CEV in the rear?"

Randy nodded but said, "I'm thinking reverse the CEV and Duster. CEV is more mine resistant; Duster has the better firepower. And we'll have to ditch the dozer. It's too slow."

"The Cat might be useful. Best traction. Slippery shit, that clay."

Randy thought a moment, rolling his shoulders and staring at the map. "No. Still think we have to leave it. We need speed. Besides, the CEV is a tank—armor, machine guns, a cannon, *and* a dozer blade." Again, he looked around, weighing the men's expressions. But everyone's expression was the appropriately neutral balance between "Oh shit, why us?" and "Can't not do it."

"Right, sir," Jarvis said. "I'll get 'em organized. Anything else, LT?"

"I'll get a bunch of concentrations plotted. Soon as everyone's ready, assemble here for orders, then we'll roll before we have a chance to start pissing in our pants." Left alone, Randy pinpointed with letters and numbers where he would have the artillery preplan targets. He also marked on his map additional *X*s with color names as checkpoints and wrote down the map coordinates of each. He passed the coordinates and identifications on to Green Granite Six-Three and to Bagger Three with a synopsis of his plan. Bagger Three replied with the news that the promised gunship had delayed takeoff as a result of technical problems. Randy signed off and stared at the map. Eight-inch howitzers threw a hell of a big shell—too big, in some respects, to provide effective close support such as they might need. "Thank God for the Duster," he said aloud, and he reviewed his plan for gaps he could do something about as opposed to gaps, like the gap in air support, he could do nothing about.

By the time he had done all this, everyone was back, ready for final coordination. When they had written down the code words, coordinates, call signs, and frequencies and understood the plan, they dispersed to their own men. They would roll in ten minutes—twenty-five minutes after Randy had been wakened and sixty-five minutes after Spooky 45 had crashed on the muddy road thirteen kilometers away. The mist had now transformed into a heavy fog.

CHAPTER 5

ROAD TO AN CAO

They started out on the Xanh La–Chu Song road, heading south over the section they had already cleared and improved. It was basically clay, but the greatly improved drainage meant that while it was slippery, it was not nearly as slick as it could have been. The greater danger was the mist and fog. Driving with just the combat lights, a driver could not even see to the shoulder of the road.

One of the infantry squads had an AN/PVS-1 Starlight scope, and Randy had planned to use it from the cab of his command truck. The AN/PVS-1 was a first-generation night vision device that took even very weak ambient light, such as starlight, and electronically amplified it to create an image on a tiny green screen inside the scope at the focal point of the eyepiece. Typically, it was mounted on an M16 rifle like a telescopic sight. But in the thick fog, the user might as well have been looking through frosted glass. That killed Randy's plan to ride. Instead he clipped a flashlight with a red filter on the back of his shoulder harness for the truck to use as a reference and took another flashlight to aim at the ground, which gave him about five yards of visibility, and he led his little convoy on foot. Frederick and Sergeant Jarvis had both volunteered for the job, but Randy had refused—partly because he thought he might be making a really stupid move and did not want to risk one of his men on something he was very uncertain about. His decision to take the point, which a leader should not normally do, was also partly because the action would divert his mind from the gnawing fear that he was facing a challenge he might not be up to, or that he might turn it into a suicide mission.

The flashlight Randy had no choice but to use cocooned him in a mist of pearly luminescence. Around his feet, the mist bled into the glistening red clay. In a weird way, the cocoon of fog was comforting, as if all fearful things beyond its pearly walls were imaginary. He began jogging slowly, realizing he didn't have to see the verges of the road; he had only to get in a rut and stay there. He counted his jogging steps, and every one hundred twelve, he ticked off a hundred meters in his mind and checked behind him to be sure he could still see the cat's-eye combat lights of his three-quarter-ton command truck.

When he had counted off nine hundred meters, he stopped, walked back to the truck, and told Esteveria to stay to his left, as he would be walking along the right edge of the road, looking for the turnoff. Esteveria nodded. Randy walked. About five minutes later, he saw the roadside ditch disappear into a culvert. They were at the turning point. It was bad enough to take a walk at night down a road that he was familiar with and had earlier swept for mines. Now it was a turn into the unknown.

The mist was still thick. There would be no thunder run in this crap. The gunship had been down well over an hour now. He turned off his bright white "Here I am, shoot me" flashlight and walked back to the truck. "Sarge. We're at the fork. A pretty sharp right turn. You want to guide them around it? Bring up the CEV to lead, then Carter's dump truck, then the rest. Swing 'em wide of the shoulder. Don't want anyone sliding into the ditch. I'll go ahead. Pull them up to my light."

Sergeant Jarvis's lips compressed into a thin crease in his stubbled face. "Sir, you don't want to go up that road alone. Dismount Carter's squad. At least that."

60

Randy put a hand over his eyes. "Okay. Right. Not thinking. Get Carter."

Sergeant Jarvis nodded but didn't move. "Sir, are we maybe ..." He stopped, reformed a thought, and said, "Battalion know what they're doing?"

"I don't know. All I know is we have a mission. A gunship's down, survivors on the ground. And what do air force types have? Just fucking pistols, right?"

"Sir. You've told higher to kind of stuff it before. When you know, like, they don't know."

"Yeah, Bagger Three sort of gave me permission to chicken out, but what do you do if you don't know you know better? You're getting me confused, Sarge. One thing we do know: we don't want a confused lieutenant running around. Bullshit's better than no shit; action beats inaction—your own words. Besides, what if it was you out there?"

Jarvis nodded glumly, left to get Sergeant Carter, and then moved up the line to brief the drivers, muttering, "Uh huh. Do something even if it's wrong!" But muttering couldn't stop the thought *What if it was me out there?*

In any event, after getting his little convoy turned onto the road to the An Cao valley, Randy continued to take the point on foot, trotting or walking as the mists and slopes dictated, sometimes almost slipping, for this road, also clay, was poorly graded, eroded in spots, and consequently as slick as ice. Still, no rocket flared out of the fog, no bullets cracked open the dark. There was only the silence of the night, made deeper by the muffled muttering and groaning of engines behind him. He had gone perhaps a kilometer when Sergeant Carter, exasperated, caught up to him. "Sir, you really need to get your ass back there. We can take point. We can follow a fuckin' road, sir." Randy relented. The hills were probably the worst place to meet the enemy. Sergeant Carter and his men were trained grunts. They would know how to handle the sort of trouble they might get into far better than he.

They cleared the last hill and the most likely ambush site. The road sloped into the valley, and they felt a slight breeze begin to shred the mist and fog. Randy realized the breeze would grow stronger in the valley, pushed by air cooling in the hills and sliding down into it.

Ten klicks to go—six miles. At a fast walk, it would take almost two hours; at a jog, an hour plus. They had already been on the road over a half hour. Time was wasting. He got on the radio. Battalion would be listening, so he didn't bother to call in. "Listen up. Looks like the fog's going to start breaking up. I'm going to take the lead again. Not walking. Jogging. Ajax, your guys on point'll be too slow, and you're carrying a lot more gear. I want you guys to mount up, now. There's a breeze coming, so it's likely to lift soon. Soon as it does, I'll mount up and we'll roll. Over." One after another, each radio replied, softly, "Roger."

Sergeant Carter couldn't decide if the lieutenant was being reckless, stupid, or smart, so he made no comment and motioned his squad to head back to their truck.

The thunder run started at a jog. As he had anticipated, air, cooling over the hills during the night, had begun to slide down into the valley under the thick overcast. His flashlight showed ragged tears in the ring of mist. His cocoon was dissipating, expanding, and then suddenly reforming. It dawned on him that at any real distance, the fog would have smothered the glow of his flashlight, but as the predawn breeze began to shred the fog, the glow of his light could be seen at ever greater distances even while there remained enough fog to make a thunder run too risky.

He might not be exactly a sitting duck, but a walking or trotting duck wasn't much better. When the fog closed back in, part of his mind sighed in relief; another part became worried and frustrated. And when the fog shredded and briefly parted, the different corners of his mind reversed feelings. He wanted to run; he wanted to hide. He wanted to charge; he wanted to retreat. Since he did none of these things, he began to feel almost as stupid as he felt exposed. Randy decided he was hating his job. He was in charge, but nothing was happening that needed his action, leaving him to imagine all dire possibilities while nothing could be done until one was manifest. He decided the drivers were the lucky ones. Their task took all their concentration: keeping their vehicle on the road, not losing sight of the faint glimmer of taillights ahead but keeping a safe distance from them. It pushed imagination aside and rolled fear into a knot that bothered but did not consume. On the other hand, the vehicle commanders had it worse. They had to stare into the night in the forlorn hope of seeing danger before it blew them up. If anyone had it worse than he thought he did, Randy thought it was the engineers and infantrymen sitting in the trucks with nothing to do, shrouded in canvas, mist, and darkness, with what flickers of light did reach their retinas mocking their inability to see. The sounds of the engines both deafened them to danger and announced to the night they were there. He could imagine them, some fleeting the war zone to immerse themselves in brighter moments in days past or days hoped to come; others blocking out fears with tunes in their head, knees bobbing, heads nodding to silent rhythms; and others still simply staring into the dark, praying, or just clamping their jaws against the urge to curse something.

Randy had jogged steadily forward for about ten minutes, covering about a kilometer, when the fog stole away in tattered, dirty sheets and the road to An Cao disappeared into the night ahead. He turned and waved the CEV to a stop. Two helmeted heads were faintly visible. One, the head of the driver, Specialist Paul Bailey, was at about eye level, peering over the top of the CEV's dozer blade. The head of the vehicle commander, Specialist Bobby Higgins, was a good five feet above him, peering over the top of the CEV's .50-caliber machine gun turret. "Higgins!" he shouted. "Frederick and I are going to ride with you! Time to roll!" Then he ran back to his command truck.

"Hey Fred! Grab your radio. I need you with me on the CEV." For some reason, this made Frederick feel better, although he felt safer in the truck, well behind the CEV. As he trotted behind Randy to the CEV and scrambled aboard, he figured the deal was that sitting on his ass in the truck with nothing to do was like being helpless. Clinging to a turret on the lead vehicle of a convoy beside the lieutenant meant there was something he could do—like call in fire on any asshole who shot at him—which meant he wasn't helpless. The stench of the big 750-horsepower diesel engine engulfed them as the CEV hit the accelerator and the fifty-eight ton vehicle lurched forward, dim combat lights off, regular headlights blazing. The thunder run had begun.

Frederick felt even better when Randy had him calling in artillery concentrations. They were fired both to distract any enemy and to serve as signposts. He knew where on the map the shells would land. Taking a bearing on the explosions told him where he was on the road. They barreled up the road at a thrilling fifteen miles an hour, sometimes spurting to almost twenty. On a starless night on a narrow dirt road coated with slippery wet clay, in a fifty-eight-ton tank, this speed was extremely thrilling. While the CEV's headlights lit up the road, the following vehicles kept just their cat's eye combat lights on. They could see only the pinpricks of taillights ahead, centered in the vague halo from the side glow of the CEV's lights. For the drivers of the following vehicles, it was somewhat beyond thrilling.

Aboard Spooky 45, the cargo bay filled with soft sounds, clanks, and thumps as Arlen Washington and Lieutenant Blagget worked on their project. The mechanical noises were connected with quick, low discussions separated by drawn-out strings of Washington's muttered curses. For him, everything was taking too long, the darkness and the sloping floor acting like molasses, doubling the amount of effort required to accomplish every movement, the sharp pains from his broken toe and headache aggravating the situation. Mostly by memory and feel, Washington removed the pod covering the gun mounted in the cargo doorway, exposing the electric motor that drove it and the cable holding the wires that supplied power to the motor and controlled firing. He set to work freeing enough of the cable to allow the gun to swing and then cutting it open to separate the wires to the motor from those controlling the firing switch.

It went more smoothly than Tom had predicted, and for good reason. Arlen Washington had stolen the gun many times in his imagination and, in a sense, in practice. He and Otis cleaned and serviced the guns between missions, and there had been times when, these chores done, Washington had hung back to explore his fantasy and learn how, in practice, to remove the gun and its vital accessories. He'd been caught at it twice—once by Lemuel and once by Chief. He'd had a more-or-less credible story for Chief, who'd complimented him only to find him his usual surly and distant self on the next mission

The part of the operation that had no precedent in Arlen's fantasies was actually hanging the dismounted gun in the door. Replicating what he'd seen in the chopper, Arlen attached cargo straps to the top of the cargo doorframe and to the gun at its balance point to suspend it a little above his waist level. A second strap was attached to the sides of the cargo doorframe and run through the handles of the gun. This strap would prevent the gun from recoiling too far when fired, and because the strap just passed through the handles without being attached to the gun, Arlen could slide the gun left and right along the strap to aim it, as well as swing it up or down. Finally there were two safety straps for the gunner. They weren't needed for firing out the cargo door but were needed for Arlen to be able to swing the gun 180 degrees and fire blindly through the other side, as Captain McLaughlin wanted. With the safety straps, he could do it, but it left his backside hanging way outside the cargo door, leaving him—illogically—feeling a hundred times more vulnerable.

Eddie had been staring into the fog for perhaps thirty minutes when he heard the gun barrels spin up and then wind down. He moved to the gun side of the plane. "Hey, gents. What's the status? Ready to blow us up?"

"Think it will work," Tom replied, "I mean, the gun spins up. Guess it'll fire too."

Eddie chanced standing at the door to look at the gun. The cluster of barrels swayed in a lazy gyration above his head. "Think you can actually hold it when you fire?"

Washington pointed to the straps passing through the handles. "No sweat, sir. No sweat." He grinned. "Want we should test it, sir?"

"Not while I'm standing here. I'll warn Otis and Hector. You sure you can turn it off quick?"

"All I've got to do is flinch," Tom replied, holding the cable up to illustrate.

Eddie shrugged and turned away to the illusory shelter of the tail, where Otis sat with his silent, clammy crew chief. He squatted by the two men. "Any change?"

"No sir."

"Hector? You hanging in there?" Hector mumbled something,

responding possibly to Eddie's voice, possibly to the squeeze of Eddie's hand on his shoulder. "You sure?"

"I can feel his heartbeat in his leg. Hand's kind of cramped."

"I can spell you."

"No sir. Don't think I can let go, anyway."

Eddie sighed. He moved closer to Otis, putting a hand on his shoulder with a helpless longing. "Arlen's got an idea about using one of the guns. We're going to test fire it." He felt Otis shrug, and a moment later, Washington and Tom heard him say, "Anytime, gents. Fire when ready."

Washington looked at the faint outline that was Tom. "Guess we ought to put helmets on, sir."

"What for?"

"Noise."

He was about to make a remark when he saw Washington retrieving his. Tom shrugged, found his in the cockpit and put it on. They took up positions, Washington holding the grips and leaning into the gun, aiming it straight out the door, Tom holding a bight of the cable. Two wires had been pried loose and cut, the insulation stripped from the ends for a short way. Tom held the bight between his palms and the two pairs of wire. "Ready?"

"Sir."

"Spin up." He touched the end of one wire to its mate. The gun motor whined, and the barrels rotated, speeding up to the slowest rate of fire. He slid the tip of one motor wire along the bared section of its mate, bringing the tips of the firing wires closer together until they touched. The blast of light and sound made his hands jerk apart. Darkness and silence then fell in like a tunnel collapsing around them. The sudden silence itself seemed deafening.

After a moment, Tom shouted, "You Okay?"

"Yes sir. Works good."

Tom couldn't see him. The gun was swaying, and Washington wasn't holding it. "Where are you?"

"Sittin' on my ass."

"What happened?"

"I leaned in on it, sir, to hold it steady. Wasn't thinkin' right. Man, it's got some recoil! Got to not lean in but pull back an' keep it tight on the recoil strap."

"Yep. Does kind of give you a start."

Captain McLaughlin's voice drifted in. "You guys okay?"

"Yes sir!" Washington replied.

"Washington, I think you hosed everything between heaven and hell with that burst. You sure you can control it?"

"Yes sir! I know what to do now. Maybe we should do another test."

"No!" Captain McLaughlin's tone was adamant. "You might just blow us all up. Let's say it works and we'll try it again if the shit hits the fan. Now, let's stay low, guys. Charlie thinks to drop a mortar round here, up there won't be the happy place."

"Oh," Tom and Washington said together. Tom jumped down. Perversely, being outside the plane made him feel more vulnerable. Washington slid gingerly to the ground, favoring his hurt foot, and looked back at the barely visible gun swinging slowly in the open door. He felt better with his hands on it, but he guessed the boss was right. He and Tom joined Eddie beside Otis and Hector.

Washington slapped Otis on the shoulder. "Hear the gun, man? We can fire up some shit now!"

"Sarge!" Otis said, "You hear the gun?"

Hector moaned, "Huh?"

"Wake up, Chief!" Otis pushed on his shoulder. "You hear the gun?"

"Gun?"

"Yeah!" Washington all but shouted. "Listen, Chief! No Charlie's gonna get near us now! So you hang in there! Don't you go to fucking sleep!"

"Sleep."

"Don't go to fuckin' sleep! Got that?"

"Don't shout," Eddie said. "We can hear you fine. And so could Charlie a klick away."

"Fuck Charlie, sir!" Washington swept an arm toward the rice paddies hidden in the darkness. "We can cut his ass to pieces now! Hey, you listenin', boss?"

"Chief to you. That flare go out?" The words were strung out, soft, wheezing, slow.

"Sure as hell did." After that, no one else spoke. Silence cloaked them as thoroughly as the night.

Eddie gave Otis's shoulder a squeeze and stood, banging his head on the underside of the plane. "Shit!" He stepped away, patting Washington on his back. Hector was hanging in or he wasn't. There was nothing he could do. There was nothing he could do to help Otis. The mist and the night hid everything: danger and rescue, friend and foe. After a moment, he said he was going to take a leak and then stand guard. A moment later, they heard faintly his stream splashing into the night, then silence, and then scrambling sounds near the right nacelle as Eddie climbed onto it. Then it was deathly quiet again, save for the faint sounds of breathing.

Tom moved and sat on the wet ground near Hector's head. "Chief. Give me some advice."

"You, LT?"

"Yeah. Give me some fucking advice. You know how us lieutenants couldn't pour piss out of a boot if the instructions were written on the heel. So give me some advice!"

Hector seemed to think a moment. "It's kind of cold."

"Yeah. Listen; is it right for an officer to admit he peed in his pants in an emergency landing?" Tom asked, scratching an ear.

"You pissed yourself?"

Tom stiffened, rolling his eyes. *Dumb question!* "No! I'm just asking the question. Like if it came up."

"Damn."

"Come on; answer the question!"

Washington blurted through tight lips, restraining a laugh, "You did?"

"I didn't! I'm getting advice from the senior enlisted man here who's in charge of training his lieutenant." Tom held his hands up as if pushing something away. "I didn't say I pissed myself, Chief Villanueva; I just asked a question."

"You asked advice. Not a question. You pissed yourself, sir. Don't ever admit it. Are you cold?"

"I won't admit it." Tom wondered why he'd suddenly posed such a stupid question. Now, if they all woke up in heaven, hell, or still here,

68

he suspected he'd be stuck with something no amount of denial was going to erase. "Shit."

"Flare got out, right?"

"Flare?"

Washington piped up. "Chief, guess he saved our ass, LT. I'd just pulled the pin on it when something hit my helmet. Near knocked me out, and I dropped the flare. It didn't go out. Fell on the floor. Chief got it, pushed it to me. Man, my head was ringing, dizzy. I tried to kick it out, but it just went backward. Chief got it out just before it went off."

"No shit? Hector?"

"It got out, right?"

"Sure did," Washington said.

"You cold?"

"Hector!" Tom called. "Does the recoil get worse the longer you fire the guns?"

"Huh?"

While Tom tried new silly gambits to harass Hector into staying awake, Washington couldn't bear standing helpless, doing nothing, staring at nothing. Quietly, he climbed back into the plane, gripped the gun, and pointed it at the open crypt of night. It felt better. He started to think of home but then began to dream of home as he thought maybe it would be when he got back. Jason said his education benefits would be his ticket to the good life. But that was a lot of work to get some piece of paper so he could sit in an office all day. The vision of a deadly Lincoln Town Car or maybe a Continental was more appealing. Girls and guns. *The* gun. He let his imagination run free, and the night took on alluring shapes.

Eddie McLaughlin had climbed onto the left wing to stand watch, only to realize the added height would not let him see the enemy any sooner. He slipped to the ground, leaned against the wing, and thought of his wife in order to not think of Hector and their situation. He calculated what time of day or night it was in San Antonio. It was two fifteen in the morning in Vietnam, one fifteen in the afternoon at home—right after lunch. The last time he had gone through this drill, she would have been getting ready for bed, and that was a much more romantic thought. He was imagining a final glimpse of a tantalizing nightie while reaching to turn out the light when the PRC-90 survival radio came to life. "Spooky Four-Five."

"You guys under attack?"

"No. Quiet as a graveyard and dark as a tomb."

"Okay. Cavalry's coming. They thought they might have seen an explosion near you."

"No. Heard some, like, artillery way off to the south. Oh! We test fired one of the miniguns for a second."

"You haven't shut down?"

"We rigged it to fire, just in case."

"Keep us posted."

"Roger that. How long before they get here?"

The radio crackled the unsatisfying reply "They're on the way. Out."

On the thunder run, six long minutes passed, each like an hour, each a clone of the last. The diesel roared in their ears, the shells exploded as planned, the night remained impenetrable, and the road remained under them. Their clothes, dampened by the fine mists, made the night air uncomfortably chilling. Frederick periodically called Battalion with the same report "No contact, proceeding according to plan. Out." This gave him something to do and kept headquaters off the LTs' back. Suddenly, far ahead, he saw a flash of light and a moment later, just registering above the noise of the engines, heard a brief sound like thunder. "You see that, LT? What the hell was it?" Frederick shouted. Higgins and Bailey had also seen it. The CEV immediately slowed, its brake light giving just enough warning to the dump truck behind to avoid rear-ending it. Randy hadn't seen the flash. Giving Frederick a puzzled look as the CEV slowed, he grabbed the phone plugged into the external intercom jack. "What's up?"

"Looked and sounded like some kind of explosion up ahead, sir," Higgins replied.

"How far?" Randy fumbled with his flashlight and map. "We'd better halt."

"Roger." The CEV slowed to a stop, and the headlights went out. Higgins broke in again, answering the first question. "Hard to say, sir. Half a klick? Five klicks? Flash and sound weren't together, but maybe more'n a second apart. Five seconds, maybe?"

Randy knew that what felt like five seconds could be two or ten. He also knew sound travelled something like eleven hundred feet per second, which would put the source at roughly 350 meters. If it had been only two seconds, less than a klick. Five seconds, about a mile, and at ten seconds, about two miles, or a little over three klicks. *Somewhere between under one and not more than three klicks.* He took a bearing on the direction Higgins had given on the flash. It was in line with their objective. The air crew could be under attack.

"Will. Radio." Frederick had scrambled close to Randy as soon as the CEV had stopped, and Randy had the handset in hand almost as he spoke. "Bagger Three, Boiler Two-Six. Saw a flash, possible explosion, in line with our objective, possibly on the objective. Can you check; are they under attack?"

Randy didn't wait for a reply. After all, they were a rescue mission. If the poor bastards were under attack, the sooner they arrived, the better. "Higgins! That flash could be on the objective. Let's move out."

The CEV lurched forward. Everyone else followed suit, aware something had happened but otherwise uninformed and unsurprised by the brief halt and the sudden start.

Randy stuffed his map under the webbing of his combat harness and keyed the radio again. "Granite Niner-One, Boiler Two-Six. Fire Alpha Papa One-One, two rounds. Over."

"Boiler Two-Six. Roger, two rounds, Alpha Papa One-One, Out." Less than a minute later, the speaker crackled. "Boiler Two-Six. Two rounds on the way. Out." A moment later, Bagger Three called. The downed crew reported no enemy activity.

Randy visualized the markings on his map. Near where the road crossed the river they were following, he'd made a small circle for the objective. A few hundred meters to the southwest of the circle, a small X annotated AP-12, the next artillery concentration he intended to fire.

A few hundred meters to the northeast, another X annotated AP-14, and right beside the circle was the annotation AP-13. This was Randy's "annihilation" concentration, plotted to land right on the crash site to destroy the aircraft remains and anyone near it.

Two eight-inch rounds, each weighing about two hundred pounds, exploded almost as one some two dozen feet above the point on the ground designated AP-11. When Randy took a bearing on the flashes, he realized they had less than two kilometers to go.

CHAPTER 6

FOG FIGHT

Sergeant Carter's estimation of what enemy might be in the An Cao valley was on the money—almost. Almost because it just so happened that a small enemy sapper team of ten men armed with AK-47 assault rifles, hand grenades, and an RPG-7 rocket-propelled grenade launcher were in the valley and not far away. The team had no mission in the valley; it was simply transiting it on a mission beyond the mouth of the valley.

They had not yet entered the valley when they observed Spooky 45 turn on its landing lights and crash-land somewhere on the far side of the An Cao stream. When they did not observe any fires or explosions, they realized there was an opportunity. It would not be too difficult to find a way across the river and determine exactly where it had come down. At night, Americans often carelessly made noise, smoked cigarettes, and even used flashlights. The enemy had had no doubt the Americans would attempt a rescue. They always did and tried to recover or destroy anything of possible use, which meant there could be an opportunity to booby trap the plane and any bodies to kill more Americans with their own munitions.

Two things helped the enemy. The rain had thinned to fine mists and, in more and more places, quit altogether. The fog that had formed was now shredding from the cool air sinking from the hills and here and there briefly clearing completely. Above the fog, the thicker cloud layers were breaking up, allowing hints of moonlight to filter through, breaking the black night into blacks of different textures—enough to reveal the plane at ever greater distances. For Tom Blagget and Arlen Washington, their efforts with the gun required them to use a flashlight, which was impossible to fully conceal. Also, another flashlight occasionally blinked as the captain checked on Timmy and Hector.

These slight things that were making work easier for the Americans were also making it easier for the enemy. These occasional gleams of light helped guide the sappers, and as they got closer, sounds also helped. Then the plane's exact location was revealed with a blinding a blast of light and sound. The wild spray of tracers streaking harmlessly overhead revealed the plane but also revealed that the American survivors were not defenseless.

Uncertain as to what defenses awaited them at the crash site, the sappers elected to do what GIs called a recon by fire. Having crept to within a hundred meters of the wreck they spread out so as not to present a concentrated target. The leader opened fire with two shots from behind a rice paddy dyke and then quickly crawled to a new spot. His shots were the signal for the rest of the team to do the same.

Most of the twenty rounds fired were high. One hit the tail fin. One passed through the fuselage near the cockpit. One hit just below the cargo door, and another hit a wing. That one ricocheted and plowed into the ground near Hector's feet. The rest gave a faint, snapping salute as they passed overhead. The fog dimmed and smeared the muzzle flashes, but it was unmistakable that they were muzzle flashes coming from a wide area.

Washington was the first to react. He had heard enough small-arms fire hits on the fuselage while in the air to recognize the sound on the ground, especially since one of the bullets had hit within a couple of feet of him. "We're under fire! We're under fire! LT! I need you!"

Tom had been on his knees beside Otis and Hector. Both he and Otis had been pelting Hector with questions in low, urgent, commanding tones to keep him awake. The sounds of the shots were partly muffled by the fog, although the distinctive sounds of the hits to the fuselage were not; nor was the ricochet that splashed mud on him. The sounds registered, but not their meaning, until Washington shouted. Only Washington, from his more elevated position, had seen any of the muzzle flashes. "What the hell?" Tom jumped up, grazed his head against the belly of the plane, slipped, and fell to the roadway. He shook his head; fumbled around for Washington's M16, which he had taken custody of; found it; and raced to the cargo door hunched over, pointing the M16 generally in the direction of the enemy, squeezing the trigger as fast as he could. But he had not first chambered a round, and the M16 remained mute. "LT! You comin'?" Washington shouted.

"Yeah, yeah!" The enemy's next volley came with a couple more hits on the fuselage. "Your damn rifle doesn't work!" Tom shouted as he scrambled on board. With a loud clang, a bullet struck the tail on a structural member just above Otis's head. Huddling protectively over Hector, he cried out, "Enemy fire!" Captain McLaughlin pulled his thirty-eight from its holster and ran to the tail. As he did, a vague flash in the fog stopped him. He used both hands to aim at where he thought the flash had come from and emptied his revolver before screaming, "Get the gun going!" He then ran to Otis. "Where's the M16?"

"LT has it, sir!"

"I need you, forty-five." Eddie felt down Otis's back to his holster and pulled the automatic free. He worked the slide and foolishly emptied the precious seven-round magazine at the night.

"Dozen or more out there, LT!" Washington shouted. "Spin her up! Hurry, LT!"

Standing in the yawning cargo door, both men felt naked, and their exposure gave added urgency to do something since they couldn't do the obvious thing and jump for the protection of the ditch. Tom flicked on his flashlight, having fitted the red filter that came with it. The faint ruby beam danced drunkenly around the interior while he fumbled for the cable ends with mud-slick hands. A bullet punched through a few feet away. His hands began to shake. Suddenly the cabin filled with a whine and the gun barrels began to spin up. "Okay, okay, LT. Goddamn, the fuckers must be gettin' close!" he hissed without any real idea of where the enemy was.

Eddie appeared in the door. "Tom! Gimme the rifle!"

"Stand back! We're going to fire! Washington, you ready?" Tom shouted. The flashlight was clipped to his flight suit, the cable ends more or less in its beam.

Eddie slid into the drainage ditch as he heard the snap of more bullets and began frantically reloading his revolver.

The Spooky 45 crew heard a whistle blow. They had no idea what it meant, just a foreboding that it wasn't good. The sappers were splitting into two teams, each sprinting closer and farther to each side. Then they fired a couple more shots and repeated the maneuver to close in for the kill from two directions, forcing the defenders to divide their firepower while the attackers could concentrate theirs.

Suddenly the spinning barrels slowed and the electric motor whine died. "What the hell, LT?"

"Sorry. Ready?" Tom stared at his shaking hands, shamed. "Dear God, don't let it end this way," he prayed aloud. Washington was too tense to notice.

Arlen's forearms began to hurt from gripping the gun too hard, waiting for the recoil. In quick succession, three more of the distinctive pop-clap sounds of a supersonic bullet punching through the fuselage punctuated his desperation. The motor began to whine again. Tom didn't notice. "God, it's not just me; it's all of us. Please! Hail Mary, full of grace." His voice trailed off, and his hands grew steady and brought the firing wires together.

"Ready, LT! Ready! Two-second burst!" Washington swung the barrel between the points where he had seen the flashes. Tom closed the second set of wires.

The mists were weird, shifting from a solid front to almost gossamer quilts of fog floating in the intense black of night that seemed to contain nothing else to scatter light. The road would be all but hidden one instant, seemingly clear forever the next; the next it would vanish under a quilt of mist only a couple of feet thick that undulated across it like some great, dissolving jellyfish, and the next, the world would be obscured to Randy and Higgins and perfectly clear to Bailey in the driver compartment a couple of feet below them. The on-again, off-again visibility produced a very lurching progress. As the CEV was the lead vehicle, the driver, knowing the urgency, went as fast as he dared, but each time a shred of fog hid the road, he had to slow, and as soon as it cleared, he sped up. He was giving the convoy whiplash—especially the poor driver of the M42 Duster at the end of the column.

Some moments it seemed to Randy that he was looking at a clear night through the slats of a vague gray venetian blind. In one of these moments, Higgins shouted, "Holy shit, LT! See that?"

A ruddy light like the sliver of the red blaze of a setting sun tearing through dark clouds split the dark and swept up and down in an arc that ended in a spray of bright stars scattering in all directions. As abruptly as it appeared, the light vanished. A distant, drawn-out hoot, as if from the throat of a gigantic owl, broke the silence shortly after.

Randy had seen it, but he'd seen something else shortly before—twinkles, no more than three or four, he thought. He'd seen it before—distant small-arms fire at night. "Hold up!" he shouted. "Kill the lights!" Then he grabbed the radio mike and said quickly, "Three-six! See that shooting? Bearing about three forty degrees. Can your guy with the starlight see anything?" He heard "Stand by. Out." He then gave the mike back to Frederick.

The venetian blinds of the night mists closed again, forcing Randy's eyes inward to gaze over the landscapes of imagination. The small-arms fire was not, this time, someone else's problem, but his. He was heading into it. A first firefight. Nowhere to hide, nowhere to dig in, just a mission to charge ahead. How many enemy? A handful? A hundred? A thousand? His mouth suddenly felt terribly dry. How far was it? What the hell was that flash? Enemy? Friendlies? He grabbed the radio mike again and called in a report and asked for an update from the downed crew only to hear a frustrating "Stand by. Out."

The combination of the invisibility of everything and the enveloping soft, penetrating noise of the idling engines, at once announcing their presence and masking other sounds, made it impossible for Randy to shrug it off. It wasn't, perhaps, exactly fear, but more like a kind of trepidation—the fear of uncertainty and possible inadequacy. As a combat engineer, he'd been trained to build things and blow things up, and to fight as infantry if necessary. At the moment, though, felt he must have slept through his little infantry training.

"Boiler two-six, Ajax one-three. Over."

"Two-six. Anything, Carter?" Staff Sergeant Victor Carter grimaced at Randy's use of his name rather than his proper call sign.

"One-three. Negative on the starlight. I and a couple of guys saw something … like a flash … but with the mist back, the starlight's worthless."

"Roger. I saw first what looked like some small arms, then a weird flash, then nothing."

"Dismount?" Sergeant Carter replied.

"No. Not yet. Stand by. Out." Randy gave the handset back to Frederick and chewed on a knuckle, hoping Bagger Three would get back to him fast.

But Sergeant Carter wasn't done. His voice came back. "We ought to kill the engines so's we might hear something, seeing as how we can't see squat. Over."

"Right. I'll pass the word." Randy felt a twinge of chagrin at himself for not thinking of that. He handed the handset back to Frederick and almost immediately heard a sound from the radio. Frederick had the handset to his ear and passed it back to Randy.

"Bagger Three, LT."

Randy grabbed the handset. "Boiler Two-six. Over."

"Two-six, the crew reported scattered small-arms fire. Incoming. No one hurt, several hits to the aircraft. Enemy estimated maybe one hundred meters out."

"Shit."

"Affirmative. Sounds like probing. Also sounds like you're pretty close. A race against time—if it's feasible."

The last three words dumped it in Randy's lap. Did this show confidence in him? Or was it just the dodging of a bullet? *Christ,* he thought, *What would Dad have done?* He instantly told himself it didn't matter. He wasn't his dad; he was himself. But he couldn't help it.

Dad had been a sergeant in an engineer unit in World War II. Randy had asked him once what he had done and was told that his unit was a support engineer unit and did mostly construction and repairs "safely in the rear." Randy had felt a little disappointed at that, though he guessed that lots of people had to do all that support stuff for an army and were just as vital as the guys up front.

One day, a friend of his father reacted to something Randy had said. Randy could not remember what he had said or what the conversation was about. He only remembered what the friend said. "Your dad was in the Two Hundred Ninety-First Engineers, son, in the Battle of the Bulge. In the heart of the Battle of the Bulge. You ask him about that, son. You ask him."

He did, but Dad had very little to say. "Well, the Germans surprised a lot of rear-echelon troops, son." Then he looked away chuckling. "Now, a buddy of mine—he was in … in another squad—he had an exciting story. They were supposed to blow a bridge, but not until—and if—the Germans got close. No one was sure what roads they'd come down, and we didn't want to blow bridges and trap some GIs on the wrong side. So my buddy's squad leader told him to go up the road a ways and signal if the Germans came. Well, the Germans came—a column of tanks. He realized the tanks were a lot faster than he was and would beat him to the bridge. So he stepped into the middle of the road, held up his hand, and shouted 'Halt!' Damned if the German tanks didn't just stop. He turned around and walked back down the road like he owned it 'til he was out of sight, and then he ran like hell to the bridge. They blew it, and the Germans were screwed. '*Halt!*'" He laughed, slapping his thigh. "Just 'Halt!' Stopped a whole column of German tanks! Ha!"

The only war story Dad had ever told was about someone else. "Somehow," Randy said to himself, "I don't think that'll work here."

He spoke into the radio. All the vehicles and the rifle squads were on the same frequency. Battalion, Bagger Three specifically, could hear and follow everything. "Listen up, Boiler and Ajax. You heard. Our objective came under small-arms fire just now. Probing, likely. So we've got to haul ass. Keep max distance from the guy in front of you, but don't lose sight of the taillights! It's maybe two klicks to the objective. We've moving out now!" Handing the handset back to Frederick, he shouted, "Higgins! Let's roll! Fast as you can—safely."

"Hang on, gents!" The CEV's headlights blazed on and filled the mist with a phosphorescent glow and illuminated a few yards of the glistening, red clay road surface. The CEV lurched forward. Higgins put his hands on the controls for the commander's turret and checked to ensure the .50-caliber machine gun it boasted was ready to fire. He called to his gunner in the main turret to ensure the cannon's coaxial machine gun was also loaded and ready. He moved his turret left and right, the machine gun up and down. If they were ambushed, the faster he could bring the heavy machine gun to bear on the enemy, the less damage that enemy could do. "The key to breaking an ambush is to gain fire superiority—fast." Those words from a classroom might soon mean something.

They were rolling, and there was nothing more Randy could do except hold on and think. His thoughts bounced back and forth between his father and his mission. He had followed his father into the army, into the Corps of Engineers, and thought to follow him into engineering. Now, suddenly, he wondered what the hell Dad had actually taught him. What had Dad learned down this same road—more or less—almost three decades before? Nothing he had passed on. "Duty, son," he remembered Dad saying the day he graduated from college with a degree in mechanical engineering and an ROTC commission as a second lieutenant. "Three things you'll always face: your duty, your mission, and the problem of how best to do your duty in any given mission without compromising your honor."

"Sounded great," Randy said to himself. "Profound. Should be engraved somewhere. I've got one hairy mission, forty-six—no, fifty-one—lives on the line, a duty to both, and no clue what to do except to keep my fingers crossed. Where's honor fit in? I could have used some real advice, Dad. Like how you did it when things went to shit." He began to feel exposed not just physically but also morally. He had no plans, no standard operating procedures or drills put in place to follow in case they were attacked on the road or while at the objective. He was winging it, and somehow that felt almost dishonorable.

In the middle of these thoughts, like a scene change in a movie, the CEV's headlights suddenly showed the road disappearing under the tail of an airplane older than anyone there and the booted legs of three men scattering as if a small formation had just been dismissed for the weekend.

The tail loomed into view so suddenly Specialist Bailey braked too hard. The CEV began to skid. After all the rain, if the CEV went into a ditch, it could be hell getting out again. Bailey overcorrected, and the CEV began to skid in the opposite direction. It slowed to ten, five, four miles an hour and, with a kind of ponderous grace like a fat woman slipping on the dance floor, eased into the same ditch that had claimed the gunship's engine. Bailey instantly put it in reverse, but the left side of the dozer blade had dug into the far bank of the ditch. As a result, instead of helping turn the CEV more perpendicular to the ditch so it might back out, it was simply digging a ditch in the near embankment that threatened to let the whole left side slide into the ditch. Bailey immediately stopped and cried, "Shit!"

The CEV's commander echoed Bailey at the same time. Like Bailey, Higgins knew exactly how much trouble they had just gotten into. Randy also screamed "Shit!" as the final bump into the ditch threw him into the rice paddy just beyond. Frederick screamed because the final bump had thrown him against one of the arms of the CEV's crane, cracking the ulna in his right forearm.

The dump truck managed to stop where the CEV would have been had it not slid off the road. The rest managed to stop without damage, but the convoy pretty much ended up bumper-to-bumper.

CHAPTER 7

A MEET AND GREET

The sweeping blast from the minigun silenced the enemy. Had they been blown away? Had they run away? Were they simply crouching out there, planning a different approach? What the silence meant was anyone's guess, but Washington cried loudly that he had "Hosed 'em!"

When the silence dragged on, they began to relax. Eddie McLaughlin quit staring into the dark where the enemy fire had come from and climbed back onto the nacelle of the right engine, which had been torn off the wing and was now resting just behind the tail, facing backward. The fog was beginning to shred, which gave him a longer view. Almost as soon as he settled himself, Eddie cried out, "Cavalry's coming!" Tom came running from the cargo door side, Washington following more gingerly on the slippery clay. Eddie slid off his perch, and without thinking about it, the three lined up as if at a formal reception.

"Headlights! Hoorah!"

"Ballsy bastards! Thank God!"

All they saw were fleeting haloed pinpricks of light in the distance, fading and brightening as the mists shifted. They could see only one pair of lights, and as the convoy drew closer and they could hear it, the CEV's engine drowned out the sounds of the other vehicles following it. "One vehicle?" Tom asked, wondering how they would get themselves and the chief on it and out without killing him. "God, please get Chief through this. Us too," he muttered.

Washington muttered over and over, unintelligibly, "Hurry up, you fuckers!" oblivious to the many times similar words had been thrown at him.

For some minutes, the lights seemed to come no closer but just fade and brighten with the shifting mists. Then, somehow, from far away, they were suddenly close, but how close the eye couldn't judge; and then they were closing fast, large, bright, and blinding. "He'd better slow down on this stuff," Tom said. "I mean like soon—like now!"

"Jesus! Run!" Eddie shouted. Washington darted to the right, Eddie and Tom to the left. Otis looked up and saw the looming headlights, but there was nothing he could do. He huddled over Hector and closed his eyes. The three ended up in the ditches, Washington scrambling frantically along as the headlights seemed to have picked him out to bear down on. He stepped on a piece of cowling that carried him forward like a boogie board on ebbing surf for a few feet before he flipped backward into the muck and the fifty-eight tons of CEV grunted to a halt just a few feet behind him. Gasping, Washington sat up, wiping muddy hands on his clothes. He shouted at the night, "Anything ever happen that ain't fucked up?"

Eddie sat up in the ditch, slimed with mud and boiling inside. They had seen the headlights from a good distance away. Why the hell hadn't they seen him or the plane? It sure as hell was big enough. But Eddie had not realized the same thing the driver and the vehicle commander had not realized. The headlights on the CEV were similar to truck or automobile lights, but barely thirty yards of road ahead was well illuminated, and the glare from the light reflected off the road, and the thin mist obscured things even more effectively than simple darkness. In addition, the low reflectance of the dull matte paint on the gunship's fuselage did an admirable job of making the plane hard to see in a foggy night.

When Washington managed to stand, the anger at being forced to jump in a ditch by a stupid accident had ebbed. *Shit happens. If this was the worst, thank you Jesus!* The monster that had just nearly pulped him looked like a tank with a bulldozer blade. He'd never heard of such a machine. Then he saw the monster wasn't alone. Behind it—or next to it, really—was another vehicle. "Jesus, boss, is that a fucking dump truck?"

"What the hell would a dump truck be—Lord! It sure as hell looks like one!" Eddie stumbled onto the roadway. "What kind of cavalry has an armored bulldozer and a dump truck?" He approached the weird bulldozer-tank thing, revolver in hand, stopping at the edge of the pool of light from the CEV's headlamps, revealing a flight suit covered in mud. Holding his hand out to block the direct glare from the headlight, he saw the helmets of the driver and commander. "Gentlemen! I could have told you. This road's a bitch to stop on. You guys have a stretcher?" He suddenly jerked his head to the right. "Washington! Otis! You guys okay?"

"Shit!"

"That a roger?"

"Nothing broke, sir," Washington replied calmly. "Just took a fuckin' mud bath."

"We're okay!" Otis called out. "They got a medic?"

The driver and the CEV commander just stared, both still thinking only of the fix they were in. He tried again. "I'm Captain McLaughlin. Welcome to wherever we are. I hope you have a medic and a stretcher." Eddie paused, beginning to wonder what it meant, in terms of bad news, that he was seeing a very big, weird-looking tank nose-down in a ditch and not moving.

Specialist Higgins recovered his wits from the shock of nearly crashing into an airplane and sliding into a ditch. "Kill the lights, Paul!" Then he repeated the command into his radio. The world suddenly became totally dark. It would be several long minutes before the eyes of the men near the plane would adjust enough to see even a hint of objects around them.

As soon as they had stopped, Specialist Vasquez had jumped up to look forward over the cab top. The darkness behind the CEV was almost absolute, but he could see the gunship's fuselage in the canted headlights of the CEV. He turned away, toward the tailgate. "We're here, Sarge!" Then the lights went out.

But Sergeant Carter was on it. Neither he nor his men had lost their night vision. "Secure your gear! Weapons safe! Boots laced, helmets strapped, asses tight, eyes open!" He didn't expect replies. They knew the drill. He wanted them alert and thinking. "First Squad, deploy left. Sergeant Warrant, Third Squad deploy right! Pierce, Hackworth! You're stretcher-bearers. Go with Vasquez. All right, go, go, go!" The men tumbled out, some slipping on the slick clay, but they all got to their respective ditches and set up a rough perimeter. Two men stayed in the cab, one manning the .50-caliber machine gun on a ring mount over the cab, the other the precious night vision scope mounted on his rifle, as he was the best shot in the squad and in fact the best in his company. For the time being, it was not useful, as thirty to fifty meters off the road, the mist diffused the ambient light into a uniform green haze in the eyepiece.

The CEV's headlights were off, but the combat lights were on. By their faint light, Vasquez could just make out the silhouette of the CEV and the tail of the aircraft looming above it. He moved alongside the CEV until he saw figures standing near it. He guessed they were the air crew. "I'm the medic. Where's the wounded?"

Otis heard him, and before anyone else could reply, he shouted, "Medic! Over here!"

Vasquez turned to Pierce and Hackworth who were right behind him with the stretcher. "Tommy! Jim! Over here!" Vasquez darted toward the sound of Otis's voice. The first thing that caught his eye was the bloody IV bag in Otis's hand. Then he was kneeling beside Hector. "What you got, man?"

As Vasquez examined Hector's wound and began working on it, he introduced himself, for he'd seen that Hector was not the only one in shock. Otis was almost babbling. "Hey, man, I'm Henrique Vasquez, who're you?"

Otis had backed up to give Vasquez room. Holding slightly trembling hands in front of him, glancing alternately at his hands and at Vasquez, he asked, almost pleadingly, "Will he be all right? I'm not a medic! I did what I could, but I don't know, I don't know if I did right, you know? Did I fuck up? Did I?"

"Is okay, amigo! You did great! Calm down, amigo. What's your name?"

"Otis. Timmy Otis. Is he …?"

"You get yourself calm, amigo; you done great, but we got work to do here, no? You tell me what happen. How he got hit—everything. Okay?"

Otis calmed down as he related the story, and Vasquez kept complimenting him, partly from sincerity, partly to make him feel better, and partly for the patient's morale and wakefulness. When Otis was done, Vasquez told him and Chief he had to go see when they'd get rolling and what truck they'd go in. He reminded both how important it was for Hector to stay awake.

Otis watched Vasquez disappear and suddenly felt more alone than before. "Chief, you thirsty?"

"Huh?"

Otis slid close, putting a hand on Chief's shoulder. "You thirsty?"

"No, no, don't think so."

"What would you like to talk about?"

"Nothing, I think." Chief closed his eyes.

"You gotta stay awake, Chief. Talking's the best way."

Chief turned his head enough to look at Otis. "So okay. How you meet your girl? Merry, right?"

"Usual way, I guess. In school. We dated. Thought about getting married, but there was the draft. Better to volunteer and get some choice, you know? So how'd you meet your wife?"

"My wife?"

"Yeah. How'd you meet her?" Otis took Chief's hand and held it.

"Ah—I don't know."

"Oh, come on, Chief. Bet she'd break your arm if she heard you say that."

"No. So long ago. Don't remember."

"Come on; think. Not like you're an old man, Chief."

"I knew her when I was a kid. First, maybe second grade, I think."

"No kidding! Like when you were six or seven?"

"Si. Yeah."

"So when, you know, you two fall in love?"

Chief managed a weak chuckle. "Don't know. Jus' one day, we're still in grade school, Maria, she asks if we're gonna get married when we grow up. I said 'Why not?' We just never changed our minds."

"Wow. Wow, Chief. That's so cool! You got kids?"

"Si. Three." Hector smiled and closed his eyes.

"So okay! How old are they?" Chief didn't respond. Loudly, he asked again.

"Oh, yeah. Two, five, and seven. No ... now, las' week! Eight, yeah, José is eight."

"So what're their names? The other two?"

"You ask too many questions. You got water?"

"Yeah, sure." Otis gently lifted Hector's head and let water from his canteen trickle into Hector's mouth. He had to tip it high, for it was nearly empty. "Okay, you know what the medic said, Chief. You got to stay awake."

"Then let me ask questions. Me, I'm *el jefe*, right? What you gonna do when you get home, eh?"

"Well, I'm not gonna tell Merry about this trip; that's for sure. She'd freak out. And what if I want to stay in?"

"Mistake, Timmy."

"Why?

"Don' hide things from her."

"I don't want her freaking out."

"You don' have to tell war stories. But be smart. Make a decision together. Before you marry, man. Then you can decide what's more important—air force or love."

"Air force or love, huh?" Otis chuckled. "One or the other?"

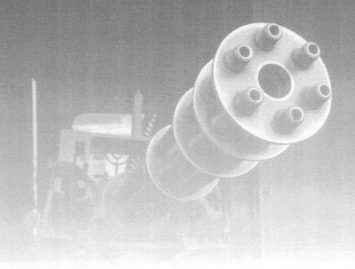

CHAPTER 8

TURNING AROUND

When he saw Vasquez and the two grunts with a stretcher slip past to the airplane, Higgins spoke into his mike to the driver. "Paul, let's see how deep this shit is." Both men climbed out of the CEV. Paul Bailey headed for the ditch, and Bobby Higgins for Eddie. "Sir, you the pilot?" Higgins asked, forgetting to salute the muddy officer with a disgusted expression. Then he realized why the officer was probably muddy. "Sorry, sir. The fog. Makes a kind of glare in headlights. Can see some of the road, but everything else is like whiteout. We just didn't see the plane. Then the friggin' mud's like ice. Sir."

Eddie stepped forward and put his hands on Higgins's shoulders. The corners of his lips twitched with a faint, rueful grin. "For a moment there, I got a bit worried you'd put a dent in my plane." He grabbed Higgins's hand and shook it. "Captain Ed McLaughlin. As you can see, I didn't do too well on this mud either."

Higgins blinked. He was not surprised to not get dressed down; that kind of thing tended to happen in the rear by sergeants with sharp creases in their fatigues. Still, he was relieved. The rule was hardly ironclad, and he'd never met an air force type. "Sir, we need to get the hell out of here. Every monkey in the jungle saw us coming."

"Not to worry. Every monkey in the jungle saw me land over two hours ago, son. They took a few shots at us, but I think we scared 'em off—for a while, anyway. You in charge?"

"Hell no sir. Lieutenant Hanley is."

"And he's here?"

"Yes sir! Somewhere." Higgins looked back toward the CEV. "Paul! Where's the LT?"

Lieutenant Hanley had determined that he hadn't broken anything, and that he was soaked and had lost his map and flashlight. Then he remembered hearing a cry of pain behind him. "Frederick! You okay?"

He heard a moan from above and then, "Don't know. Banged my arm. Hurts like hell."

Then Randy heard Higgins call to Paul. "I'm on the ground. In the mud. You okay, Higgins?"

"Yes sir! Got the pilot here, sir. He's a captain."

"I need a flashlight. Got to find my map."

Frederick said, "I got mine, sir."

"Can you get down?"

"Don't know. My arm."

"Okay, don't try. Call Battalion. Tell 'em we're here. Linkup successful. More later." He stumbled toward the front on the CEV, noted dismally the depth of the ditch and the angle of the CEV, scrambled up onto the road, and, in the dim light of the CEV's combat lights, saw two strangers. "Hey, Higgins. Can you and Bailey help Frederick, then find my map and flashlight? Lost them when I got thrown off. Left side. Then I guess we'll see what we can do about a better parking spot." He looked at the strangers dressed in what looked like muddy overalls. "You have a wounded man?"

"Yeah, my crew chief. Your medic's already with him—thanks. We might want to move. We got shot at from over there—not too far, either. I'm Captain McLaughlin. Eddie McLaughlin. Formerly pilot in command of this once lovely lady. My copilot, Lieutenant Tom Blagget."

They shook hands. Randy said, "Sir," and gave a quick salute.

"Lieutenant Hanley, sir. Second Platoon, uh, augmented; A Company; 134th Combat Engineer Battalion."

"Engineers? What the hell you guys doing way out here?" Eddie asked. He then added, "Now what?"

Randy looked blank. Then he tossed the ball back. "What do you want to do about your plane, sir?"

"Do about my plane? My *MaryAnn*? Want to do? *Want* to fly it out of here." Eddie laughed, jerking his slumped shoulders up. "But since she's missing a wing, both engines, and a runway, I guess the next option is to put poor *MaryAnn* out of her misery." At that he almost choked. He had named the plane after his wife, having told others "MaryAnn" was the name of his first girlfriend, which was also true. And now, in an instant, he felt almost bereaved, as if he were losing the real MaryAnn.

"Right, sir. Uh, anything we need to salvage?"

Washington had gotten out of the ditch and joined them. "Sir. The guns and ammo."

McLaughlin looked at the army lieutenant. "Might be nice, but do we have time?"

Randy rubbed his eyes with both hands, turned to look at the CEV, and turned back. "Probably do, sir. We have to get this guy out of the ditch and rig your plane."

Just then Sergeant Jarvis joined the group. "Sir, I've had the crews dismount, left and right; everyone's locked and loaded. Haven't seen any activity out there." Just then, glancing toward the CEV, he shouted, "Bailey, how'd you manage this fuckup?"

"Not his fault, Sarge," Higgins answered for him. "You know we were hauling ass. Headlights making the fog like a fucking frosted window. Both of us straining eyeballs, but suddenly that plane was right in front of us and Bailey might as well have been trying to stop this thing on an ice rink!"

"What pla—" He cut himself short, suddenly aware of the vague shadow in the mist he had not even noticed. "Oh."

Randy stepped in and introduced Sergeant Jarvis to the two officers. Stepping forward to shake Sergeant Jarvis's hand, Tom pointed to the muddiest of them. "And Airman Second Class Arlen Washington, gunner, general pain in the ass, and life-saving master improviser."

"Sarge," Washington muttered. He then added, "Could use some help. We can salvage the guns and ammo. Won't take long. Then we can book outta here."

"Guns?"

"Three miniguns. Got one remounted so we can aim it. Blasted the shit out of Charlie when you guys were still coming. He was shooting at us, but ain't heard a peep since I hosed 'em." Washington grinned what was really a beautiful smile, and then snorted.

Randy said, "That, like, flash of light we saw?"

"Yeah, could be! Yes sir!"

Just then, Vasquez appeared. "Sir, how soon can we leave? Our WIA, we got to get him help fast, sir. *Fast.*"

"Right." A whirlwind of thoughts filled Randy's mind. The CEV, nose-down in a ditch, loomed large behind him; the plane that needed to be destroyed loomed large in front; an unknown enemy loomed large in the darkness; all obstacles ranged against him and Vasquez's wounded man. He looked around the cluster of muddy men and thought he should at least feel a bit heroic, cavalry to the rescue and all, but he simply felt, at least for the moment, paralyzed.

Sergeant Jarvis broke into his reverie, "Sir?"

Randy almost laughed. There seemed to be a hundred different inflections a sergeant could give that one little word. This one had the inflection of a good sergeant giving his lieutenant one last chance to not look stupid. "Right," he said again, and he paused, rubbing his eyes. "Get Mancini and his guys to help with the salvage from the plane and rig it for demo. Lassky and his boys, help Higgins with the CEV. Get Warrant and Carter to set up defense. And that night-vision thing, the starlight scope—pick a good spot, but not too far away from, uh, me. Ask what they think about maybe a patrol."

"Right, sir. Carter's already got the grunts deployed. You know, if these airmen shut Charlie up, at least for now, with their minigun, maybe a little show of our firepower? The trucks' machine guns, the CEV, and the Duster? A little mad minute? Make the little shits think twice, sir?"

Uncertain, Randy stiffened, looking away from Jarvis and out into the night. After a moment, he looked down the nearly invisible column of his vehicles and cleared his throat, waving vaguely at the night. "Wouldn't that, like, give us away?"

"Shit, sir," Higgins broke in, "the pilot said they're out there, so they sure as hell know we're here. Maybe they can't see shit, but they sure heard us. But they don't know what we got. Taste of our firepower could make 'em think twice. And maybe that buys enough time to get our asses out of here in one piece."

"Would you be okay with that, Captain McLaughlin?"

"Hey, I fly planes, I'm not von Clausewitz. In the air, I'm boss. Crazy or not, what I say goes. On the ground at base, what my crew chief says goes. On the ground here, crazy or not, what you say goes." He grinned and added, "Just hope you're not *too* crazy."

"Oh, he ain't *too* crazy, sir," Jarvis said.

"Okay. Uh, sorry, I missed your name." Randy was looking at Washington.

"Washington. Uh, Airman Washington, sir."

"Right. So we could maybe fire everything from your gun, the CEV, and all the way back to the Duster. A few seconds of show-and-tell."

Tom raised his hand like a schoolboy in class and asked, "What's a CEV Duster?"

Randy pointed. "That's a CEV, sir. Duster's bringing up the rear." He explained what it was.

"Well, that's sure nice to have, seeing as our backup gunship's still on the ground," Tom replied, looking at Eddie.

Sergeant Jarvis looked at Randy impatiently. As far as he could see, they were sliding into a bullshitting session, not hustling. "Sir," he said, nodding vigorously, "I'll get on it."

Vasquez returned just as Sergeant Jarvis left. "Sir, we leave, now?"

"Can't just yet. Got to get the CEV out of the ditch and rig the plane for demo; then we'll roll."

"Carajo! Sorry, sir." Vasquez took a deep breath, looking around. If it were up to him, he'd just leave all this crap. It wasn't important in his mind—certainly not like a life. "Can we get a medevac here? If no, maybe take a truck and get him out now, sir?"

Higgins reappeared. "Found your stuff, LT," he said, handing him his flashlight and map. "Also, sir, got Frederick down. Will's got a really bad bruise or maybe broke his arm. But he's vertical, and the radio still works."

"Good, good. Oh, Lassky and some of his guys will be up to help recovery." Randy wanted to rub his eyes again, but now his hands were full. He started to look at Vasquez but didn't. Every option seemed reasonable, after a fashion, and every option had a risk. And every risk was incalculable. *How the hell do you choose among incalculable risks? Engineer officer school didn't teach the stuff I really need to know.* He forced a look at Vasquez. "They've been telling us nothing can fly. Why we were sent. Maybe there's a change. I'll check." Then he looked at Captain McLaughlin. "Sir, I've got to get on the radio. A Specialist Mancini will be up shortly with some men to help with salvage and, uh, rig the demo. If you could let 'em know what to salvage, whatever needs special attention for demo."

Saluting Randy, Eddie said, "You got it, partner," but he did so in the tone of a grieving man.

"Vasquez, when you get a moment, can you check Frederick's arm?" Vasquez nodded and followed Randy. Frederick was leaning against the rear of the CEV, cradling his arm.

"Battalion's been calling, LT. Reception's turned shitty, though, sir."

"I'll go to the truck radio. Vasquez here'll look at your arm."

Randy turned to head back to his command truck and ran into Sergeant Carter. After getting his men into position, he'd come forward to learn what the flyboys had run into. Eddie passed him off to Tom, who gave him a rundown on what they had encountered and what they had done. "The minigun seems to have shut them right up, Sergeant. Guess they're gone?"

Carter shook his head. "Not likely. That first pattern of shooting was probably just to get you to shoot back so they could get an idea of what you had. The second bunch sounds like they thought they had your number and were trying to close in. We got here pretty quick after your little firefight, sir. Likely they're still out there, probably considering options. Opportunistic thing."

"You think they're still out there, like waiting."

"Yes sir. Maybe, maybe not, but best bet is they're there. Hate to say it, but probably haven't been hurt."

"Huh. Everyone's going to fire all the big guns. Our baby, your machine guns and tanks. Send a message. Which I guess they'll get if they're still here."

"A mad minute." Carter shrugged.

"Something wrong?" Tom asked, curious at the flat, dismissive tone in Carter's voice.

"It's okay, sir. Just that the message 'We've got big guns' is also gonna tell 'em 'and here's just where they are.' Hope they don't have an RPG."

"Oh." Tom wasn't sure what was wrong with that, but if it didn't make the sergeant happy, it didn't make him happy, either.

Crawling into the back of the three-quarter-ton truck to his so-called command post felt like crawling under the bed covers as a boy. Not one iota of vulnerability had eased, nor one iota of responsibility, yet he felt comforted by the invisibility of the world outside. He turned on his flashlight and spread out his map. Staring at the map was little more than an effort to reduce fearful reality to a map exercise—academic, not real. "Bagger Three, Boiler Two-Six. Over."

Bagger Three had been rubbing his eyes every few minutes, figuratively biting his nails since Lieutenant Hanley had reported his arrival at the crash site. He had gotten impatient after some long minutes had passed and had tried to call Boiler Two-Six, receiving no answer. That had pushed his anxiety meter into the red zone, but there was nothing he could do except imagine a hundred grim reasons for Boiler Two-Six not to answer. He could not even follow the army principle of "Do something, even if it's wrong." Frustrated, he called Green Granite Six-Three, the fire direction center of the supporting heavy artillery battery, to see if they could reach Randy. But they quickly replied in the negative. Was the silence from signal loss, enemy action, someone simply not listening? It was impossible to know. Since there were no even marginally useful somethings to do, he decided on a useless something—finding some coffee. That did the trick. He wasn't five yards from the operations tent when the radio operator called to him that Boiler Two-Six was on the line. He ran back into the tent.

"Bagger Three. What's up?"

"No further enemy fire since the first report. An accident with the CEV, and it's in a ditch. Recovery may be, uh, problematic. Take a while, anyway. Main issue is the WIA. Medic says he needs a hospital ASAP to survive. We need … we need a medevac. We can light up a landing spot. Over."

"Right where you've been drawing enemy fire? Christ, Two-Six, they're all grounded anyway. Over!"

"The weather seems to be better. The fog's not nearly as bad as it was. Over."

"I'll call. But it's no chance, really. How long to get the CEV out of the ditch? Over."

"Don't know. Still, uh, assessing. Over."

"I'll call about the medevac. You call me back with a time estimate, ASAP. Over and out."

Major Gridley put the mike down and looked at his assistant operations officer and his operations sergeant, both of whom were awake and sporting bloodshot eyes, one having been awake twenty hours and the other eighteen hours.

"I'll call the One Thirty-Ninth again," the assistant operations officer said, reaching for a different radio.

"Looks like maybe it's one or the other, the CEV or the WIA, sir?" the operations sergeant asked.

"Maybe. That'll be the CO's call. Damn, don't want to lose either. The WIA comes first, but, crap, we don't know enough."

The operations sergeant stood and stretched his lanky frame. "Hell, sir, out here, a lot of what we do are shots in the dark. Want some coffee?"

Major Gridley pushed himself erect. "I'll go with you, Sarge. Want to breathe some fresh humid air instead of stale humid air. You be okay for a few, George?"

"Got it."

"Bring you a cup, sir?"

"No, a Coke if there's any."

"It'll be warm. Or hot."

"So's everything else."

Outside, the major let himself vent a little. "How the hell could they put the CEV in a ditch so that recovery is needed?"

"Well, sir, they did report the road was wet and slick. Having those track pads may be nice on paved roads, but they make it dicey on that red clay when it's wet."

"Guess you'd know. It's just … we don't need complications."

"Who does, sir?"

Five minutes later, they were back sipping hot, weak, bitter coffee and more or less regretting their choice of beverage. Major Gridley was thinking that drinking army coffee was like being a lemming. It didn't taste good, especially when it wasn't fresh, and at two in the morning it was about as stale as it could get, leaving the mouth tasting horrible and doing nothing to wake one up, yet just about everyone did it. "George, anything?" he asked as he stepped back into the tent.

"Medevac says no can do. They say cloud and fog's usually worse in narrow valleys like the An Cao, and they're still pretty much socked in anyway."

"You tell 'em the case is, like, desperate?"

"Yeah. They did ask if we could get the medic on the line. I passed it on."

"No reply yet?"

"No sir."

Major Gridley sat down heavily, and as he did so, the radio crackled to life. "Bagger Three, Two-Six. Over."

"Bagger Three," the assistant operations officer answered.

"Negative contact with Red Hen. Over."

"I was kind of afraid of that. Out of your range, I guess. Your medic with you?"

"Affirmative. Over."

"Have him tell me everything he can think of about the wounded guy. I'll pass it on to Red Hen. Maybe they can think of something." The assistant operations officer took notes from Specialist Vasquez and then called the air medical evacuation battalion and passed it on. In the end, there was little anyone could do. Vasquez had suggested a field blood transfusion if the right blood type could be found, but he was turned down. The antiplague vaccines all soldiers in Vietnam took made their blood unsuitable for transfusion. All blood for transfusions had to come from outside the country.

When that had been passed on, Major Gridley took the mike. "Two-Six. Status on the CEV? Over." But all he got in reply was a "Wait. Out."

Washington hurt. His long toe hurt. There was a steady, dull pain and then a stabbing pain when he placed his foot wrong. His head still throbbed dully. With the help of some engineers, he and Otis had dismounted the other two miniguns and hauled them to the dump truck, along with most of the ammunition. He'd insisted on keeping the door minigun in place, even though it made carrying stuff out awkward.

As he and Otis were carrying the first of the GE guns out, Washington noticed the crowd of soldiers around the CEV. "What they doing?" he asked no one in particular.

Otis replied, "Trying to figure out how to get it out of the ditch, I guess."

Washington had been looking at the ground, favoring his foot. His head jerked up to look at the CEV. "Hey! We're leaving the fuckin' plane. Bet it's a lot more expensive. Why not leave that thing too? We got to be gettin' outta here!"

"Hey, Arlen! You want to save our guns. Don't you think they want to also?"

"Yeah, okay; we only need a few minutes, Timmy. That thing don't look like it's goin' anywhere. Wastin' time is what I think—and maybe us."

Otis didn't reply. With the two GE miniguns stowed in a dump truck, they returned for the flares and ammunition. The remaining flares, they decided, would be part of the demolition. Washington felt he couldn't wait to see those fireworks. Now it was time to move it. He didn't want to. Lieutenant Blagget called up, "Ready to cut the gun loose?"

He wasn't. He held on to the handles. "Sir, we ought to keep it ready, like, to the last minute. Only take a minute to cut it loose. Till we're ready to roll, wanna be able to hose 'em, right, sir? And besides, they gonna do that mad minute thing; we supposed open up too, right, sir?"

"Okay, makes sense. What about the ammo and the chute and the cables? I mean, you can't man it alone."

"Got Otis. He's free now. Medic's taking care of Chief."

"Okay. He's getting Chief back to a truck. They're going to send a truck back with Chief."

"Why don't we all go, then, sir? Why the hell hang around?"

"They got that tank out there stuck, and we've got to blow this plane. Going to take a while."

Washington didn't reply but looked alternately disgusted and afraid. He looked away and peered into a darkness made deeper by the hints of glowing mist from the flashlights and the memory of bullets punching through the fuselage. In the air those sounds, muted by his helmet and the noise in the cargo bay, had not been as frightening. On the ground, they had been much louder and so had seemed much closer.

At home, you didn't stand still when being looked for by cops or kids from a different street. You flew. That was what they did in the air—fly, keeping ahead of the bullets. Being stuck on the ground was like running into a blind alley. His thoughts bounced among present fears and hopeful fantasies about the gun, and memories of childhood escapes—and failures. The latter didn't help for memory locked on the worst escape—hiding in a Dumpster behind a restaurant.

Tom left him, and a few minutes later, Otis reappeared. "The army's taking care of Chief now. I can't help him anymore. You need help?"

"Yeah, man. Takes two to fire this sucker. Come on up." As Timmy climbed aboard, he bumped into the straps rigged across the cargo door to limit the recoil and fell backward, but Arlen grabbed his arms and pulled him in, laughing. "Gotta look where you're goin', dude!"

It took only a few minutes for Otis to understand how they had rigged the gun. Washington was all business until he knew Otis could handle the firing. "They gonna do what they call a mad minute," Washington said, "All their machine guns and cannon and shit at the same time. Man, wait'll they see what this sucker does!"

"Makes one hell of a noise when you don't have your helmets on."

"Yeah. You got yours?"

"Somewhere in here, I guess."

"Better find it."

A few minutes later, helmet found, the two were standing by the gun, staring into the dark. "He's still out there," Arlen said, breaking their mutual silence.

"Who?"

"Charlie!"

"You ... you think so?"

"Why would he leave?"

"You said you hosed 'em."

"Yeah, course I did. But who knows how many out there? They know exactly where we are, man. Don't have to hunt for us. Just get organized and close in!"

"We have the army here, and with a tank too. We're going to be out of here soon."

"That fuckin' tank's stuck in a ditch! What good's a tank what gets stuck in a ditch? Its gun is aimed at the dirt, just like ours were. How long they gonna screw around with it? Like that fuckin' tank's more important than you or me."

"No, it isn't! But they got to try. Just like we had to try to save the guns, right?"

"We ought to be moving, I tell you man! I'm from Baltimore." Arlen hunched slightly, his hands pushing out almost as if he were holding pistols. "You think Chicago's the tough city! Might have the rep, but Baltimore's tougher. Fuckin' Charm City," he snorted. "Cops or some other gang come 'round, you fly!" His imaginary pistols aimed at Otis. "Now, you're from Pussyville, and you wouldn't know. Think of the movies, man. The hero? He always stay ahead of the bad guys' bullets. *Ping, splat*, they hit the ground, the walls behind him, but he stays ahead—like when we're up there, in the air, where we supposed to be! The dumb ones? They stop to shoot back or hide, and they're the sittin' ducks what get wasted. In the air, it's like running, staying ahead of the bullets. Here it's like being the dumb ones, the sitting ducks!"

"Maybe. But we did get shot down. Up there wasn't all that safe."

"Yeah, yeah, maybe." Abruptly, Arlen laughed and his bitter tone changed. "Man, it be so cool to have this baby back home. Ain't no one mess with me or mine then!" He patted the gun. "Poor baby. Got shot down and lost."

That comment reminded Timmy of the partly overheard conversation between Arlen and Lem in the mess hall. Was he maybe serious, or just daydreaming? He couldn't decide, and his thoughts bounced back to the present moment and Arlen's fear of being a sitting duck. True enough, and maybe the tank was useless. And if there were a lot of enemy out there, maybe they were just a bigger target. The ability to aim and fire the minigun loomed more important. But would it work for long?

Imagining hundreds of enemy closing in as they had on the grunts they were supporting when they'd been shot down, Otis had a frightening thought. "Hey, Arlen. The plane's a wreck. We always have engine power when we fire. We only have batteries now. How long can we fire on only the battery? And we already hauled off most of the ammo. Maybe we should just let the army guys shoot."

"I don't know, man. All I know is we shoot till we run outta juice or ammo. Then we're dead or we're outta here. We do this mad minute thing to show Charlie we got too much firepower to mess with. Won't be long. Couple of seconds for us, like."

"Okay, okay." Otis nodded. "Oh. They're sending Chief ahead on a truck; hope to God it'll be in time."

"So why aren't we on the truck? They supposed to save all our asses, right? We should all go with Chief. They can stay here and do whatever they think they gotta do."

⚓

Specialist Fifth Class Marco Mancini was stocky and had a permanent five o'clock shadow. If he had been an actor, his main roles would have been Mafia hit man and enforcer. He appeared at the cargo door. "Anyone on board?"

"Washington answered, "Yeah. Two gunners an' a gun. Who you?"

"Marco Mancini. I'm here to blow this fucker up. Who're you?"

"I'm Arlen, This here's Timmy. We're manning the gun. We took a bunch of shots from Charlie, and if they still out there, they might need another dose."

"Okay guys. Just don't get trigger happy. I'm gonna have two guys with me: Privates Brown and Stanislaus. We're gonna rig the cockpit radios, and I understand you got flares on board. Show me where they are, 'cause we want to rig them too. Also what's to salvage."

Washington took charge. "Right. We already got the salvage out, Sarge," Otis replied.

Washington immediately added, "Except this gun here. We save it last. Timmy here, he'll show you the flares. I'll keep the gun safe—an' ready."

Mancini and his helpers got busy. When Otis showed him the flares, Marco got excited. "Man, are we gonna light up this place!" All the activity gave Washington hope. They were at last about to haul ass. Soon bricks of plastic explosive and thermite grenades were set in key places, all connected by redundant ropelike lines of high explosive called det cord and electric blasting caps attached to the ends. The caps were then connected to a reel of communications wire that was rolled out the cargo door and down the road. Just as they were done, they all heard a loud chorus of curses.

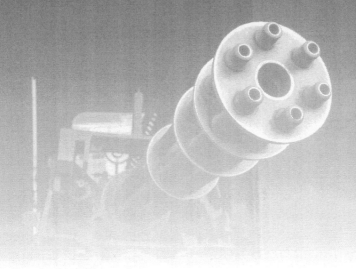

CHAPTER 9

IN THE FOG

Randy put the mike down after cutting Major Gridley off. Several minutes earlier, Sergeant Jarvis had announced they were ready for their mad minute to impress Charlie, and a moment later, Vasquez had appeared to ask anxiously if they were ready to let him go ahead and, when Randy's answer was vague, to beg for some faster action. He felt a small and petty annoyance at Vasquez's pleading for his patient. He knew it was unfair, but Vasquez had kept calling the wounded man by his name, Hector. A WIA was bad enough; a man called Hector was somehow more real, evoking more empathy—and more guilt. Sending a lone truck ahead was a risk; not sending it was another risk—both incalculable. "Screwed if you do, screwed if you don't. Do something, even if it's wrong," he muttered to himself.

"LT?" Sergeant Jarvis's tone was pitched for a gentle hint of impatience.

"Right. Give me a couple of minutes. I'm going call in some eight-inch to go along with our little demo." Two minutes later, Randy stuck his head out into the night. "Sarge?"

"Sir."

"Give the word."

"Roger that. Hey, Will. Call Bobby. Tell him to fire." Thirty seconds later, they heard the .50-caliber machine gun on the CEV hammer the night, then a second .50-caliber cut loose, and then they heard the deeper, slower hammering of the Duster's twin forty-millimeter cannon, which was almost instantly followed by bright flashes and sharp cracks of the shells exploding in the rice paddies. At the same time, there came the loud, mournful hoot of the minigun. The brief show climaxed with the earth-shaking thunder of eight-inch shells exploding. For a minute or so afterward, it seemed all light and sound had been sucked from the night as eyes saw only afterimages and even the insects were cowed into silence.

Randy looked around blindly, blinking as if that would speed up the return of his night vision, and broke the silence. "Okay, men, I'm sure Charlie has pissed his pants. Sarge! Let's get the vehicles turned around. Put Warrant and his squad on Jersey's five-ton with Vasquez and the WIA. I'm going to send him ahead. Charlie's either going run or focus on us. That'll give the five-ton the best chance to make it out. Best chance for the wounded man."

"Jesus, LT. You sure?"

"I can't think of what else to do, Sarge. Going to take a while to finish rigging that plane. And I don't know if the CEV is a real problem or not. Do you?"

"Nope. They've been making noises. We should have brought the dozer."

"Shoot, Sarge, I'd love to have it, but we'd still be on the way here."

"I guess." Jarvis shrugged, thinking, *Got a dozer we sure could use, got a dozer we can't use.* "I'll get things moving, LT. But one thing: where's Jersey gonna take the WIA?"

"Xanh La. They only have a medic there, but more plasma. Then, if it looks good, on to Tranh Xa, and hopefully by then a medevac can get to him. Be close to morning."

Sergeant Jarvis nodded and left. As he walked away, he thought, *No way that poor guy will survive the night, so why waste a squad of men going it alone?* But his next thought was *Would I want someone thinking that about me? Shit, no, Mister Jarvis, you'd be begging, "Gimme a chance! Miracles happen!"* He cleared his throat and realized it wasn't a snotty shot fired by the angel on one shoulder at the devil on the other but a real question. A shitty question, but a real one. He decided he was glad he didn't have to answer it, that LT did. Same with the dozer. If they'd brought it, they might not even be here yet. On the other hand, with it, getting the CEV out of the ditch would be a snap, but the wounded guy'd likely be dead. *Guess LT's right, maybe. When you've got no good choices, go for the miracle.* With that last thought, Jarvis pushed them all aside and got to work.

Randy looked at his watch. It was two forty-five. They'd already been screwing around for a half hour. He got out of the three-quarter-ton and made his way toward the CEV. He was just killing time—and maybe killing a man. He could not improve on the expertise already being employed to get it out of the ditch. He could see how the demolition prep was coming, though again he knew he couldn't improve on the expertise already at work there either. He could hear voices and see the diffuse, dancing glow of flashlights ahead. *I should feel heroic,* he thought. A *leader of a daring rescue attempt, not a mouse hiding in the dark. Those guys. My guys. They have the cojones. Flashlights to get the job done as fast as possible. And they know Charlie's right out there! And you're standing in the dark, Lieutenant, oh, great leader!* It was one thing to bear responsibility when he could act and be confident in his actions, but he was beginning to realize the burden becomes infinitely heavier when acting in a fog of uncertainty.

He shook his head, pushed his shoulders back, and walked toward where the mist was aglow. The CEV loomed, still canted nose-down in the ditch. "How're we doing?"

"Dicey, LT," Higgins said morosely, meaning they weren't doing well. The first thing they had tried was to back the CEV out. But the CEV was in the ditch at an angle. The right front was fully in the ditch, the left front somewhat higher, as the left track had partially climbed the rice paddy dyke that formed the far side of the ditch. The two tracks had differing degrees of grip on the road surface, and trying to back out had slewed the vehicle further to the side, risking dropping the entire left track into the ditch. The next thing they tried was to get the

CEV more perpendicular to the ditch, putting the left track in reverse and the right in forward. For a moment, it seemed to work, but then it lurched leftward again and the nose of the CEV tipped further down as the churning tracks tore away at the rice paddy dyke. Had there been a sturdy tree anywhere near, they could have winched it out. But there were no trees of any kind within a hundred yards.

"If we got the Duster up here, could it help? You know, maybe with the CEV backing up and the Duster pulling?"

"Hell, sir, the CEV is twice its size. And the Duster could only pull down the road, which would tend to pull the rear closer to slipping into the ditch."

"Anything we can stuff under the tracks to get better traction?"

"Nothing we've got with us." Sergeant Lassky had joined Higgins. When nobody spoke, Lassky looked at the plane. "What if we use the crane. Hook a line to the plane. Winching in might pull the ass of the CEV toward it. Then maybe it can back out of the ditch?"

They tried it. The CEV moved a slight bit; then the plane began to move. They gave up.

"Any more ideas?" Randy asked.

"Might try rocking it. Build up some momentum then gun it on the backroll." Sergeant Lassky paused and then added, "You know, when they send out a CEV alone like this, it'd be cool to make an anchor part of the gear."

"An anchor?" Randy blurted as Sergeant Jarvis returned from his errand just in time to hear the last word.

"Yeah. You know, a boat anchor, like for a yacht. They dig in when you pull on them. Winch yourself out."

"Well, I don't see any anchors here," Sergeant Jarvis said, a bit sourly, still thinking of the order to send one truck back alone.

Sergeant Lassky replied laconically, "Nope. Don't suppose the plane carried one, either."

"What, for, like, an emergency brake?" Sergeant Jarvis almost snorted. Like Lieutenant Hanley, he was feeling helpless, an NCO without solutions. Not supposed to happen.

"Joking, Floyd," Lassky snorted back. Jarvis and Randy nodded, and so they tried Lassky's last-chance idea.

Bailey had a light, sure touch on the controls. The CEV began to rock back and forth gently, and there seemed to be no inclination to slew left. As the momentum built, Bailey gave it more throttle. Because the dyke on the far side of the ditch was weaker than the elevated road surface, the forward lurches tended to carry the CEV further forward, chewing into the dyke, than the backward lurches carried it backward. Still, the backward lurches were beginning to carry it higher and farther. It looked like it just might work.

Bailey was focused on his machine, sensing the ground through the action of the treads. Higgins was in the commander's cupola on the turret, staring at Sergeant Lassky, who had positioned himself on the dyke well to the left, where he could see the overall motions of the CEV. The rest of the crew were standing in the road, watching the action of the tracks. Randy had crossed the ditch to stand on the dyke and watch on the other side of the CEV. Sergeant Jarvis had left to find out why he hadn't heard a five-ton drive off.

The CEV lurched forward and almost topped the dyke. It looked good for the momentum needed going backward. Lassky waved at Higgins, and Higgins told Bailey, "Now!"

Bailey shifted smoothly into reverse, smoothly gunned the engine, and felt the tracks gain traction. The CEV surged backward as if it would leap onto the road. It was going to work.

Until it didn't. Both tracks had been digging into the road embankment. Now the right track suddenly got more traction than the left, and the CEV slewed left. In an instant, the slide became irreversible. Ponderously, the entire left side of the CEV slid into the ditch to the tune of half a dozen men crying "Oh, shit!"

Randy and Sergeant Lassky instinctively jumped off the dyke and into the sodden rice paddy as the rear of the CEV swung toward them. A sheet of water from the ditch flew up and came down on them like a brief downpour. Specialist Bailey's head was slammed against the side of the driver's cupola, and he passed out. Higgins had been able to brace himself. "Bailey! You okay?"

When Bailey didn't answer, Higgins scrambled awkwardly to the driver's compartment and found him unconscious and bleeding.

"Medic!" he screamed, forgetting that Vasquez had gone with the wounded Chief.

Randy and Sergeant Lassky, both drenched, looked at each other for a long moment, and almost in unison, both said, "We're fucked."

The "Oh, shit" chorus died out, and the men stood around in a stunned silence, waiting.

Then everyone heard Higgins cry out.

Randy, Sergeant Lassky, and Higgins's gunner and loader scrambled onto the CEV to help and promptly got in each other's way. But moments later, they had the unconscious Bailey on the makeshift litter that had been set up under the plane's tail for Chief Pastor-Villanueva.

"He's got a gash on the head, LT," Lassky said. "He's breathing, and his pupils look good. Think he's just knocked out. Should have had his helmet on."

Randy felt relief both at Lassky's news and at his competence. He could leave things, for the moment, in his hands. "Thank God. Okay. I've got to report this. Be back in a few."

Back on the road, he bumped into Sergeant Jarvis, who had returned and was standing with Specialist Mancini. "Looks like the CEV's fucked, sir," Jarvis said.

Just then, Sergeant Lassky joined them. "Well, we gave it our best shot," he commented in a flat tone.

Sergeant Warrant shook his head. "We're gonna have to blow it, sir. There goes half our firepower."

"Okay. Sarge, I'm going to the three-quarter. Figure out how to blow the CEV. I'll get Battalion's okay, though. You keep Frederick. That way you can move around and we can stay in touch. I'll keep you posted on what Battalion says."

When Lieutenant Hanley was out of earshot, Sergeant Jarvis got on the radio, called Sergeant Warrant, and told him to call when he had a clear shot past the Duster, but not to move until he got an order from him or the lieutenant. Then he turned to Mancini. "Marco, how long to rig the CEV?"

"Should be no sweat. Higgins still has his basic load of HEP rounds. A little det cord and we'll have a fifty-eight-ton bomb. Plane's already rigged. I'll rig the CEV and wire it into the line for the plane, blow both together. Have to do it that way anyway. Not enough commo wire to run separate lines to the CEV and the plane from a safe distance. We'll want to be a good two hundred meters downrange. Chunks of that thing are gonna fly."

"All the stuff to salvage?"

"Got everything except one of their miniguns. Two airmen have it rigged so they can sweep the paddies with it. They're manning it now. Claim just a couple of minutes to get it out. But they're nervous as cats in a dog pen."

"Huh. Hell, aren't you? Okay. Have a couple of guys get up there and stand by to help 'em. Put the stuff in the dump truck with the other salvage. Hugo, take your guys back to your ride. Defensive positions. Take Bailey with you. Bailey seems okay, except for a blazing headache, but have Vasquez check him—you know, should he be evac'ed with the WIA or not."

"Right, Sarge." Lassky began gathering his men.

When Bailey came by Sergeant Jarvis with Lassky's squad, he tried to apologize. "Can it, Bailey. You did your best, and no one could have done better. Shit happens. Doing it right don't always work. You'll get another ride. Now get moving."

Higgins cried, "I'm screwed!" His gunner added, choking on the words, "What're we gonna do now? We got nothing," and his loader, the most junior of the CEV's crew, just coughed. But even his cough had a despairing quality.

Hearing them, Specialist Mancini, tasked to blow the CEV up, slapped Higgins on the shoulder. "It's just a goddamned machine, guys! Here's what you guys are gonna do. First, get your stuff off it, and any of Bailey's he left. Then help us rig it to blow. Then you're gonna stick with me, and we're gonna get out of here. Hell, you're engineers and my squad's short. Then we're gonna get you a new one, 'cause we can't do without. Got it? Hey?" No one replied.

Back in his "office," Randy rested for several breaths, hiding from the realities outside. Then he gathered himself and called Bagger Three with the bad news. Bagger Three's reply was "Wait. Out." Randy sagged back under the imaginary bedcovers, feeling very tired, his tiredness exacerbated by the awareness that any rest for him was yet many hours away.

A pair of shadows—one long and lean, the other shorter and wider—appeared at the cargo door and made a noise. "Hey, you airmen there?"

"Yeah," Washington and Otis said together. Washington added, "Who're you?"

"Bert and Ernie. For real. I'm Bert," the lean shadow said. "Bert McAllister. And this here's Ernie, Ernie Friendly, if you can believe that. We've been told to help get your gun and stuff over to the dump truck when we get the word."

"Soon?" Washington asked.

"Yeah. Soon as the CEV's rigged for demo."

"CEV? That tank you got? What's—why?" Otis asked.

"Can't get it out of the fuckin' ditch. Can't take it with us, so we blow it or make Charlie a present of it," Bert said. "Anyway, want to show us what's what? What's to move?"

"No goddamn cannon, man," Washington grumbled. "We take this gun down, our asses are in the wind. We got no firepower."

"Come on, man! We got fifty-cals on the trucks; we have the Duster, two squads of grunts. So let's get it in gear, huh?"

Otis ignored Washington and began telling Bert and Ernie what they would have to move. Faint red beams from their flashlights danced over the cargo bay as Bert and Ernie were shown what to take: the gun, the electrical cables, an ammunition feed box, and the ammunition feed chutes between the remaining box and the gun. They were also shown what to avoid—in particular, the explosives and lines of det cord and wires that would ignite the *MaryAnn*'s funeral pyre.

While Washington held on to the gun, the three began to review everything to move and how to move it. Washington interrupted. "Hey, man. All this shit's gonna go in your dump truck? There any way we can mount it? Like it is here, you know, so I could swing and aim it and fire it? Need electric for it."

"Mount it?" Bert asked. "Huh. Our trucks have ring mounts over the cab for a fifty-cal. This thing got a fifty-cal mount?"

"Don't know. Never seen one up close."

The red lights winked out. The men shifted discussion from salvage to how they might mount the minigun on the dump truck, the whispered discussion an armor against the darkness and the dangers it hid. Three sat in the cargo door, legs dangling; one stood apart, nursing the handles of the gun.

A red beam swept the cargo door. "Well, well. Workin' hard, boys?" Specialist Mancini asked pleasantly.

"Ready to roll," Bert replied.

"Then roll. We're ready to blow. "Soon's you got the shit stowed, convoy's going to roll, and you two and me are going take a little stroll. We got to lay a good two hundred meters of commo wire."

"Two hundred?"

"That CEV's gonna go sky high."

"Oh." They got to work. When the gun came free of the webbing he'd rigged in the door, Washington suddenly felt naked as he rushed to help speed the salvage of the gun.

Lieutenant Colonel George Short was awakened for the third time, this time by the operations sergeant because it was his turn. "Sir. The CEV in the An Cao … looks like it can't be recovered."

Colonel Short swung his bare legs off the cot, planting his feet on the canvas tent floor. "Can't? *Can't?* How'd they fuck that up? Tracked vehicles were invented to cross ditches!"

"Well, sir, you know those clay roads are like ice when wet."

"A fifty-eight-ton CEV is not a bloody hockey puck." He stood. "You certain?"

The operations sergeant bit his lip. "I can't say for certain, sir. I'm not there. But from the situation, it will take a recovery vehicle to get it out. We can't see that being possible."

"Damn! Losing a CEV in a noncombat situation! A CEV on bloody loan to us! Know what that will look like? Make us look like hell!"

"Sir, yes sir. But there has been enemy fire. Charlie's there. It does look like a combat situation, sir."

"Shooting at the air crew, before Lieutenant Hanley ever got there."

"Well, yes sir. Yes sir. But I guess Lieutenant Hanley's got to assume the enemy's still there. That shooting was probably a recon by fire. He's got to assume it was kind of a prelim to something else, I guess."

"Yeah, yeah. But I want that vehicle back. Tell him to try again, dammit!"

The operations sergeant felt suddenly at a loss. If he opened his mouth too much, he might put his own rear in a wringer. "Sir." He saluted and turned to the tent entry. There he took a sharp breath and turned. "Sir, you know, they gave us this rescue mission. We got there, got the air crew, and one of 'em is badly wounded. Looks like he'll die if we can't—don't—get him out ASAP. If he dies because we spend extra time, uh, trying to recover the CEV, well, I don't know."

Colonel Short chewed on a nail for a moment. "Right. Do whatever's necessary to save the airmen. We'll deal with the fuckups later."

"Sir!" The operations sergeant vanished.

⚭

Randy had been left a bit confused by Bagger Three's slow-in-coming response to his report on the CEV's hopeless condition: "Six says do what you have to."

"Do what I have to. Great!" Randy almost threw the handset down. Lips pressed to a thin line, he thought, *Old Shorty's not sticking his boots in this swamp. Okay. Just get home. Become a civil engineer. More money, less stress. Hope you don't mind, Dad, if I come home a very nonhero owing Uncle Sam whatever a CEV costs. "If" ... that is one big-ass word. If everything turns to shit, if everything comes up roses. If, if, if.* Energized by a fresh fatalism, he flung himself out of the three-quarter-ton and nearly landed on Sergeant Jarvis. Straightening up, he said, "Yo, Sarge. Battalion okayed blowing the CEV. Sort of."

"Sort of, sir?"

"Never mind," Randy replied, shrugging a shoulder. "Jersey on his way? I heard the Duster guys report a wide enough spot."

111

They were standing almost nose-to-nose, and Jarvis took a small step back. "The CEV's rigged, sir. I, ah, told 'em to hold a sec. I think we can all get out together."

Randy nodded, accepting Jarvis's decision. "Heard from Mancini?"

"Running the commo wire. Needs two hundred meters, he figures." He gave a quick grin. "CEV's just a big bomb now."

"Oh. Let's get 'em rolling. I'll go up front. You bring up the rear with Mancini and his guys. Get a head count. Air crew?"

"In Mancini's dump truck."

"Okay. The Duster moved about two hundred meters, he said. Soon as we catch up, we should close up, then blow everything." Randy put a hand on Jarvis' shoulder. "Keep Frederick. How's his arm?"

"Hurts, but he's doing okay, sir." They parted, and Randy trotted through the dark, giving orders to each vehicle in turn. The last was Lassky's five-ton, and he jumped on the running board. The road filled with noise and flickering lights as the vehicles carefully turned around. Lassky's five-ton got turned around and followed the taillights of the truck ahead. Moments later, it stopped, as had the rest of the convoy. There was only one thing left to do, and Mancini would do it. Then they could get the hell out of the valley. Randy let go of the truck's rearview mirror to jump off and find Mancini somewhere behind him.

At almost the same instant, there was a loud crack and flash of light toward the head of the column, followed almost instantly by an explosion a couple hundred yards down the road. As if it were a twisted echo, a scream of pain followed. Partly from the concussion, partly in surprise, Randy fell off the running board. A soldier in the truck ahead shouted, "I saw it! I see them!" And then Randy heard a .50-caliber machine gun open fire. Within seconds, M16 rifles from Sergeant Warrant's infantry squad in Jersey's truck joined in, concentrating where the .50-caliber's tracers were hitting. Seconds after the M16s had opened fire, one of Warrant's men, armed with an M79 forty-millimeter grenade launcher, fired.

The grenade exploded several yards from where the two enemy were crouched, but its flash illuminated them. They crawled frantically along the back side of a rice paddy dyke, but the elevation advantage gained from standing in the bed of a truck allowed Warrant's men and the .50-caliber gunner to get hints of their movement. There was really no escape. The third grenade from the M79 detonated between the two enemy soldiers, killing one and wounding the other. The wounded one tried to turn back to his companion but passed out. Both having fallen flat, they were out of sight, so no one realized they had been hit, and the firing continued.

Vasquez leapt out of the truck and ran to the Duster. The Duster's armor was only an inch thick, and the rocket-propelled antitank grenade blew a good-sized hole in it, killing the driver and riddling the loader's legs with shrapnel. The two others were stunned and deafened, and their legs peppered by hot bits of spalling armor the size of birdshot. By the time Vasquez arrived and shouted at them, they were able to gather their wits, and the first response Vasquez heard was "Oh, Christ! I think Kevin's dead!" Then another voice, the loader's, clearly in pain, shouted, "I'm hit! God, I'm hit! Medic!"

Sergeant Warrant was the first to realize there was no incoming fire. He turned to one of his men. "Jordy. We're not getting any incoming."

"Shit, don't look like that up front, Sarge!"

"I mean no small arms, just one RPG." Sergeant Warrant told Corporal Jordy Hicks, one of his fire team leaders, to take his team and see what was really out there. The rest of the squad would provide covering fire if needed. They briefly discussed directions and distances. "Got a flashlight?" Jordy nodded. "Red filter?" He nodded again. "Take it. Keep it pointed toward us so we can track you. Got it?"

"On it. Sammy, Rube! Follow me." They did, scrambling over the truck's tailgate, dropping to the ground, slipping to the left side of the truck behind them, and stumbling into Randy.

"Where you guys going?" he blurted after a moment's panic that they were enemy.

"Who the fuck are you?" Jordy Hicks had dark skin and large eyes. All Randy saw were the whites of his eyes all around the dark irises—eyes that seemed to be floating in the void. For a split second, he thought he was seeing the Grim Reaper.

"Lieutenant Hanley," he croaked in reply.

"Oh. Sir. Corporal Hicks. Sergeant Warrant's squad. We're going find what's really out there."

"Just you three?"

"No small arms, sir. Just the one RPG. Rest of the squad's covering us."

"Oh." Randy didn't know what, if anything, to add. Jordy and his men slid past him and vanished.

Randy's encounter with Corporal Hicks had the effect of settling some of the confusion in his mind. An emotional impulse was to run to the Duster. Responsibility told him to run to the radio in his truck and get in control. It was one thing to plan and direct. That's what engineers do. It was a vastly different thing to think in the chaos of even a small fight. The one thing he could do was call in artillery. But where? What targets? And now some of his men were maneuvering out into the dark. He could never bring eight-inch artillery in for close support. He ran to the Duster, which, amazingly, was not on fire.

Sergeant Jarvis had been walking with Specialist Mancini behind the dump truck as Mancini paid out the commo wire from a large reel when he heard the explosion from the RPG. "What the hell?" He stepped to the side of the road, but there was nothing to see until he saw the .50-caliber's tracers. He grabbed the radio handset from Frederick just in time to hear Sergeant Warrant's voice over the radio. "RPG fire! Listen up! Listen up! RPG hit on the Duster! Right flank, maybe fifty meters out, fifty ahead! Repeat! RPG fire from the right flank! Duster's hit! Returning fire!"

Jarvis immediately ordered Sergeant Carter's squad to dismount, but Carter was already doing just that. He called Randy but got no response. Then he heard the small-arms fire add to the machine gun, and then grenade explosions. *Warrant's firefight—for now, anyway*, he thought. Then he turned to Mancini. "Where are we?"

"Where we want to be. Just about two hundred meters from our big bomb."

"Hook it up, and holler when you're ready." A moment later, Mancini hollered. The shooting had died down. Jarvis shouted aloud and into the radio, "Fire in the hole! Fire in the hole! Fire in the hole!" At the third repetition, Mancini gave the handle of the detonator a hard twist.

The explosion was spectacular. A pair of bright orange-and-black fireballs like a pair of giant incandescent Halloween pumpkins blew away the night. By their light they saw the turret of the CEV fly fifty feet in the air. Out of one pumpkin fireball bits and pieces of two dozen flares arced hundreds of feet through the sky like sun-bright roman candles, giving the mists a fluorescent glow that hid the world as effectively as had the darkness, except in one particular case.

Having passed the second truck behind the one he'd just left, Jordy Hicks led his men to the right side of the road, where they could just make out the ditch and the dyke on the far side. When they crossed the ditch, they saw they were next to a dyke perpendicular to the ditch, leading to the next parallel dyke. Crossing the ditch, their boots had made squelching sounds, and creeping through the rain-soaked paddy ahead would be just as noisy. Hicks decided the safest bet was the fastest. They'd go in file on top of the perpendicular dyke as fast and as quietly as they could.

Hicks had just reached the next intersecting dyke, the one Warrant suspected the enemy had fired the RPG from, when Mancini set off the demolitions. Hicks and his team jumped off the dyke into the rice paddy. The mist glowed from the flares arcing high above. While most quickly fell to earth like little meteors, the parachutes of a couple had deployed. The mist itself did not quite reach the ground, and under its soft glow, the ground was clearly visible.

Sammy suddenly moved, shoving his rifle in front of him, not quite bringing it to his shoulder. "Jordy!" he whispered. "Chinks!" And then he fired a half dozen shots. Sammy had pointed his rifle but not really aimed it. The first shot went a little high, and the rest higher.

With Sammy's first shot, Rube jerked down into a crouch, facing away from Sammy, clutching his rifle to his chest. When the firing stopped, Rube could hear is own rapid, shallow breathing but no one else's. A paralyzing fear that Sammy and Hicks were dead gripped him; the paralysis was broken in the next second by Sammy. "I think I got 'em!" Sammy said in a loud whisper.

Hicks had noticed two things: no bullets kicking up dirt or making bodies jerk, and the bodies not moving. "What's the rule, Sammy?" he hissed angrily. "Don't shoot unless you're shot at or you're told to. Besides, they're not moving. I'll check 'em out. You and Rube cover me. Rube, keep that light pointed at the road."

Hicks crawled over the dyke and, at a crouch, moved slowly toward the two figures that lay only about twenty yards away. As he approached, he heard one moan. Getting closer, he could see an AK-47 lying beside the figure that had moaned and an RPG launcher strapped to the back of the other. They looked like Vietcong: black shirts and trousers, sandals. He quickly closed the distance and kicked the AK-47 out of reach, feeling an impulse to shoot the man just to make sure, but the moan he'd heard stopped him. He nudged the body with his boot. Another moan. He'd heard that sometimes they played dead or wounded, hiding a grenade or pistol under their body. Then, when a GI got close enough, they would go out in a blaze of glory. Both were facedown, but the moaner had both hands out, as if he had been trying to drag himself. Jordan bent and gingerly turned the body over, jumping back a couple of feet.

The face was muddy. He looked as if he were too young to shave, but he was breathing. A little froth of blood bubbled in his nostrils. "Hey," he called softly to Sammy and Rube, "this one's alive. They seem to be alone."

"Finish him off!" Sammy said.

But Sammy was not seeing the face. "Shit, man, this guy's war is over." Hicks straightened and walked over to the other body and prodded it with his foot. One hand was not visible; the other was. Pointing his rifle at the head, he stepped hard on the outstretched hand. No reaction. Then, with his foot, he turned the body over. The man was dead and looked no older than the other. "Sammy, Rube. Come on here."

They met standing over the wounded man's body. "These dudes were alone," Hicks said.

"You sure?" Rube asked, tearing his gaze from the enemy forms to look around.

"Nobody shooting at us. Wouldn't you be shooting if you saw three enemy hanging around your buddies?"

"I guess." Just then the first man moaned again, still unconscious. "Shit. I guess we should put this asshole out of his misery," Sammy said.

"You wanna shoot him?" Hicks asked sourly.

Sammy looked at the face. "I mean, he's got no medics around. I mean, you don't leave a wounded animal out to die."

"No," Hicks said. No one spoke for a long minute. Sammy and Rube avoided the issue, turning their eyes from the sight of the wounded man to the surrounding darkness as if to seek an answer or at least a diversion in it. Finally, Hicks said, "Guess we got to take him to Vasquez. I think it's what we got to do. Anyway, no more Charlies out here."

"I never saw a guy I shot," Sammy said softly.

"I think Marco's M79 got him. Look at his legs."

"Oh."

"Disappointed?"

"I don't know."

The froth in his nostrils indicated some wound to the lungs. They stripped the wounded soldier of his bloody shirt and used field dressings to bandage the punctures in his back. Then Sammy and Rube shouldered their rifles and pulled the wounded man to his feet between them, each wrapping one of the man's arms over his shoulder. The three climbed onto the dyke and returned to the convoy with their prisoner. "Think he'll be okay?" Sammy asked. No one answered.

Lying on his cot, Lieutenant Colonel Short looked at his watch and got nervous. Some time had passed with no updates on the rescue mission or the status of the CEV. He pulled on his boots and strode to his operations center, arriving seconds after the latest grim update had been received. "What's the status on the CEV?" he demanded.

Major Gridley spoke first. "Sir," he said. He then paused, trying to frame a reply.

The operations sergeant spoke next and filled in the blanks. "Boiler Two-Six just reported an enemy attack, sir." He cleared his throat. "Including RPGs, sir. Afraid they lost the Duster. Uh, one KIA and another WIA."

"Jesus Christ!" Short's tone was somewhere between disgust and horror.

"Yes sir," the operations sergeant said. "Uh, looks like there was more to things than just a probe of the downed aircraft, sir. They might be there in strength now."

Major Gridley found his voice. "Lieutenant Hanley's men counterattacked, sir, and apparently have driven the enemy off. at least for the time being. At least one enemy KIA and one wounded enemy captured."

"This is a clusterfuck! What about the CEV?"

Major Gridley and the operations sergeant looked at each other. The assistant operations officer, barely able to keep his eyes open, looked at the floor. Major Gridley spoke up. "Clearly, sir, there's an enemy force of unknown size in the An Cao no one knew about or at least didn't tell us about. Given the nature of his mission and the time constraints, there was no way to get there undetected. If, uh, he's going to save the air force crew, especially the WIAs, Hanley's going to have to break contact and get out of there as fast as he can."

"You're saying the CEV's still stuck in a bloody ditch."

"Yes sir. Too risky now to keep trying."

"They need to get the WIAs evacuated ASAP, sir. Guess that's the priority," the operations sergeant added.

"Goddamn! All right! Get 'em out of there. But we'll investigate this mess later. Get to the bottom of it."

CHAPTER 10

THE ROAD BACK

At the Duster, Randy had found Vasquez in charge and the two lightly injured crewmen helping him. There being nothing he could do to help, the firing coming to a halt, and the demolition part of the mission clearly having been accomplished, he ran to Sergeant Warrant for an update.

"We're not getting any return fire, sir. No sense in wasting ammo. Corporal Hicks and his team are coming back. That red light over there—moving toward the road. Might have just been, like, a lone shooter." Randy nodded and ran to his truck to report and—somehow—get organized, or at least feeling organized. At least Battalion did not give him any grief when he reported the loss of the Duster, just to keep them posted. He got an update on the demolitions and told Jarvis to get the Duster prepped. He learned that no other vehicles had taken any fire. He ordered his convoy to move until safely beyond the ruined Duster. Then he ran back to Jersey's truck to get it moving as soon as the wounded were ready.

Jersey's truck, now the lead vehicle in the convoy, was still the ambulance because Vasquez insisted on not moving Hector. The Duster's commander, Sergeant Bud Newsome, and his gunner, Private First Class Stephan Wodzinski, both of whom had only minor burns and cuts, joined Jersey's crew to be with their comrades, the poncho-wrapped corpse of the driver, and the more seriously wounded loader, who now lay between Chief Hector Pastor-Villanueva and the wounded enemy soldier who was lying between the Chief and the corpse.

Randy decided to ride in the lead vehicle, mainly because he'd feel useless passively riding in his "office" in the middle of the convoy. Frederick would monitor the more powerful radio in the three-quarter ton, and Randy would take the backpack radio with him, switching the three-foot standard antenna for a ten-foot whip antenna to get the maximum range, which might let him talk directly to headquarters or the artillery, and if not, Frederick could always patch through. Sergeant Jarvis would ride in the last vehicle, a dump truck, with one of the engineer squads and the airmen. He assigned Newsome and Wodzinski to sit at the tailgate of Jersey's truck to keep an eye out left, right, and rear. Since Jersey's truck had an M60 machine gun on a ring mount above the right of the cab, the duty of machine-gunner fell to Randy. He wedged himself and his radio into the ring, checked the ammunition feed, verified it was ready to fire, stifled an urge to test fire it and waited for word from the squad leaders and Sergeant Jarvis.

In the back of the truck, Randy heard a soft but acid conversation. Newsome wanted to know "Why the fuck we got a wounded chink with us? He's got to be the shit who killed Kevin."

"He's wounded, man. Can't leave him since we found him," Vasquez explained.

"Should have shot the fucker."

"Can't do that, man."

"I could shoot that shit right now. Everyone would understand why. Think I'd get in any trouble? They'd pat me on the back is what!"

"*I* give you trouble is what."

"You don't even pack, Enrique. Goddammit, you give this little shit as much attention as the flyboy here and Rockefeller together! Whose fuckin' side you on?"

"No, I don't pack. You wanna kill him, you kill me first!"

"Man, you are shit for brains!"

"He was just doin' his job, man. If you'd seen him first, you'd have done your job and blown him to bits, no?"

"Yeah, and you know what they do to prisoners."

"*Si*, I hear. But we ain't them."

"He's right, you know," Courtney Rockefeller, the wounded Duster loader said, and he gasped in pain.

"We're a team, dammit!" Newsome grimaced as if Rockefeller's pain were his own. "Kevin was part of the team! Part of us! This little shit killed him"

"Maybe, Sarge, maybe. But Enrique's still right. I feel just like you do, but … but …" He grimaced in pain again. "Fuck it; he's right."

"Bullshit. Bullshit!" Kevin wasn't his friend. Didn't even know him that well, as he was the newest crew member. But Kevin had been his responsibility. Logically, there was nothing he could have done, but logic didn't drive feeling, didn't numb pain, didn't ease an irrational sense of failure. Newsome swung his rifle and pointed it at the prisoner. Vasquez moved closer to block the line of fire. Newsome's finger slipped onto the trigger. The rifle wavered, and then Newsome jerked it vertical. "Bullshit!"

They fell silent. Hector mumbled, "Que pasa?" The wounded loader from the Duster eructed a little gasp and asked, "Hey Vasquez, man, legs hurt. You got … got any more juice?"

Vasquez said he didn't want to overdose. That would be worse for him. "Soon, soon, Rocky, we get you to the hospital, but we can't risk an overdose, man." Vasquez knew he had just about run out of morphine, and if the prisoner awakened, he might need it even more than Rocky. He closed his eyes, trying to pray. *Yes*, he thought, *they're all God's children*. But this was Rocky, one of his—his sort-of family. Who had priority? *What*, he asked God, *do you do when you don't have enough?*

Wodzinski asked Vasquez, "Hey, Enrique, how come you don't pack a gun?"

"My religion don't allow it. We're what they call COs—conscientious objectors."

"What're you objecting to?"

"War. Killing."

Sergeant Newsome cut in. "Hey, I know that if you're a conscientious objector, man, you don't have to be here. They put you in safe places. Isn't that right?"

"Yeah."

"So what the hell you doing here, you being all against war?"

"I'm a medic. 'Cause I'm a CO, they make me a medic. They made me a medic, so here's where I belong. Don't have to carry a gun, just my kit. All I need."

"You need more smarts is what," Newsome muttered.

When they fell silent, Randy decided not to butt in. Then, one after another, everyone reported ready. Randy called Sergeant Jarvis. "We're moving out. Call when you get past the Duster a safe distance to blow it. Then we'll make it a thunder run. Over."

Randy took a deep breath and told Specialist Jersey, "Okay, crank up and roll. Combat lights only." It was three fifteen. They had been at the crash site an hour. Ten minutes later, Jarvis called and the convoy halted. Mancini came on and said, "Thermite grenades in the breeches set, detonator wired. This is a gas buggy, so we're just gonna torch it. The ammo'll cook off once it gets hot. Ready to roll. Over."

"Do it. Out," Randy said, and he looked backward. A moment later, a ruddy light grew in the mists. "Hey, Jersey. Headlights on. Roll as fast as you feel safe." He called Battalion and reported, "We're rolling, out." If they wanted to ask questions or chew ass, they could call. Lastly, he called Green Granite and called for them to fire—in fifteen minutes— the "annihilation" concentration: battery, three rounds. Since Green Granite's battery had four guns, this meant a total of twelve heavy artillery shells—more than a ton—would fall on the remains of the gunship and the CEV and, they hoped, not only destroy anything left but also kill any curious enemy rummaging through the remains.

No one shot at them. After a few minutes, Randy began trying to contact Red Hen to tell them he would be at the road junction soon. He wanted to try one more time for a medevac.

Red Hen Three responded and informed him they were still zero-zero for flying weather.

Randy tried again. "Red Hen Three, we're not zero-zero here; the rain has pretty much stopped, fog seems to be lifting. We can see a good way on the ground, couple hundred meters. Over." He exaggerated, but the truck's headlights were revealing a mist hovering above the ground, and the road ahead disappeared into the dark where the headlights didn't reach, and not into a fog wall. Three did not seem impressed. But then a new voice came on.

"Boiler Two-Six, Red Hen Six. Over." The voice was deeper, somehow calmer.

"Boiler Two-Six. Over."

"You now have three WIA, I understand. How serious are the other two?"

Randy didn't know how to answer that in any technical way. "One's got multiple fragment and burn wounds in the legs, upper and lower, from an RPG and is in big pain. The other has multiple frag wounds in the back and legs from an M79 grenade, probably one or more lung punctures. He's semiconscious. Over."

After a seemingly long pause, Red Hen Six came back. "You're still in the An Cao valley? Over."

"Roger. ETA the Xanh La–Chu Song road in ten minutes."

Another long pause followed, and then Red Hen Six responded, "Can you be prepared to mark an LZ on the An Cao, QL-99 road junction when you arrive?"

"Roger that, Six. Over!"

"Good. Keep me apprised of any activity. I'll be on your push. Six out."

Randy felt a weight lift, fumbled to make an opening in the canvas covering the truck bed, and shouted, "Vasquez! We're getting a medevac when we get to the junction! Ten minutes!"

"Yes sir! Bless, you, sir! Gracias al Dios!"

Randy got back on the radio. "Boiler Two-Six. Listen up! ETA to the road junction, ten minutes. When we get there, Jersey will turn right and stop. The rest of you turn left. Soon as Two-Five clears the junction, all stop, dismount, and secure the convoy. Leave one squad of grunts at the junction to clear and secure an LZ in front of Jersey! Medevac is on the way. Let me hear a roger from all of you. Over!" He did.

A few minutes later, he heard Red Hen calling. "Boiler Two-Six. Over."

"Red Hen Six. Am en route. ETA one-five. How will you mark your LZ?"

"Vehicle headlights and an orange panel. Vehicle will be on north side. Over."

"Roger. Out." As they progressed back down the An Cao road, Randy found himself biting down on the edge of a thumbnail, making little clicks that were loud in his head, each click punctuating a worrisome thought. Sergeant Carter had thought there'd be no real enemy in the An Cao, but they'd been attacked—not by many, but was that just to hold them while more slipped around to cut him off? What about his own base? He'd lost a CEV and a Duster. Had he also lost the dozer and grader? He asked Battalion for any new intelligence on enemy in the area, but there was no useful or satisfying intel—just vague high-level stuff, no details. About all he could get out of the intel was that now might be a good time for R&R.

It hadn't really rained in over an hour. The road was far from dry, but it wasn't as slick as on the trip in. Jersey sped up a little, and a very few long minutes later, the culvert loomed at the edge of the pool of light from the truck and they were there.

It was time to hustle. They staked out the orange panel, and the infantry squads deployed. Randy ordered Jersey to cut the headlights until they heard from Red Hen. Sergeants Jarvis, Warrant, and Carter and Randy stood together beside Jersey's truck as each gave a quick status. Just as they were wrapping up, Red Hen Six called again. "I'm on the road just north of Xanh La. Altitude twenty to fifty feet, depending on the mists, landing light on. You should see me any minute. Over."

Randy was still wearing Frederick's backpack radio. All four could hear Red Hen. Randy told Jersey to turn the headlights on and replied, "LZ is marked and lit. Out." He then turned toward the back of the truck. "Vasquez! Newsome! Get the patients ready. Their ride is coming!"

Jarvis asked, "Red Hen Six?" Randy nodded.

"That'd be the CO?" Carter said. "CO of the medevac battalion?"

"I guess," Randy replied.

"A friggin' colonel? Flyin' straight up the road under fifty feet with his damn lights on? Now there's cojones, sir." Jarvis suddenly laughed. "Hey, sir, he's as crazy as you. Maybe you'll make colonel too."

Carter laughed. "Hey, LT! You like going down the road with a flashlight. You should be a pilot. Pays better!"

Randy didn't know how to take all that. He bit his lip, looking away from the older, seasoned sergeants. In the backwash from the headlights, Sergeant Jarvis saw it. He said sharply, "All this leadership in one spot makes a great target." Carter and Warrant got the hint and moved off. "Sir, I'm gonna check on the men. We going back to our base?"

"I guess. No orders otherwise. Our mission hasn't been cancelled."

"Right. Sir?"

"Yeah?"

"Don't worry, sir. You've already taken point three times tonight. You got to be charmed." Sergeant Jarvis saluted casually and disappeared into the darkness.

Red Hen Six had grown up in the same Baltimore neighborhood as Arlen Washington but almost a generation earlier. He had been asleep when Spooky 45 went down, but something had awakened him about an hour later, and realizing he probably would not get back to sleep right away, he'd wandered into his command bunker to see what was what. Learning of Chief Pastor-Villanueva's condition, a glance at the map and the weather confirmed his staff's appraisal that it was not feasible. Now, almost three hours later with two more wounded at risk, he reconsidered.

Visibility in narrow valleys like An Cao was predictably worse than the broader, flatter area the Xanh La–Chu Song road, QL-99 on the map, ran through. The small base at Tranh Xa a few miles south of Xanh La had a landing strip used for army Hueys, air force Caribous and smaller Air America aircraft, and an air traffic control setup, consisting of a jeep with a radio. He thought one could navigate by dead reckoning at a safe altitude until close enough to Tranh Xa to be heard, use the controller there to help drop down low enough to see QL-99, and then follow it visually to the pickup.

The big risk was that he'd be flying up QL-99 below a hundred feet and with lights on—an open invitation to be shot down. Local intel was so paltry it made the risk completely unknowable.

He looked at the notes on Hector's condition. He could order the alert crew to fly it or ask for volunteers and knew he would get some. The very nature of medevac missions made it a very high-risk job. Sometimes the best thing to do was be an example. "Jerry," he said to the operations sergeant on duty, "Alert Chang, will you? We're going to fly a mission."

"Boiler Two-Six, Red Hen Six. Over."

"Boiler Two-Six. Over."

"I think I see your headlights. Over."

"Roger! I see you!"

"Understand you still have one KIA, three WIA. Over."

"Roger. I also have four more of the air crew."

"I can take two more, max. Over."

"Roger. Over."

"Red Hen Six. Out."

"Sergeant Jarvis! He can take two more besides the wounded. Get the air crew!"

Captain McLaughlin, Lieutenant Blagget, and airmen Washington and Otis were standing together when Sergeant Jarvis gave them the word. Captain McLaughlin immediately said, "Otis, you and Washington go. We'll help pilot the dump truck for a while and catch the next flight."

Washington's beautiful smile flashed for a second but clamped shut when Otis said, "Sir, me and Arlen are needed here. You go."

"Needed here? We ain't *needed*"—Arlen fairly screamed the word—"anywhere, 'cept back at base!"

"We are too! They got no firepower left except our guns! And like you said, we could mount the door gun on one of their trucks. And we're the only ones who know them, Arlen!"

"That ain't our problem, man!"

"Without them, Chief'd be dead and we'd have been screwed. Think we could have held Charlie off all night? Or longer? You saw what they did to that other tank! We owe 'em!"

Eddie didn't know what to do. Surely it was wrong for officers to run out on the enlisted, but Otis made sense. Yet how could he order Washington to stay while he flew home to a nice bed? Lieutenant Blagget took half his problem away. "Hey, Otis," he interjected, "I helped Washington set it up. I know the drill. Washington, you go with Captain McLaughlin. Otis and I'll stay. We can't be arguing all night."

Washington looked as if he would explode. Tom and Timmy stared at him. Tom almost laughed. Washington was clearly desperate to get out of there. Of course, so was Tom himself, but he thought there was some kind of qualitative difference he couldn't define but that left him feeling that Washington's desperation was somehow more cowardice than simple fear. Maybe the difference was that if Washington went while Otis volunteered to stay, Otis would be the hero, the man, and Washington's fearfulness, and maybe cowardice, would be exposed.

Otis had similar thoughts, but then he saw Washington's head jerk around for a quick glance at the truck carrying the guns.

Washington indeed felt as if he would explode. Just seconds ago it was simple. Now it was so fucked up. If he took the lieutenant's offer, kiss-ass Otis would be Otis the man, the hero, and Washington, just a chickenshit; there was no way it could be seen differently. As he tried to swallow that, he had a second thought. *The gun. That sucker's out of the inventory. Walk away from it and lose it.* "No sir, no sir. Otis is right," he blurted before he could stop himself. "Him and me need to crew that gun. Him an' me. We're the gunners, right? Our job."

Feeling half ashamed, the two officers followed Sergeant Jarvis to the light. On their way, they broke into a run, for they all heard shots. The chopper was on the ground. The wounded had just been loaded. Some local Vietcong were reacting. Randy ran for the machine gun on Jersey's truck, but Jersey had already scrambled to it. The shots were coming from the side where Sergeant Carter had deployed his men, and they began returning fire.

The firing indicated maybe only three or four Vietcong, but they seemed determined and braved the return fire. As was usual, especially at night, both sides tended to shoot rather high. Still, as McLaughlin and Blagget ran toward the chopper, they could hear the snap of passing bullets and the all-too-familiar pop as one hit the chopper's aluminum skin.

They stumbled on board and were shoved roughly to the rear bench seat by the crew chief to keep them clear of the wounded, and as soon as they were more or less inside, the chopper immediately lifted a foot and slid to the side and forward to get out of the truck's headlights and put the truck between it and the incoming fire. Then Red Hen Six doused his own lights and pushed the engine to maximum power, lifting the overloaded machine almost straight up to disappear into the mist.

With the targeted chopper having escaped, the Vietcong slipped away as fast as they could to escape what they assumed would soon be a hail of artillery fire.

The copilot took control, and the chopper leaned forward and rapidly gained speed, climbing at a more sedate rate and with much less stress on the engine. The copilot was flying because Red Hen Six had to bandage his own leg. Just as he had lifted off to slide behind the truck, a bullet had punched through and cut a furrow across the top of his thigh a few inches above the knee.

Tom Blagget breathed a deep sigh of relief as the chopper rose, losing itself in the utter blackness of the low clouds. It seemed to him his mind, breath, and heart had all stopped when the shooting began. Now he was back from Zombieland, fingering his rosary and thanking God. Then he found himself praying for the safety of Otis and Washington, and then, in the faint light from the cockpit instruments and a tiny pen light the medic was using, he couldn't help but stare at the patients—and the poncho-wrapped body. He jerked his mind away from the body and shouted at the medic, "How's Chief?"

"Chief? Who's Chief?"

"The man you're looking at!"

Hector was awake, and Vasquez could not bring himself to shout out the truth of Hector's dire condition while he could hear. "Hanging in there. Gonna be all right, sir! Yes sir. You're gonna make it, man! Keep your eyes open, buddy; don't go zone out on me, right?"

The medic's voice dropped, focusing on Hector. Tom's gaze turned away to fall on the body, and he felt an odd pain in his chest. "You died for me," he said to himself. "You didn't mean to, didn't want to. God, how old are you?" It was a stupid question. Lying next to him, on his side, for his wounds were in his back was the prisoner, likely responsible for the body next to him. Suddenly he was aware of Eddie's voice in his ear.

"We never see this in the air—this up-close, bloody, dirty side. We take part but never see it." Eddie's hand appeared in Tom's view, pointing to the prisoner. "How many of these guys have we shot to pieces? Killing to save lives? This guy's lucky. How many crawl off and die in the woods like a wounded deer?" He couldn't find words for the agonies imagined.

Tom didn't reply. The wounded man from the Duster suddenly gasped and moaned loudly enough to be heard. Eddie said loudly, "You okay, son?" He waved his hands vaguely in response. "Stupid question. Sorry." He leaned forward and took one of Rockefeller's hands and squeezed. "Only a few minutes, friend. Only a few more minutes. What's your name, son?"

"Rockefeller. Courtney. Ah!" Rockefeller squeezed back. "Sorry. It ... hurts like ... hell." His eyes squeezed tightly shut, and his lower lip disappeared as he bit down on it. Panting, he added, "Everyone calls me ... me ... Rocky."

Just then, roused by the loud voices or Rockefeller's movement, the prisoner coughed, and blood seeped at the corner of his mouth in a kind of froth. His free arm jerked up as if to scratch his head. On impulse, Tom took the hand. "*Hoa binh*, how bin, peace, peace," he said, over and over. He felt his eyes wet. He couldn't stop thinking of the boy who was dead and the boy in pain, and the boy who'd probably done it, whose hand he was holding, and the confusion it all brought. He hadn't been to language school, and the words he uttered had come from his antiwar sister. "Hoa bin, hoa bin. Vietnamese for 'peace, peace,' Tom. That's what you need to be taking there, not guns!" she had said just before he'd shipped out. Confusing, such a noble sentiment without a hint of how.

Eddie kept hold of Rockefeller's hand, which squeezed back spasmodically. But Eddie's mind was on his wife's name. That the plane had the same name, *MaryAnn*, was no coincidence, but somehow he felt as if he had, in some way, betrayed her—let her down. Maybe it wasn't in naming his plane in a naive confidence that her name would be safe with him. Maybe it was that he had actually volunteered for

Vietnam—volunteered to leave her. He saw her again standing by their car at the terminal as he took his first parting steps, her eyes glistening, her smile brave. She had never looked more lovely.

Shortly after, the chopper began to descend.

CHAPTER 11

HANGOVER

At four fifteen in the morning, Randy Hanley's platoon was back where it had been four hours earlier, minus three men, one M42 Duster and one M728 combat engineer vehicle, but plus two airmen, three miniguns, and the news that Hector had had only minutes left when he was rushed to treatment but that he and the other two would survive.

They could not know if their old positions had or had not been booby-trapped while they were gone. The platoon had spent the rest of the night in their trucks and ditches along the road, alternately sleeping and keeping watch. Even then, they had carefully felt along the ditches for punji stakes and trip wires, though they found none. The ditches were wet, their clothes were wet, the sodden air was cool, but they slept, too tired not to.

With sunrise, the platoon searched their old positions and the vehicles they had left behind, finding no booby traps or any sign the enemy had paid a visit. With everything seemingly in order, Lieutenant Hanley had the simple task of nodding assent to Sergeant Jarvis's suggestions for reoccupying their old positions, getting some rest and recuperation to dry out, getting at least a little cleaned up, and preparing to get back on the road-opening mission the following morning. Although the goal for the day was mostly rest and recuperation, vehicles needed to be serviced, security patrols had to be put out, weapons cleaned, and more. They might have wanted their camp to mimic a village at siesta time, but the best they could do was halfway between a siesta and a bustling market.

In resting and recuperating, the engineers had an advantage over the infantrymen who were providing security, for the former had vehicles they could stow duffel bags with extra gear in, such as shelters, air mattresses, and changes of clothes, whereas the infantrymen had only what they could carry in their packs. Consequently, once they had secured their campsite, Randy, for one, was able to put on relatively clean and dry fatigues. The infantrymen's solution was to organize a bath and laundry party at a nearby creek.

Randy got on the radio to see if Battalion would be sending him another CEV and another Duster, and how soon, but all he got was an impression that there was nothing in motion to replace them and that the battalion commander was apparently unhappy with him. Disgusted with the tepid response and his own self-doubts, Randy left the radio and found Frederick with Vasquez, who was checking the splint on his arm. "How's the arm?"

"I'm good, LT. Doesn't hurt much now."

"Probably broken, sir," Vasquez said, "but, like, maybe just a hairline fracture, you know. When we can, should get it checked by a real doctor. Meantime, need to keep it immobile, like. No stress on it—none, Will. Don't lift, push, drag, carry nothing heavy—like your radio. You a one-armed radio man now. Comprende?" Frederick nodded. Vasquez turned to Randy. "We should have medevaced him last night, sir. But dumb Willie here wouldn't go."

Randy was glad he hadn't, but he glared at Frederick anyway. "Dumb Willie is right. You eaten this morning?"

"Yeah, yes sir. You going to be moving around, sir? I can backpack."

"You can get the radio on your back with one hand? No, Will, you stick with the truck and Esteveria. Take care of that arm. I'm not going anywhere. I'll be close enough to hear if you holler."

Randy caught up with Sergeant Jarvis, who was standing by the road. "Sir, for tomorrow, I talked to Carter. We agree we should have a full squad, not just a fire team sweeping ahead of the mine-detector teams. We'll get 'em going first thing in the morning, if that's okay, sir." Randy nodded. "You know, sir, the farther we get up the road, the more time we lose minesweeping before we can get any work done."

"Beats not doing it. But you're right. We're going to have to pull up stakes and move the camp soon. By the way, I called Battalion, and for the moment anyway, they don't seem to have anything going to replace the CEV or the Duster. Probably get a resupply truck tomorrow, though."

Jarvis turned sharply, facing Randy. "And the mission's still on?" Randy nodded. "They think we can just waltz up this fucking road with no firepower?"

"I get the impression they think I fucked up in losing them," he replied softly, almost guiltily.

"They gave us a mission to make a goddamn midnight run up a fuckin' unknown road into bandit country and are pissed because we took losses? Tell 'em next time they can take their own candy asses on a thunder run!"

"Right, Sarge. Let's tell 'em together! We'll get medals for courage in the face of the chain of command." Jarvis's indignation made him feel better, and he laughed.

"Anyway, there's the two airmen and the guns they salvaged. They volunteered to stay behind with them—sort of payback. Sarge, think we could get them operational?" Randy rubbed his face, feeling the stubble and the crusty, greasy feel of dried sweat and grime. He started walking up the road just to move.

Sergeant Jarvis caught up. "Back there they dismounted one and hung it in the door. Worked. Yes sir, we can make it happen."

Randy tapped him on the back. "Good. Use Lassky? He's clever like that."

"I'll get him on it. Feel half naked without Newsome's and Higgins's firepower." They turned back toward camp.

Timmy Otis and Arlen Washington had spent a miserable remainder of the night in the bed of the dump truck, which was now cluttered with three miniguns, boxes of ammunition, and tangles of ammunition-handling gear. There was a canvas cover that had been stretched over the truck bed to keep rain out, but nothing remotely soft to try to sleep on. Hovering in a twilight zone between fitful sleep and awareness of their discomforts, they didn't notice the arrival of daylight until Sergeant Newsome pulled back the canvas cover and peered in. "You two look like shit," he said by way of greeting.

"Yeah?" Washington muttered, not recognizing the figure silhouetted by the morning light.

"And you look like you rolled in it," Newsome added. "Take it you guys haven't had anything to eat?"

Otis came alert at the last word. "Eat? Don't remember when we ate. There a mess hall here?"

Newsome laughed but looking around the truck bed. He saw the guns and ammunition but no packs or duffel bags. "You guys get any of your personal stuff off the plane?" Otis and Washington looked at each other. It had never occurred to them. Arlen announced he had his M16. "Great. All right, get your asses outside; it's warmer out here. You might start drying off. I'll be back." The silhouette disappeared.

Getting off the truck, Arlen came down on the wrong foot, and a bolt of pain shot up from his toe. He grunted, embarrassed at his clumsiness. The driver, Hutchinson, had just gotten out of the cab. "You okay?"

"Yeah. Just stepped wrong."

"Oh. You guys sleep okay back there?"

"Shit no. Where'd you sleep?"

"In the cab. Kind of cramped, but a too-short padded bench seat beats hell out of a muddy steel floor."

Sergeant Jarvis saw Otis, Washington, and Hutchinson come around the side of the truck as he approached, and he noticed Washington limping. Looking at the two airmen, he greeted them. "You two look like shit." He couldn't remember their names. "How come you're limping, son?"

"Uh, hurt my toe, Chief, when we was gettin' shot down. Just now, gettin' off the truck, put my foot down wrong."

Jarvis realized he hadn't really given any thought to what these two kids might have gone through in being shot down, crash-landing in no-man's-land, and getting shot at again. "Okay. I'll get our medic to look at it. You hang tight." As he started to turn away, Newsome and his gunner, Wodzinski, appeared, carrying a sandbag full of C-ration boxes. Newsome announced that breakfast was here. Jarvis turned back, looked at the airmen, and asked, "Either of you a sergeant?" Both shook their heads. "Okay. Newsome here is a sergeant and, for the time being anyway, has no job. Sorry, Bud. So I'm putting him in charge of you three. Hutch, we're gonna try to make a gun truck out of your ride. So you'll answer to Newsome instead of Mancini until I or Lieutenant Hanley says different; got it?" Hutchinson nodded.

Jarvis looked at Washington. "We got introduced … too busy to hold on to your name. And son," he added, turning to Otis, "I don't think I ever got yours."

Everyone got introduced, even shaking hands, and then Jarvis wrapped it up. "Okay. Sergeant Lassky'll be up here later to help. He's good at, you know, improvisation. In the meantime, Sergeant Carter and his grunts are setting up a bath party. Bud, you get these two mud pies down there and cleaned up. And see if you can't scrounge up something for them to wear. Those flight suits or whatever need a bath too. You two have canteens?"

Newsome replied, "They didn't get any of their gear off the plane; just the guns and ammo."

"Too bad. Well, there are priorities. Glad you got the guns off. But they need water, Bud. See what you can do."

Wodzinski piped up. "We got Kevin and Courtney's stuff, Sarge. You know, you told me to get all the personal gear out."

Newsome pinched the bridge of his nose and ground a knuckle into his forehead as if hit by a sudden headache. "Their stuff in Jersey's truck?" Wodzinski nodded. "Okay. I'll go through it. Personal stuff to … to send back. I'm gonna go do that. Get these guys breakfast, and after Vasquez is done, take 'em to the bath party if I'm not back."

After Sergeant Newsome had left, Wodzinski dumped the sandbag contents on the ground. "What's your favorite?" he asked no one in particular.

"Favorite what?" Otis replied.

"C-Ration."

"I don't know. Never ate any."

"You're shittin' me!"

"No. We go to the mess hall. We got flights coming' and going all the time. Mess hall's a twenty-four-seven deal."

"No shit. I can see why you joined the air force."

"Yeah, it's a pretty good deal," Otis agreed. He opened his mouth to add something, but Washington cut him off.

"Till now, anyways."

"We're pretty damn lucky, Arlen. If they hadn't come for us, we'd be dead. Think. The rocket that got that tank could have gotten us."

"Yeah, yeah. You got it, all right! Those assholes could've shot that rocket at me! But I tell you, man, we're sitting ducks here just like we was back there. Up there, man"—he pointed upward like a preacher calling down heavenly wrath—"up there we're a moving target. Harder to hit."

"You did get shot down," Wodzinski interjected with some acid in his tone.

"Yeah, yeah, but we been shot at lots of times," Arlen exaggerated. "You poor suckers? Sitting ducks. That dink took one shot and bang! You're tank's history. That's what I mean, man."

"Welcome to the ground-pounder's war, my friend," Wodzinski replied, again acidly. "At least you're all alive." He took a breath and added in a mutter, "Kevin isn't, and Court's got his legs tore up."

Arlen didn't have a quick response for that and fell silent, as did the others, but after a moment, Otis broke the quiet. "I know, I know. Hector made it, and your guy didn't. Sorry."

Sergeant Newsome had turned back to ask the airmen a question that, on hearing Otis' comment, was shoved out of his mind by a sudden anger. "My guy? My guy?" he almost shouted. "My guy was Kevin Blackstone, in country barely a month! Nineteen. Nineteen fuckin' years old."

"I'm sorry. I am. Heck, this morning I was thanking God Chief's going make it. But you know, I just couldn't think, just didn't know what to say to God about your g ... Kevin. You know? Why Chief and not him? Why him and not the enemy guy?"

Newsome looked at him, cocking his head slightly, puzzled. He took in a deep breath and blew it out noisily, as if that might clear his mind. "Shit, kid, it's a fucking war. Shit happens. Just be glad your ass is still in one piece is all."

"Amen, bro," Arlen muttered as Newsome left them again.

Approaching the dump truck, Vasquez shouted, "Hola!"

"You the medic?" Arlen replied.

"That's me."

"Can you look at my foot, man? My toe hurts bad."

"Sure, man. What you do to it?" Arlen limped to the cab and sat with his legs dangling out the open door. He told him. "Well, let's get the boot off."

Arlen didn't move. "What if I swell up and can't get it back on?"

"Think I got X-ray eyes? Listen, man; you might have a broken foot or toe, or just a bruise! Either way, we wrap it tight and get the boot back on. Or cut the toe off."

"Cut off my fuckin' toe? No way, man!"

"Not your toe, man, the boot's toe."

"Oh." Arlen began unlacing his boot.

A few minutes later, Vasquez had splinted the broken toe by taping it to the next toe and a thin splint. He managed to get the boot back on, and gave Arlen a pill for the pain. Then he turned to Sergeant Newsome. "Yo, Sarge. I come here to look over your and Stevie's wounds."

"Fuck off." Newsome was still pissed at Vasquez's treatment of the enemy.

"Want me to get LT to order you, Sarge? You got burns, cuts. Don't care if they're small. In this country, everything that can get infected does. I need to look at them. Daily."

"They're on my legs. You want I drop trou right here?"

"Drop your pants wherever you want, Sarge."

"Huh. Over here, behind the truck."

"Okay. Stevie's next." Newsome sat on the tailgate and pulled his trousers down to the tops of his boots. "Okay. No infections, yet," he said, applying an ointment to the various injuries. "I can write up a Purple Heart for you."

"Purple Heart? For these scratches? When Blackstone's Purple Heart goes straight to his mother? Save your Purple Hearts for real wounds. And I'll break all your fingers if you write up the Chink for one."

"He'll have to wait till the war's over. Maybe his army will give him whatever they give for wounds."

"Shit, they'll probably shoot him for letting his ass be captured."

"They do that?"

"They're a bunch of commie assholes. Course they do that."

The skies seemed to be clearing, and Washington thought deliverance might be at hand, but Sergeant Jarvis dropped by, interrupting Newsome's opinions about the enemy with the news that that they would be getting a resupply truck the next day and it would take them back. Otis pointed to the clearing sky and asked if a search-and-rescue helicopter couldn't come from Nha Trang and get them. "No idea. All I know is when the supply truck gets here tomorrow, to put you two on it for a ride back, at least as far as Battalion. And don't let the pretty morning sky fool you, friend. It's going to thicken up in a few hours and rain again this afternoon, which reminds me." He turned to Newsome. "Hustle these two to the bath party. Don't want to miss the chance to get their clothes dry."

As Jarvis left them, Otis looked at Washington. "Not today, but tomorrow, he says. Maybe a good thing, you think, Arlen? Give us time to set the gun up so they can use it, huh?"

"Yeah, yeah, whatever."

"You don't mind putting another day out here as a sitting duck?"

"Course I do, man. But, hey, you said we owe 'em. Guess you're right."

"Sure I'm right. Glad you see it," Otis laughed, not really believing him, and he went off to find a latrine or at least a bush.

When Otis returned, Newsome and Wodzinski had gone somewhere and Washington was alone. Otis could hear him muttering in the bed of the dump truck that there had to be a way to keep "it" and wondered what "it" was.

Otis climbed up the side. "Got to be a way to keep what, Arlen?" Arlen was staring at the minigun, the one with handles. "You're kidding! You really want to"—Otis broke into a laugh—"keep that?" He laughed again. "Think it'll fit in your duffel bag?"

Washington looked up sharply, his eyes wide, mouth agape. Then he shut his mouth as his nostrils flared like an angry horse. "No! What? You think that? Well if I was, I sure ain't now, 'cause kiss-ass Timmy Otis would sure as shit rat me out, wouldn't he?"

Otis stiffened; his smile shut down. The epithet stung. "What makes you think I'm a kiss-ass? 'Cause I do my job? I tell you, Arlen, you want to steal that gun, go ahead. I'm mum. Won't say a word. 'Cause I won't have to. You try, you'll sure as shit get caught. No way you can smuggle that out of country."

They stared angrily at each other for a long minute. Suddenly Arlen stepped away from the gun to the other end of the bed of the dump truck and spun to face Otis. "You think I'm just a dumbass, don't you? Too stupid to figure out a way to get that if I want it!" He snorted. "Huh, Timmy, it's you what never had to think. Just follow the rules, do your homework, 'Yes ma'am, yes sir, whatever you say, sir!' You never had to figure your own way where they ain't no rules but one: look out for yourself! Then you get smart or you don't get nothin'!" Abruptly, Arlen's body relaxed. He shrugged and eructed a harsh laugh. "If I wanted to, man. Rat me out all you want; I'd still find a way. *If*, man, *if* I wanted to." He stepped back to the gun and slapped the cluster of barrels. "But right now, like you say, we got to figure out how to get this sucker to work here, right?"

Otis gaped, wondering if Arlen was half right and that it was he, with his upbringing, who really didn't know how to think. Or maybe stealing the gun was just a joking fantasy to Arlen and Otis had been reading everything wrong. He didn't have a chance to dwell on the problem for long, because just then Newsome and Wodzinski reappeared. "Bath party, gents!" Newsome announced. "Got some rags for you too."

The bath was a shallow creek a few yards wide that flowed out of some hills to the north and passed about a hundred yards from the perimeter of their camp. The spot they used was screened by some brush and a few trees. A number of bodies in varying states of undress also helped screen the water from view as Washington and Otis approached. Newsome called out, "Hey, Jordy! You in charge here? Don't see Warrant."

"No one said, Sarge. Got a problem?"

"Two. These here are Airman Washington and Airman Otis, two of the dudes we had to pick up last night. As you can see, their cleanliness is way below army standards. Maybe you could show 'em your good hygiene practices and don't let 'em get lost or drown?"

"Sure, Sarge. I'll even let 'em use my soap." Corporal Jordan Hicks looked at the two airmen and held up a shiny bar of soap. "It's got a string on it, so you shouldn't drop and lose it, 'cause if you do, we'll shoot you."

Otis stepped forward and reached for the soap. "I'm Timmy Otis. He's Arlen Washington. We won't lose the soap. Will we, Arlen?"

"That how we get clean?" Arlen asked loudly, pointing to a white guy and a black guy in the middle of the stream scooping handfuls of mud from the bottom and throwing it at each other.

Corporal Hicks shouted, "Jude! Ricochet! You're settin' a bad example for our air force guests!" When both turned their attention from each other, Hicks continued. "Say hi to Airmen Arlen Washington and Timmy Otis." Turning to the airmen, he added, "The white mudball is Ricochet, and the black mudball is Jude Jefferson."

Ricochet said, "Hi! Hey, Jude! We have us another president *and* an elevator! Maybe together you two together can outrank the big prick and call off the war, and elevator Otis can lift us out of here, and then ..."

"Yeah, whatever, smart-ass," Jude interrupted. "And by the way, you got a leech on your calf."

"I do? Where?"

"Back of your right calf, man."

"Ah, shit." Ricochet waded ashore, picked up his helmet, and pulled a small plastic bottle from the camouflage band.

"A leech?" Washington asked. "What's that?"

Ricochet, stepping out of the water, said loudly, "A bloodsucker!" and turned his leg to show him what looked like a two-inch slug sticking out of his calf. Seeing the revulsion on Washington's face, he went on. "Sucks the blood right out of you, and if you don't get it off right away, turns you into a zombie. Living dead."

"And you play in the water with them things around?" Washington asked, horrified. Living on an air base had not exposed him to tropical ecosystems.

Ricochet took the cap off the bottle and squirted a few drops of its contents on the leech. Jude said, "He's shitting you, man. No big deal." A moment later, the leech dropped off him.

Arlen and Timmy sat down to remove their clothes, and then Timmy noticed Arlen's bandaged toe. "Hey, Arlen. Should you go in that water with your toe?" Turning to Hicks, he went on. "Arlen's got a busted toe; could he get an infection from the water?"

Hicks peered at Arlen's toe. "Get cut?" Arlen shook his head. "I know we don't want to splash around with open cuts or sores, especially the muck on the bottom. Better safe than sorry."

Arlen found himself standing naked on the shore while Ricochet used his helmet to scoop up water and pour it over him both to let him wash up and to rinse him off. It was very odd to him because he felt something but didn't know what the feeling was. No one had done anything like that for him before. At first he thought he hated it. But almost against his will he found himself enjoying it. The enjoyment began with his comparing his larger, fitter, darker body with Otis's thinner, paler one; followed by an emerging atavistic pleasure at being in an Edenic setting free of all encumbrances of pasts and futures; and then something very rare for him: he found himself enjoying just laughing and joking with the men around him—strangers who didn't feel like strangers.

Corporal Hicks did the same for Timmy, who then braved the stream to wash the mud, blood, and grime from their flight suits, socks, and underwear. He was kneeling in the creek, finishing up the laundry, when he suddenly jumped up with a low shriek. "Something wriggled past me. Big!"

"Did it bite?" Hicks asked.

"No!"

"Then don't worry. Hey, you do have a couple of leeches on you."

Timmy looked down and saw one on his thigh, close to his crotch. "Shit! Oh! What do I do?"

"Good thing it's not on your dick. There's another on the back of your right leg," Hicks said calmly, adding, "Don't let them clothes float away." Otis hesitated between the desire to get out of the water as fast as possible and the sight of a flight suit and a pair of shorts drifting toward the main current. Finally, he lunged for the clothes, scooped them up, and sloshed toward the shore.

"You got the soap?" Hicks demanded.

"I—I don't know! I must have dropped it!"

"I'm gonna shoot you."

Arlen laughed. "It's hanging from your wrist, Timmy."

"Oh," he replied, stepping onto the grass. Ricochet had retrieved his plastic bottle and, telling Otis to stand still, squirted the two leeches.

"Man, this jungle shit sucks. Bad enough flyin' over it. But standin' in it really sucks."

"You call this jungle, Washington?" Jefferson snorted. "You're all safe and cozy in a nice little base camp. Jungle is where you patrol under triple canopy and can't see the sky, and you damn near choke on the air 'cause no breeze can reach that deep. Where you need a fuckin' machete to clear enough crap just to see your boots. You ain't in any jungle here, friend. You're in a park."

Arlen swallowed. The leeches fell off Otis. He had a vision of the little ant figures swarming around Queen of Hearts. He wanted to say something back. "My captain said there's tigers in the jungle. Guess you seen some?"

"Nope, thank the good Lord. Guess they could be there, but there be other goodies: cobras, bamboo vipers, and—oh! Jordy! Tell him about Warrant and the panther!"

Jordan Hicks laughed. "Un-fucking believable! We're on ambush, lying by a trail as still and quiet as can be. Sarge is maybe six feet from me. He hears a, like, snuffling in his ear. He thinks it's me. He whispers, 'Jord, what the …' and stops there. He's turned his head, and there's just enough light to see he's nose-to-nose with a big-ass black panther!"

"A panther?"

"Five foot long if an inch, man! When I looked, I saw it too!"

"You're shittin' me!" Arlen couldn't resist asking. "What'd he do?"

Hicks reached for his helmet, put it on, and, from the elastic camouflage band, retrieved a small bottle just like the one in Ricochet's hand. He held it under his eye, pointing at Washington. "Real slow, he got this, took the cap off and put a squirt right in the panther's nose. Fucker ran off like it was on fire!"

"Mosquito repellent!" Ricochet laughed, holding his own bottle out. "Repels mosquitos, knocks off leeches, runs off panthers—you name it. Never leave home without it."

CHAPTER 12

IMPROV

It was pushing noon, the air hot and humid under a bright but cloudy sky. The airmen's suits were drying on the hood of the dump truck along with their underwear. Timmy Otis was wearing Kevin Blackstone's extra pair of jungle fatigues, which were slightly large for him. Arlen Washington was wearing Courtney Blackstone's fatigue trousers, but not the shirt. Arlen was one of those men born with genes for broad shoulders and slim hips. Courtney's trousers, although too short, fit Arlen's slim hips, but his shirt was uncomfortably tight across Arlen's shoulders.

They were standing in the bed of the dump truck along with Sergeant Lassky, pondering the three miniguns. The breathlessness of the late morning was amplified within the steel sides of the dump truck, and all three were sweaty even though they'd simply been pondering and talking.

They'd soon realized they had only enough gear to service one gun and that the Aero-Dillon with its handles was the only one they could effectively control. It would have been simple if they could have swapped the minigun for one of the heavy machine guns on a truck ring mount, but the mounts were not compatible. Also, the dump truck did not have a ring mount, and Washington argued for mounting it on the dump truck to gain what he saw as the added protection of the dump bed's steel walls. He even argued for coming up with a mount that would allow the gun to be pulled down behind the walls if it came under fire.

Sergeant Lassky countered it would be way too complicated, and besides, a machine gun hiding behind a wall is useless. They made no progress for some time. Washington finally asked if they could make a frame to act like the gunship's door, and then they could use the straps he'd used before. Lassky had been trying to imagine solutions based on typical machine gun mounts—a single point of attachment to a ring, a tripod, or a post—but the mechanics of such an attachment eluded both his imagination and, he knew, their tools and resources.

It took some effort for Lassky to free his imagination from his preconceptions and grasp Washington's suggestion and decide it could work. They climbed out of the dump truck and found a piece of flat, bare ground to use as a design board. Otis was sent on an errand to get a measuring tape, and the two sat down to sketch out a design for a wooden doorframe. What they came up with was a wide doorframe shape supported and braced by a boxlike timber frame that would be wedged tightly against the sides of the dump truck bed.

Lassky stood up. "Okay, my man, we got a plan. Let's go take some measurements and I'll send my guys out to get materials." Washington looked up at him, watching him turn away, but then Sergeant Lassky turned back and said, "You know, we're damn glad to have this gun, considering." He paused, stroking his stubbled chin. "But this wouldn't work without you. Not sure we'd have ever come up with your doorframe idea. I know this is no picnic for you, but I'm really glad you're here."

Something in Lassky's tone brought Arlen up short, and he stifled a dismissive knee-jerk reply. Surprising himself, he confessed, "Nobody was ever glad I was around."

Sergeant Lassky blinked, opened his mouth, and decided that while there was something there to explore, it was not the time. He smiled. "First time for everything. But I meant it, my man." He headed for the dump truck, patting his pockets. "Crap. Forgot my notebook. Be right back."

For a few moments, Arlen didn't move, alternately staring at the design scratched in the dirt and back at the dump truck. His thoughts bounced around like a pinball. The army guys wanted his gun set up badly. *They must need the firepower, for sure as hell they don't feel safe without it. They put me and Timmy on that supply truck tomorrow, no way they going to let that gun go with me. The GEs maybe, but not the good one. And that means the army guys are pretty sure not just that shit can happen but that shit* will *happen. In the gunship, when shit happens, the captain can always go up, out of range, or into the clouds.* Washington had never actually experienced that on a mission. The main thing was that he could if he wanted to. This was no gunship. *Shit happens here, there's nowhere to run, nowhere to hide.* His thoughts bounced between tomorrow's supply truck and the dump truck. The first equaled safety but no gun. Alternately, he could do what Timmy did—volunteer to stay and be the army guys' gunner. They'd need a guy who really knew the gun. Just an extra day or two, maybe, for sure the army would get them new firepower, new tanks. *But sure as shit, in my life, if shit can happen, shit will happen.* There it was: safety but no gun, or gun but no safety.

He had no idea how long he stood there, trapped between a truck to safety and a truck with the gun. His paralysis was broken by the approach of another truck, this one loaded with men of Sergeant Lassky's squad, tools, and timbers.

Not far outside the engineers' defense perimeter lay the ruins of a tiny hamlet, the victim of some earlier battle fought and forgotten before any of them had arrived in Vietnam and now a convenient source of the timbers Sergeant Lassky needed to build a mount for the gun.

They were pretty sure they could have the gun operational by evening.

The dump truck was becoming a gun truck with a crew of five. Hutchinson, the driver, was happy to drive and take care of the truck but wanted nothing to do with what he saw as the misuse of his truck as an experiment in turning it into a combat vehicle with no real armor. Sergeant Newsome knew nothing about dump trucks or miniguns. Nevertheless, he was in charge because he was a sergeant. Sergeant

Lassky was okay but had his own duties. He would help get the gun mounted, but then he would be off.

As the work progressed, arguments broke out. These were not so much about how to get the gun installed as they were about who would be operating it, and they were triggered by Washington's vacillation on the matter. Newsome wanted everyone trained on all the tasks involved in controlling, firing, and feeding the gun. Washington seemed at once both intent on keeping control of it and exhibiting all the signs of a man reluctant to take the responsibility. Newsome tried to play on that, pointing out how much safer a man would be lying down in the bed of the truck, helping keep the gun fed with ammunition, than exposing himself to aim and fire it.

At one point, Arlen needed to relieve himself. Newsome asked if he needed toilet paper. Arlen nodded, and Newsome dug into his pack and pulled out some packets and pointed Arlen to the most distant latrine. When Arlen had muttered a thank-you and left, Newsome turned to Timmy. "What the hell's wrong with him? He think he owns that thing?"

Timmy laughed. "That one's special. I think it is like his girlfriend—if you're the type of guy who thinks he owns his girlfriend."

"Huh!" Newsome snorted. "If it's his girlfriend, he seems as much afraid of her as he wants to own her!"

Wodzinski chimed in. "Arlen wants to be the gunner, but he's the most nervous guy I ever saw! If Charlie comes and he's on the gun, he going to shoot or just wet his pants?"

"Aw, come on," Timmy said defensively, "We've been on a bunch of missions, and we've been shot at." He gave a snort. "And shot down." Newsome and Wodzinski just stared at him until Timmy felt he had to say more. "I think it's like not being in control. If you're just out for number one ..." Timmy paused, cocking his head while trying to organize his thoughts. "I think, you can't just go along for the ride, can't like put your trust in others. Arlen hates the missions. We're both gunners. That's our job title: gunner. Except we're gunners that don't gun. We just keep them operational and fed with ammo. The captain—the pilot—he's the real gunner. He has the switch. He aims the guns. Us? We get to hear bullets punching through, but we can't do a damn thing except stand there. Like, you ever get nervous riding in a car when someone else is driving?"

Wodzinski chuckled. "Sometimes."

"I think that's what it is. I think it's easier for Chief and me and Lemuel, 'cause we trust Captain McLaughlin and each other. But it's like Arlen doesn't trust."

Washington returned, and there were no more arguments, as Sergeant Newsome had decided that when the time came, he'd just give Washington an order, and if he didn't carry it out, he'd throw him off the truck.

Newsome, Wodzinski, and the driver left to hunt up jumper cables to connect the truck's battery to the gun's power and control cables. Left alone, Arlen and Timmy were laying out the ammo boxes, figuring out how to configure the flexible ammunition feed chute and linking belts of ammo together. "You could've asked, you know," Arlen blurted.

"Asked what?"

"Asked me, man. 'Stead of volunteering us both like that."

Otis looked at Arlen, who was avoiding eye contact. "Hey, the lieutenant offered to stay, didn't he?"

"Yeah, and make me look like a pussy."

Timmy didn't reply immediately but thought a moment. "Okay, so if I hadn't said anything and we'd gotten a ride, you wouldn't have looked like a pussy, huh?"

"None of us would, man."

"Okay. We wouldn't look like—you know, that. These guys lost all their heavy firepower saving our butts, and us walking out on 'em, even though we can give 'em a lot of firepower back, that's okay so long as we don't look like we're chicken."

"Look, man; we took our chances and got our asses shot up. They took their chances and got their asses shot up. It's even, man. Don't owe 'em shit."

"We owe what we can do." Timmy heaved a sigh. "Think this'll work?" he asked, heaving the end of the feed chute to approximately where the gun would be.

"Maybe. Looks okay. Won't know until we try it. Might need more slack."

"Okay. Let's load the belts." They set to work again.

After a few minutes, Arlen asked, "Owe what we can do? Hell's that supposed to mean?"

"Come on, Arlen; you know what I mean."

Arlen sort of snarled and looked away out over the deep, alien greens of the rice paddies and jungles slashed by the long, ochre scar of the road. Antagonistic visions tugged in his mind, not quite in images, not quite in words; Big Ma's fat, comforting hand, words long forgotten trailing vague sentiments too close to Otis's for comfort; Jason and the teachers, almost the same if for different reasons—toe the line, keep your head down; the rule of the streets, look out for number one; and the vision—Arlen and his gun, terror and the hero of the streets.

Timmy snorted. "So you didn't take the lieutenant's offer 'cause you didn't want to look like a chicken, but you're pissed at me 'cause I volunteered to stay with these guys. That mean you're a chicken, just don't want to look like one?"

That snapped Arlen out of his confusing reverie. "Who you callin' chicken!"

"Not me, man. Just wondering what you think."

"I'm no pussy, man. No kiss-ass either. Just I know no one gets anything 'less he does for himself. Man's gotta be for numero uno!"

"Just askin' Arlen, not saying."

They fell silent, but Timmy's remarks seemed to have stung. After a while, Arlen said, "Don't know what they needed them tanks for anyway. Hell, these guys are just a bunch of road builders. Got to be pretty safe where they let a bunch of road builders loose. Probably got 'em just to, like, calm their nerves."

Timmy didn't reply. Arlen pressed on, forcing himself to test an option. "That Sergeant Jarvis. He said a supply truck is comin' tomorrow. We're supposed to go back with it. We could put the two GEs on it, you take 'em back. Then, when these guys think it's safe or they get new tanks—can't be too long, probably a couple more days max—I bring this baby back."

Timmy wanted to laugh. "Hey, I volunteered. I could stay with it."

"Nah, I know this gun. I got it all figured out. Nah, better be me," Arlen said, thinking there was always a chance, somewhere, somehow.

149

Shit always happens. Just have to be smart enough to find the opportunity in it.

Timmy chuckled. He wouldn't look directly at Arlen as he replied, "I guess you're not chicken. Sorreee," drawing out the last word in a falsetto tone. He thought Arlen made no sense. He chewed on Arlen's behavior, half-transparent, half-murky, but it just got him confused and irritated. He tried pushing him out of his mind by thinking of Merry. But thoughts of Arlen's unpleasant peculiarity intruded and he bounced between the desired and the undesired thoughts. Thinking of Merry was also like trying to put together a puzzle without a full picture to go by. Chief talked about strong women. Merry was sweet, and kind, but was she strong? What did that mean, really? He tried to think of signs of strength—signs of a strong woman. Suddenly he wondered whether Arlen was strong. His immediate response to the thought was blurted out loud: "Hell no!"

"What's that, man?"

"Nothing, Arlen; just thinking."

"Sound pissed off, man. At what?"

"Ah, you know, general, uh, stuff. That's all." Timmy went back to his thoughts. He started to think of Merry, but a different thought jumped at him. Arlen was selfish. Did that make him strong? Maybe. But he decided no, it didn't. *If I was selfish*, he thought, *I'd make lots of friends and then use them.* He tried to think of someone he knew like that, but his mind jumped back to Merry. She was the opposite, but then he thought of Tiffany, head cheerleader at school, queen of the senior prom, arm in arm with Mike Palace, quarterback and movie-handsome super stud. She dated her way up the status chain in the team, dumping them in turn, as cold as ice to the last as soon as the next one showed up. She got Merry kicked off the squad because Merry was dating Dick Price and Tiffany wanted him next. Merry had told him the story after they had been dating awhile.

"Got me on the rebound?" he'd dared ask.

"No," she replied, with a light squeeze of her hand. They were walking down a street. "You got me earthbound." Timmy wasn't sure what that meant and said nothing. But after a minute, Merry said, "I cried, of course. The next school day was a Monday, so I had all weekend to feel sorry for myself—and did. And on the way to school, I had the bitter thought that Tiffany will always win. She'll probably go to her grave a winner—at least in her mind. But then I realized I didn't want to be her, because she might win all the time, but she'll never be happy."

"Why not?" he asked with the first thought that came to mind. "You know what they say: 'Winning isn't everything; winning is the only thing.'"

Merry snapped back, "You don't believe that!"

"Well, I guess I don't really want to, but don't most people?"

Merry had said something snappy in response, but he couldn't remember it; he recalled only a kind of irritation rising up, prompting a fear of a fight he didn't ever want.

Suddenly "I'm for Numero Uno" Arlen was back in his thoughts. He didn't like Arlen but didn't want to really admit it, just as he didn't really want to believe winning was the only thing. He felt doing right should be. But what was that? Wanting to escape into thoughts of Merry, home, tomorrow, but unable to without irritating intrusions of thoughts about Arlen, Timmy gave up and turned his mind back to the tasks at hand. It didn't work. The thoughts kept intruding like squabbling siblings in the next room. But he managed a kind of focus by forgetting each intruding thought almost as soon as it burst in on his concentration.

As they worked on building the crib for the gun, morning passed into afternoon. The clouds darkened, heavy with impending rain. Their now dry flight suits and underwear were stuffed safely in the truck's cab, and they worked with growing urgency, wanting to finish and get canvas over the truck bed before the rains arrived.

The timber doorframe and the supporting crib were completed and the gun mounted in the same manner it had been jury-rigged in the gunship's cargo door. It could swing vertically about thirty degrees before the recoil straps that ran between the sides of the frame restrained it. It could swing left and right about 160 degrees. To aim in the other direction, the gunner would need to remove the recoil restraining strap, swing the gun around, and then reinstall the recoil strap. That still left arcs of about twenty degrees around the posts supporting the frame that could not be covered. This was not considered a problem, as the truck could always be maneuvered.

Washington wanted to test fire it. Sergeant Newsome sought out Sergeant Lassky to get permission. Lassky climbed into the truck, looked around, and shook his head. "Can't do that, man; not yet anyway. We don't know where everyone is."

"Just rice paddy out that way, Sarge. I don't see no one," Washington argued. "I got to have something to aim at. No sights on this thing. Got to get a feel for it, you know. Like that bush out there in the middle of that paddy."

"That's a hut."

"That little thing? They got midgets out there?"

"No. Don't know what it's for."

"Looks like a bush."

"It's a hut, and you can't shoot it. For all we know Carter's got an OP there."

"What's that?"

"Observation post—like a lookout."

"Well, gimme a place to shoot."

"I told you," Lassky began, but he stopped himself. No one wants to rely on a weapon that hasn't been test fired—especially one with a jury-rigged mount. "I'll go find Carter. Hang tight. Don't shoot nothing."

When Lassky left, Sergeant Newsome coughed. Since they had started work building the frame and mounting the gun under Lassky's supervision, he'd seldom spoken but had worked quietly at the labors involved. When he had offered an occasional suggestion, it had been brief and in a somewhat surly, offhand manner. Now he suddenly spoke like a sergeant. "We ought to mark sectors."

"What's that mean?" Washington asked.

Newsome put one hand on Arlen's shoulder, pointing with the other out over the fields. "Look out there. You can see fine now, but Charlie most always attacks at night. Maybe you can see him; more likely not. Then the fireworks start, and that screws your night vision. We have a wide sector to support." He made a wide sweep with his hand, and Arlen swung the gun, following, squinting down the barrels. "So we need a way to mark targets so you can aim even if you can't really see them." Arlen looked at him, puzzled, unable to visualize what Newsome was saying.

Newsome saw Arlen's blank, wide-eyed expression. "It's like having preplanned targets. LT does it all the time. Every night. Like that hut out there. He figures out the coordinates and sends it to the redlegs. Then they figure out all the angles and shit and come back and give LT a name, like Tango Three-Three. So a fight comes and LT calls them up and says something like Tango Three-Three, right fifty meters, and the redlegs blow the crap out of whatever's fifty meters right of Tango Three-Three."

"Yeah, yeah, Sarge, in the dark. I get it"

"Sarge," Otis chimed, "coordinates with names won't do us any good."

"Yeah, Sarge," Arlen added, "we've no way to set angles and stuff on the gun; it's all hand and eye."

"I know. But I've been thinking. Say we get with Warrant and Carter. They pick out some reference targets, like that hut—whatever—and give 'em names like Red, Blue, Alpha—whatever. If we got illumination, the grunts can radio us. 'Hose 'em at Blue! Fifty meters right!' Something like that, see? We'll already know Blue. No one has to try to point it out or describe it. Be too slow to try."

"How can we do that?" Washington grinned, now intrigued by the idea. Red, Blue, Alpha. He could see himself swinging from target to target, blowing the VC away.

"But if, like you say, we can't see the target, we can't see the reference either," Otis interjected, covering his eyes with one hand and pointing aimlessly with the other.

Arlen's grin faded. "Well, I think I have an idea," Newsome replied. "I'm thinking we can identify reference targets out there—Red, Blue, and so on—and mark out a kind of aiming system to each target. Won't be right on, but close, and with this gun, close will be good enough."

"How would that work?" Otis asked.

"Don't know just yet. Something we've got to figure out, 'cause we're really going to need it." Newsome replied.

Just then Sergeant Lassky returned with Sergeant Carter and the first of the afternoon rain. Fortunately, Newsome and the crew had spread the canvas over the truck bed in time but would have to pull some of it back to shoot. By the time Sergeant Carter had a good look, the rain had turned heavy and visibility was poor. Instead of test firing, Carter made sure they had a radio on the right frequency and could maneuver on call. The truck had been parked with other trucks, not assigned to any part of the defense, because no one knew whether the gun could be mounted and operational.

Earlier, around midafternoon, Bagger Three-Five, the battalion's operations sergeant, called Boiler Two-Five, Sergeant Jarvis, with a question. "What base were the fliers out of? Oh. You on speaker?"

"Nha Trang, and negative on speaker. Over."

"Roger. Uh, you get their unit? Or, like, the pilot's name? Over."

"Unit? No. You want a name over the air? Over."

"Uh, guess not. Uh, don't know how to ask. Everything go okay, you know, from your view?"

"What? Shitty weather, slick roads, enemy fire—sure, everything went perfect!"

"Look, sorry, Two-Five. Didn't mean it that way. Sort of meant it worse. Like, any fuckups. Over."

"Three-Five, we can tell war stories over a beer someday, but not here! Shit happened, but nobody fucked up to make it happen."

"So, uh, shit happened but nobody fucked up? Over."

A sudden suspicion formed, and Jarvis replied harshly, "Don't fuck with my LT, Three-Five! Sure, he's got no more experience than a draftee, but he's as good as they come, and he's got balls!"

"Roger, Two-Five. No sweat. Out." Jarvis wondered what the hell that might be about; he then put it out of his mind to give his attentions to tomorrow, when they would have to get on with their mission.

CHAPTER 13

ON WITH THE MISSION

Otis and Washington's second full night on the ground was much less uncomfortable thanks to the ponchos, poncho liners, and inflatable air mattresses Newsome provided from his missing crewmen's gear. The weather pattern of the previous day continued with intermittent partial clearing in the morning that let bits of sunshine through—a prelude to yet more rain in the afternoon. The dump truck crew spent a relatively pleasant morning improving the jury-rigged control of electrical power for the gun. The cables salvaged from the plane extended with jumper cables brought power from the truck's twenty-four-volt battery and sixty-amp generator. They wanted to avoid the clumsy process of having one man aiming the gun and an assistant gunner firing it by trying to touch the right sets of bare wires together, and with advantages of daylight and tools, they were able to wire it into the gun's trigger controls, enabling the gunner to both aim *and* fire.

Otis, noting the better weather, kept expressing hope they might be picked up and not need a ride to just another army camp. Washington kept silent on the matter. Wodzinski kept looking for the supply truck, and when noon was an hour past, he began asking every few minutes, "Where's the damn supply truck? They said it would be here right after lunch."

Finally, they were allowed to test fire the gun, and it worked. Washington could now both aim and fire.

Though weak and mostly hidden, the morning sun rapidly raised the temperature and dried whatever was exposed to it, including the hood of Lieutenant Hanley's command truck, where he had two maps spread out: one a standard military topographic map and the other a larger-scale photographic map that more accurately showed the locations of buildings, vegetation, and cultivated land. He still had the mission to clear the road to Chu Song, but now it was looking both riskier and more complicated.

Barely two kilometers beyond the farthest point they had cleared, the rice fields ended and the forest closed in on the road. On the photomaps, the road was traced by overprinting, for the forest canopy otherwise hid it. To clear the road though the forested section, they would need Rome plows—the twenty-eight-ton D7-type Caterpillar tractors with very large and specially angled blades that could cut through trees over a foot thick. They could rip through jungle like a barber's electric shears could rip through a thick head of hair. Ideally, the plows worked in groups staggered in echelon, clearing swaths of jungle forty to one hundred or more feet wide in a single pass. Normally they would want to clear the jungle back from the road one to two hundred or more meters. The reality depended on the evenness of the terrain and the age and density of the jungle. The photos told him where the jungle was but gave little hint of its density or how mature the trees in it were. They could be fifty-foot trees with trunks barely a foot thick, or one-hundred-fifty-foot trees with six- to eight-foot-thick trunks. The photomap did show there were very few clearings in the forest.

Randy didn't like the thought of using Rome plows. As a Boy Scout he'd learned to love camping and hiking in the forest with other kids and hunting with his father. He thought, *Tearing down forest and not even harvesting the timber for any good use—is, like, sacrilegious!* As he completed the thought, he uttered the last word aloud.

"What's sacrilegious, LT?" Sergeant Jarvis asked.

"Oh. Thinking about the Rome plows. What they'll do to the all that jungle. Kind of raping it."

"Better it than us, LT. Shit, this is a war. Don't that make the whole fucking thing sacrilegious?"

"Could be. Shitty for sure."

"Amen, LT." They peered at the maps together. After several minutes of comfortable silence, Sergeant Jarvis uttered an opinion, pointing to the photomap where the jungle swallowed the road as if it were vanishing into a tunnel. "Six klicks to the objective as the crow flies, LT, but not on the ground. Got several switchbacks through the jungle here. Been pretty flat for us so far. Be a different story when we hit the hills in that jungle. Twenty-meter contour interval. All kinds of rugged crap can be hidden between those contour lines."

"Yeah, and perfect terrain for Charlie."

"No shit. It's going to take weeks. And good old Second Platoon won't be enough—no way."

"Don't think we have weeks."

Both realized that two squads of infantry were way too little. At minimum, they'd need the protection of a full infantry company, plus replacements for their CEV and the Duster.

"Any word from the minesweeping team?" Randy asked, staring up the road.

"All clear, sir. They're as close to the wood line as seems safe."

"I think we need to go up and look."

Nodding, Jarvis asked, "Ask for a chopper?"

"I'll call Battalion. If they can rustle up a bird, great, but I'll bet that before they can, the rain'll be back. I think we need to drive up and see what we can see."

"Yes sir. I'm with you on that. And Battalion needs to fish or cut bait." Randy headed toward the back of his command truck to call

Bagger Three, but halfway there, Sergeant Jarvis had a thought. "LT? What's artillery support look like up ahead?"

"Let's see." He returned to the maps on the hood. "Only unit in range is Green Granite, here at Xanh La. Their eight-inchers can reach, what, like sixteen klicks. We're sitting at twelve."

"So we run out of eight-inch support shortly after we get into the woods here."

"They have two eight-inchers and two 175s. The 175s can reach twenty-two klicks."

"Sir. The 175s have a flatter trajectory. Good chance of hitting a tree before they reach the target. Depending on the terrain, could detonate right over us unless they fire high angle; then their accuracy is for shit anyway."

"Good point. And us with no CEV or Duster. The army unit at Chu Song may have artillery support we could use. Okay, I'll stick that in Battalion's ear too." But when Randy laid out all his issues to Bagger Three in the person of the battalion operations sergeant, he got no real information other than that there were apparently some mission changes coming down from on high. Randy tried to take that as good news. Maybe Battalion was ahead of him, realizing the jungled part of the road would require more resources than he had.

They folded the maps and headed up the road.

Captain Eddie McLaughlin left the Nha Trang field hospital depressed. He had slept like a baby between clean white sheets, and as soon as he woke, he had made his way as quickly as he could to the hospital, but Chief was gone. He'd been evacuated to Japan. He'd get the very best of care for his wound, but he would not get a goodbye. Eddie felt derelict, as if he'd failed again. He headed for his squadron headquarters. At least he could make sure Otis and Washington got back safely.

But headquarters was pissed at him. The very first thing all headquarters want when pilots return from a mission is a debriefing. He'd gotten back to base at an awful hour and almost literally dead tired, so they had waited until he'd gotten some sleep. But in the morning, his mind on Chief, he'd forgotten the debriefing. When he arrived, Tom had already been debriefed, and not wanting any mix-ups or misinterpretations, he had waited for Eddie. The debriefing covered every moment of the mission and rescue. When he described their escape from the valley, he mentioned they still had to rescue Washington and Otis.

"Why weren't they evacuated with you?" the squadron commander spoke up, having just walked in. He'd heard Tom's earlier debriefing, but he wanted Eddie's take, as all decisions in his crew were his responsibility.

"Oh, they were evacuated with us, sir, but they're still with, uh, the army engineers who picked us up." He explained the gutsy air evacuation by the commander of the air medevac unit.

"You left them behind?" The commander's tone clearly implied that officers don't leave their men behind. Eddie explained what had happened.

"They volunteered?" the commander asked coldly. "You didn't, say, suggest it?"

That stung. Eddie's posture stiffened. "Yes sir, they volunteered. As I mentioned, sir, the engineers lost their two combat vehicles. Otis and Washington thought they could jury-rig one of the miniguns, like they did at the crash site—provide some substitute firepower until they could get reinforced or replacements."

The commander relaxed slowly, clearing his throat. "Damn fine of them."

"I thought so. Anyway, far as I know, they're still out there."

"You know the unit?"

"I know the leader's name. A Lieutenant Hanley. That right, Tom?"

"Randy. Randall, I think. Randall Hanley. An army engineer unit. They were building or repairing a road."

"Okay, gentlemen, we'll find them and get 'em back. Maybe the army's already evacuated them. We'll find out. You guys get some rest, food, drink—whatever. That kind of adventure takes some unwinding. By the way, You might have screwed up parking that historic relic, but otherwise you guys did a damn fine job. Mission accomplished."

"Yes sir. But we need to get our crew back."

"I know; I know. They're my crew too, gentlemen. So unwind. That's an order." The commander turned to leave. Eddie and Tom saluted.

"Sir! We ... do we still have a job? I mean a flying job?"

"No. Not immediately. We're transitioning to C-130s. Talk about firepower, now. We're getting one soon for testing and training. Pilot in command will be a Major Elliot Richardson. Richardson's been with it all through installation and testing the guns and mods. Rest of the crew we want to make up with guys with in-country experience. That'll include you and Tom. You're both rated. Co-pilot and navigator. If you all want it, that is. Getting shot down can drain a guy's enthusiasm sometimes. Especially guys with families." The commander completed his exit, and suddenly Eddie and Tom were alone in the debriefing room.

"So," Tom said into the chilly silence of the overly air-conditioned room. "You want it?"

"You?"

"Yeah, I think so."

"Why?"

Tom didn't reply right away. "Man. Hate that kind of question like you hate the word 'should.' Partly, it's what I came here to do. Someone's got to push pencils, I know, but I don't want it to be me. And, hell, the other part is, well, the kind of aura of it—losing your nerve."

"You're disgustingly honest, Tom. So we go for it?"

"Why not? Right now, though, no plane, no job, no crew. Mitchell's still in hospital. Buy you a drink?" They both stood as if on command, but neither took a step immediately. The story had suddenly ended, and they were no longer living it. Everything ahead was a different story unfolding. There passed between them a collective sigh—a sense of loss mixed with a reluctance to take the next step, to turn the new page. Finally Tom spoke again. "I can't tell. Colonel trying to make us feel good or looking down his nose?"

"Feel good, I'd say. He got shot down in a P-51 in Korea. Walked back through enemy lines."

"Oh. And I'm bitching because we had a bumpy ride."

"Let's stop at operations on the way. Maybe there's news of Otis and Washington." There wasn't any. But there was a message from a Sergeant Victor Thompson, army, 134th Engineer Battalion, asking for Captain McLaughlin by name to please call back and ask for Sergeant Thompson by name. "That's weird. Why me by name and this sergeant by name? Why not just a nice message: 'Hey, your boys are safe,' or something?"

"Something worse?"

"Shit, Tom, don't go negative on me." Eddie turned to the desk sergeant. "Hal, how can I call this guy back?"

"I'll put it in right now, sir. Now, we don't have a private phone booth, so don't talk dirty and don't give away any secrets. Everyone from Ho Chi Minh to the CIA are probably listening in."

A few minutes later, Eddie was on the phone. "Sergeant Thompson? This is Captain McLaughlin. You left a message for me to call?"

"Yes sir."

"One Thirty-Fourth Engineers. That the outfit that rescued us?"

"Yes sir. Actually, Second Platoon of our A Company, sir. They're the ones who ran the rescue mission. Ah, we come under Second Corps headquarters."

"Were you one of those guys?"

"No sir. I'm the battalion operations sergeant. Uh, you met the lieutenant?"

"Yeah. Hanley, Randy—Randall Hanley. Give him my best."

"Yes sir, that's what I'd, uh, like to do. But, uh, I called because, like, there might be sort of a problem."

"Problem? Those guys all right? Two of my crew may still be with them." Eddie looked sharply at Tom, who shrugged, looking puzzled.

"Oh. Yes sir! They're okay, far as we know. They're a godsend, sir. But, uh, that's not, like, the issue. Uh, what I mean, sir, is, did they, uh … did Lieutenant Hanley, he do a good job? I mean, as far as you could see?"

"Good job? Hey, I'm standing here cool and dry, and my chief is on his way to a hospital in Japan instead of being shipped home in a box thanks to your guys! You said problem? Can we cut to the chase here?" Eddie had been slightly hunched over the phone and now straightened in irritation.

"Yes sir! Uh, can you hold on for a minute?" Sergeant Thompson seemed to vanish, and all Eddie could hear was a sort of muttering in the background and occasional radio static. It was almost two minutes before Sergeant Thompson came back on. "Yes sir! Sorry about that. The problem, sort of. The lieutenant lost two vehicles on the mission and—"

"I know, Sarge! And I lost a plane!"

"Yes sir. Ah, well, in a, uh, headquarters, marks on a map are cleaner and neater than what's maybe actually going on. Uh, gets hard to assess; something bad happens, like is it negligence or bad luck or, you know, REMFs: rear echelon mother—"

"Yeah. You're asking about the tank thing that got stuck in the ditch."

"Some, uh, thinking they might not have lost either vehicle if, uh, the one hadn't gone in a ditch and delayed the, uh, withdrawal." Eddie noticed that now Sergeant Thompson was speaking softly and the background noises were muted as if he were cupping his hand around his lips and the mouthpiece.

"Well, lot of fog and mist. First, nothing visible. Then headlights suddenly there, closing fast. And only when it's just yards away, I finally see it's a tank. Just as I couldn't see that tank until it was about to run me over, that tank couldn't see my plane until it was about to crash into it. It went into the ditch so it wouldn't run over me and my crew! Negligence my ass, Sergeant. Call it the fog of war. Shit happens. You can't stop it. All you can do is deal with it."

"Yes sir! Sure. I—we—was wondering if maybe you might write something up. A letter or, like, a commendation. You know—outside observer, witness."

"To straighten out the REMFs? Be glad to. I'll send it straight to you."

"Oh, not me, sir!"

"I mean your commander."

"Ah, sir, it might be better, uh, if maybe you—or even better, your CO—could send it, like, to Commanding General, Second Corps. We're a Corps unit."

"To a three-star?" Eddie laughed. And, of course, then no REMF could dare bury or ignore it. "You've got it, Sergeant. Let me add your outfit's damn lucky to have you." Eddie laughed as he hung up, flexing the stiffness of irritation from his shoulders. He then explained the whole exchange to Tom.

Slapping Tom on the back, Eddie concluded, "Know what, Tom? Whoever it was that made the NCO corps separate from the officer corps was a bloody genius." They headed for the officers' club.

Lieutenant Colonel George Short sat at a table in the battalion headquarters mess tent, which he used as a conference room for staff meetings and briefings. His elbows rested on the table, hands laced together, chin resting on his hands, and his eyes fixed on a burned-out bulb dangling from the peak of the tent. He had received an order from Second Corps to expedite the clearing of the road to Chu Song so that the heavy artillery battery now at Fire Base Chrome near Xanh La could deploy to Chu Song. He had immediately replied that the unit on that mission was recovering from the mission to rescue the downed air crew, but Second Corps didn't seem impressed. He'd then protested that all his assets were committed. He would need more to expedite opening the road to Chu Song. He was told that Second Corps realized he was overcommitted and that he was to reallocate his assets based on the new priorities, and if he still needed more, to ask.

Colonel Short had also received Lieutenant Hanley's list of issues, needs and concerns—or, as he thought of them, his list of whines. He had not received a suitable report on the loss of the CEV, which reinforced his intuition that the story was not a good one. He had called a staff meeting to deal with the issues and had arrived early for several reasons. The weather was oppressive, and the mess tent had a good fan. A fresh pot of coffee had been brewed, and he wanted a cup before it started to get stale. Lastly, he wanted time to think through how he would handle matters. He did not want to appear indecisive.

Presently, his staff began to arrive, get coffee or a soda, and take their seats. His sergeant major arrived first, followed by his senior staff. His executive officer, who would normally facilitate such meetings, especially if briefings were involved, was thoughtlessly on R&R leave in Hawaii. Half a dozen junior officers and noncommissioned officers pulled up chairs behind their bosses. The last to arrive was his logistics officer, or S-4. As the S-4 settled his bulk onto a chair, the sergeant major rose and rumbled in a voice that seemed to come from deep in his large barrel chest and that could probably have been heard in Hanoi, "Sir, the staff is present."

"Thank you, Sergeant Major. Gentlemen—"

The sergeant major interrupted. "Sir, should the S-2 give an update?"

"Oh. Of course. Polk?"

Lieutenant Harry Polk, the S-2, or intelligence officer, jumped to attention. "Sir! No real change in the weather forecast. Continued heavy overcast, intermittent rain. Sometime in the next forty-eight to seventy-two hours another tropical storm will arrive, hitting us as heavy rain. No change in enemy activity reports. No new activity reported in our areas of concern."

"Road to Chu Song? QL-99?"

"Nothing new, sir."

"What about that earlier report, where was it, northeast of Xanh La?"

"No updates on that, sir. Have to assume no movement."

"Right. S-1?" But before the personnel officer could open his mouth—he was always slow to speak—the S-4 raised a plump hand and spoke at the same time.

"Beg pardon, sir, but I have a gun truck with the supplies Lieutenant Hanley needs ready to roll. If it leaves now, it can get there; drop off the supplies and a nice, hot meal; and be back well before dark."

"Send a truck alone?" the commander's tone sharpened.

"Sir, it's a gun truck. Armored, three machine guns. Hanley's low on ammo, rations, and fuel. No enemy activity reported. We'd be sending it anyway in the morning. This way they won't have to spend another night short on ammo."

"Right. Go ahead. Oh, have it bring back those airmen and the Duster and CEV crews. And whatever was salvaged from the aircraft." The answer seemed forced on him, as any other would look indecisive or worse. "Okay, Odom?"

The gist of the S-1's drawling report was that the executive officer was back in country from his R&R and would arrive on a flight with half a dozen replacements the following day, weather permitting.

"Which it probably won't," Colonel Short said. "S-3? Bob?"

Major Gridley rose. "Sir. We've been reviewing what it'll take to speed up the QL-99 mission. We should call for the Rome plows to move up in the next forty-eight hours. The main issue will be security. The last several kilometers are heavily wooded. We'll need stronger security." He paused for a breath and continued, "Hanley estimates a company, but frankly, sir, more likely a battalion is what'll be needed. That's the big deal. Corps needs to act on this, sir."

"Company or a battalion? I've heard of no enemy activity in that area. You, Harry?"

"None reported, sir," Lieutenant Polk interjected. "This comes from Corps and Division assets in the area, a few long-range patrols, IR and SLAR flights." The S-2 shrugged, ran a finger over the map board, tracing highway QL-99. "No signs of any significant enemy activity near the highway. Quiet."

"Okay. Good." Colonel Short abruptly stood, clasping his hands behind his back. "Then we may assume the enemy is not a significant factor between Hanley's current position and Chu Song. Still, inform Corps that we must stand down B Company from its current mission to assume the QL-99 road clearing mission. Attach Hanley to B Company if Captain Crendall thinks he can use him. Also, we need an infantry sweep of the forested area ASAP, prior to our getting there. Let's get a timeline on that and schedule the Rome plows accordingly. Oh, Alert B Company to be ready to roll in the morning, assuming we get approval."

No one brought up any other issues. Colonel Short had one more question for his personnel officer. "Jeremy," he said jovially, "any lieutenants in that packet of replacements coming in tomorrow?"

Jeremy looked surprised for a moment, for all new officers were assigned through a different channel and by name. "No sir. Just six new guys fresh out of AIT."

"Ah, okay. Thank you, gentlemen."

CHAPTER 14

BEST LAID PLANS

Randy and Sergeant Jarvis had driven up the road as far as the minesweepers and Sergeant Warrant's infantry squad had dared, close to the edge of the wood where the road vanished as if into a tunnel. "Road surface actually gets better the farther up we come," Sergeant Jarvis pointed out. "Hell, we can clear up to this point in next to no time, LT."

"Yeah. But we're just about in RPG range from the jungle," Sergeant Warrant said, "and we are standing within sniper range."

"We are?"

"Yes sir. Not that their snipers are very good shots." He shrugged.

"Okay, got the point." Randy stared at the peaceful countryside and thought back to the length of road they had traversed to get where they were. He pulled out his map and stared at it. The two sergeants watched. "Well, one good thing. We're not looking at triple-canopy jungle. Second-growth stuff. Forty- to maybe some sixty-foot trees, heavy underbrush. At least that much'll be easier for the Rome plows.

Okay. We passed a kind of broad hummock back a klick or so. See this little bump in the contour line near the road where it bulges out into the rice paddies? I think that's it." The sergeants nodded. "I think we ought to pull up stakes and move there. Less minesweeping to do to get to work. And we've been sitting where we are for a good while."

"More'n long enough for Charlie to scope us out in detail," Sergeant Warrant agreed. "I noticed it coming up, but we should take a closer look-see on the way back, sir."

"Sure." Just then Frederick came walking up from the command truck. "Hey, LT! That supply truck should be arriving at the CP in an hour or so. Ammo, water, rations, mail, *and* a hot meal from the Battalion mess! Also they want to pick up the airmen and take 'em back to Battalion."

"Great! Oh, hell! If the airmen go, what about the gun they're mounting? There must be something we can do to keep it—on loan or whatever. I guess we'd better get back. Let's recon this spot for a new position on the way. We'll want to move tomorrow. Soon as we get back, get the word out, and I'll see about keeping the gun."

The crew of the gun truck with the supplies and hot dinner had been on their toes and alert; they just hadn't been alert for the right thing. The men manning the machine guns on the gun truck had constantly scoured the fields on both sides, and the driver and forward gunner had kept their attention intently on the road, looking for any disturbance or discoloration that might indicate a mine. The things that looked like twigs blown across the road didn't register on anyone even as they drove over them. The twigs proved to be steel caltrops—simple contraptions made of four steel spikes welded together such that however they were dropped, three spikes rested on the ground, forming a base for the fourth, which pointed up. The caltrops punctured both front tires and two of the eight on the tandem rear axles.

To the disappointment and likely salvation of the waiting Vietcong squad, the truck did not even slow but rumbled on as if on invincible tires. They fired an RPG after them but missed the fast-moving target.

A couple miles down the road, however, the tires went flat and that was what delayed the supply truck for several hours. When they did arrive at Second Platoon, it was already forming up to relocate to its new campsite father up the road. The gun truck with the supplies would have to join and follow. At any rate, it was already clearly too late to get back to Battalion headquarters before dark—especially in view of their experience with the caltrops and enemy fire. They would spend the night and return in the morning.

On arriving at the new location, Sergeant Carter directed the dump truck crew and their minigun to a position behind a low rise that would protect the lower part of the truck from rifle fire. On the other side of the rise, men were already preparing foxholes. Sergeant Carter pointed out the land beyond the low rise; perhaps150 yards of rice paddies split by the road, and just beyond, the edge of the forest. Pointing toward where the forest edge was closest, he said, "That's the most likely direction for an attack to come from, gents, so keep the gun ready and your powder dry."

"Powder dry? What powder?" Arlen asked, but no one answered.

Resupply always seemed to animate the vital notion that someone cared, that they were still connected to the world, and it brightened a creeping twilight of loneliness, especially when it included mail, which Sergeant Jarvis went around handing out. Arriving at the dump truck, he announced that Otis and Washington would be liberated the next day, going back with the gun truck to Battalion and then by some as-yet-unknown means to Nha Trang and the air force. For a second, the news delighted Washington, but then he frowned. "Both of us? What about the gun we just rigged?"

"LT wants to know if we can keep it. This one anyway. Until we get a new Duster. Orders are to bring all the hardware back with you, though."

"I can handle the gun," Sergeant Newson offered.

Arlen had been leaning on the gun and now stiffened and stepped back. Pointing at it, he snapped, "No you can't, Sarge."

"It's a fucking machine gun. Handles and triggers like a fifty-cal."

"It's electric. Ammo feeding and all. Complicated. You know how to feed it, Sarge? No kinks?"

Sergeant Jarvis cut in. "The main thing is, can we keep it? Say yes and we'll forget to send it back and you can heroically remind your air force bosses to come back and get it later. How about it?"

"Keep it!" Washington said, looking at Otis and then breaking eye contact. Tomorrow, one way or another, he'd stay with the gun, let Otis go back.

Naturally, there was no mail for Washington or Otis. Washington never got mail anyway. Wodzinski and Newsome did get mail, and there was a letter for PFC Kevin Blackstone. Someone in personnel had screwed up, bundling it with a letter to another private named Blackmun.

⚭

Sergeant Newsome took the letter, which put him in a dark but determined mood, as an idea for aiming the gun at night had been germinating in his mind—a spin-off of a somewhat impractical idea Kevin had come up with a week earlier. Newsome secured a length of stiff baling wire, bending the ends into two legs with a foot-long section in the middle made as straight as he could. This he wrapped thickly with silvery duct tape. Then he secured the legs to the gun with more tape. "What the hell's this, Sarge?" Washington asked as soon as he saw it.

"Your sighting bar."

"It's not lined up with the barrels! I aim with that, I'll just be shooting clouds! Anyway, how'm I gonna see it in the dark?"

"I'll show you, amigo; just be patient. Here come Carter and Warrant. The two infantry sergeants picked out the reference targets, two or three in each quadrant, labeling them by the alphabet: Alpha, Bravo, Charlie, and so on. Washington aimed the gun at the first one, and Sergeant Carter allowed him to fire a couple of bursts to get his eyeball aim on target. Then, holding the gun steady, he looked down Newsome's sighting bar to a spot on the dump truck's side. There

169

Newsome used duct tape to fix a small square of white paper with a cross and the letter *A* beside it. So if he sighted down the sighting bar to the letter *A* cross, the gun would be aimed at target Alpha. They did this for each reference target. At night, they would use flashlights with red filters to illuminate the sighting bar and the appropriate letter.

Washington was impressed. Over and over, he pointed the sighting bar to one target letter after another and then looked along to gun to see what he was aiming at. The late afternoon rains came, and they stretched the canvas over the truck bed and ate a cold supper. By the time the rain eased off, it was dark. Washington was eager to practice in the dark, which they did, but when he begged to test fire again, the sergeants said no.

By then everyone was bedding down for the night. The infantrymen were in their defensive ring of foxholes; the engineers in their ditches, trenches, or foxholes; the gunners and drivers of the gun truck and the trucks with machine guns manning their gun or asleep nearby. Half the men were asleep or trying to be, and half were on watch. It was another night in the country. It began to drizzle. The tarp over the dump truck bed kept most of the rain out, but it had to be open in a couple of spots for men to keep watch. The world fell into a tomb-like silence broken only by the occasional soft and distant crump of an artillery shell and the soft patter of water sliding off tarpaulins and vehicles. The misty drizzle was virtually silent.

Sergeant Carter's warning had left them nervous and edgy. Otis and Washington took first watch. Washington had thrown the front of his poncho over the gun to keep it dry and stood inside the timber crib, gripping the gun handles. "You got the power on?"

"Yeah, Arlen. Push your buttons and it'll go."

"I'm gonna spin it up. Test it."

"Sarge said no firing."

"Just spinning it up, okay?"

"I guess."

He pulled the poncho off. The gun spun up; a loud whine rose and ebbed away. Sergeant Newsome cursed. "What the hell?"

"Just testing, Sarge."

"You're gonna test that sucker to death."

The world went silent again, and after a while Otis broke it. "Say, Arlen, what're you going to do when, you know, this tour is up? Re-up? Go to school? There some job for you back home?"

"Re-up? No way!" Washington grinned wolfishly, his hands caressing the gun handles. "Hah! I'm goin' home and make my own job and be somebody. Get respect!"

"Well yeah, like, what kind of job?"

"Like I said, my own job. Arlen works for Arlen."

"Start, like, a business?"

"Yeah. A business. Arlen Inc.!" He laughed. He didn't elaborate but asked, "You? What's Timmy Otis gonna do?"

"One way or another, I'm gonna go to college."

"Be a big businessman, huh? Big office, fancy suits and all?"

"Nah. Most of the guys in high school that could go to college right off, that's what they were after. Business, law, medical, that kind of stuff. I don't want it. I want something real."

"Hey, man, you'd make a good doctor, way you was all over Chief. They make good money. Hey, be a women's doc. Have fun and get rich."

"Oh, no. Tell the truth, Arlen, every minute of that with Chief, it was all I could do not to throw up. Don't want to ever see more blood. Blood makes me feel seasick. I think maybe some kind of engineering. That's something you can get your hands on."

"Yeah." Washington grinned. "That's me. Something I can get my hands on."

⚬

Some fifteen kilometers to their south, there was a bridge, about eighty feet long, where highway QL-99, the road to Chu Song, crossed the An Cao river where it meandered out of the valley.

The bridge was well guarded by a reinforced platoon of South Vietnamese provincial forces and a small flock of geese. The geese virtually guaranteed that a surprise attack was impossible. The provincial forces were well armed and defending from stout bunkers. Moreover, they could be reinforced relatively quickly by other provincial or American forces. The nearest Americans were at Fire Base Chrome, currently home to the heavy artillery battery that had supported the rescue mission and the bulk of Charlie Company, the parent unit of Sergeants Carter and Warren, who were providing Randy Hanley's infantry support. In addition to the two rifle squads detached to support Randy, Charlie Company had a platoon on the south side of the An Cao river supporting the security of the bridge.

It had been assumed that if the enemy should attack the bridge from the north side of the river, infantry from Charlie Company at Fire Base Chrome could provide support if needed. The platoon from Charlie Company on the south side of the river was there to reinforce, if needed, in case the enemy attacked the bridge from the south side. In any event, the enemy attacked the bridge neither from the north or the south, but from the river itself.

A short distance up the river, out of sight of the bridge, the enemy sapper team that had attacked at the crash site were now carrying out their main mission, supported by a half dozen local Vietcong. A coffin-like box packed with hundreds of pounds of explosives was eased into the river, where it sank. The box also contained a bladder. Using a bicycle tire pump, an enemy soldier inflated the bladder until the box gained enough buoyancy to float just below the surface. With the aid of other soldiers, the box was pushed into the middle of the river channel, where a small sampan was anchored. They attached a line to the box and soldiers in the sampan slowly fed the line out, letting the box drift downstream just below the surface. When the soldier feeding the line out felt a knot slip past his fingers, he stopped. With a sharp jerk on the line, the bladder was punctured, air rushed out in a froth of bubbles and the box sank to the bottom directly under the bridge. The soldier in the sampan pulled up the anchor, paddled to shore, and joined his comrades, and they disappeared into the night.

Twenty minutes after the box had come to rest on the river bottom directly under the bridge, a timer in the box ended its countdown. Tons of river water were thrown violently upward, smashing into the bottom of the bridge like a giant sledgehammer. The entire bridge span was ripped from its abutments and lifted several meters. Then, buckled and twisted, it fell into the river, leaving an almost ninety-foot gap in highway QL-99.

CHAPTER 15

LONELY NIGHT

Captain Christopher Cornwell, commander of A Battery, First Battalion, 115th Field Artillery, and custodian of the two eight-inch howitzers and two 175-millimeter long-range cannons at Fire Base Chrome, sat up on his air mattress. He had heard something that awakened him, and as if recalling a fading dream, it seemed he'd heard an explosion—not the sharp hammer blow on the ear drums of one of his guns, or the almost as sharp crack of an exploding shell, but something more like a bolt of thunder. One of the last things he wanted was more rain, especially in the form of a sudden thunderstorm with thunder and lightning. He slipped on his boots, leaving them unlaced, and stepped out of his tent. All was very dark and quiet. His watch told him it was shortly after one in the morning. "That you, Captain?" a voice asked.

"What're you up to, Johnson?" It was quite dark, but Captain Cornwell recognized Johnson's Louisiana bayou drawl.

"My shift on watch, sir." Johnson reminded Chris Cornwell of Paul Bunyan—big, tall, broad-shouldered, and slim-hipped.

"You heard that?"

"Sounded like an explosion, sir. Off thataway. Pretty far, so maybe a big one—yes sir, big."

"Not thunder?"

"No sir." Johnson paused a moment and added, "I could feel it in the ground."

"Huh. And just one? Not like a bombing."

"Yes sir."

"Shit." Just then both men saw a wavering red light on the ground approaching.

"Who goes?" Johnson called out, gripping his rifle.

"The Grinch."

"Captain?" Johnson asked.

"Ev?" Chris Cornwell asked.

"Yeah. Just got a call from Third Platoon, south of the river. They're reporting a big ass explosion." Ev was Everett Rosen, commander of Charlie Company, Second Battalion, Twenty-Second Cavalry, whose company had been detailed to provide security for Fire Base Chrome— an assignment that had not made him happy. To Everett, sitting on his butt providing static security was not what cavalry, especially air cavalry, was for.

"Know what it was?"

"Nope. George said it felt like an Arc Light, except only one bomb."

"One bomb? Who drops one bomb?"

"He said it was in the direction of the bridge. Anyway, they're checking it out."

"Crap." To Chris Cornwell, the bridge had seemed very well secured, looking as bunkered as Fort Knox when he crossed it. "If it's the bridge ..." Chris began.

"We're likely in deep doo-doo. And it's likely part of something bigger." They immediately agreed it was time to go on 100 percent alert.

Both officers returned to their tents, which were also their command posts. Captain Rosen picked up a radio set to his company frequency and sent out his alert. He then grabbed a second radio and reported the skimpy facts to his battalion headquarters. Captain Cornwell did much the same, except he went to the battery fire control center to issue his alert. Suddenly the little fire base was filled with soft, furtive sounds as men not on watch were awakened and scrambled to their duty positions. The two captains hunkered by their radios, listening for reports from their subordinates and for any intelligence from higher headquarters. They got the reports but no intelligence.

Thirty minutes passed, and nothing happened. Then Rosen's platoon on the south side of the river reported in. The platoon had had an ambush set up only a few hundred meters from the bridge. They had gotten close enough to use a starlight scope, which revealed a missing bridge and numerous figures wandering around on both sides of the gap. Had there been any small-arms fire or geese honking their warning prior to the explosion, the men on the ambush reported, they would have heard it. When Everett passed this on to Chris, he growled, "How the hell can you blow up a bridge without taking it first?"

"They have a secret air force?"

After a moment, Chris said, "We're cut off from the rear. And you from your platoon. And we're maybe screwed. Blowing that bridge has to be about something north of it. That's us, The engineers and—"

"My two squads with them."

"Right. And ... and maybe Chu Song."

"Chu Song can look out for itself. I'm going get George back. Somehow. I can't leave him cut off from us and any reinforcement like that. And you're right, Chris; if the shit's gonna hit the fan, it'll hit on our side of the river."

"Tonight, you think?"

"It's after oh-one hundred. Maybe yes, maybe no. Anything from your OPs?"

"Nada." Captain Rosen paused a moment and said, "Shit, he probably knows already, but I'm gonna call Hanley. My two squads with him need to know."

Captain Rosen went to his own command post to call the engineers and to consider the options with his second in command and his first sergeant, the latter being the most experienced soldier in his company, both in combat and otherwise. "The bad guys aren't messing around," he said, "Sneaky, them being able to blow the bridge without attacking or even, apparently, doing anything to alert the bridge defense."

The first sergeant broke the short silence. "However they did it, they could have done it anytime. There's timing to it, like it's a preliminary to something."

"Preparing the battlefield," his executive officer commented, academically but pertinently.

"For somethin' north of the bridge," the first sergeant added.

With two of his rifle squads detached to provide security for the engineers, and one platoon stuck on the south side of the river, Captain Rosen was left with roughly fifty-five men to defend the perimeter. Subtracting his radio operator, first sergeant, a mortar squad, and two four-man outposts, that left roughly twenty-four yards per man on the perimeter. He did have seven machine guns, which included four machine guns loaned by the artillery gun crews, as they would be much more effective on the perimeter than on vehicles.

If their fire base was the target, the enemy clearly was not pussy-footing around. He decided he had to get Third Platoon back—not just for their sake but also for the sake of his primary mission to defend the battery. The question was when and how. Helicopters were still out, and Rosen didn't want to ask Battalion's permission. They might hem and haw and have to get permission from someone higher. He thought it better to act and ask forgiveness later than sit on his ass and wait for permission. Besides, the platoon's mission had been to provide an outer security screen for the bridge. The bridge was now gone, so he figured the mission was gone too.

"We can rig a one-rope bridge," the First Sergeant suggested.

"River's couple hundred feet wide," Rosen countered.

"Not everywhere," his executive officer said. He pulled out a photomap and ran his finger along the river downstream from the bridge. "Thought so. Saw it from the air week or so ago coming back from Battalion. See the bend here and the light spot? It's like a little beach. Less than half the width. Max fifty, seventy-five feet."

"Tie a good rock to a hundred feet of commo wire, and a good arm'll get a line across easy. Then pull a climbing rope across," the first sergeant said. "Also need some air mattresses to float gear across."

"Not a problem; we have that," the XO said. "Dark as dark out there, though."

"Man, it's between a rock and a hard place. We need them now, in case we're the real target. But sending even a squad out at night—split our force even more, and maybe just as we're attacked?"

The first sergeant said, "Sergeant Torres would volunteer, and he'd be best man for the job. He's volunteered for two of those long-range recons Brigade sends out. There'll be three, four guys'll volunteer with him."

"Let's call Lieutenant Bromley and get his input."

Everett called the platoon leader and briefed him, switching on the radio's speaker so the XO and first sergeant could also hear. His reply surprised them. "Six, I don't know. I'll have to send out a patrol in the morning to find it."

"You've been patrolling the river, right?"

"Six, affirmative."

The first sergeant mouthed a name—Monet. Everett said, "Check with Five. He may remember. Or your other NCOs. Over." They waited. Bromley's platoon sergeant, Sergeant Monet, came on the radio. "Six, this is Three-Five. Roger on the bend with a beach. Know the spot. Over."

"Can you get there tonight?" There was a long pause. Then Monet got back on the radio. "Three-Six feels it's not, uh, wise. Over."

"Could you lead a patrol to secure that spot yourself?"

"Uh, affirmative. Over."

"Roger, put Three-Six on."

"Uh, Three-Six. over."

Everett ordered Lieutenant Bromley to assemble his platoon and take it to the bend with the beach as soon as possible and arrive within an hour and a half. "Don't worry. No enemy activity in your area. Your Five knows the way. We'll have a team there with a one-rope bridge. Okay? Now get rolling and good luck. Keep us posted."

The first sergeant said, "I'll get Torres, sir," and he left.

The executive officer said, "I'd have been a lot more comfortable if Malcom's platoon had been given that mission."

"I know. Malcom's a natural, and George isn't. Maybe not really cut out for infantry. Maybe he can learn, but everyone's got to take their share of the higher-risk missions, just like everyone's got to take their turn on point."

"I think I ought to go with Sergeant Torres."

"Come on; you—an expert in night patrols?"

"Hell, no. I'm just thinking I'd give Torres some weight with George. As you've counseled him, he doesn't listen too well to subordinates—that kind of mix of pride and insecurity."

PFC Frederick woke Randy. "Radio, sir."

"Battalion?"

"No sir. Ajax Six."

"Six? Carter's CO? What the hell?" He took the handset. After a minute, he gave the handset back to Frederick. "Get Sergeant Jarvis. Have him round up the squad leaders. Oh, and Newsome, and Corporal Belli—he's in the gun truck. Then call Battalion. Tell them the bridge over the An Cao has been blown up. And tell them we got that report from Green Granite and Ajax."

"That the bridge back down the road?"

"Yeah. We're kind of cut off now."

"The supply truck's screwed."

"Yeah." Something suddenly occurred to him. "But hey, look on the bright side; we have ourselves a gun truck."

Sergeant Newsome trotted back from Randy's briefing and banged on the steel sides of the dump truck. "Up and at 'em, guys! Like they say in the navy, general quarters!"

Washington and Otis had fallen asleep curled up under the ponchos they'd been given shortly after Wodzinski had relieved them on guard. He was not at the minigun but was leaning against the truck bed's high front side, cradling the M60 machine gun they had salvaged from the Duster, peering into the night through the gap between the truck's steel sides and the tarp they'd rigged to ward off the rain.

Otis made waking sounds at Newsome's call, but as Washington remained motionless, Wodzinski kicked his foot. "Washington! Wake up, man! General quarters!"

"What the—general what?"

"General quarters!"

"Who the hell's general quarters?"

"Not an officer, Washington! Means we're all on alert!" Newsome replied, climbing into the truck bed. "Get the gun ready!"

A wave of sheer fright took Washington by surprise. He remained motionless, rigid, the whites of his eyes showing all around his dark irises. It took Otis poking him hard to make him move. He pulled his boots on, got into the crude gun mount, and gripped the handles. Beyond the vague shape of the gun and the faint, straight rim of the dump truck's sides, he could make out nothing. Although the sky was a moving mosaic of shades of charcoal painted by an unseen moon struggling to shed light through layers of wandering clouds, the earth seemed to absorb what feeble light reached it, revealing nothing to the nervous eye. Otis prodded him through a checklist, and they spun up the gun for a second to verify it had power.

The dump truck was now a miniature steel fort with four pairs of nervous eyes staring out over the steel walls. Newsome, satisfied that they were as ready as they could be, explained that the bridge had been blown and that that likely meant they could be the target of an attack. "Looks like you two flyboys are stuck on the ground with us a bit longer."

"How long's that going to take to fix?" Otis asked, disappointed and fearful of what might lie ahead the longer they were stuck with the engineers.

Sergeant Newsome had no answer. Days, weeks—he didn't know. Washington muttered a litany of brief curses as if he were reciting a four-letter rosary. He was not cursing the fate of being stuck there, but rather his conflicting feelings: anger at the fact that he wouldn't be able to send Otis on while he bravely remained behind to give fire support to the engineers until he could get the gun evacuated and "lost" at the same time, and fear at what now might happen—that he might not get the gun but die with it.

After what seemed to Otis a long while, he halted his litany and fell silent.

The soft rustling and metallic clinking that had filled the night when he had been booted awake, giving it a kind of substance, faded into silence. It was as if one was in a void, empty except for the self, what the hands touched, and the substance of the void itself, which was a miasma of not exactly fear or trepidation but of doom—a doom as unfathomable as the night. Washington couldn't stand it. He whispered urgently. "Timmy, got the flashlight?"

"Yeah, sure."

"Let's practice. Be ready."

"Okay."

"Alpha."

Otis shone the red filtered flashlight at the gun, found Newsome's aiming bar, and then illuminated the white card labelled "A" until Washington could align on it. Washington whispered, "Wham. Okay, man. Bravo." They swung the gun from one letter to the next until they got tired of it and it no longer distracted from the vague sense of doom.

When a minute or more had passed and Washington had not called another target letter, Otis whispered, "Guess we're good to go."

Washington grunted. "You know, I don't see how anyone can do anything in the dark. I mean dark like this."

Sergeant Newsome heard him and said, "Get your eyes off the flashlight. Even with the red filter, it robs some night vision. There's some light out there. Wait. Let it reach you." Otis turned his flashlight off, and gradually the blackness began to yield a few secrets and they could make out hints of a world in the void. First they saw the patterning of the clouds, then the vague line between earth and sky, and then even hints of pattern in the earth, the roadway, paddy dykes, jungle edges. Yet the very sense of features dimly perceived only emphasized the sense of foreboding, for the shapes they could discern mocked them with a thousand shadows hiding what they couldn't see.

After a long silence, Washington muttered, "Man, fuck this shit." For an instant, it made him feel better, but an instant later, he felt worse with the awareness that there was absolutely nothing he could do. Anywhere else, the comment would be a prelude to turning around and walking away. There was no walking here—nowhere to go and no way to get there.

Otis, close by, heard Washington's muttering. When nothing followed it for a minute or two, anxious to get his imagination free from the darkness, he asked, "Arlen, what'd you join up for?"

Arlen took his time replying, sorting through a blizzard of possible answers. Somehow honesty won out. "So's I wouldn't get drafted and end up in a shithole like this."

After a moment, Otis laughed. "No kidding. We both joined up for the same reason!"

Arlen couldn't help but laugh too. "Lotta fuckin' good it did us."

"Well, we get through this, we're back in clean sheets."

"Yeah. *If.*"

The forbidding gloom of night and the sense of isolation it brought, amplified by the knowledge that they really were cut off, made conversation too difficult to maintain. Occasionally Newsome and Wodzinski whispered together, but they, too, soon fell silent.

When conversation no longer distracts and daydreams wear thin, the last defense is to become like a dog in the night: eyes open, ears alert, but the mind blank, the switches to the powers of thought and imagination turned off, awaiting some signal. Soon the four men in Fort Dump Truck, like most of the unseen engineers and infantrymen around them, had become just watchdogs in the night. And so they remained until the first hints of dawn turned the mental switches on again.

✀

Earlier that evening, Major James Graham had been awakened by a knock on his bunker entry. The young Vietnamese soldier who had knocked simply said, "Thieu Ta, Dai Uy," which translated to "Major, the captain."

Major Graham replied, "Cam on ban," meaning, he hoped, "Thank you." Vietnamese was a tonal language, and the same syllable could have different meanings depending on the inflection, and he had frequently made his counterparts laugh at his efforts, which were still very clumsy in spite of six weeks of language school. The soldier slipped away in the dark as Jim slipped on his boots while listening for sounds of war but hearing only the whispers of a tropical night.

Dai Uy was Captain Thieu Van Chien, commander of First Battalion, Fifty-Fifth Regiment, Thirty-Fifth Infantry Division, Army of the Republic of Vietnam. Two months earlier, when Major Graham had arrived in Vietnam and been given his assignment, he had been told, "Congratulations, you've just been assigned to the worst battalion in the worst regiment of the worst division in the Vietnamese Army." He was on his second tour in Vietnam, had commanded an infantry company on his first tour, and had made early promotion to major. He was sort of a golden boy. He assumed his unfortunate assignment was because of really bad luck or because he'd pissed someone off. He had no doubt in his mind that he'd pissed people off now and then.

When he arrived at Chu Song, where the battalion was stationed, he discovered that the battalion had just been placed under the command of a young captain and not a lieutenant colonel, as the position called for. Captain Thieu had been in command only three weeks, but Major Graham quickly sensed he was both a leader and a fighter. He also sensed a wariness in the captain about his American advisor, so he had made a point of learning from the captain, not trying to teach or impress until he could overcome that wariness.

Captain Thieu spoke English pretty well. He also did not have the patience to help Americans make it in his language. When Major Graham knocked, he said, "Ah, Major, come in, please. I have been given a mission, and it may be difficult." Graham was very lean, with pale gray eyes, sandy hair, and a narrow, handsome face. At six-two, he had to fold himself carefully to enter Captain Thieu's command post.

The battalion's mission had originated in Second Corps Headquarters but had been triggered by the 134th Engineer Battalion's report that an expedited opening of the road to Chu Song would require a strong infantry force to clear and secure the forested section of the road. Having concluded the enemy was maneuvering for an offensive in the heavily populated areas and that the strategy would be defensive in hopes of destroying the enemy when they attacked and exposed themselves, Second Corps did not want to divert forces securing the populated areas to clear the road. That meant giving the mission to forces near Chu Song—the Vietnamese battalion, "the worst of the worst of the worst," or the small American task force securing the airfield at Chu Song. The airstrip was vital, and the American force small. That left the "worst of the worst of the worst." If there were no enemy in the woods, fine. If there were some, it still might work. If there were more, well, they'd find out and then decide what to do about it. So the mission had been passed to the Thirty-Fifth Division and passed on down to Captain Thieu.

"Tieu Ta." Captain Thieu pointed to a spot on his photomap. "It is two kilometers from here to the start point. Nine kilometers from here to where the forest ends. My heavy mortars only reach seven kilometers."

Major Graham looked at the map and the locations Captain Tieu had marked on it. They discussed the artillery support available. The problem was that if fighting broke out in the forest, it would be at pretty close quarters and the artillery available would be close to their maximum range and too inaccurate for effective close support. Graham suggested he have his companies take their light mortars with them. "In my experience when I was here before, it was surprisingly easy to find enough of an opening in the trees for a mortar to fire close support. We found one only needed a small hole in the trees."

Captain Thieu, doubtful about the using mortars in thick jungle, didn't comment. His eyes flicked alternately from the map to Graham's shoulder as he thought. Finally he asked, "Can you explain to my commanders using the mortar in the forest?"

Graham nodded. "My deputy, Lieutenant Klegg, knows mortars very well and speaks better Vietnamese."

"Good. We take tomorrow to prepare. I make a start line here." He pointed on the map. "We cross at maybe ten hundred the following morning."

It seemed like an overly long time to Major Graham, but he didn't question it, assuming Captain Thieu must have a good reason. He was, after all, trying to both lead and reform "the worst of the worst of the worst." They discussed the mission in general. Chu Song had been isolated for a decade. Both the Vietnamese and American forces in

Chu Song had been airlifted in. The road hadn't been used, at least for military or commercial purposes, since the French had left; as Captain Tieu put it, "The last Anglo to use this road was French."

Major Graham had chuckled and corrected, "'Anglo' refers to English. We Americans call the French Frogs."

"Frogs?"

"They eat frog legs, which to Americans was very strange."

"Ah. Anglo more polite. Did not French conquer Anglos of England in 1066?"

"Touché." Major Graham's confidence in his counterpart grew. They turned back to the maps. In the morning, Graham would brief his advisory team and they would take off to coordinate what support they could, gather intelligence, and monitor Captain Thieu's preparations. With that, he went back to bed thanking God that the "worst of the worst of the worst" did not include Captain Thieu.

Washington and Otis slowly came out of their watchdog coma. Above them, the gray morning was a mix of gray sky and darker clouds. Otis hoped they might send a helicopter now. Washington grimaced and sidestepped the issue. "Hey, Sarge, any breakfast?"

"Sure 'nuff! Army's best C-rations. Here!" Sergeant Newsome reached in a box and tossed Washington a small cardboard box. There were two cans and a couple of paper packets inside.

"What's this shit?"

"Read the label, man." The labels told him he had a can of peaches, a can of ham and eggs, a packet of cocoa, and a packet of instant coffee and plastic dinnerware. What it didn't contain was a cup for the coffee or cocoa or a plate for the food. Newsome instructed them on the skills of the grunt: how to use the tiny P-38 can opener provided, and how to roll up a small ball of C-4 plastic explosive, set it alight with a match, and heat the rations or water with it.

"Ham and eggs?" Washington snorted when he had opened the can. "Looks like an old turd."

"Tastes like it too," Wodzinski said. "But if you don't want it, I'll take it off you." But Washington was too hungry. He washed out the can and used it as a cup to heat water and make a mix of cocoa and coffee, which, he was assured, made the coffee bearable.

If breakfast was bad for Otis and Washington, the morning was worse. They were detailed to dig new latrines for the platoon, much to the amusement of the infantrymen and engineers. The afternoon was not much better. Among the supplies the gun truck had brought were hundreds of empty sandbags to help strengthen the defenses. The infantry squad leaders, trained in air mobility, did not much believe in sandbags. To them sandbags required lots of time and sweat for little benefit, since they tended to move daily.and their tactics dictated foxholes and camouflage. To them, sandbags were just signs advertising "Here I am; shoot me." Sandbags were worth the effort for units that stayed in place for longer periods or had equipment to protect. The dump truck fell into that category, and Otis, Washington, and Wodzinski spent the afternoon filling sandbags to line the steel walls of Fort Dump Truck.

No helicopters came. Far to the rear, at least in the army chain, the two airmen were forgotten in the consternation of the loss of the bridge and new intelligence flowing in, and unaware of developments in the army's sphere, the air force chain assumed Otis and Washington were being efficiently transported out of harm's way by the army. A day of broken cloud cover and relatively easy flying passed, and the sun again set behind the hills. No helicopters came; nor did any word about when the road might be open again. What did come was an unhelpful warning that intelligence indicated enemy movement possibly aimed at the road, the engineers, or the artillery unit.

Randy stared at his NCOs. "Men, I guess fifty percent alert for everyone again. The intel doesn't tell us squat. Enemy movement. Strength, purpose? Unknown."

"Sir, if there was bad shit out there, they could have brought reinforcements anytime today," Sergeant Jarvis said sharply, jerking his shoulders in irritation.

"Coulda, woulda, shouda," Sergeant Carter said. "Maybe HQ knows what's going on; maybe they're as clueless as we are. They're there, sir; we're here."

"So make the best of it. Right. Any suggestions?"

"No sir," Sergeant Carter replied. "We're about as ready as we can be. I'm putting my man with the starlight scope in the dump truck with the minigun. Gives him a radio and a three-sixty field of view. With the two M60s from the gun truck, we've got nearly three-sixty coverage with machine guns all crisscrossing and nearly all grazing fire. The minigun truck is covering the critical sector. The fifty cals on the gun truck and the two other dump trucks cover the rest of the perimeter."

After Sergeant Newsome briefed Wodzinski, Otis, Washington, and PCF Rick O'Day, the sharpshooter with the starlight scope, on how they would work together if shooting started and divided up their shifts, Otis muttered to Washington, "You know, we should have kept the radio."

"What radio?"

"The prick-ninety, the survival radio the captain used to call for help."

"We gonna call for help here?"

"It talks to our guys, not army. I was thinking if we could have called them, they could have got an air rescue team in here today, no sweat."

Washington did not know what to think about that. While another day and night in the boonies was the last thing he wanted, rescue from the air force was not what he wanted either. He shrugged. "Maybe, maybe not. Anyways, we ain't got it."

"Like I said. Should have kept it. But we didn't."

Darkness closed in, and Washington tried to settle in for a repeat of the previous night while feeling grungier, more tired, and sorer than before. Vasquez's bandaging of his toe had helped in curbing the pain, as had the pain pills, but it now throbbed from the stresses of the day's work, and he couldn't get to sleep when his turn came.

CHAPTER 16

OPENING BELL

PCF Jude Jefferson and his usual buddy, PFC Rick O'Day—or, as Jude and most others called him, Ricochet—had started to dig the new foxhole they would share. But about halfway through the effort, Sergeant Carter came by and told O'Day he would be posted in the dump truck with the minigun that night to have a better view of things from its height, and Jude's buddy for the night would be PFC Bert McAllister from one of the engineer squads.

Although this was not the first time they'd been separated, it did not make Jude very happy. This separation happened from time to time because Rick O'Day was a crack shot and, consequently, the custodian of the squad's starlight scope.

Jude had seen McAllister off and on while his squad had been attached to the engineers, but McAllister was still an unknown quantity, whereas O'Day was not. He and Ricochet had each other's measure and confidence. Wisely, Sergeant Carter had made his decision early enough in the day for McAllister and Jefferson to get somewhat acquainted, and wisely, both knew they had better make the best of the time.

The foxhole was finished and camouflaged. Supper was also finished, and the last of daylight was fading. In Fort Dump Truck, PFC O'Day used the waning twilight to recognize the lettered targets in his starlight scope and to use them in his regular sweeps of the surroundings and to show Wodzinski how to use the scope so he could relieve him on watch. In the foxhole, Jude was educating Bert.

"Man, you as pale as Ricochet. Face like a streetlight. Just draw the enemy fire right on us."

Bert considered this. "Well, hell, man, it just means they'll be shooting at me, not you."

"Yeah, but they'll be shooting this way, not some other way. Shoot out there all they want. Shoot this way, man, they just might accidentally hit me."

"You got a point. I'll just curl up in my poncho; you take the night watch, and I'll do the day." Bert began to do just that.

"Hey, I'm just shitting you, man."

"I know." Bert grinned. "But you do have a good point." He didn't move to get back up.

"Come on, man. Besides, you got to know our SOPs."

"SOPs?"

"Don't know what a fuckin' SOP is?"

"Course I know. Standard operating procedure. Like vehicle checklists and stuff. Didn't know grunts had any."

"We do. And tonight, you're a grunt."

Bert got up. "Hey, I've done grunt duty before, man. Okay. So?"

Jude lectured about who was on their right and who on their left, what weapons they had, what their sectors of fire were and where they overlapped their own assigned sector, and where the machine guns in their sector were and what they covered. "Specialist Hicks, he's got the M60 on our right. Next foxhole past Marty and Joe. He'll lay down enfilade fire right down that dyke what runs at an angle in front of us. See that?"

"Yeah, I see the dyke. What's enfilade?"

"Enfilade. It's like flanking fire. Means Hicks don't shoot straight at the enemy like you would with your M16. He lays down, like, a wall of bullets right across our front." Jude used his arm to indicate bullets flying across their front. "That way the enemy's got to walk through that wall of bullets to get at us. Got it?" Bert nodded and repeated back the names of the soldiers in the neighboring foxholes, their weapons, and their assigned sectors. "So, see, Hicks's M60 is the primary defense in front of us."

"What about the gun trucks?"

"We got the dump truck behind us with that minigun. They're all set up to shoot where the action is. Jarvis and the LT take care of that shit. It's behind us 'cause this way's the best direction for an enemy to attack from. Sergeant Carter says one of our jobs is to protect the dump truck. Don't want some asshole getting close enough to use hand grenades or satchel charges on it; get it?"

"Okay, right. They could use an RPG."

"Yo. Just better hope we see the man with the rocket before he gets a shot off. Now our shit. Me, I have an M79. You know what it does?"

"Sure. It shoots grenades. Us engineers *do* get infantry training, you know."

"Yeah, okay. Not puttin' you down, man. Just to say I'm pretty damn good with it. Like having a really good arm for throwing a baseball from outfield to first base. I can drop 'em in a ditch on the other side of dykes there, or across the road that way. That's my job. Cover the ditches and the dykes in our sector. So the M60s cut 'em up when they move; grenadiers like me blow 'em up when they hide."

"Okay. So what's my M16's job?"

"Keep my ass alive."

"Okay. I'll just cover up and lie down here so my pale face don't give you away."

"Bullshit. Now, how many grenades you got?"

"Four. Basic load."

"Me too. We take 'em off our belts, lay them out between us on this ledge—what we cut out for our elbows when we shoot." When they'd laid out the grenades, Jude continued. "Now the phone. Right behind you. Links the whole perimeter and the CP. Used one before?" Bert knew about the phone communications but had never used one. After demonstrating its use, Jude concluded, "Oh, one last thing, McAllister. You see or hear movement, or think some one's shooting at you, don't shoot."

"Why the hell not?"

"Your muzzle flash gives you away. If it's close enough, we throw a grenade. Farther out, I'll take 'em out. M79's got almost no muzzle flash, and the sound is hard to pinpoint."

"Shit, man. What if I can see 'em—like, there's one shooting at me and I can see him?"

"Then shoot. We just don't want guys wasting ammo and giving themselves away shooting at shit they can't see."

"You're the boss."

"Good. How long you been in country?"

"Two months. You?"

"Eight." Their voices dropped, and they settled into whispered exchanges about themselves. As complete darkness fell, the whispers died out, and around the perimeter, men began to fall asleep or again become watchdogs in the night.

PFC Wodzinski responded to PFC O'Day's gentle kick. "Midnight already?"

"Half past, Stevie."

"Uh." A few minutes later, he was up, boots laced, eyes rubbed clear of sleep. "Anything?"

"Nope. Dead quiet except for the bugs and bats."

"Shit, it's almost cold."

"Uh huh. Where's your rifle?"

"What for?"

"Hey, man, wake up. I don't want to lie down without my hand on one."

"Oh, yeah, Ricochet, sure. Sorry." Wodzinski handed his M16 to O'Day, took O'Day's and sighted through the starlight scope. "Cool. You really can see in the dark with this."

"Let's take a look all the way round. Then I'll catch some z's."

Wodzinski rested the rifle on the edge of the truck side and began to softly call out each feature that marked a scanning sector as he swept the rifle in a slow arc, interrupted by slow up-and-down movements to scan farther out and closer in. "Hey, why they call you Ricochet?"

"I'm the best shot in the company, man; why else?"

Wodzinski chuckled. "Thought 'ricochet' meant you missed. But it does go with the name too. How they know you're the best shot?"

O'Day laughed. "I told 'em. They said I was full of shit. We had a contest. I won."

Suddenly the night was torn apart by a painful crack and blinding flash followed instantly by what sounded to the imagination like large buzzing insects zipping past and hammers pounding on the walls of Fort Dump Truck. "Shit!" both cried. They heard similar words coming from beyond the truck but no cries of pain or calls for a medic. They stared all around into a darkness made deeper by the flash, numbed and uncertain.

Thirty seconds later, as the others in the truck were stumbling to their feet and O'Day and Wodzinski were foolishly staring inward toward the source of the sound and flash, there came a second, more blinding, flash, and crack. Wodzinski felt something hit his arm, but it didn't hurt. Someone in the perimeter screamed "Incoming!" and from inside the truck bed, they heard Sergeant Newsome cry out, "Mortar! Get your asses down!"

Wodzinski and O'Day dropped, but O'Day grabbed the rifle with the starlight scope and shouted to the others, "If a ground attack's comin' it'll be comin' soon! Gotta see!" He activated the scope, put it to his eye and peered over the side of the truck, looking for signs of movement. Freed of the rifle, Wodzinski rubbed his hands together as if he were chilled and felt wetness. He traced the wetness up his sleeve to a tear and discovered he'd been wounded.

"Hey Sarge, I been hit!"

"Bad?"

"Don't know!" he paused. "Guess not. Don't hurt. Bleeding, though." Newsome shouted for Otis and Washington to man the gun and then was beside Wodzinski.

Otis pushed Washington. "Arlen; get up! We've got to get the gun going."

"Nothing to shoot at! I can't shoot down a mortar!"

"You hear Ricochet? Ground attack might be coming!"

"He's got that scope, and he ain't seen anything yet!"

Every thirty seconds—the time it took the enemy mortar crew to adjust aim on the mortar and drop another round into the tube—another shell exploded. The adjustments between rounds were made to create a grid of impacts intended to cover the engineers' position.

Somewhere in those long seconds, the mind begins to hope the last was the last, and then the flickering hope is blasted away again. But once men sensed it, the regular intervals were also a blessing, for they could safely raise their heads and look around, and then duck back down before the next round hit.

In Fort Dump Truck, Ricochet used the intervals to scan with the starlight scope. In the foxhole, Jude and Bert took turns peering over the berm for signs of enemy movement. After an explosion, one would pop up and survey the night for a count of ten and then duck down again. Bert usually forgot his count, being so intent on what his eyes might pick up, but Jude would count for him and then jerk his sleeve. "Down, man!" The silence between mortar shell explosions was broken by a burst of automatic rifle fire off to their left. Bert jerked his head up to peer over the berm. Jude said, "Fucking engineer."

"Could be enemy!" Kneeling, Bert's long frame still left him head and shoulders above the berm of their foxhole.

Jude was sitting, knees tight against his chest, rifle between his knees, head bent. "That's an M16. Don't hear any AKs. Some dumb fuck is shooting at the dark, no one shooting at him."

"I don't see anything."

"Get your head down," Jude hissed.

Bert sat back on his heels, still peering over the berm. "One of your guys?"

"We know better." Jude's head jerked to stare in Bert's direction.

"Maybe. But you grunts come and go. I've seen grunts pop off at shadows."

"Not us, man! Not us." Jude poked Bert's thigh with his elbow.

Another shell exploded, and Bert ducked as low as he could. It was Jude's turn to keep an eye out for enemy.

Now Jude had lost count, and he started over when the next mortar shell landed, catching him by surprise. He swore, decided he wasn't dead, and then froze, for this explosion was followed by a second, softer one that lofted a fireball into the night, bathing the land around him in a bloody light. After a stunned few seconds, he pulled his eyes away from it and by its light saw two figures slipping across the road to his right, headed toward his sector. They vanished into the ditch on the near side. Jude aimed his grenade launcher at the point where they had disappeared and fired. The grenade exploded against the edge of the roadbed. He reloaded, adjusted aim, and fired a second grenade; then he grabbed the phone to report what he'd seen and done.

As Jude was reporting, he heard Ricochet scream, "Jesus! The supply truck blew up! Oh, shit, they, they … God! No chance! Oh, God, no chance! Oh, man!"

Sergeant Newsome had just bandaged Wodzinski's arm. He jumped up and looked. The gun truck was engulfed in flames. He saw Sergeant Jarvis and Vasquez running toward the burning truck. The truck had been nearly blown in two, and only the driveshaft connected the front and rear halves. Pieces of armor plate, two bodies, and a .50-caliber machine gun lay next to the truck, just outside the circle of flames. Even to Newsome, it was clear they were dead.

Vasquez, seeing them, began to sprint ahead of Jarvis. But Jarvis had a sudden premonition and flung Vasquez to the ground, landing on top of him an instant before the next mortar shell exploded some twenty yards away. Jarvis felt a fragment hit his helmet as if it were a hammer. The shock numbed him to another piece of shrapnel that struck his thigh. The rest of the shrapnel whined harmlessly over their bodies, some bits pinging the sides of Fort Dump Truck.

Vasquez writhed to get free of Jarvis, who held him tight. "They're dead. They're gone. You can't help."

"You don't know! You don't know that!" he cried, trying to wriggle free.

"I know dead when I see it! Back to our hole. Now! Others will be needing you, Enrique. Let's go! Now!" He dragged Vasquez up and jerked him around toward the command bunker. Vasquez gave up, and they ran back. Then Jarvis felt the pain in his thigh.

The first mortar shell had landed only a few yards from where Randy had dug in his little command post, and the blast had shredded the tent that made his roof and almost knocked him insensible. The second explosion, fortunately twenty yards farther away from him, brought him out of his confusion. He grabbed his radio and immediately called Green Granite to report the attack and ask whether he was under attack also. Green Granite wasn't and was ready to support.

As a matter of course, Randy had preplanned artillery concentrations around his position and defined points for illumination flares. He asked Green Granite to have a gun ready to fire illumination over his position and reported the barrage to his battalion headquarters. Then he put the phone connecting his perimeter defenses to his ear, hearing just nervous communications checks and sergeants telling soldiers to shut up unless they had something to report. He felt helpless, thinking he should be doing more but not knowing what. He put the phone down to find his rifle and extra magazines, fearing he might need them, and missed Jude's report.

When the gun truck exploded, he didn't see it but heard the shouts of those who did. He crawled out of his shallow hole and stood up, almost mesmerized by the flames. He saw Sergeant Jarvis and Vasquez run toward it, saw Jarvis tackle Vasquez just before the next explosion, and then saw both return. Foolishly, he kept standing amid the slow barrage. Pulling his eyes away from the burning truck, he turned full circle, trying to see who was hurt or not, learning nothing and somehow not being hit by shrapnel. Only when it occurred to him that he had left his rifle behind did he get back in his dugout. He then had the presence of mind to get on the phone for an update.

"Jarvis."

"Any hope, Sarge?"

"No sir. Killed instantly."

"Any others?"

"Not yet. Jefferson in Carter's squad reported movement, fired at it. No results, no report of incoming fire."

"Okay. Clark? Warrant?"

The reply, if any, was cut off by the next explosion. Randy put the phone down. There was nothing he could do that hadn't already been done. The ball was still in the enemy's court, and that made the waiting between explosions all but unbearable.

It was again Jude's turn to take a look, and he saw a figure come up out of the ditch where he had fired his grenades and run toward him—not directly but more toward the dump truck. "Ricochet! Get your M16 up here!"

"I'm Bert, man!" Bert appeared beside him.

"See there! See the fucker? Shoot him!"

"You said don't shoot!"

"Fuck what I said! Shoot him!" Just in case Bert remained too stupid to react, Jude pulled out his .45-caliber pistol.

Bert aimed, but in the faint and wavering light from the burning supply truck, he could not get the rifle's sights aligned on the dark figure a hundred yards away. He aimed ahead and began firing as fast as he could, thinking, *A wall of bullets.*

Almost at the same time, Ricochet, on the dump truck, caught sight of the figure in his starlight scope and also began firing. The figure stumbled and fell.

In the foxhole, Bert cried out, "I killed him! Oh, man! Oh, God!" He began to hyperventilate. Jude grabbed him in a bear hug, squeezing hard.

"Okay, man, okay. Hold your breath. Hold it!" Bert gulped air, clamped his mouth shut, and, after a moment, burped loudly.

A few seconds after the next mortar shell explosion, there came another explosion when the bulldozer, parked almost in the center of the perimeter, exploded in flames. But someone on the perimeter had seen something and cried out, "RPG! Incoming RPG!" M16s in that sector opened fire more or less in the direction of the flash of the RPG launch.

Ricochet, guided by the direction the warning cry had come from, caught the RPG team in his starlight scope and also began shooting, calling for Washington at the same time. "Get the fucking gun going! We got targets!"

"Nobody seen shit, man!"

"I've seen 'em asshole! What you think I'm shooting at?"

Otis pushed Washington toward the gun mount. "Arlen! This is it! Go, go!"

Washington clambered into the crib-like mount. "Power?"

"Ready!"

"Feed?"

"Good to go."

"All right, all right! Shit!" Another mortar shell explosion caused him to duck and bang his head painfully on the crib.

Otis called, "Where's the target?"

O'Day wasn't sure. He couldn't remember exactly what predefined target letter was closest. "Fire just over the burning dozer and sweep left!"

"Got that, Arlen?"

"I hit my head. Shit!"

"Arlen! Get up, for God's sake!"

Washington stood again, grabbed the handles of the gun, and swung it where Otis directed. Then he fired a sweeping two-second burst, unleashing a hundred rounds.

Under the hail of blindly aimed M16 fire from the nearest foxholes and the more accurate fire from O'Day's M16, the RPG team withdrew, and in doing so, they ran into the brief storm of Washington's bullets. O'Day saw them go down and shouted, "They're down, man! They're down!" After a moment, he added, "Could be you got 'em, Arlen. Saw a lot of tracers. God, I hate RPGs."

"We done? It's over?" Washington asked breathlessly, half smiling, pleased that he'd hosed the enemy.

"Not likely," Sergeant Newsome said. "Get your asses down. O'Day, keep your big eye out."

For a moment, the night was quiet, and then another mortar round exploded, but this one was almost a hundred yards away.

When Sergeant Jarvis had himself and Vasquez back in their hole, he confessed to his wound, which was fortunately a gash and not a penetrating wound. While Vasquez dressed it, Sergeant Jarvis called Lieutenant Hanley. "LT! We need illumination! Sure as hell there could be a ground attack coming, and we've had movement and some ground fire!"

The thought of a ground attack should have frightened Randy, but he felt more relief than anything. There was something to do, action to take, and he called in the request to Green Granite.

After the gun truck was destroyed, Sergeant Carter ran to each foxhole in his section of the perimeter and then to the dump truck, giving the same message. He'd gotten a picture in his mind, based on his assessment of the terrain and the reports of enemy from Jude, Ricochet, and others, as well as the absence of reports from other sectors. "Listen up, guys," he said to the dump truck crew, but mainly to Newsome. "Movement we've seen means a ground attack. Most likely gonna hit this sector. May hit others too, but I'm betting the main one's here. Usually two waves: first tries to make a breach; second comes in to exploit the breach then overrun if they can. We're not a big outfit, but them making a ground attack means likely a hundred or more."

"Hundred?" Washington cried, or at least tried to; it came out as a squeak.

"So keep your fuckin' eyes open! Be ready! If they're comin', it won't be long! Ricochet! I want you scanning three-sixty; got it?" Ricochet nodded. Washington made a whining sound. Another mortar shell exploded outside the perimeter behind them. Carter disappeared to run to the next position before the next shell hit.

Before Newsome could say anything directive or even reassuring, the first wave surged forward, but not in a charge. Across their front, small teams of enemy soldiers ran forward a few yards then threw themselves down while other teams fired to give them cover; then they fired while others dashed forward. The black night began to shatter like glass with the cracks of passing bullets, the twinkling lights of muzzle flashes, and the streaks of tracers soon followed by the flashes and cracks of exploding M79 grenades. The enemy's method of attack was slower than an all-out charge but kept the air filled with bullets seemingly as thick as a hailstorm, and for the men in Fort Dump Truck, it even sounded like hail.

But the first wave was not surging toward the blasted, decimated defense they hoped for. The enemy's calculations for aiming their mortar had not been quite correct, and as a result, many of the mortar rounds had exploded outside the perimeter, and most of those that had landed within the perimeter hit toward the far side from where the enemy was now attacking.

Ricochet was not the first to sense the attack but was the first to see the scale of it. "Enemy attack! Alpha and Bravo! They're coming! Washington! Get the gun going! Alpha! Alpha first!"

Washington didn't move. Newsome and Otis both shouted at him. Washington remained hunkered in the timber crib that was his weapon mount. He could hear the bullets. They were all around, as if he'd kicked a hornet's nest, with the sounds of firing and the cracks as they passed overhead, as well as the louder, hammer-like sounds as some struck the truck. He didn't feel fear—at least not the paralyzing sort he'd felt the night before. It was just that for Arlen, the world just needed to go away for a while. He closed his eyes and put his hands over his ears. But then someone grabbed his wrist and jerked his hand away from his ear, and Otis's voice shouted into it. "Arlen! For God's sake! Get up! They're coming! You got to shoot!" Arlen didn't move. "Shoot, God damn you! Or get yourself killed and all of us!"

That stirred him. Timmy hardly ever swore. He jerked his hand free, reached for the gun handles, and pulled himself up. Now he could see the blinking lights of the muzzle flashes, the streaks of tracers arcing across his view, and, here and there, flashes from grenade explosions. Just then, the first illumination round burst overhead.

He had seen it before. But from a thousand feet, they were just little black ants scurrying about, nonhuman, unreal. This was very different; these were not little ants but larger, human-shaped ninja-like shadows, not remote but near and nearer. He screamed something at Otis. The barrels began to spin. He ignored the aiming bar and the letters taped to the truck's sides. He could see well enough. He saw Otis was standing close beside him and staring with him at the enemy. "Get your head down, Otis! Ammo!"

"Got it!" he cried, but he didn't duck.

Ricochet again shouted, "Alpha!" Washington looked that way, swung the gun toward Alpha, and pressed the trigger.

A lance of neon fire severed the night with a roar like an enraged beast, sweeping through a wide arc. The ground the gun was pointed at was a hundred or more yards out. The gun swept across the arc and then back again; a total of no more than four seconds passed before Washington let up on the triggers. Four seconds, and two to three bullets swept through every yard of that arc that encompassed some thirty Vietcong. Ten were hit, four dying immediately and six falling with wounds of varying severity.

Ten casualties in a few seconds was not enough to stop the Vietcong push. But as with the enemy assault against Queen of Hearts, the shock of the unexpected weapon was enough to make it falter. A few still strove to move forward while some began to crawl backward, but many simply hugged the ground, uncertain what to do.

When the minigun opened up, Ricochet, Wodzinski, and Newsome also stopped firing, shocked into silence by the machine that had suddenly become a fire-breathing dragon. All around them, the sounds of small-arms fire diminished as defenders saw less to shoot at and attackers hugged the ground more than their triggers.

The light of the flare began to fail. Green Granite had fired another illumination round, timed to ignite as the first faded, but it was a dud. The flare had illuminated the battlefield, but it had also killed the soldiers' night vision, and now the battlefield faded into a total darkness as frightening as what the light had revealed earlier.

"Jesus!" Wodzinski said over and over. Newsome and Ricochet said nothing, and as the darkness returned, Ricochet put his eye back to the starlight scope. Washington, realizing he had at least fired several hundred rounds, shouted to Otis to check the ammo belts.

Darkness became complete. When Randy called anxiously for illumination again, Green Granite realized they had fired a dud and hastened to fire another. In the darkness, Washington called to Otis again, "We good? How much do I have?" But Otis didn't answer. "Hey, man! We good? We good to go?"

In front of Fort Dump Truck, Jude and Bert's exclamations at the effect of the minigun had died down, and Jude leaned to his left and called out in a low voice, "Ned, Tom, you guys good?" They replied they were. Then he leaned right and called for Marty and Joe but heard no answer. He called again, more loudly, but again received no reply. "Shit."

Bert said, "Think something happened to 'em?"

"Well, they're not deaf. Least they weren't."

"I'll … I'll go check on them."

"Shit, could be anything out there. They could just be nervous. Trigger happy. Could get yourself shot."

"Well, shit, we got to know, don't we?"

"I oughta go," Jude whispered.

"Why you?"

"I'm trained. Experienced."

For some reason, that stung Bert. "Fuck you, buddy. Anyone can crawl." Before Jude could reply, Bert crawled out of the foxhole toward Marty and Joe's. He could visualize the direction and distance from when they had been digging in that day. Unlike most of the grunts, Bert had a flashlight strapped to his combat harness. Like many others in his unit, he not infrequently needed it to service a vehicle or find tools in the dark. And like most others, he kept a red filter on it. With the flashlight in one hand and his other gripping his M16's pistol grip, he slid forward on his belly. He counted each time he pushed forward with his left knee. Two times, one yard. He guessed it was twenty, maybe twenty-five yards to Marty and Joe's foxhole.

Thirty pushes. Bert figured he'd crawled fifteen yards. He wanted to call out but was afraid of giving himself away. He heard nothing from the direction of the foxhole. He began to feel stupid and exposed, for he just didn't know what the smart thing to do was. He knew Marty and Joe like he knew the other grunts, casually. But he couldn't just turn back without knowing. Bert took a deep, slow breath, shoved his rifle in front of him, holding it by the pistol grip, and slipped his finger onto the trigger. He pushed his flashlight out to his left, aimed it toward where the foxhole should be, and turned it on.

The first thing Bert saw was the soles of a pair of combat boots, toes to the ground, and beside them the top of a helmet. For a split second he wondered why in hell someone would take his helmet off, much less his boots. He didn't try for an answer, as some vague feeling, at once cold and hot, gripped him. He heard a faint gasp and swept the dull red beam to the right. It revealed a face and three black-clad figures pulling hand grenades from a cloth sack, their Asian faces staring blankly at him, confused by the unexpected appearance of a red light. It confused them for just a second too long. The meaning of the boots became terribly clear. "You fuckers!" he screamed, and he pulled the trigger again and again.

Bert rose to his knees and then to a crouch and charged, firing until he had emptied a twenty-round magazine. When he got to the edge of the foxhole, still jerking the trigger of his now empty rifle, the three Vietcong were dead. He shone his light on them, and then on Marty and Joe, whose bodies had been shoved out in front of the foxhole like sandbags—a revetment of flesh.

Gagging, Bert ran back to Jude, crying, "They're dead! They're dead! I killed 'em, I killed 'em."

Jude grabbed him, pulling him roughly into the foxhole. "You fucking shot Marty and Joe? Fucking shot my buddies, you dumb shit?"

Bert couldn't answer, because he was trying not to retch and Jude was shaking him. Finally he managed to gasp, "VC! VC there!"

Washington had been staring into the darkness. Wodzinski whispered hoarsely, "Lordy, but you hosed 'em good, Arlen!"

Yeah, I hosed 'em good, Washington thought, letting his mind drift toward the hope of morning. Surely it couldn't be far off now. The firing had died down. But the burst of fire from Bert, only a few yards away, brought him back, and he again called to Otis for an ammo status. He could make out the clouds again, charcoal against dark gray. His eyes were again adjusting to the darkness, and by the faint moonlight that managed to penetrate, when he looked down he could make out shapes inside the truck. Otis was looking at him, one eye wide open, the other half open. A spot like an inkblot marred his pale forehead. He let go of the gun and jumped out of the crib. "You dumb fuck! I told you! I told you to stay the fuck down!"

Just then Ricochet saw movement through the starlight scope. "Oh, shit!" he cried out, "They're coming again! A shitload of 'em! Enemy! Alpha! Alpha and Bravo!"

Sergeant Newsome, still holding his M60, jumped to brace it on the rim of the truck side, calling to Wodzinski for ammo and to Washington to crank up the minigun. Newsome didn't hear Washington respond. What he heard was a wailing curse. He looked but couldn't really see Washington. He pulled his flashlight from his harness and turned the red-filtered light on. Washington was not at the gun. He was kneeling, holding something in his lap. "Rosie!" he wailed. "I told you! I told you! Stay put! Stay down!"

"Rosie? What the!" Newsome cut his words short. The object in Washington's lap was Otis's pale face. "Oh, no!" he whispered; then, hearing Ricochet's rifle bark, he called to Wodzinski. "Stevie! Take the M60! Get with Ricochet!" Then he went and knelt by Washington. Now he could see Otis was dead, Washington was crying, tears flowing, and crying the name Rosie or the word "rosy." He couldn't tell.

"Arlen! Arlen, man. I'm sorry! Sorry, man, but you got to get up. We need the gun, man! They're gonna fucking overrun us! Get up! You've got to get your ass on the gun!"

"I told the fucker to stay down!" He was rocking, holding Otis's head. "I told her! I told her!"

Newsome put his hands on Washington's shoulders and squeezed. He had no idea what was going on inside the man; he only knew he had to get him onto the gun. He shook him. "Listen! Damn all! The enemy's attacking again. We're in deep shit, Arlen! We need you on the fucking gun! Come on, please! Get up!"

"I told her!"

"I know, I know! Here, let me take care of him." He pulled Otis's head and shoulders from Washington's lap. Washington didn't resist. He lay Otis down and shouted to Wodzinski, "Steve! Forget the M60! You know how to feed this thing ammo, right?"

"What's with them, Sarge?"

"Otis is dead."

"Oh, shit, no!"

"Get over here." Newsome turned his attention back to Washington and grabbed him, heaving him upward. "Get your ass on the gun, Arlen! The fuckers who killed Otis are coming for us! Get on the fucking gun!" He had Washington up and slumping against the gun crib. Just then, a flare ignited high overhead, illuminating the battlefield, and two 175 mm shells exploded two hundred yards from the perimeter, loud and earth-shaking but harmless to friend and foe alike. Newsome and everyone else on that side of the perimeter could see well over a hundred enemy swarming forward, firing from the hip, less than a hundred yards away. Newsome grabbed Washington's head and turned it. "Look! Look, goddammit!"

Washington saw, and it struck him like a slap in the face. He felt something—not quite fear, not quite rage, but something like a towering wave of injustice about to crash on him. And then, defiance. He got to the gun. "Ammo? We got ammo?"

"Yeah, yeah! Go!" Wodzinski shouted.

He could see them, the ninja shadows, larger and closer than ever. He screamed at them, swung the gun, pressed the triggers.

There had been three Vietcong that had made it to Marty and Joe's foxhole, but one had gone back to report the breach in the enemy perimeter, and that was where the second wave focused its assault. Specialist Hicks had been wounded and his machine gun was out of action. That meant than in the space of those three foxholes, from Jude and Bert on the left, to Hicks and his companion on the right, only two M16s were firing. Toward that stretch of weakened defensive fire, the enemy assault automatically drifted, creating a smaller and more crowded front. And into that front began to pour fifty bullets a second.

Nothing seemed to happen between that moment and sunrise—at least nothing he could remember. Sergeant Newsome tapped him on the shoulder. "Hey, Arlen. You okay?" No reply. Washington did not feel bad or good. He was standing in a dump truck on a road in Vietnam, gazing at lush green fields and dark jungle-forested hills and not seeing them; touching the now cool metal of the gun and not feeling it; seeing Timmy's blank face in the bloody, ruddy light of Newsome's flashlight and not recognizing it. It was as if a bullet had severed the nerves that carried feeling to his mind; as if awareness and feeling used different circuits and he'd been left with one but not the other. And for a reason he couldn't fathom, tears were flowing again and he would not look at anyone.

CHAPTER 17

TO CHU SONG

The medevac helicopters were gone. Lieutenant Colonel Short's helicopter was gone. The wounded were gone. The dead were gone. Only the whole and the lightly wounded who refused evacuation were left. Sergeants Jarvis and Carter and PFC Wodzinski were among the wounded who stayed behind. The mental numbness that follows the draining away of adrenaline was beginning to wear off, and the varied, complex reactions to stress set in. For men in foxholes on one side of the perimeter, the night had been one of riding out a storm like a hurricane or a tornado, full of sound and fury, tension and fear; and then the storm had passed. For those on the other side, it had been the same until the veils of the storm had parted to loose the terrors of hell, for none of them had ever actually seen enemy the way they were seen that night, and none had ever actually shot at another being one could see large and close, however distorted by the swinging glare of flares. Some of the grunts had been in firefights before, but the experiences had been brief spates of bullets coming from or fired into walls of darkness or foliage and fleeting, shapeless shadows; lightning filled squalls that struck, engulfed, and fled as quickly as they had come.

Lieutenant Hanley could remember only fragments of the rest of the night and early morning after the moment he called Green Granite for illumination. He had fragmentary memories of calling for concentrations to be fired, hoping to hit something but not daring to bring them as close as the action was; of hearing shots and picking up his rifle only to put it down again; of listening to the phone until he realized that at some point it had gone dead; of seeing the four dead wrapped in ponchos, wondering who had done it; of noting their names and serial numbers and of listing the names of the wounded in his notebook with numb hands and mind; of looking at the dead faces: Marty, Joe, Timmy, and one of his own men, Irving, and feeling nothing; and, finally, of looking at Sergeant Jarvis's haggard face.

"You okay, sir?" Sergeant Jarvis asked, his brow furrowed, staring at him with unusual intensity.

"I couldn't look at the guys from the gun truck. Mancini got me their dog tag info."

"It's okay, sir. Not pretty."

"It's no guts, Sarge. I looked at the others. I feel nothing. Just nothing. Something is fucking wrong with me. I didn't do shit last night."

"You did your job, sir. We all did. You put the pieces in place. And each of those pieces knew what to do. That was your job, and you did it."

"So why don't I"—he hit his chest—"feel like I did? Feel anything?"

"Shit, there's a limit, sir. Then if we're still busy feeling every fucking thing, we couldn't handle it. Think they'll come back?"

"Don't know. You have a guess?"

"I think they shot their wad, sir. Carter thinks so too. They left, like, at least twenty-five bodies behind. Lot of blood trails too. Means they dragged off a lot of their wounded and KIAs. But leaving that many bodies behind? One, it means there was a shitload of them. Two, it means they got their ass whipped."

"Can we … what do we do now?" Randy looked almost forlorn. He had never experienced an attack before.

"What's the colonel have to say?"

"I should have dispersed the trucks better, had a tighter perimeter, and not been so panicky."

"Panicky?"

"When I estimated the enemy at two hundred or more."

Jarvis snorted. He agreed with his lieutenant's estimate, but there was nothing he could say about it. "The major give any news?"

"He patted me on the back. Told me we still had a road to clear. Asked me what I needed, besides a new D7." Randy paused, his mind shifting to the mission more as an escape than anything else. "Well, hell, let's go look at the road—see if there's anything we actually can do."

Sergeant Newsome, PFC Rick O'Day, PFC Wodzinski, and Arlen Washington sat beside the dump truck, eating a breakfast of C-rations and drinking C-ration coffee made from some ancient powder that had perhaps been a coffee bean when their parents were kids. No one spoke. They ignored the comings and goings of helicopters, shutting out the sounds of the day as they shut out the memories of the night. They threw the empty cans and packets into a pile. Wodzinski finally said, "Timmy was a good guy, you know. A really nice guy." He coughed and cleared his throat. "Good guy." Abruptly, Arlen left them and climbed back into Fort Dump Truck.

Wodzinski looked around, pained. "What'd I say?"

"Nothing," Ricochet said. "He's just, you know, having a hard time."

"Guess so. Guess they were buddies."

Newsome stood. "You guys wanna take the trash to the pit?" Without waiting for a reply, he turned and followed Washington into the truck. Washington was staring out over the rice paddies, gazing well past where the dark shapes of enemy dead still lay scattered. Newsome stood beside him for several minutes before speaking. "You know, you, you and your gun saved our ass last night. No way—no way—could we have stopped that many VC from breaking through. Especially, *especially*, with Marty and Joe gone, Hicks wounded. No way. You saved our asses. Want you to know that."

Washington coughed. But the thought crept in that the sergeant was right—that he had really done something. He didn't feel like he had done something, even while Newsome was saying he had. But maybe he really had. Something like pride seeped in for a second, but then he saw Otis's dead face, and his budding pride was crushed by a feeling of failure. He tried to shrug it off. "I saved my ass. Told that fucker to get down."

Washington didn't look at Newsome but continued staring out over the battlefield and the bodies. Newsome stood silently, wondering. The man he'd been crying over was now "that fucker." It made no sense, and it angered him.

Newsome poked Washington with an elbow. "See that foxhole there—the one almost in front of us? Jefferson and McAllister were there last night. You didn't save your ass, buddy; they did!"

Washington's didn't respond.

"The VC that got Marty and Joe had a bag of grenades. They were after this truck. You'd have never seen 'em until too late, man. Jefferson and McAllister got 'em. They got another one, too, coming in over there. Guy had a satchel charge. Meant for us. Saved your ass again."

"Yeah, Washington," Newsome added, "you saved their asses when the big attack came, but they'd already saved yours and mine twice. See? They're still kickin' because of you, but you're still here 'cause of them. We save each other. Comprende?"

Beyond another grunt, Washington said nothing, and another few minutes passed. "You okay?" Newsome finally asked.

"Huh? Sure, Sarge. I'm good."

"Who … who's Rosie?" Arlen looked startled. He clamped his mouth shut. "Who's Rosie?"

"Rosie? What the—what're you talking about?"

"When Otis got shot, you were crying, man. Calling Rosie, crying you told her to get down, stay put. Otis, Rosie, him, her, stay down, stay put—all mixed up. There's something there, man. Made me curious." Arlen looked away, the muscles of his jaw bunched. Newsome thought the kid was used to flying around above it all, remote, looking down onto some kind of game board—nothing close like last night. *Hell*, he thought, *I'd never been so close either, but living on the ground where it could happen, one sure as hell worries about it.* Impulsively, he put his arm around Washington. "Sorry, man. Forget I asked. Not my place."

Arlen felt something he'd never felt before. He could not fathom what it was, but it gave him an impulse to speak. "Rosie. Rosalind. My little sister. She was two, two and a half, maybe. I was eight, almost nine, maybe. Told to watch her. All the time. Lots of times. But this one day, I … I look away a sec, and she run out. Run out into the street! Into the fucking street! And this asshole, speeding, speeding like shit! No chance—she had no chance! I told her, man! 'Don't go nowhere, stay put!'"

A multitude of thoughts struck Newsome and struggled with each other as if half a dozen different people were in his head, all arguing over what he had heard. He felt contempt for the carelessness, empathy for the terrible burden, curiosity about how long that "sec" really was, anger at whoever gave a kid that responsibility, and more. He squeezed Arlen's shoulder a little tighter as he sorted through his thoughts.

Arlen suddenly said, "I was reading a Superman comic. Fucking Superman."

"Arlen, you told Timmy to get down; I heard you."

"I did. I told him."

"Well, he was as grown up as you. And he decided to stand up like you were standing up. That bullet could have hit you just as easily as it hit him. Don't beat yourself up, man. Like the guys on the line, like all the others, you two were doing what needed doing. And we're still here thanks to that." He patted Arlen on the back and left, leaving Arlen alone.

The heavy air drifted by slowly, carrying broken clouds and a few glimpses of blue above. The soft grumblings of engines and the distant mutterings of voices seemed to emphasize the quiet. The slivers of blue sky showing and the quiet brought to mind the sounds that had filled the air shortly before: the *thump-thump* of rotors and the whine of turbines as the medevacs and bosses had come and gone. No one had come for him. No pilot had been given the mission to retrieve Airman Washington.

Ricochet went to rejoin his squad. Hutchinson, the dump truck driver, was digging a new prone shelter ten yards from his truck. He'd prepared a prone shelter for himself under the truck, thinking that the safest place from enemy fire and weather. But when he saw the blast-shattered gun truck, he'd decided to move.

Wodzinski, left alone, went back to the dump truck to join Washington. "You okay?"

Washington didn't reply. He wasn't at the gun but was leaning against the side of the truck, staring off to the green hills on the far side of the road. "Sorry about Otis, man."

Washington muttered, "Yeah."

"Real sorry. I mean I only knew him what, two days? But he was, like, a good guy. Really good guy, you know."

Washington cleared his throat twice and then replied, "He had a girlfriend—Merry. Were gonna get married soon's he got home. Guess she'll have to marry a fuckin' corpse now." It wasn't the words but Washington's voice that struck Wodzinski. The words were almost contemptuous, dismissive, full of schadenfreude, but the voice was tight and high, full of pain.

"How come you're still here? You could've gotten a ride out."

"No one come to get me."

Wodzinski was quiet a moment and then said, "Maybe they were planning on using a truck so they could get the guns back too. But then the bridge got blown." When Washington didn't respond, Wodzinski rambled on nervously. "Guess it sucks for you, but for me, guess I'm kind of glad. I mean, another thing like last night? Without your gun? We'd be up shit creek."

Wodzinski left, and Arlen returned to staring at the dark line of trees far across the road, not really seeing it. Could he have gone on one of those choppers? Why hadn't he? Why had he just sat in the dump truck like a bump on a log? Otis was dead. Otis dead was a convenience—an opportunity. Otis dead was another failure. Otis dead was Rosie, was Big Ma, was shit happening to make life shit.

He tried imagining getting out with the gun, but every scenario that started to form immediately collapsed. Who'd help him? The last thing these guys wanted was for the gun to go away. He could have gone empty-handed maybe, but that thought brought on a great reluctance to be parted from the gun, almost as if the gun needed him as much as he wanted it.

Maybe there had been a chance, but it had come and gone. He felt strange, but what he didn't feel was the wash of anger when fate once again had had fun jerking the rug from under him.

Walking back from the latrine, Bert McAllister bumped into Ricochet. "Hey, man," Ricochet asked, "You doin' okay?"

"Yeah. Why not?"

"Hey, Jude told me about last night. You took out three Charlies."

"Didn't help Marty and Joe any." That made for an awkward silence. They walked together a few yards. Ricochet patted Bert's shoulder but didn't say anything. Bert said, "When it got light, I looked. A grenade got Marty and Joe. Tore 'em up." Bert stopped and faced Ricochet. "They were right next to me! Not twenty yards! Didn't hear or see anything. We're supposed to be, like, mutual support. We weren't. I wasn't."

"Don't beat yourself up, man. Look; Marty and Joe must've not seen 'em. I didn't see 'em, and I had a starlight scope! Can't be looking everywhere all the time. You did good. Jude said so."

"Shit. Man, that's something I never want to see again. Want to forget I ever saw it."

"Yeah. There should be a forget-shit pill. Hey. I'm looking for some coffee. Wanna come?"

"Nah, I just got to get my head together. Then get my stuff cleaned up, you know."

When Ricochet walked off, Bert found himself staring at the road grader. It was not far from the shattered hulk of the bulldozer, and that morning they looked completely out of place, which was strange. When it and the dozer had been attached to Second Platoon for the road-clearing mission, it had seemed perfectly normal for a mission to repair a road. But that morning, it didn't belong somehow. A soldier was walking slowly around it—short guy, blond and slim. Lucius. He walked over to him. "How's it going?" he asked.

"Okay, I guess." Lucius gave him a brief, blank stare and then turned his attention back to the grader. "Not a scratch," he said.

"Where's your partner? Preston, right?" Lucius stopped, looked at Bert, and suddenly looked lost. He didn't reply. "He okay?" Bert asked, afraid of the answer.

"I … I guess. Got medevaced. He … he kept getting up and looking around. A piece of shrapnel got him. Right under the chin." Lucius's pale face looked even paler. "I keep thinking. An inch higher, it would've taken his jaw off. An inch right, it would've tore his throat open."

Bert thought about that. "Guess he's lucky."

"Guess so. But now he's gone. Guess he'll go home. It was a big gash. Bled a lot. A *lot*. He shouldn't have stood up like that. Now I got no mate. It's a two-man rig." Bert saw it was much more than that. Lucius was now alone. He wasn't really part of Second Platoon. He was attached, making him even more alone.

Randy and Sergeant Jarvis were standing in the road watching the minesweeping team get organized when they both saw a jeep coming down the road toward them. "What the hell?" Randy exclaimed, "You see that? Where'd it come from?"

"Jesus, sir! He's come out of the woods there!"

"It's … it's a jeep—an M151."

Randy trotted back to their three-quarter ton and pulled a pair of binoculars from the cab. Sergeant Jarvis called to the mine detector team and the infantrymen with them to alert them. Peering through the binoculars, Randy said, "GIs. Helmets, jungle fatigues."

"Could be a trick."

"Get the men off the road and take cover. I … I'll wait by the truck. That'll put you guys on the flank if it's a setup. I'll get Esteveria and Frederick to cover from the ditch." He fell back to stand by the truck. The jeep slowed as the men on the road dispersed, and then it came forward, the soldier in the passenger seat rising to stand. It stopped a few yards from Randy, who called out "Halt!" and immediately felt a bit foolish, remembering his dad's war story. The two men in the jeep were clearly Americans. "Who're you?"

The tall, lanky man standing in the jeep said, "Uh, Major James

Graham, senior advisor to the First Battalion, Fifty-Fifth Regiment, Thirty-Fifth Infantry Division, Army of the Republic of Vietnam." Pointing to the driver, he added, "And my ops sergeant, Mike Beeker. Who're you?"

"Uh, Lieutenant Randall Hanley, 134th Combat Engineers, sir. Did you, like, just come from up there—from Chu Song?"

Major Graham returned Randy's salute and replied, "Extremely embarrassed to say yes."

"Embarrassed, sir?"

"I can't find my battalion."

"I haven't seen them, sir. Could have used them last night."

"I hate to confess this, especially to a lieutenant, but I seem to have fucked up." He dismounted from his jeep and walked up to Randy, explaining that his battalion had been given the mission to clear and secure the road from Chu Song to roughly where they were standing. The battalion was to have kicked off the mission at 0900. He had decided to make a final check with the American force at Chu Song to see if there was any new intel. When he arrived several minutes late at where the mission was to kick off, he'd found no one there and concluded that his aggressive counterpart had already moved out. His deputy advisor had been left behind to advise the battalion's heavy mortar platoon, which meant there was no American with a radio with his counterpart and he had no way to communicate with him except face-to-face. "I'm supposed to be with him, not sitting on my ass chatting by radio. So I figured I'd have to catch up with him. Here I am. Clearly Thieu delayed for some reason."

After taking a moment to digest the major's story, Randy said, "Sir, you just drove all the way from Chu Song?"

"Uh huh. The drive down was kind of nervous, you know? But the drive back is going to be really nerve-racking. If Charlie was asleep when I drove by, he's awake now. Damn."

"Can I ask, sir, what the road is like? Its condition?"

"Road's fine—almost all macadam. The macadam peters out just this side of the jungle. No big potholes, no washouts. Jungle's pretty thick there. Like driving through a tunnel, almost. Probably protected the roadway."

"Good enough for heavy vehicles? Tracked vehicles?"

"Hm." He looked back at the jeep and called, "Hey, Sarge! The road we came down—think it'll hold tracked vehicles, like tanks?"

"Yes sir. APCs? Sure. Not too many tanks, though. Tracks'll start tearing it up. Macadam's not that thick. Yeah, I think so."

The major turned back to Randy. "Answer your question?"

Sergeant Jarvis had joined them. "What're you thinking, sir?"

Randy answered, directing his words to both Jarvis and Major Graham. "Our mission is to clear the road to Chu Song so that a heavy artillery battery can get its guns there. Everyone's in a hurry to have it happen, and no one up the chain seems to see we can't make it happen by ourselves. No dozer, no Rome plows, and not anytime soon, because now the bridge above Xhan La is blown. Just had a brain fart that maybe the road is already clear. Or clear enough. Why not just haul ass?"

"Think Battalion will go for it?" Sergeant Jarvis asked.

"No clue. Or if the redlegs will."

It was an incredibly stupid idea for a lieutenant on a mission defined by Corps to have by himself—at least that was one of Randy's thoughts. Still, all they could do was say no, so he decided he would run the idea by Major Graham and then Green Granite. "Sir, the outfit you checked with—they have any good intel?"

"No, not really. They say something's up. But they gave me nothing actionable."

"Huh. Something was up last night. We nearly got overrun."

"Good God!"

After some prodding, Randy told the tale of the night and ended by asking, "Would you call me when you get back to your unit, sir?"

"I sure as hell will, Lieutenant. And I'll keep you posted on my counterpart's progress—if he doesn't shoot me for dereliction or desertion." Major Graham got back in the jeep. It turned around and sped back the way it had come.

Randy got on the radio to Green Granite.

The commanding general of Second Corps waved his chief of artillery to a seat. "What's up, Fred?"

"That heavy battery we're trying to get to Chu Song."

"Still stuck, I gather. Engineers can't get Rome plows up there until they can get a bridge unit in place."

"Yes and maybe no. The engineer unit that's been trying to clear the road was attacked last night."

"Got that report. Any updates? This another setback?"

"Well, it looked like it. They lost their bulldozer and a gun truck. I came about a request from the battery commander. Apparently the engineer unit that has been clearing the road has info that the road is clear all the way—no mines and usable, actually macadamed from near where they are all the way to Chu Song. Apparently someone just drove the whole route." The artillery chief passed on the story of the inadvertent linkup between Major Graham and Lieutenant Hanley.

"So your battery commander is getting this from an engineer lieutenant, and he wants to roll on it?"

"Right. Question is, do we let him? Because if so, it should be ASAP."

"Your opinion, Fred?"

The chief of artillery gave a shake of his head and smiled. "Bold thinking. I like that. His battalion CO's brand-new, but the XO thinks well of him. And with the bridge on QL-99 blown, we don't have good prospects otherwise. We could go for it. Or wait two weeks at least."

The corps commander leaned forward, resting his elbows on the desk and his chin on his interlaced hands. He returned the smile with a tiny one of his own. "I received a message this morning from the commander of the gunship squadron at Nha Trang effusively praising the courage, leadership, and initiative of one Lieutenant Randall Hanley, 134th Engineer Battalion, to high heaven for rescuing one of his crews a couple of nights ago. This the same outfit?"

"Yes sir."

"We're running out of time, here." The general leaned back, hands together as if about to pray. "Fred, you know the intel this morning. First the bridge, now the engineers, not Fire Base Chrome. It seems

215

to me their interest is not in the guns, per se, but that they *not* get to Chu Song."

"Protecting their flank?"

"Right. This monsoon season's giving us a record-breaking drenching and near constant bad flying weather. This favors the enemy launching his offensive sooner rather than later. Once they get their licks in, however successful, they'll want to get back to their sanctuaries while the flying weather is still bad."

The chief of artillery nodded, adding, "And Chu Song would seem a tougher nut to crack than an engineer unit." He paused, tapping his lips with a finger. The corps commander waited. "Sir," the chief of artillery continued, "that could imply they don't have that much to work with in the area, so the attack on the engineers could've been trying to hit the weak spot."

"Makes sense. But they failed. So what's their plan B?" The general paused, picked up a phone and asked his chief of intelligence to join him.

"Manny, what's up at Chu Song? What's the enemy have in that area?"

"Well, sir, we've got an ARVN battalion and a reinforced infantry company from the Seventh Division there, and the opposition could probably put an NVA regiment—two battalions, anyway—and a VC regiment there in a few days. The NVA regiment is probably in the pipeline for their offensive. But it's in the area, so it could be used. All told, maybe three thousand men. Maybe half that could actually be committed." The intelligence chief paused, stroked his broad, flat nose, and added, "The ARVN battalion doesn't have a good rep."

"I know."

"But it does have a new commander."

"Any evaluation from the advisory team there?"

"Don't know off the top of my head. I'll check."

The artillery chief said, "Sir, if plan B is Chu Song, given what could be thrown at it, Chu Song could use some reinforcement. I'm thinking go for it. Make up a task force from Battery A, the infantry company from the Cav that's been providing security, and the engineer platoon. The battery commander's the senior officer. It's his mission. He works well with the infantry commander and obviously has confidence in the engineer lieutenant. It would almost double the forces at Chu Song."

The general looked down at his desktop and rubbed his eyes. Looking up again, he said, "Let me think out loud about this a moment." The general was silent for a moment and then said, "It'll be a task force, you say, which means throwing together a bunch of young men who don't know each other that well and haven't trained together, and sending them on a mission that could be putting them in a crunch. Do we really want to do that? Are they, in their invincible youth, proposing something that's actually reckless?"

"You were at Normandy, sir."

"I was, yes, and young and reckless, Fred, but I got swept up on that beach with no more say than a bit of driftwood on the tide. Besides, I was second wave." The chief of artillery's expression remained bland. The commander put his hands flat on his desk and cleared his throat. "Hell, I'm probably just getting old and querulous. Okay. So go. Get 'em rolling. Make sure you get a take from Manny on that ARVN battalion ASAP. If it's very negative, we may want to rethink."

The chief of artillery smiled, waved a half salute, and slipped out.

The day passed quietly for Lieutenant Hanley's men, suffused with an eerie boredom, a mix of easy routine and lingering numbness from the battle. The road was swept for mines all the way to where it tunneled into the jungle, with none being found. Vehicles—those still in one piece—were serviced, hose leaks repaired, minor damages jury-rigged one way or another. Ricochet rejoined his squad; Washington and Wodzinski serviced the gun and spent a good deal of the day simply waiting. They talked very little. At least this was true until midafternoon, when a jeep came up the road from the direction of Xanh La carrying Captains Everett Rosen and Christopher Cornwell, followed by a truck with a squad of Rosen's infantrymen. Everett immediately went to see his two squad leaders to learn firsthand what had happened in the battle and collect information and personal effects of the men who had been killed or wounded. Then the two captains and Lieutenant Hanley got down to business.

"You had quite a night last night," Everett said as kind of an opening.

"Basically, sir, I spent the night scared shitless."

"Well, you covered it up well on the radio," Chris said. "Hell, on the radio we'd have thought it was just a training exercise."

Everett cut in. "My guys say your minigun saved the day. Night, rather."

"Yeah, but Captain Cornwell's illumination made it possible, sir."

"So, okay, Hanley, you hear anything from your chain? Orders? News? Intel?" Chris asked.

"Status reports. Or, rather, requests for status."

"Okay." Chris Cornwell stood, somewhat dramatically. "Gents, on orders from Second Corps, we're here to organize Task Force Nickel, a combined artillery, infantry, and engineer task force to get my guns"—he spread his arms like a bad Shakespearian actor—"and my ass safely to Chu Song ASAP! In short, we're going to implement your idea, Randy."

"No shit?"

"No shit. How are you on gas?"

"Okay. We can get that far, no sweat. Thank God we unloaded the supply truck. It took a direct hit."

"Good. Our biggest problem may be my men," Everett said. "We're air cav. No wheels. Division flies us around when they've a mind to. Otherwise we walk."

"This mean we move up the road at a walk?"

"Not if we can ride. I've been ordered to leave a platoon to reinforce security at the bridge. I'm going to give them two of my mortar crews. Ten men. And my XO. Battalion said they can get my other two mortars up to the bridge site. They're bringing up some engineers to put in a temporary one. So it's not like I have to move everyone." He shrugged. "Crap. I hate security missions. They suck. The whole friggin' concept of cav is offense. Maneuver, move fast, do the unexpected. Ah, never mind. Sorry." Everett shrugged and grinned. "There has been one advantage, though."

"What's that?"

"We don't have a mess team. Outside of a battalion or brigade base, we live on C-rations. Cornwell's battery has a damn good one. Three hots a day does kind of compensate."

"Well, Ev, we've got trucks and tracks. One way or another, you're not walking, and we sure as hell hope we're unexpected."

There was just a jeep in front, pulling a trailer. There was a driver, two grunts in the backseat with M16s, and a third riding shotgun with an M16. The jeep was "point," the lead vehicle in the convoy. Arlen Washington stared at it. He had been staring at it for several minutes since their convoy had started off around midmorning. He had been staring at it because he was waiting for it to blow up. He was sure it was going to.

But his attention was soon drawn ahead of the jeep to the wall of the jungle, where the road disappeared as if into a dark tunnel cut into a green cliff. It seemed to be closing in on him as if he were a minnow in a stream being swept by the current toward the gaping mouth of a shark.

When Sergeant Newsome had announced to the crew that they would be moving out the next day, Washington had shouted, "Hoorah! Army's movin' us, right?" and then, grinning, he muttered to himself, "Outta inventory, man, outta inventory. And no Otis." But with the last three words, his grin vanished. An alien feeling of being derelict again swept over him. He had really told him to get down. He had. It took effort to shake the feeling off until Sergeant Newsome interrupted his thoughts, spreading a map and saying, "Here's where we're headed."

Maps didn't mean much to Washington, and he asked, "How close to Nha Trang is this Chu Song place?"

"It ain't. Nha Trang's that way. Chu Song's that way," he said, pointing in the opposite direction.

"Yeah," Ricochet added, staring at the map. "Hey, you can almost spit into Cambodia from there."

"Cambodia?" Washington had squeaked. "That's where the enemy hides out, right? Their turf, ain't it? We can't fly there, shoot there, do squat there, what I heard!" He took a step back as if the word had tainted the map. An image popped into his mind, from when he was a young boy, of a wooded park in his neighborhood—Castle Park—where kids were told never to go lest they just disappear. If he had to walk past it, he

219

walked on the other side of the street. The park was where everything scary hid out. It tempted and it terrified.

"We're not going to Cambodia, for Christ's sake, Washington! Just in that direction. And nowhere near spittin' distance, Ricochet!" Newsome had been staring resolutely at the map, and now he looked up at Washington. "Hey! They have an airstrip there. Your boys can come get you tomorrow." He smiled. "If the weather's okay."

The tunnel into the green wall ahead seemed like a tunnel into Castle Park. That was why he had been waiting for the jeep to blow up. As soon as it did, everything would stop. And then they wouldn't go into the tunnel.

But the jeep didn't blow up. It disappeared into the shadows of the jungle, which in turn engulfed him. He wanted to duck down, get down like Otis should have. He glanced back to see what others were doing. The truck was crowded—jammed, really—with Sergeant Carter's and Sergeant Warrant's infantry squads—or, rather, what was left of them. Fifteen men crowded the truck bed. The platoon's other trucks had shuttled down to Green Granite's base to load up on all of Captain Rosen's infantry they could carry in addition to their own crews.

No one in the dump truck looked afraid. They all had blank expressions. Sergeants Carter and Newsome were closest to him. Three of Carter's men were in the leading jeep. Carter said, "Hey Washington! Got your eyes peeled?"

"Yeh, Sarge. Sure."

"Okay. Good. But listen up. Fingers off the trigger. You don't shoot anything 'less I give the order, got it? There may be ARVN, South Vietnamese troops, along the road, or maybe off the road, providing security. So don't shoot. Wait for me. Got it?"

"How do you know you'll see 'em first, Sarge? I got eyes!"

Carter's eyes blazed, and he took a sharp breath to control himself, which worked a little. "Great! You've got eyes. So use them! But if you try to shoot before I tell you to, I'll shoot *you*. Got that?"

Washington said he did. But it didn't really make him feel safer. He had no opinion about the ARVNs; it was simply that he did not like to be told not to shoot. What if Carter didn't see them first? Or got shot? Or froze? Any of these things could get himself killed. Washington felt he shouldn't even be here. Only his rotten luck had put him here. But he took his hands off the gun handles and gripped the sides of the crib. Wodzinski came and stood beside him. "Don't mind Carter. He's just nervous."

"No shit? So everything's cool? Sarge just nervous?"

"Come on, man; don't be negative. Hey, see there? They got patrols out." Wodzinski pointed to a small squad of ARVN soldiers walking along the side of the road.

"I can see further than them, man. Big deal. Ain't none of us can see what's around the corner! I ain't supposed to be here. Just my rotten luck. Always fucks me."

"Well, you got better luck than Otis got."

"Shut up about Otis!" he replied sharply, and he then, more softly and slowly, added, "I told him to get down! I told him. Told him, told him, I did." His voice trailed off.

The convoy rumbled on. While his body stiffened and his hands trembled as they approached every curve, nothing happened. No one got shot, nothing blew up, and the only sounds that reached him were those of running engines, rolling tires, muted voices, crackling static from radios, and occasional alien sounds from the jungle.

And then they emerged into the light again. They came to a road junction and turned right. There was an airstrip on the right of the road, and even a line of telephone poles, and on the left, a firebase of some sort. Sandbagged foxholes, revetments, bunkers, tents, mortar pits, gun jeeps, and GIs were walking around. And then, up ahead, a little past the end of the airstrip, there was what looked like a grass-covered levee or wall eight or ten feet high. The jeep ahead slowed and stopped just past the wall. Washington could now see that the wall enclosed a compound of maybe two acres or more. The wall facing the road was cut with an entry. It was not a direct opening but an overlapping of two walls on that side so one could not see or shoot directly into the compound, which decades before, he would soon learn, had been a fort built by the French.

For perhaps an hour, little happened that affected Washington. The first thing was the infantry dismounted, and small groups of them spread out to inspect outside, inside and on top of the walls. Then the big, self-propelled artillery pieces were maneuvered into the compound. Then came the engineer trucks, the road grader, and finally his dump truck.

As soon as it pulled in, he felt safer, surrounded by the high earthen berms. He saw they were sloped enough that one could climb them at a run or using hands and feet. On the inside, the berm was stepped. About halfway up, a ledge, now weathered to perhaps a foot wide, had been cut in all the way around.

CHAPTER 18

FORT FROG

Everyone had something to do—infantrymen, artillerymen, engineers—each with his specialties and the usual "extra duties." But there were no duties or specialties for an airman, and Washington was disassociated from the organized disorder, an uncomprehending and rather lonely observer. Ricochet was back with his squad, Wodzinski and Newsome were helping service vehicles.

Washington was alone with his gun. He began to clean it. He had cleaned it before, in the long day after the battle, but now he found himself cleaning it again just to do something. Then he checked everything—the electrical connections, the ammunition feed, the soundness of the mounting straps—and suddenly realized that the earthen walls were too high. Standing in the bed of the truck, he could see over them, but the gun, a good foot lower, could not shoot over them.

Bored, restless, and now nervous, Washington gazed around the now bustling compound and saw Sergeants Newsome and Jarvis together.

Both were being barked at by a small brown-and-white mongrel with a bent tail. He hesitated but then scrambled out of the truck and walked up to them. The dog immediately began barking at Washington. He jumped back, eructing a grunt of pain. The little dog jumped forward. Washington shook his boot at it, which made his toe hurt more. "Get away, mutt! Git! Oww!"

Sergeant Jarvis laughed. "He's not gonna bite, son."

Washington stood still. Nervously, he said, "Don't like dogs."

"Everyone likes dogs," Sergeant Newsome snapped. "What's your problem?"

"Nothin'! Hear the locals eat 'em. What's a mutt doin' here anyway, Chief?"

"Chief? Where'd you get that?"

"Sorry, uh, Sarge. Always call my—our—sergeants Chief."

"Well, I'm no Indian. And Sparky here—looks like he's the battery mascot. No idea where they got it. Anyway, forget him. He barks at everyone he doesn't know."

Washington looked at the little mongrel. He decided to ignore it before the sergeants could laugh at him. "Anyway, Sarge, how long we gonna be here?"

Sergeant Jarvis answered for Newsome. "Not a fucking clue, son. Our mission's done—we think, anyway. Got no new mission, but we also got no way to get back. Anyway, nice airstrip out there. Your buddies can come get you anytime."

"So what's up, Arlen?" Newsome asked.

"I can't shoot over the wall. It's too high."

"So get on top."

"The gun, Sarge. It don't sit high enough."

Newsome looked at the gun and the wall. "Oh, shit. You're right. Got any ideas?"

Washington's first thought was that Newsome was the sergeant. He was supposed to have the answers. "You're the sergeant, Sarge," he blurted before it occurred to him that the whole thing had been his idea in the first place. He looked back at the truck, but no ideas came to mind.

Newsome gave him a brief glare, shrugged and climbed to the

top of the wall to look around, partly to get a feel for what the gun should or could cover, and partly in hopes of getting an idea for the gun. No bright ideas sprang to mind, and he climbed back down to glare at Washington again. "Yeah, I'm the sergeant," Newsome snapped, "and you're the snotty airman whose bright idea it was— thank God—to get that sucker mounted. So as your sergeant, for the time being anyway, I'm giving you an order, Arlen: come up with another fucking bright idea." Newsome then left him alone to carry out his order.

No bright ideas came to mind, and nothing seemed to happen for quite a while. Washington sat idle and anxious, for the wall did not feel nearly as safe as it first had, because he couldn't shoot whatever might come at them.

His idleness ended when Captain Rosen; his two infantry platoon leaders, Lieutenants Harris and Malcomb; Sergeant Carter; and Lieutenant Hanley came to Washington to discuss the gun. When Captain Rosen said he needed his help, Washington looked blank. Officers didn't ask for his help; they only wanted him to do this or that or, more often, just be ready to do this or that, as if there were a button on his back they could just push. This had not actually been his experience; it was simply how he had chosen to see it. After a moment, he managed to ask, in an almost suspicious tone, what kind of help Rosen wanted.

"This minigun you rigged up is the most powerful weapon we'll have here." He chuckled, pointing to the four big guns in the fort. "If someone else is attacked, those guns'll be great, but if we're attacked, they'll be useless. Sergeant Carter says you broke the attack on your guys the other night. I want to understand the best way to use it. Let's get up on top, have a look around, and discuss it, okay?"

Shortly before this, Major Jim Graham had appeared, looking to see how they were settling in and, more importantly, to coordinate fire support for his Vietnamese battalion. He, too, was first greeted by a small brown-and-white mongrel with a bent tail that barked at him continuously until Captain Cornwell assured Sparky, the battery's mascot, that Major Graham was "Okay." When Graham mentioned his Vietnamese unit had heavy mortars that could support the defense of the battery if needed, Cornwell helped him find Captain Rosen, who, with his lieutenants, was on top of the wall, and they climbed up to join them.

Now Arlen found himself standing on the top of the wall of the old French fort, the center of attention of six officers and a sergeant. After introductions which included a brief explanation of the minigun and Washington, Captain Rosen turned his attention from the gun to Graham, asking, "Sir, could you first sort of orient us as to what's what around here?"

He could. "So, we're looking more or less west here." The fort was at the end of a thirty-three-hundred-foot airstrip that could handle up to four-engine C-130s. Having no control tower, it was a fair-weather airport, but still it was what made Chu Song important. It ran parallel to the road they'd arrived on, and between the runway and the road, not far from the fort, there stood several large tents surrounded by low walls of sandbags. These served as a supply depot for fuel, rations, and ammunition. He pointed out that his ARVN infantry battalion occupied a low knoll beyond the trees at the far end of the runway. "So," he concluded, "you see bad guys on the airstrip, try not to shoot high; you'd be shooting into our fire base."

He led them to the south side that overlooked a wide draw running parallel to the airstrip. Graham pointed out that it grew gradually shallower and narrower to the west, eventually wrapping around the ARVN position to peter out in the hills beyond. It was mostly jungle forested, but near the fort it was mostly scrub wood and thick brush— the jungle reclaiming what had once been farmland. "I point this out, gents, because it is probably one of the best approaches for an enemy attack force."

They walked around to the east side. There they saw a gentler landscape of fallow fields and scattered gardens and paddies and, less than half a mile off, the village of Chu Song, apparently at the end of the road they had come in on. Graham pointed out that the road continued on through Chu Song, but deteriorated into little more than a cart path. The villagers didn't use the good road they had arrived by, because it had become bandit country since the French left. Local trade used the cart path that skirted the jungle.

Chu Song, he noted, was defended by an understrength provincial force platoon. They were not to expect them to be an effective block to any attack from the east but would give early warning. Wrapping up, Graham concluded, "Oh, yeah. There's a spook station there too. Don't know how the hell they survive."

"Spook station? Who? Like, what do they do?" one of Rosen's lieutenants blurted, speaking for the first time.

"My guess is they run a kind of local spy network. Maybe even across the border. Maybe they're CIA—or maybe not. What I know is they have a damn good liquor cabinet and their info seems credible." He paused and smiled. "Or it could just be the booze that comes with their briefing."

They walked back around to the northern end of the west wall, where they had a good view of the American positions. "Task Force Baker. Basically it's a reinforced company from the Second of the Tenth Infantry. It's a Seventh Division outfit. They have a major in command of the whole thing, the infantry company, a battalion recon platoon, and a battalion mortar section of two four-point two-inch mortars. The company has three eighty-one-millimeter mortars and two antitank guns." He cleared his throat. "Both the major and the company commander are very new in country. Have you met them yet?" They had not. "But aren't you attached to Task Force Baker?"

"Not that I know of," Everett replied. "Right now I report to Chris here; he's our task force CO. When we were given the go to come here as Task Force Nickel, that was directly from Corps Artillery."

Graham looked at Chris. Chris shrugged. "Far as I know, Corps."

Everett interrupted, being more interested in something else Graham had said. "Antitank? You mean like one-oh-sixes on jeeps? Charlie have tanks up here?"

"No. Not that we know of, anyway. They're just part of the infantry company's organization, so they have them."

"Oh. Right. They're regular infantry. Have more firepower than us air cav grunts, and I only have one of my mortars with me."

"One?" Graham asked.

"We're air cav. Once we're on the ground, we walk. One we can handle. Try to carry all three mortars and ammo for them, we don't walk far or fast. Anyway, we were on patrol when we got lifted out to protect Chris's battery. Usual story. We came with what we had."

"Uh huh. So. Questions, gentlemen?"

For a moment, no one spoke. Everett was noting down the weapons that could possibly provide support if he needed it—the Vietnamese and American heavy and light mortars. He didn't note down the antitank guns, because he didn't see any use for them. Then he looked up and asked, "Any artillery in range?"

"Oh, yeah. Nearly forgot. A Seventh Division fire base has two one-oh-five batteries east southeast of here. We're close to their max range, though. It's why they have the heavy mortar section with them. I have the call signs and frequencies. I can introduce you to the major over there and my battalion CO too. Might be good. Also, you guys might want to clarify the chain of command here with your bosses."

Chris did not make a note of Graham's last advice. He had a good feeling about Major Graham, but on balance, he didn't want to be subordinated to a major just new in country. He did not see majors as being much more experienced than himself. Corps artillery had two things going for it in his mind: it was far away and out of his hair, and it had far greater assets to call on than what he saw across the road.

For a while, no one spoke. Everett, his two infantry platoon leaders, and Lieutenant Hanley gazed around, thinking of defense. Washington coughed. He had listened intently throughout the walk on the wall—or had tried to. At one point, when Major Graham was discussing the valley on the south side, he'd lost interest, for the valley was confusing. He was used to seeing terrain from above—a vantage point where, to him, the slopes and folds of the earth had little meaning.

"Yeah, Washington?" Everett asked. "Got a question?"

"Uh, yes sir. Where's Cambodia?"

"That way." Major Graham pointed across the road to the north. "Five, six klicks."

Washington swallowed. "So Charlie's gonna come from there, right, sir? So we put my gun on this side?"

One of Everett's platoon leaders answered. "Brings up a point, sir." He turned to Everett. "What about defending this side with friendlies just across the road?"

Washington frowned. He hadn't thought of that.

Everett glanced around and quickly settled it, deciding to have positions prepared along the north wall for the reserve to occupy just in case but man only one position on the ground to cover the entrance with an M60. He asked the major where he thought an attack was most likely to come from.

"Hard to say," Graham replied, stroking his chin, thinking. "Shortest approach and withdrawal route is from the north to hit Task Force Baker. Downside is Baker has great fields of fire and visibility on that side. A lot longer route to use the draw on the south side. Upside, great concealment. They could get pretty close without being detected. If they're aiming for this fort, straight out of the draw at the south side. If aiming for the supply dump or Task Force Baker, sweep across the airstrip out of the draw. Downside? Longer, more vulnerable withdrawal routes." They walked back to the south side and paced up and down, examining the ground beyond. Then Everett asked Washington's opinion.

For a moment, Washington gaped at Captain Rosen. He swallowed and coughed and finally found his voice. "Uh, ah, first problem, sir—the dump truck's not high enough to let me shoot over the wall. Like maybe a foot. Need to get it higher somehow, like this much over the wall." He held his hands about belly high.

"Can't we just take it off the truck and put it up here?" Everett asked.

"No sir, don't think so. I mean, it's mounted in that wood frame so's I can aim it and handle the recoil."

"Huh. I see. Got any ideas?"

He had. It had come to him as they had walked atop the wall, seeing the landscape outside and the dump truck below him inside. "Can we maybe make, like, a ramp, like three, four feet high? Back the truck up to it, then raise the dump bed so, like, it's level again."

The officers and the sergeant all looked back and forth between the truck and the wall. One of Everett's lieutenants asked, "Why so high? Like you said, it's only about a foot too low."

Washington mimed firing the gun. "Got to be able to shoot down, sir."

Everett looked at Lieutenant Hanley. "Can we do that? Make a ramp?" Randy nodded. Turning back to Washington, Everett asked,

"So, think we put it in the corner here so you can cover both the south into the draw and west over the airstrip?"

"Yes sir," Arlen replied.

"Okay, I guess we have a plan for the minigun," Everett said, but then Randy asked about his men. "Shit. You're right. Hold on. Chris, what about your guys. I mean, in defense?" This triggered a lively discussion. Randy's engineers basically no longer had a mission. Like Washington, they were simply stuck there. On the other hand, if they came under attack, Chris's artillerymen might well be busy providing fire support to some other unit. In the end, Everett decided to use Randy's platoon as the reserve instead of his own weapons platoon, which he could now use to reinforce his two rifle platoons. Chris would organize his gun crews into a backup reserve.

And that became the plan for the defense of what was officially designated Fire Base Nickel. It might have been Fire Base Nickel on the maps and status reports in various headquarters, but once the men of Task Force Nickel learned they were occupying an old French fort, it became "Fort Frog." No one could say who first came up with the name, but it stuck.

About the middle of the next day, they had completed the ramp, backed the dump truck onto it, and raised the bed to be level. At last Washington could unlimber the gun and swing it to cover the western and southern quadrants and survey his fields of fire. He did so and grinned, but the grin faded when he looked back and down at the ammunition feed. No one was there. He put a fist to his mouth and muttered over and over, "I told you to get down. I did!" until he noticed Wodzinski approaching, carrying two metal ammo boxes.

"Hey, Arlen! They got tons of machine gun ammo in the tents over there!"

"No shit? Well, we only got maybe six thousand rounds left. Let's load up before someone says no."

An hour later, they had appropriated almost ten thousand rounds and hauled them to the dump truck. No one had appeared to tell them no or ask for paperwork or anything. "Hell, out here, I bet I could walk off with the gun. Take it home as a, like, souvenir!"

Wodzinski laughed. "No problem taking it out of here, except for maybe eighty guys here would kill you to keep it. Unless maybe we got a new Duster; then we wouldn't care so much. Course, you might have a little trouble getting it on the plane for home."

"I don't know. Disguise it? Shit, there's always a way."

"Maybe," Wodzinski laughed again. "What in hell would you do with it? Hang it over your fireplace?"

"Fireplace?" Washington shook his head. "Use it; that's what."

"You're too weird, man."

"Serious."

"Right. Can't use it for anything legal. So use it at all and a million cops'll be on your ass."

"Blow 'em away."

"Yeah! Go out in a blaze of glory—really dumb glory."

"You take the fun outta it. Anyway, I'd just scare some assholes with it. One look down the barrels of that baby and they'd piss their pants."

"Then the cops come and you get your blaze of glory. Bye-bye Arlen." This banter went on as they arranged and linked the ammunition for the gun and returned to the storage tents to appropriate more. When Washington didn't reply to his last comment, Wodzinski added, "You have a truck to mount it on?"

"Nah." Almost eagerly, Washington described a big Lincoln sedan with its huge trunk that could hold a big store of ammo and the back seat removed to make room for the gun and a gunner and a mechanism to raise and lower it through a hole in the roof.

"You got one hell of an imagination! Got to admit, though, it would be fun to see!"

"You think I'm just shittin' you?"

"You think I'm dumb enough to believe you?"

"Maybe I'm just shittin' you, 'cause if I was serious, I wouldn't tell you shit, would I?"

Wodzinski laughed. "Now you've got me thinking maybe you're crazy enough to be serious!"

They had finished with the ammunition and were standing by the gun crib, looking around. They could see all around for miles—all the way into Cambodia, it seemed. They heard aircraft engines. When he looked up, Washington saw a twin-engine Caribou drifting on the downwind leg, just below the cloud cover. Shortly it banked, turned onto its base leg, banked again, lined up with the runway, and then seemed to drop like a rock to a smooth landing and quick stop, almost disappearing behind a fine spray of muddy water thrown up by its reversible-pitch propellers. It taxied close to the storage tents, and men appeared to unload it.

Wodzinski said, "That's air force. Maybe they're here for you?"

"Dunno," Washington said morosely, as if he didn't care.

"Just leave the gun behind," Wodzinski said.

"I don't see nobody coming here. Back at Nha Trang, you hear 'Aircraft down!' everybody gets all excited. Boom, choppers, fighters, whatever, all zoom off. Save the crew! Save the crew, man! Where are they now? Like they don't give a shit." The unloading was done in minutes. They watched as the engines powered up. The plane turned and took off abruptly, airborne almost as soon as it started rolling, and quickly disappeared into the clouds. Arlen stared at the clouds the plane had disappeared into with two conflicting disappointments: that no one seemed to care, and that another potential opportunity had been lost because he didn't have a plan.

Arlen turned his back on the airstrip and found himself staring across the fort at the village of Chu Song. The roofs were metal or thatch mostly, the walls mostly mud colored. He could just see a man pulling a wagon down the road—a scene as alien from his neighborhood as alien could be, yet something about it resonated with his own memories. Wodzinski interrupted his vague, molasses-like thoughts. "What're you looking at?"

"Huh? Oh. The village. Think anything goes on there? Like any bars or girls?"

"Out here?" Wodzinski snorted, then had a second thought. "Bars? Who knows? What the hell else is there to do? Girls? Maybe, but sure as hell they're not inspected!"

"Think they'd let us go see? We kind of done here."

Wodzinski shrugged. "No one asked us anything when we went to the ammo tents." Minutes later, they walked casually past the guardian machine gunner who paid no attention as they turned right toward Chu Song instead of left toward the tents.

The thin macadam lay in broken bits like fractal tiles, gradually being swallowed into the red clays of the road. A couple hundred yards along, they passed the first structure and the road surface smoothed out as if the village traffic had pressed all the macadam into oblivion. The road turned into a dirt street meandering between houses and trees. Above, low clouds drifted by, rarely letting show a sliver of blue sky. And then they saw children—skinny boys and girls in shorts and worn cotton dresses appearing out of the houses and shadows to stare at the Americans. As if the soldiers were pied pipers, as they passed, the children followed. They came upon a solemn boy, perhaps nine or ten, missing two fingers from his right hand and with a scar across his torso, and a little girl, perhaps two, clinging to the remaining fingers.

The toddler suddenly broke free of the boy, running on her dirty bare feet out into the road and Arlen cried out, "No!" swept her up in his arms, ran to the solemn boy, and, putting her down, started to say something, but on seeing the boy's maimed hand and scar, his voice choked. He turned away and rejoined Wodzinski.

"What was that about?"

"Nothing! She—too little to play in the street is all." Arlen turned a full circle. "Nothin' here, man. Let's go back."

Shortly after Wodzinski and Washington left to visit Chu Song, Captains Cornwell and Rosen left to meet Major Baker, who was commanding Task Force Baker. From their perspectives, the meeting went well; they were briefed on Baker's defenses, frequencies and call signs were exchanged, and fire support was coordinated, but mainly no one raised the issue of overall command. The bulk of Task Force Baker was dug in to face the main threat of attack from the north out of nearby Cambodia. Heading back to the fort, Captain Rosen suggested they take a look at the Task Force Baker defenses facing the road and airstrip, as they would be involved if any fighting broke out around the fort, especially on the airstrip side.

They strolled past a few foxholes reinforced with sandbags and then came upon what looked like a low, wide mound but was actually a sprawling camouflage net made more inconspicuous by tufts of grass stuffed in the netting. The only opening appeared to face inward. They could see something was there but could not tell what it was. Stopping by it, Chris Cornwell wondered aloud, "What the hell is that for?"

"Supplies?" Everett Rosen offered.

The netting at the opening fluttered, and a soldier with staff sergeant's stripes emerged, walked around the mound to them, and saluted. "Sirs? Can I help you?" The voice was deep, rumbling, and powerful, reminding Everett of a subway train approaching, and it came from a towering six-foot, four-inch; broad-shouldered; deep-chested body of close to 250 pounds.

The captains returned the salute, and Everett replied, almost timidly, "We were uh, wondering what that is, Sergeant. We're from the fort there."

"Sir, that is a jeep-mounted one-oh-six recoilless rifle, sir."

"No kidding!" Everett replied, looking along the road at the uncamouflaged foxholes and adding, "Damn good camouflage!"

"Thank you, sir," the sergeant boomed. "Don't want my guns to be a target. Least until they have their own targets in their sights." The sergeant pointed down the road to another low mound beyond the storage tents. "The other gun, sir. Weapons section has two."

"How come you're set up on this side?" Everett asked.

"Sir, this the safest side. Commanders feel if shit hits the fan, it'll come out of Cambodia, hit the north side. From here we can maneuver to where we're needed. Shoot and scoot—what we're designed for."

Chris remembered his manners and introduced himself, Everett, and their mission. He extended his hand, and it disappeared in a big chocolate paw with a surprisingly gentle grip.

"Sirs. Staff Sergeant Nelson Ferreia, antitank section chief. Good to have that fort occupied. Your big guns'll give Charlie some second thoughts about messing with us."

On their way back to Fort Frog, Chris remarked he hoped the sergeant was right about his "big guns," and Everett replied incongruously, "Damn good camouflage. Great location—for us."

"Where are my crewmen?" Eddie McLaughlin was in the squadron's personnel office, and no one there yet knew where Airmen Timmy Otis and Arlen Washington were. He was assured they were looking. They had expectations. They were trying to get the story. But they were talking up an air force chain that was talking down an army chain. These were administrative, not combat, channels, and while routine matters generally flowed smoothly and quickly through them, nonroutine matters often did not. Frustrated, Eddie returned to the squadron's operations center and people he knew better. He found the desk sergeant and said, "Hal, you remember that sergeant from that engineer outfit—the one that picked us up when we went down? Could you get him on the phone again?"

"I can sure give it a shot, sir. Let me finish this telex and I'll get on it. Everything okay?"

"No, I'm still missing two crewmen!" he all but shouted. He then took a breath and began chewing his lip. Much more softly, he added, shaking his head, "I should have made them get on the chopper." If he had heard Eddie, the desk sergeant didn't respond but concentrated on his telex. About ten minutes later, the desk sergeant did not have the sergeant Eddie had talked with on the phone, but he did have Major Gridley, the 134th Engineer Battalion operations officer on the line.

After introductions, Eddie blurted, "Sir, it's been four days since your guys rescued me and my crew. Two of my crew have never been returned. I mean, it's been four days!"

"Oh, shit!" Gridley said. He collected himself and tried to explain. "I'm really sorry, Captain. I ... let me get ... perspective. How'd we get you back to your base?"

"Your guys managed to get a medevac. Took yours and my wounded out. The pilot said he could carry two more. There were four of us left: me, my copilot, Otis, and Washington. I told them to go, but they volunteered to stay behind with the miniguns salvaged from the plane since they knew the guns and your guys had lost all their heavy firepower rescuing us."

"Oh, yeah. Yeah." Major Gridley cleared his throat once, and then again. He stared at the operations map propped on an easel, a grease pencil line still marking the road up the An Cao. "The next day we sent a gun truck up the road to resupply Lieutenant Hanley's platoon; they were the guys who picked you up. They were going to bring your men back, but they were delayed by enemy action and arrived at the platoon too late to return the same day, so they stayed with the platoon overnight. That night, the enemy blew up a bridge, cutting them off. The next night, Hanley's platoon came under heavy attack."

"Jesus, Major!"

"The gun truck took a direct hit, and everyone on board was killed."

"Jesus! Were … were they on it?"

Major Gridley did not know, but he made a supposition. If the airmen had stayed behind to mount miniguns to give Hanley more firepower, in his mind the logical vehicle to mount them on would be the gun truck for its armored sides. Just then, the operations sergeant, Sergeant Thompson, who had walked in moments before and heard most of what Major Gridley had just said, spoke up.

"Sir, there was an airman KIA. They brought his body back with the others."

Gridley put his hand over the mouthpiece. "We know who it was?" Thompson said he would check, and Gridley asked Eddie to hold on. A couple of minutes later, Thompson gave him the answer. "Captain McLaughlin? Sorry, I had to check something. I … I'm afraid one of your crew, an Airman Otis, Timothy Otis, was killed in the attack. I'm sorry." He hated what he'd had to say. He'd never lost a man in combat. This was his first tour, and as a staff officer, none of his staff had become casualties. So far, his headquarters had never even received a single mortar or rocket round. He could not think of what—indeed, if anything—Captain McLaughlin was feeling.

What Eddie felt was a sudden, crushing guilt. The image of Timmy's face hit him like a thrown brick. He was the quintessential nice kid. The quintessential good kid. And he'd thrown his life away because he'd let him volunteer for something he had no business doing. A second pang of guilt hit him with another thought: *Why couldn't it have been Washington?*

"Washington?"

"Captain?"

"My other crewman, Airman Arlen Washington. He okay?"

Gridley again cupped the mouthpiece and asked Thompson, "The other crewman, Washington, what about him?" Thompson shrugged. He didn't know. He took his hand off the mouthpiece and said, "I don't know, Captain. He wasn't listed among the KIA or WIA from the fight. Since he was supposed to be brought back, he may have been evacuated with the others. Can I check and get back to you?"

When he had put the phone down, Major Gridley sat heavily into a folding chair and looked at Sergeant Thompson. "We rescue a couple of airmen only to lose them? How did we fuck that up? How can we not know where this guy is?"

Thompson shrugged again. He could see the major was feeling bad about the news he'd had to convey. Finally, he said, "Shit happens, sir. We know that."

A corner of Gridley's mouth twitched. He coughed a rueful laugh. "Great answer. Covers it." He crossed his arms over his chest and leaned back for a moment. "Huh. If they were both on their minigun on the gun truck, the second airman, Washington, would be dead or wounded. If somehow he wasn't on the truck, he'd have been evacuated with the wounded or still be with Lieutenant Hanley, right?"

"Sir."

"So let's check with the medevac and also see if we can get a message to Hanley if anyone survived that mortar hit on the gun truck."

"Sir."

It didn't take long for the answers to come back. As to the first question, the body of an airman had been evacuated, but no wounded or uninjured airman had been. As to the second, no one on the gun truck had survived. But no one had actually asked whether Washington was still with Lieutenant Hanley's engineer platoon. Consequently, Arlen Washington was officially listed as missing in action—probably dead, his body not having been recovered. When feasible, a team would be sent to examine the ruins of the gun truck to look for unrecovered human remains that might be identified.

A sedan pulled up in front of the steps to a narrow, seedy brownstone in an old section of Baltimore. The driver said, "Damn, look at that. Luck's with us. A space right in front, sir."

"Great. We can keep an eye on it while we do our thing. Maybe save the hubcaps," the passenger replied. Both got out at the same time. The driver was an army master sergeant in dress green uniform with four overseas service stripes on his sleeves and four rows of ribbons and parachutist and combat infantry badges on his chest. The other was an army captain, also in dress greens, with no overseas service stripes on his sleeves and two rows of service ribbons on his chest. Both were serving with an army ROTC detachment at a local college. Both were slightly overweight, and the captain had clearly been slimmer when his uniform had been fitted. The sergeant had a clipboard with a notepad, and the officer a fat manila envelope. He double-checked the address.

The officer looked around. It was a beautiful day. The sky was a pristine blue, dotted with a pattern of cirrus clouds in narrow bands, the air having been cleansed by a recent rain. Even the temperature was nearly perfect, although the officer was sweating slightly, mostly from nerves. "How … how do they react?" he asked the sergeant. They were on the sidewalk.

"Only done this duty once, sir—for a KIA," he replied. After a moment, he added, "I'm told MIAs are the hardest."

"Why? I mean, with an MIA, there's always hope, isn't there?"

"Almost always MIA just means they haven't got the body. And it means we stick with the family, holding their hand while they wait until the body's found. Or, if they're really lucky, he's found alive."

"That sucks." They climbed the steps together and pressed the doorbell, the officer half hoping no one would answer. The woman who finally came to the door after half a dozen rings appeared to be under the influence of something, or at least disoriented. The officer introduced himself and the sergeant.

"If you recruiters, my boy's already in. He's in the air force." She peered intently at the uniforms as if puzzled by them. She was slender, almost emaciated. Her eyes were bloodshot and rheumy, her afro style hair shot with gray. She reminded him a bit of an aunt, a permanently unhappy aunt, and he felt a sudden pity for her. A happy life may provide some resilience to the blow he was about to deliver, but an already unhappy life would surely have little defense.

"Ma'am, we're not recruiters." The captain straightened stiffly, sucking in his stomach. "We, uh, we are representing the, uh, Secretary of Defense. I, uh, I, the Secretary of Defense, uh, well, regrets to inform you ..." The captain stopped. He'd forgotten to introduce himself.

The woman cut him off with wide eyes and a deeply furrowed frown. "You army! What you doin' here? My boy's already in! An' he's no draftee!" She stiffened with a prideful squaring of her shoulders. "He's air force! No sir! Now you all get along! You ain't sellin' your army here!" she almost spat the words.

"Sorry, ma'am. Uh, is your husband home?"

"Husband? Ha! Never!" she snorted. The door slammed shut. The officer and the sergeant stared at each other, mute. The sergeant had never seen this reaction. "You suppose a neighbor?" the captain asked. The sergeant shrugged with a nod, and they went next door. No one answered. They went to the other next door.

An elderly woman answered. She was quite short, with well-tended white hair, a surprisingly smooth complexion and bones, and a matronly form that, like a sunset on a beautiful day, recalled a lovely youth and dark eyes that looked both wise and sad. When they asked if she knew a Mrs. Washington next door, she paused a long moment. Her eyes misted. "I seen you, long time ago." She looked away from them at a spot on the doorframe for a long moment and then spoke again. "You here about that boy of hers."

They nodded. "Yes ma'am."

CHAPTER 19

SETTLING IN

Washington forgot about the plane and the seat he didn't have on it when he heard Sergeant Newsome shout that it was chow time and it was Wodzinski's turn to wait for the second serving. It was only heated up B-rations made to look, more or less, like a real mess hall meal, but that was a great step above C-rations. They sat on the ground to eat, those who could leaning against a truck wheel or sandbags to relax. The small group was mostly other engineers because they knew each other.

"Hey, Washington," one asked, "when you getting your ride outta here?"

"Hell, I don't know! You heard them planes come and go. Weren't no seat for me on 'em," he replied, almost bitterly. It would have been completely bitter except for his lack of a plan.

"Well, you can stick around till my tour's up. Only a month left, man. No sweat."

"Yessir! Keep our asses safe so we can sleep like babies while you send the chinks to hell!"

Bert McAllister was one of the engineers, and he piped up. "You think the chinks we kill go to hell?"

Sergeant Newsome gave his opinion. "They're dirty commies. Where else would a dead commie go?"

"Think they're all commies?" one soldier piped up. "Poor shits get drafted by the commies, don't make them one, does it? I mean, I got drafted; that didn't make me a—who the hell's in charge? Anyway, doesn't make me part of his party."

"Shit, man, kill a chink in this godforsaken place and he's being let outta hell," another said.

"Amen!" another said.

Bert said, "I have an aunt. Great aunt. Nutty as a Planters bar. Every big family dinner—Easter, Thanksgiving, whatever—she always asks, 'You think this is purgatory?'"

"What's purgatory?" several asked at the same time.

"It's a Catholic thing," Sergeant Newsome said. "You a mackerel snapper, Bert?"

"Nah. The aunt is. As I understand it, if you're really a saint, when you cash in you go straight to heaven. If you're really an ass, you go straight to hell. But if you're just a normal, run-of-the-mill fuckup, you go to purgatory, where I guess God takes His time sorting you out or maybe giving you time to straighten up. Something like that."

Sergeant Newsome smirked. "So your family reunions were purgatory?"

"Come on, Sarge. Just telling about a nutty aunt."

One of the men laughed. "Maybe she's not nuts. Here we are, a bunch of normal fuckups in a giant clusterfuck." More laughter followed.

Another piped up "Look at the bright side. We only got to be in this clusterfuck twelve months, and I'm halfway through. And Tommy here, he's like, what, eleven months through!"

"Yeah, well, you got to keep your ass in one piece all that time," another said. "When I was on R&R, met this guy. He'd caught a ride to Bien Hoa with a couple other guys. One of 'em was on his last day. His flight home was that night. When their Huey landed at Bien Hoa, they discovered the guy was dead. Shot in the head. He'd taken a fuckin' stray bullet at a thousand feet doing what, over a hundred miles an hour! On his last day. His last friggin' day."

"Hey, men, it's chow time," Sergeant Newsome said in his best authoritative sergeant's voice. "Let's relax. All this negativity's bad for the digestion. Hell, you can go home and get run over by a bus. Bad luck is bad luck anywhere."

Bert said, "Yeah. My old aunt I was talking about? Yeah, she's nutty, but the real thing is she's got a like permanent negative attitude, and that's why she thinks she's in purgatory. It's attitude, man. Like, if I think I'm gonna make it, I'm better off. Even if I don't, I'm still better off up till when I don't, right?"

Hutchinson, Fort Dump Truck's driver who seldom spoke, nodded vigorously. "Yeah, you got it. You can look both ways crossing the street, but you can't do squat about some drunk running a red light, right?" He blew his breath out sharply. "Besides, we got Arlen here and his badass gun, and I reckon my ass is still here thanks to it, man."

That brought on a moment of silence, and Bert again experienced a mental movie clip that kept recurring. First came the image of doom—a horde of dark shapes spitting sparks, rushing inexorably toward him and the pitifully inadequate power of his rifle. And then came a torrent of tracers from behind, shattering and scattering death.

Sergeant Newsome broke the silence. "Yeah, you can say that." He looked at Washington. "You can say that. And it's true. Damn true. But McAllister, you and Jefferson shot a chink trying to get to our truck. Next morning, we find he had a satchel charge. And them that got Marty and Joe? They had a bag of grenades. They were aiming for our truck too. You know that. Take out our heavy firepower. Like those assholes took out the Duster—and Kevin—not one of the trucks. So yeah, Washington saved our asses, but only 'cause you and Jefferson saved his ass—and mine." He paused to rub his nose hard, as if it itched. "We get through shit like that 'cause we've got each other's backs. Right? Am I right?"

Arlen stood in the gun crib that night, not holding the gun handles but a canteen cup filled with a mix of water, powdered coffee, powdered cocoa, and powdered creamer and sugar. It wasn't very hot but was at least warmer than the cool night air. The moon was waxing and the cloud cover thinning, revealing the world as a dark etching. A couple of golden pinpricks of light punctured the black outlines of Chu Song; the intermittent glow of cigarettes being drawn on gave faint hints of life to the bunkers and foxholes across the road and inside the fort. Everywhere else, the world was black and gray. Somewhere in the fort, someone was snoring loudly. Muted voices filtered out of the fire control tent. The dark outlines of the big artillery pieces looked sinister and powerful in the dark, like sleeping dinosaurs. Next to his truck, the sharp, awkward lines of the lonely road grader were incongruous and out of place. Shapes of sleeping soldiers littered the ground along the base of the walls.

He thought of dinner, and it felt good, like the cup in his hand. It didn't occur to him that back in Nha Trang, he seldom ate with his crewmates but usually alone or with his one friend, Jason. Looking down into the fort from his vantage, he felt strong and something else—almost protective—standing watch over them all with his badass gun.

Wodzinski came and stood beside him, cradling a canteen cup of the same mix. He chuckled, looking at Washington's cup. "Home, I'd pour this crap down the sink. Hell, I'd never think to make it, even with real stuff instead of powdered shit. Right now it's almost as good as a cold beer."

"Crap is right," Arlen replied, taking a sip.

"Supper weren't bad. Real cooking for a change."

"Got that right." Arlen grinned. "Couldn't hardly move my elbows, though." Wodzinski looked a question at him. Washington elaborated. "Huh, back in Nha Trang, always plenty of room. Maybe Lem, maybe Jason and me—table to ourselves, you know. Better chow too." He didn't add that a lot of times it was just himself for company at a table.

Arlen looked into his cup, took a sip, and said, "I don't mean that bad, Stevie. Best chow since I got shot down, for sure." He smiled, and in the dark, his teeth gleamed as brightly as the whites of his eyes. Wodzinski smiled back, wishing he had teeth as white and even as Arlen's. "You and me, we got about the lowest rank here, but ha! We the highest up! Can look down on everything. We're, like, in a fuckin' dirt castle, but we the tower," he said, sweeping his arms across everything in the fort. "They can sleep, man, safe under my badass gun in the dump truck tower!"

"Captain Thieu. Good evening." Major Graham bent to duck through the entrance to his counterpart's command bunker.

"Ah. Good evening, Major. How you say, what's new?"

"Well, the heavy battery is operational. They have the concentrations you wanted plotted. The station in Chu Song reports the enemy is preparing to do something soon, probably here, meaning us or the Americans up the road."

"I agree. A patrol sent out this morning to the south return maybe hour ago. They find fresh trails going east–west, made by many feet." On a map he pointed to a spot about a kilometer south and slightly west of them.

"Going for our boys, then. Any sign they could be closing on us here?"

"No. Patrol cross trail at one point. Many men. Some footprints in both directions, but most go east. I will send more patrols out in the morning." He pointed in multiple directions. "I hear no intelligence from my headquarters. You?"

"No. But Division is pretty far away. I think they are more worried about activity near the population centers."

"Yes, I agree. Few days ago, my regimental commander said I should not worry about anything—that the enemy is planning an offensive much closer to the coast. Not in his area."

"Yes, but that does not explain trails with many feet here."

"No," Captain Thieu said. "Also does not explain blowing up bridge on Chu Song road and attack on your unit working on the road."

"The enemy has some interest here. Some part of his plan is here. Soon, from what you have found."

"Ah, but we are not to worry. You have not been told to worry; I have been told not to worry. Well then. Let us share a drink to no worries."

The next day, hot, breathless, and humid, passed quietly, almost. The enemy was quiet, but some higher headquarters were busy. The first disturbance came when Captain Cornwell's brand-new battalion commander swept in for a visit. Lieutenant Colonel Sherman Greystone was particularly interested in visiting Battery A because a number of years before he had briefly commanded it. His UH-1 Huey landed as close to the wall as was safe, somewhat to the annoyance of men working on the walls of Fort Frog.

He jumped out of the helicopter and immediately straightened, which was a bit reckless since he was a tall man and the ground sloped upward. The still-spinning rotor blades just missed his head, and the whine of the engine spooling down drowned out the shouted warning of the copilot. He strode rapidly, hands clasped behind his back, his bearing perfectly military and a bit Napoleonic as he strode between the overlapping walls that made the fort's entrance. There he found himself marching into the face of a machine gun manned by a shirtless soldier.

"Soldier!"

The machine gunner jumped to attention and saluted. "Sir!"

Colonel Greystone gave the soldier his sternest look. "I'd return your salute if you looked like a soldier! Where's your shirt?"

"Uh, over with my stuff, sir." He pointed into the compound.

"Well, soldier, you go get your shirt on right now!"

"Sir, uh, I got duty here, and—"

Colonel Greystone cut him short. "Move!"

Moments later, the soldier was back, shirt on. "Shouldn't you be up there?" Colonel Greystone demanded, pointing to the top of the wall.

"Uh, no sir. We're covering the entry."

"From down here? Huh. Very well. What's the password, soldier?"

"Sir, don't have one. Daylight we can see who it is, and at night, sir, we don't ask; we shoot."

"Not smart. You with Battery A?"

"No sir! Charlie Company, Second of the Twenty-Second Cav, sir!"

"Huh. Where's the battery command post?" The soldier pointed. He saw the CP and decided that he'd take advantage of Captain Cornwell's ignorance of his presence to look around and assess without interference. Interference came anyway, in the form of the battery's mascot, Sparky, who quickly detected the intruder, found him, and trailed him, barking a warning to all while Colonel Greystone did his best to ignore the mutt. It did not take him long to see the dump truck in its peculiar position and to see a shirtless Airman Washington working on some weird thing rising from the dump bed. He'd already passed several shirtless soldiers, all of whom had been sent scrambling. While the topless soldiers were scrambling to cover up, a sergeant ran to inform the captains of the invasion by a superior officer. "Soldier! You! Up on the dump truck! What the hell is this?"

Washington had again been enjoying the view. He looked down and saw a tall, lean man with a long, narrow face that made his helmet look too big, and a long nose hooked over a pencil mustache. His jungle fatigues looked too clean, the trousers had sharp creases, and he was wearing his pistol in a shoulder holster. *An officer.* "What's what? Sir."

"What the hell are you doing with this truck? Making an elevator?"

"No sir. It's a gun. Got to get it high enough to shoot, sir."

"Where's your shirt, soldier!"

"In the cab, sir."

"Well, you're a disgrace to the army! Get down and get in proper uniform!"

"I ain't army, sir. I'm air force," Washington replied defensively.

Captain Cornwell ran to see who the invader was and caught up to him just at that moment. He could see it was a lieutenant colonel, but he had no idea who. "Sir!" he called out, and he saluted. "Captain Chris Cornwell, Task Force Nickel commander! What can I do for you?"

"Nickel? Oh, yes. Task Force Nickel. Captain, I am Colonel Greystone. Took command of First of the One Fifteenth day before yesterday."

"Sir! Ah, well, welcome." *This does not bode well*, he thought, hoping he was wrong.

"Listen here, Captain, what the hell is this? Turning a dump truck into a convenient elevator? Letting soldiers go around shirtless? And who in hell is that soldier? He just told me he's not even in the army!"

Taken aback, Chris Cornwell was speechless at first, merely stammering. Finally he replied, stiffening his posture and his tone.

"He's correct, sir. He's air force. And uh, the dump truck is in that, uh, configuration to elevate a minigun so it can fire effectively. Part of the defense, sir."

"The air force sent you a minigun on a dump truck?"

"Well, no sir." He explained sparingly how Washington and the minigun came to be there.

The colonel looked up at Washington, who was still looking at him. "You, son! Understand you really are air force. But while you're here, you'll act like a soldier! In a proper uniform! Get your shirt on!" He turned to Cornwell. "Walk with me." It did not take Colonel Greystone long to complete a circle of the compound, giving it a thorough critique. Back at the entry, he said, "Captain, let me give you some advice. We're Vietnamizing this war. Got it from the highest authority. Turning it back over to the Vietnamese. They're to take on the fighting. And that means it's time for us to get back to being a professional, by-the-numbers, spit-and-polish army. That's what I expect to see here. Discipline and good order tend to get slack in the field. My predecessor allowed it. I'm not blaming you. But you do get my message, don't you?"

"Sir! Yes sir!"

"And I'll see the air force comes and gets that man."

When the colonel's Huey left, Everett Rosen and Lieutenant Hanley were standing beside him. "I think I'm fucked," he said.

Everett said, "No sweat, Chris. We'll whitewash some rocks, lay 'em out pretty like it's a Fort Riley motor pool, and whenever a chopper lands, we'll make sure all the troops have shirts and pants on."

"Your CO like that?"

"No, he's got his shit together, thank God. Hell, we're the air cav. We get the pick of the litter."

"Thought they chose you guys for small brains. Airheads. Easier to lift."

Everett chuckled. "Hey, you guessed it. Course you know it's similar criteria for redlegs, except for stuffing the empty space with cotton to protect the little brains from shell shock."

The second disturbance came later that afternoon when Major Graham appeared to share his gossip. The officers gathered in the fire control center to hear what the major called his gossip. "Pretty vague, sir," Everett Rosen said. But then he pointed to a point on a map set on an easel. "Here, you say, sir? Many feet, as it were, moving east?"

"Yep."

"Into the draw here?" Captain Rosen asked, pointing southward.

"Maybe. Maybe just passing through."

Captain Cornwell had met the major commanding Task Force Baker, but neither had gone beyond the courtesy of introduction. "Uh, the Seventh Division guys? They hear anything?"

"No, nothing that'd make them bite their nails."

"So how do you read it, sir?" Everett Rosen asked.

Graham rubbed the day-old stubble on his chin. "We all know the general intel that an enemy offensive is brewing, likely targeted on the more populated areas. Chu Song's, well, not in that picture." Graham cleared his throat. "But we are on the enemy's flank." Chu Song and the airstrip and Task Force Baker were not a real threat, Graham pointed out, until Chris's heavy artillery battery arrived. His guns have the range to cover many of the enemy's exfiltration routes." He chuckled. "Assuming they can put guys where they can tell you when and where to shoot."

Captain Rosen drummed his fingers on his folded map. "Charlie took out the bridge and tried to take out Randy. Here was their last chance to shut Chris down."

After Major Graham left, the officers sat silent, the lieutenants waiting for a captain to speak. Everett noticed Chris was staring at nothing, his chin propped on balled fists. Chris broke the silence. "I think we can stick with fifty-fifty alert. Don't want the men getting worn down only to find nothing happens or it doesn't until, like, next week."

Everett said, "Makes sense, but I'm going to put an OP down in that draw." Chris cocked his head as if puzzled. "Chris, OPs on the wall can see a long way over the jungle, but they can't see *into* it. An OP down in the weeds can't see any better, but they can *hear.* Banking on their ears, not their eyes."

"Okay. You know best." Chris leaned back, clasping his hands behind his head, and scanned the faces around him. "So the shit may hit the fan; we just don't know how or when." He gave a fatalistic chuckle.

"We need to ensure we've got all possible fire support coordinated. Seventh ID's one-oh-fives, Baker's four-deuces and eighty-ones, the ARVN's four-deuces."

"Right," Everett said, adding, "let's also see if we can get some aerial infrared or side-looking radar recons in the area." There followed nods, and then idle chatter broke out, easing the tension Graham's news had brought. The meeting broke up when Chris rose, suddenly feeling the weight of responsibility heavier than ever before.

⚮

Washington, Newsome, and Wodzinski decided to stretch their legs and hopefully find some coffee. After all, now there was a mess tent, and in the field, mess sergeants, if they were any good, always had coffee on, and A Battery's mess sergeant was very good. And since it was getting close to supper time, the coffee would be fresh.

It was, and they weren't the only ones craving a caffeine fix. Several soldiers, including Vasquez and another medic, were nursing mess hall Bakelite coffee cups. "Hey, Sarge, Stevie!" Vasquez called when he saw him. "How're your wounds doing?"

"I don't have any!" Newsome grated in reply.

"Sarge, don't care what you call 'em: injuries, a rash, acne. Like I tell you before, got to think infection. You too, Stevie. Any reddening? Tenderness?" They both denied any problems.

"So, Wash, how's the toe doing?"

For a fleeting moment, he worried about Newsome's stoicism, but he shrugged. If he acted as if it were nothing, it probably was. "Only when I walk on it."

"Swelling?"

"Don't know. Haven't took my boot off."

"But it still hurts, especially when you walk on it?"

"Sorta. Sometimes."

"Lemme look at it."

"Don't wanna take my boot off."

"Don't sweat it, man. We'll get it back on. Besides, with the other company medics here, we have more stuff that might help, you know?"

249

"Okay, Henrique!" Newsome cut in. "I'll drag him over to see you—after we get our coffee, okay?"

"Sure! Then I'll also check your teeny-weeny probably infected scratches too, no?"

A makeshift table with a couple of canvas folding chairs and stools made from empty ammunition boxes was set up in one corner of the tent. The table was for officers and senior NCOs, but since none happened to be around, several soldiers were taking advantage of it to rest their elbows and coffee cups.

Sparky the mascot was lying under the table, his bent tail thumping the floor, full of hope and confidence that someone coming to the table would share something with him. Washington paused when he saw it. "That dog okay?"

"Sparky? He'll rip you to pieces you don't give him something," one of the men at the table said.

"Arlen," Newsome said, "don't pay him no attention. Look. He don't even bark at you anymore. We're part of his pack now."

"Pack, my ass. Aw, okay." He surveyed the men at the table. One was properly dressed to Colonel Greystone's standard, one wore a T-shirt only, and a third was bare chested. When he noticed the latter, Washington blurted, "You didn't get your ass chewed by that colonel for no shirt?"

"Sure did, partner!" he replied, looking up with a slight smirk. "Saw him fly away too!"

"Yes sir! Outta sight, outta mind!" T-Shirt added.

"What about the officers? Bet that colonel gave their asses some shit about it."

"Yeah, but I guess they understand better'n rankers with their air-conditioned trailers."

Newsome nudged Washington in the ribs. "Guess you miss your air conditioning, huh, Arlen?"

"Damn right, Sarge."

As they sat down with their coffees, the fully dressed one asked, "So, you some kind of REMF? Who'd you piss off to get sent out here?"

"Yeah, man," Wodzinski laughed. "Arlen's about as REMF as you can get and still be in country!"

"What, you in Saigon or something? Must've really pissed someone off. What's you do? Tell General Abrams to stuff it?"

"Nah. If I'd seen him, maybe I would've," Arlen replied with a snort and a jerk of his shoulders.

Newsome cut in. "Worse, man. Arlen here's air force. He got shot down the other night. Our outfit picked him up. Haven't been able to get rid of him since."

"You a pilot?"

Washington didn't reply. For reasons he didn't quite grasp, Newsome's quip had hurt.

"Nah, and a good thing too. Arlen here was a gunner on a Spooky gunship. When we picked him up, he had the wits to salvage the miniguns—and one of 'em we were able to get mounted in a fuckin' dump truck, no less. He's our badass gunner now."

"No kidding?" Shirtless said. "Shot down and you're not a crispy critter? Or worse, caught by Charlie? Someone's smiling on you, brother."

"Right. And I'm having a beer in my hooch with the AC full on!" Washington grumbled, shaking off the odd pain.

"Beats a hot beer in hell, don't it?" Shirtless said.

Washington glanced at him and saw a smile that seemed to say the words were truly sympathetic, and something about the smile made him smile back. "Yeah. Ain't much worse'n hot beer."

Just then a platoon sergeant walked into the tent and noticed the men. He came over and stood facing Shirtless and T-Shirt. "Are you gentlemen disrespecting the CO's new dress code policy?" Both men stared at the platoon sergeant almost sheepishly. Neither replied. "Well?"

After another awkward moment, Shirtless spoke. "Yes, Sergeant, we totally respect all uniform policies. Absolutely."

"And you're full of shit as usual, Jackson. Your position ready?"

"Yes, Sergeant. South wall, between Dirksen and Channing on our left and Jefferson and O'Day on our right, Sarge," T-Shirt proudly replied for Shirtless and himself.

"You turkeys know I know if you're bullshitting me. In case you haven't noticed, these walls are really berms. With a good head of steam, a man can damn near run up them from the outside. You know the scoop, so don't let your asses get complacent."

The men at the table said nothing. "So if your shirt's not on, keep it close. Hear a Huey coming in, put it on. Now. Chow for the first and weapons squads in half an hour. Fifty-fifty alert again tonight. Enjoy your coffee."

Washington stifled an urge to laugh with a sour thought about the chief. But with that thought came images of Chief, the last he saw him—Chief on the stretcher being carried to the chopper, glancing at him in passing with a sort of dazed look and a weak smile. It made him uncomfortable. And then he was gone. Then a second image came—that of Chief chewing him out as usual. Then came the last, and most uncomfortable, image: Chief waving at him, shouting at him to come sit with him and Otis. Arlen glanced from the sergeant to Shirtless and T-Shirt and inexplicably it felt good, right then, just being there, and he did laugh aloud. "Right, Chief."

"Who you callin' chief, soldier? Oh, you're the airman."

"Sorry, Sarge. Just used to calling my, uh, sergeant Chief. Our way."

"Lucky man he wasn't on your plane."

"He was," Washington said sharply. "Got a twelve point seven through the leg. Near bled to death. And he saved our ass. A flare, uh, malfunction. Nearly threw his own ass out of the plane gettin' it out before it burned us up."

"Shit. He make it?"

Washington leaned back, looking surprised, almost embarrassed at his own vehemence. Other than Wodzinski and Newsome, he didn't know most of the men there, but his gaze swept over all of them. With the same vehemence, he said, "Yeah, Sarge, he made it. Jus' barely, man, but he made it. He's goin' home. Wife 'n' kids 'n' shit." He was looking at Newsome again. Newsome blinked and looked away. Arlen glanced from the sergeant to Shirtless and T-Shirt. "Yeah, he fuckin' made it."

"And so far, so have we," Shirtless said, and Arlen laughed aloud, took a deep breath, and put his hands flat on the crude table, fingers spread wide, his coffee cup between them.

The platoon sergeant promptly ignored the three men and turned to Sergeant Newsome. "Bud? Your team set up? Good to go?"

"Good as we can get it, Sarge," Newsome replied.

"And what's that mean?"

"South wall, we can cover up to about twenty meters of the base of the wall, maybe thirty toward the east end. The way the truck had to be positioned, the gun's farther from the edge of the west wall, meaning the closest we can cover is maybe seventy-five meters out."

"Let's take a look. We might want to move some M60s." Somewhat reluctantly, Newsom left with the platoon sergeant to take a look. Finding nothing to change, they ended up in Captain Rosen's command post tent with the other officers and senior sergeants. Captain Rosen wanted a final review of their defenses before it got dark. The consensus was that their weaponry was disposed about as well as it could be.

Three issues did come up. First was that one of their two starlight scopes had a malfunction, leaving only one—Ricochet's. Accordingly, Ricochet was once again taken from his buddy Jude and posted to Newsome's dump truck, where he could observe over both the south and west walls. Second was the problem of "dead space"—those areas close to the base of the walls where machine guns could not reach and riflemen would have to dangerously expose themselves by standing up in order to fire down close to the wall. The solution was to order every position to have extra quantities of hand grenades.

The third issue was a weakness at the southwest corner of the fort, for while the ground in front of the walls was generally clear, at that corner a gully had eroded and was full of brush right to the base of the wall. They finally decided that a double extra supply of hand grenades for the men in the OP at that corner, backed up by Newsom's M60, was the best they could do.

"Okay," Captain Rosen summed up. "If anyone comes, we should be able to keep 'em from getting close. If they do, guess we have that covered. Weather's too crappy for any recon flights, so no news there. The terrain says that for us, the biggest risk is on the south and west walls. That brings me to our best weapon, the minigun. Who's manning it?"

"Guess I've got it, sir," Sergeant Newsome said. "The airman, Washington, he's the gunner."

"He's still here? An air force Caribou came in a while ago. No one put him on it?" Everett asked, surprised.

"We were still setting the gun up, sir. No one from the plane came to get him."

"He going to be okay? I mean, he's not—hell, he's never even had army basic training."

Lieutenant Hanley spoke up. "He did okay when we were attacked the other night, sir. His gun pretty much saved the day."

"He is kind of flaky, though, to tell the truth," Sergeant Newsome added.

Everyone stared at him. Lieutenant Hanley, after a moment of hesitation, blurted, "He did save our asses the other night!"

"The gun did, sir. I had to kind of push and shove him to get him into action."

"His crewmate was killed, for God's sake. That's going to unnerve anyone."

"Yes sir! I know!" Newsome replied bitterly. "I lost Kevin while we were saving his ass! Washington needed prodding before Otis was killed." Newsome blew out a breath of air. "Though once he was on the gun, he was good. But that's what I mean by 'kind of flaky.'"

"Anyone else know how to shoot it?" Captain Rosen asked.

Sergeant Newsome replied, "Wodzinski and I do. But Washington knows it inside and out. We get a misfeed, some other problem, he might be the only one who can fix it—or at least fix it fast."

"Well, if the shit hits the fan, think you can push and shove him again if he needs it?"

"Yes sir!"

Captain Rosen nodded, went over a few other administrative matters, and the meeting broke up as the sun kissed the treetops in the west and the vivid greens of the jungle began melting into muddy browns and grays.

Shortly after Newsom returned from the meeting, Ricochet climbed aboard. "Looks like I'm stuck with you guys again. Now, I don't want no repetition of the last time I was stuck with you."

"Amen!" Sergeant Newsome said. "Where's your buddy Jude? Who's babysitting him?"

"Jude? Sarge, if there's any babysitting, it'll be Jude doing it. Anyway, he's right over there, less 'n ten meters. We're kind of stretched thin, but there's guys on both sides not more 'n five meters from him. Anyway, if shit happens on that side, I'll be covering him. If it gets real close, I'll join him."

It got dark, though not totally dark. A waxing moon was marginally successful in getting some light through the cloud cover—just enough for the world to have some semblance of shape in various shades of charcoal and ash. Washington found himself on watch with Ricochet. Arlen watched Ricochet fiddle with his starlight scope, put the rifle to his shoulder, peer into the eyepiece, and scan. He heard him say, "Shit!"

"What?"

"We got fuckin' ground fog. Just a thin layer but can't see through it for squat."

"Can I look?"

Ricochet handed him the rifle. "Don't shoot anyone."

"Even a chink?"

"Don't want to give our position away," he replied soberly, and then he chuckled.

Arlen laughed. "Hey, cool! I can see the tents! Most of 'em, anyway—not the bottoms. Yeah, now I see the fog." Bored with the film of ground fog that hid the airstrip, he aimed the rifle inside the fort. There was no mist inside. Cannon, trucks, and tents all jumped into view, as did huddled forms of sleeping soldiers. Bright points of light appeared and faded as some who were awake took drags on their cigarettes.

For Ricochet, it seemed minutes passed as Washington examined every corner of the Fort through the starlight scope. Washington raised his aim slightly and sighted along the walls. Niches had been cut into the walls, sort of half foxholes, and he could see two men in each, one standing, peering out, and one with only his legs showing dangling over the ledge, the body slumped inside the niche, sleeping or trying to. Arlen suddenly handed the rifle back to Ricochet with a single word. "Shit!"

"What's shit?"

"Enemy come up them walls, I can't hose 'em. Our guys are right there. No way to miss 'em! I can't—can't protect 'em! Shit!"

"Can't aim in front of 'em?"

"No sights. Can't hold it that steady anyways. Enemy gets close, man—like, up on the walls—I can't hose 'em."

"Then I guess we'd better hose them out there, huh?"

"Guess we'd better. But with that fog, how we gonna do that?"

"It should go away or lift soon," Ricochet replied, hoping it was true. Conversation stopped as Ricochet returned to scanning with the starlight scope, trying to see hints through the thin blanket of ground fog. Washington stared into the dark, occasionally biting his nails until he managed to turn off his thoughts and imagination to again become just a watchdog in the night.

CHAPTER 20

ROCKETS' RED GLARE

The attack came in three waves—the first from the north, aimed at Task Force Baker—and began with a barrage of rockets. For the enemy, the weather was perfect. The light ground fog that had frustrated Ricochet had persisted, and thickening cloud cover blocked almost all moonlight, providing a perfect cloak.

With the first rocket explosion in Task Force Baker's area, sleeping soldiers jerked awake, among them Staff Sergeant Nelson Ferreia, roaring his men out of their sleeping trenches and to their guns while he stood, assessing what was happening. He had twenty years in. He had been a private in the Korean War, had risen to corporal and been busted back to private, made sergeant, lost his stripes again, and finally made master sergeant, but a year ago, he had lost a stripe again. Temper control and suffering fools were not among Nelson Ferreia's strengths.

By the luminous hands of his watch, he saw it was twenty minutes past one in the morning. Sergeant Ferreia's gun jeeps were powerful weapons. They could destroy any known tank up to a mile away. But they were designed for warfare on the rolling fields and forests of Europe. Having no armor protection and it being impossible to hide the brilliant flash of flames when fired, they were designed to shoot from ambush and then quickly move and hide before the enemy could fire back. In static positions, such as Task Force Baker's, they were vulnerable to both rocket grenades and small arms. So Ferreia had dug his guns in, using jeep-sized holes about two feet deep with ramps at the rear so they could pull in and out. Walls of sandbags rose another foot or so. The walls couldn't hide the guns, for they had to be able to fire, but they did offer some protection for the crews. In his first exposure to combat in Korea, Ferreia had learned to value concealment—hence the sprawling camouflage nets made more inconspicuous by tufts of grass stuffed in the netting. In daylight, one could see something was there, but not what, and at night they looked like low hillocks.

The enemy's 122 mm rockets had large warheads and screamed through the air but were very inaccurate compared to artillery or mortars. They seemed to land randomly, more often striking outside the defenses than inside. The first had exploded between two bunkers on the northern side of the perimeter. The second, a minute or so later, fell on the airstrip, not too far from one of the bunkered storage tents. "Jesus!" he cried; if one hit the ammo bunker, his men would be toast. Grabbing his PRC-6 platoon radio, he jumped back into a shallow trench beside the jeep's dugout and called his platoon leader, who could not enlighten him. He asked for illumination, and his platoon leader said he would check with the CO. Two rocket explosions later, he was informed that the CO did not want to make it easier for the enemy to adjust fire and that there was as yet no sign of enemy movement to the front.

Ferreia knew "front" meant the north side of their perimeter—the side facing Cambodia. But the ammo and supply tents on the airstrip seemed at least as likely a target for a ground attack. If an attack did come on his side, Ferreia realized that it would come out of the low ground on the far side of the airstrip; and with the ground fog, the enemy could be almost on them before anyone could see them. Even the new guys in the old fort were unlikely to see the enemy before he did.

Almost a mile to the west, Major Graham did not hear the rockets striking, for he was asleep, and at that distance, the sound was not enough to waken him. But he was awakened by his operations sergeant, who had been on watch. Surrounded by a few hundred South Vietnamese troops, his team did not usually maintain a night watch. But he had had an intuition that something might happen. He could not get out of his mind the possible import of the "trails of many feet" Thieu's patrols had found. "Major." Sergeant Beeker shook him awake. "Second of the Tenth's got incoming!"

"Any details?"

"Rockets. From near or across the border."

"Okay. Let me get my boots on. I'll go see Captain Thieu. See what you can get from Green Granite."

"Right, sir." Just as Sergeant Beeker turned to leave, Captain Thieu knocked on the bunker entry.

"Tiu Ta?" Moments later, Thieu and Graham were looking at a map in Thieu's command bunker. "What do you think, Major?"

Graham wasn't quite sure what he thought. The one report hardly painted a picture. While he was stroking his chin and searching for a reply, Sergeant Beeker stuck his head in. "Sir. Green Granite reports no activity on their side. Just rockets coming in on Second of the Tenth's positions. One did hit on the airfield."

"None around them?"

"No sir."

"Thanks." Graham turned back to the map, standing beside Thieu. "Rockets here, not here. Many feet here. What do you think?"

Captain Thieu waggled his fingers in front of his mouth, struggling to find a word. "Disguise? Hide true act."

Graham reached to his left, wriggling his fingers. "Distraction over here?" Then he reached out with his right hand and seemed to grab something in the air, "But the tiger is here?"

Thieu chuckled. "I make poor English, you make poor Vietnamese, but I think we say same thing." After a brief silence, he added, "I call regiment. No authority to help."

"Ah, I understand." Graham waited, sensing that Thieu would need permission from his superiors to actually do something.

Captain Thieu returned from his radio, stared at the map a moment, and then turned his gaze from the map to Graham. "But maybe danger to my base. I say maybe I send patrols out to check for enemy. Regiment say okay."

Graham nodded. "Good. Where?"

Captain Thieu pointed to the draw that ran along the south side of the airstrip. His finger touched where the draw crossed the highway and then petered out by the hill his battalion occupied. "I will keep defense strong. Send reserve company with recon platoon to check for enemy here." He ran his finger a short way down into the draw. "What you think, Major?"

"Strong patrol."

"Maybe many enemy, yes? My patrols found sign of many feet."

"Yes. Good idea to find out."

"Tres bien. We go."

"We?" Graham smiled. Captain Thieu wasn't sending a patrol; he'd be taking it.

Captain Rosen had placed two-man OPs at each corner of the wall, and a full squad on an OP some two hundred meters down into the draw south and slightly west of the fort. For clear communication and reference, each was given a letter. On the fort, Alpha was the southwest corner—the most critical corner, in Rosen's mind—lettered clockwise to Delta on the southeast corner and Echo for the OP in the draw. The soldier on watch in OP Bravo on the northwest corner of the old fort happened to see the distant streak of fire marking the launch of the first rocket. It was pencil thin and seemed quite far away. He had never seen anything like that before and idly wondered what it might have been until he heard its screaming arrival and explosion. He still didn't know what he'd seen, but he knew it wasn't good news. He called it in and woke his companion.

The explosion woke Captain Rosen, and a moment later he heard of the report from OP Bravo. As he scrambled up the slope to the OP to see what was happening, he heard the second rocket hit. As soon as he got to the top, the soldier told him what he'd seen. "First one hit over in Second of the Tenth's area. Second just now hit on the airstrip, sir."

"Sounds like rockets, Carson. Where'd you see the flash?"

"That way, sir."

"Got a compass?"

"No sir."

"Huh. All ops should," he snorted. "I should have thought of it. Anyway, here's mine. Aim it best you can where it went off."

"Sir." As he aimed the compass, he saw a third flash. "Shit, sir! Another! Just about the same direction." He aimed the compass. "Uh, looks like azimuth 340." Just as he said the last word, they heard a shriek in the air and then an explosion, this time well away from the airstrip and inside Task Force Baker's area.

Everett called OP Alpha on the southwest corner. They did have a compass, and he told them where to look and to get a bearing on it. Turning back to the men in OP Bravo, he ordered, "Keep the compass for now. Get a bearing on the next one. Call it in." He scrambled down the bank and ran to the battery fire control center. Chris Cornwell was already there. He took a piece of paper and borrowed a ruler and compass from the plotters. He drew a line representing the west wall and marked the distance between the two OPs. Then he drew another representing the relative direction to the flash. There came a fourth explosion, and both OPs reported the direction to the flash of the launch. He drew another line and had a triangle. Then he used the known length of the west wall to measure the distance to where the two sight lines crossed. It was between ten and twelve kilometers.

Chris translated the direction and distance to a map. "Looks like the bastards could be in Cambodia," he announced, "or just this side, maybe."

Everett asked, "We can do counter battery fire, right? We are being shot at!"

"I'll have to check with Battalion, Ev." Chris called Battalion, which passed the request to Corps. Several more rockets landed, and with more bearings, they got a better fix on the launch site, which now looked to be on their side of the border. They did get permission to fire if the target was inside Vietnam. They did, knowing their fix on the launch site would not be very accurate and it would be dumb luck to actually hit a launcher. It might scare them, though.

The dump truck had been pulled partway down the ramp to get the gun out of sight but still high enough to let a man in the truck bed see over the walls. Wodzinski had been on watch, cradling Ricochet's M16 with the starlight scope, and heard the first rocket explode. Partly because the walls of the fort and the truck muted the sound, it seemed rather distant, and he didn't get very concerned. The second, landing on the airstrip, woke the rest of the crew. After Wodzinski updated him on what little he'd seen and heard, Sergeant Newsome told Wodzinski, "Give Ricochet the scope and get Hutchinson up. If this shit keeps up, we might need to back up onto the ramp." Then he clambered out of the truck and onto the wall to talk to the men manning OP Alpha.

Arlen was the last of the four to drag himself out of his poncho liner. Standing at his gun, he was head and shoulders above the wall, but there was little he could make out beyond the hints of the fort as he scanned a full circle, nervously asking what was going on. No one answered, because no one knew. Then another rocket struck. Washington heard the scream as it fell, saw the flash of light from the explosion reflected off the low clouds, and heard Ricochet curse as the flash was amplified in his eyepiece. With no muting barriers between it and his ears, it was not just a loud noise but a concussive blow to the eardrums. Even though it was some distance away, it was clearly bigger and meaner than the mortar explosions he'd experienced in the attack a few days before. The flash and sound of the mortar round that had blown up the gun truck jumped into his thoughts, and he began to imagine the same fate coming to his dump truck. *It would. Just my fucking luck.* But he had happened to be looking across the fort when the rocket struck, and by the flash of the explosion faintly reflected from the low clouds, the interior of the fort was revealed like an underexposed photograph—a frozen moment of men scrambling among a welter of equipment and the four massive guns. In an instant, his mind shifted from imagining the next rocket obliterating him and his gun to it landing in the middle of the compound, obliterating all those guys while the steel sides of the truck spared him. Abruptly, he felt torn, inexplicably uncertain which would be worse. Just as these thoughts—or, more accurately, feelings—were expressed, they seemed to explode into reality in a series of fiery flashes and concussive blasts of sound in the heart of the compound.

With a silent curse of dismay, he slumped down in the gun's crib, eyes shut and hands over his ears. A moment later, he couldn't bear just sitting there; he had to see. He pushed himself up and forced his eyes to the interior of the compound just as a second series of blasts hammered him. This time he recognized what they were; the sleeping dinosaurs had awakened and belched great tongues of flame. It was fascinating as each illuminated a giant smoke ring that flew away into the night. Weirdly, it brought a memory: an old man, his tight curls perfectly white, sitting beside Big Ma on the stoop, smoking a fat cigar and blowing perfect smoke rings for a little boy.

"Hey, Stevie!" he shouted, using Wodzinski's first name for the first time. "Something's up. Something's up!" Then he noticed that Wodzinski was the only other one of the crew still in the truck bed. "Where's Sarge and Hutchinson?"

"He's over at the OP seeing what's up. Hutch is cranking up in case we have to get the truck up into shooting position. I'll check our ammo."

"I'll find what goin' on." Arlen abandoned the gun, and as he scrambled out of the truck to follow Newsome, he glimpsed the red glow of Wodzinski's flashlight as he inspected the ammunition feed for the gun, and the sight sparked a brief sense of comfort. He could just make out Newsome's prone form beside the deeper, uneven muddle of the two men in the OP dugout. "What's up, Sarge?"

"I'd get my ass down if I was you, Arlen. Rocket attack. Coming from over yonder. Maybe from across the border. Smithy here says they're mostly landing around the grunts across the road. Looks like Charlie's after the boys over there."

After a long moment of silence, Washington asked, "Back the truck up?"

"No. Not yet." Arlen crawled back to the truck. Deciding OP Alpha had no useful information, Newsome followed Arlen.

They would halfway hold their breath, waiting for the next rocket, and then empty their lungs in a rush when it screamed in and they discovered it had not been close and they were still there.

The dinosaurs fell silent, and at some point, the next rocket did not come, but there began a series of smaller, more familiar explosions, closer together in time—mortar shells, one every fifteen to thirty seconds, marching across the western part of Baker's perimeter. This was soon followed by the sound of small arms in the distance. "Looks like the grunts across the road are getting it," Sergeant Newsome said. Just then one of the men in OP Alpha called to the truck, "Hey guys! OP Echo just called in. Sounds of movement close by. Echo's pulling back."

"Movement? What—where?" Washington blurted.

Newsome gestured to the southwest. "Over there, down in that jungle."

Washington stared into the darkness. "There" felt a hell of a lot closer than the shelling and shooting in the other direction. "Pulling back? What for?"

"So they don't get fuckin' overrun! You hear movement in the jungle, buddy, it ain't a mile away; it's a few meters is all!" Arlen felt a chill sweep over him as he again saw the host of shadows that had swarmed at him before.

Sergeant Newsome poked him. "Get the gun ready, Arlen." Then he shouted, "Hutch! Back this bastard up!" He then yelled to one of the men in OP Alpha, "Smithy! Call for some illumination!"

The news from OP Echo spread like wildfire, fanned by a brief but close burst of small-arms fire not from Task Force Baker's side but from the southwest, where OP Echo had been. The men of the engineer platoon, the fort's primary reserve force, assembled almost as if on parade. Everett Rosen's First Sergeant strode up to them. "You men have been in a firefight before. You clean your weapons since?" They all had. "You check your magazines, the last one you used, to make sure it's full?" Not everyone had. "Fill 'em up, meatheads!" He pointed to Lucius, the grader operator. "You, son! Know where the ammo is?" He didn't, but the man next to him did, and they both were ordered off to get ammo to distribute. "You guys have your selectors set on auto?" Most did. "Then switch them to semiauto! Never go on auto unless you absolutely have to!" The faint sounds of selectors being reset followed. "Hand grenades?" As the first sergeant stalked among the men, he cussed them through a checklist that seemed to cover everything except retirement benefits. Then he began going over contingencies. Some of Randy's men had met Everett's first sergeant. Some had seen him, but none knew him. Yet his abrasively commanding manner was not so much comforting as invigorating. He was a grunt, and he had lots of stripes, so he must know his shit, so they must be in good hands.

The sounds of mortar explosions and small-arms fire continued, somewhat muffled and seemingly more distant because of the fort's walls. The men were no longer strangers to such sounds, and their very distance seemed to push attention away from them.

Up in the dump truck, the sounds of battle were distant but not so muffled. Washington was at the gun, and he and Wodzinski verified all was ready for the gun to fire. Ricochet's starlight scope revealed the ground fog thinning some, undulating and showing gaps from a fitful breeze, but enough remained that the scope was still not useful. They had spent time during the day relocating the taped letters to mark new sectors of fire. Now, in the dark, Washington practiced with Wodzinski holding the light, to the accompaniment of the distant crack of rifle fire, burps of automatic weapons, the crumps of mortar shells exploding, and the softer crumps as Task Force Baker's mortars fired back. As they practiced, they all gnawed on a question: if the enemy was attacking the north side of Task Force Baker, what the hell had OP Echo run into?

Captain Rosen was busy on radios. He could not get a clear status report from the group across the road. He hadn't heard from OP Echo since the burst of small-arms fire. Major Graham had called, and he had passed on what he knew. Graham reminded him he could call on Captain Thieu's heavy mortars. "The Baker guys are firing some illumination, eighty-ones, but off to the north. Not helping us much here. I've only got five illumination rounds. Over"

"Okay. Where do you want it? Over."

"I don't ... hell ... the wind ... I don't know. Over."

"Can't be much wind anyway. How about fifty meters west of you and on the south side of the runway? Then see how it drifts. Over." Rosen agreed, and Graham replied, "Nothing going at my end. Expect illumination in two, three minutes. Out."

Everett alerted his OPs and platoon leaders.

Major Graham informed Captain Thieu of the request and then passed it on to Sergeant Beeker, who had remained behind with his deputy while he and Captain Thieu had accompanied the reinforced reserve company on his "security patrol."

On the northern front, the enemy sappers were maneuvering to get close enough to fire RPGs at the sandbagged defensive positions. This was challenging, because on that side the Americans had cleared most of the undergrowth out to a good distance from the perimeter. Defenders and attackers were exchanging small-arms fire at ranges of over two hundred yards, the fire from both sides being largely ineffective. This was in part because the GIs in their bunkers were tending to hunker as low as they could because of the continuing mortar fire, and that caused a tendency to fire high; and the relatively more exposed enemy, now also subject to both mortar and artillery fire, crouched as low as they could in what shelter they could find and so also tended to fire high.

All this was drawing attention and firepower to the north side, confirming the task force leaders' preconceptions.

Anxious to see what the illumination round would reveal, if anything, Everett scrambled up the inner face of the west wall to join his platoon leader responsible for the western half of the fort's defenses. The first illumination round from Captain Thieu's heavy mortar ignited

266

high overhead and revealed empty swaths of runway and thinning patches of ground fog.

As he watched the flare drift ever so slowly northwestward and downward, Everett couldn't decide whether he was relieved or disappointed. It seemed pointless, for the moment, to call for another, and he returned to his command post to let Major Graham know the negative results.

For Arlen Washington and others on the wall who were in a position to see, the flare brought a flood of relief, tempered somewhat by the concealing darkness beyond its reach.

Walking beside Captain Thieu as they crossed the macadamed surface of highway QL-99, Major Graham felt as if he were in an adventure, not a war, and the queer lightness in his mood gave him pause. There was nothing visible or audible to account for it—no exhilarating vistas or musical breezes. Quite the opposite; he was surrounded by the cloying darkness of an overcast, humid night suffused with the disembodied sounds of shuffling feet and of brush grasping at clothing. He should be filled with the trepidation and glumness suited to an approach march toward a possible battle of completely uncertain nature and outcome. But he wasn't.

They crossed the road near a large culvert where the highway crossed the draw and descended a gentle brush-covered slope into the draw that, widening and deepening, eventually led past the south side of the old French fort. It came to him that the night felt like an adventure because he was with Captain Thieu, and it was his almost entrepreneurial, insouciant boldness and initiative that flavored the night. Soon he found himself among trees, and there the brush thinned somewhat, making walking easier, but shortly after, the column stopped. He was about to ask what was up when he felt a tug on his sleeve. Being shorthanded, Graham had shown up for the patrol carrying a radio on his back, for the only radio that had the range and reliability needed on the patrol was the PRC-25 backpack radio.

When Captain Thieu saw him, he announced it was improper for an officer to be so burdened and appointed a soldier to carry it over Jim's weak protests. The soldier spoke no English, but all he had to know was to stick close to the American major and get his attention whenever a sound came over the radio. He took the handset, announced his call sign, listened a moment, and closed the call. Just as he did, Thieu's radio crackled and his radio operator handed him the handset. After several soft-spoken exchanges, Thieu explained to Jim, "Scouts find two trails, come from south, turn east. What do you think, Major?"

"East along this draw?"

Captain Thieu nodded. "Where do you think they go?"

"I think they are up there, somewhere. Preparing to attack."

"Da. I will send scouts ahead. We wait here with the company. See what they find." Thieu smiled at Jim's nod and added, "Major, you like to go with them?"

Jim laughed. "My duty is to support you, Captain."

"Yes, but I think you maybe crazy enough to want to go."

Graham replied with his best poker face, "I'm trying not to be crazy, but very, very, very, very cautious like you."

It was Captain Thieu's turn to chuckle. "No, I think you cannot change craziness. Cautious soldier would drive down Chu Song highway maybe a few hundred meters then come back to fire base, find out where I am. No, only crazy soldier goes all the way. And only crazy man drives from Chu Song at night dressed like Vietcong, shouting 'Shoot! Shoot!'"

"I was shouting 'Friend! Friend!'"

"Ha! My sentries say you cry 'Shoot!' and one say you cry 'Shoot Bread, Shoot Bread!' No one heard 'Friend!' You forget to make sentence. Shouting one word very confusing, especially with bad, ah, inflection. Yes, inflection." He chuckled again. "Better shout in English next time. Then guards know for sure you not VC."

Thieu knew the Americans had something in Chu Song Graham called a "station" that he'd been visiting that particular evening. The station agents who might have been CIA but never said so were very hospitable, generous with good scotch and bourbon, and had offered a maid to launder their dirty clothes during his visit, giving Graham and his driver pajama-like shirts and pants to wear while waiting for the maid to return with the clean uniforms and underwear. Unfortunately, through some sort of miscommunication, the maid had gone home for the night with the uniforms, leaving them in black pajamas. They could have spent the night at the station, but Graham convinced himself that would be the night Captain Thieu would have desperate need of American fire support, leaving him with no choice but to drive in the dead of night from Chu Song to Thieu's base through local force roadblocks and Thieu's outposts dressed like Vietcong.

"I am supposed to be your advisor. I'm afraid I am doing far more learning than advising. For example, I learned that wisdom and caution fade after three glasses of scotch."

"Then we will work together; you not too crazy, me not too cautious. Make harmony and balance." They both laughed.

To Everett it seemed a long time had passed since the illumination round, and he cursed himself for not noting the time that the flare had revealed an empty airstrip. OP Echo had stumbled into an enemy patrol. Their exchange of fire had been brief as both parties separated in opposite directions. Echo had then laid low for a few minutes before making it back to the fort. Everett radioed news of that brief contact to Task Force Baker and to Major Graham, also asking Graham for another illumination round. Then he headed to the center of the west wall to see the lieutenant leading the defense of the west wall. Just as he arrived, the next flare kindled its brilliant white light, and it was as if a hundred hearts suddenly stopped beating. "Jesus Christ!" he and his lieutenant shouted in unison.

CHAPTER 21

OVERRUN

Everett Rosen's education had included military history, so he knew how enemies adapt dynamically to each other; sometimes before conflict but always in the course of conflict, as they learn the habits, capabilities, and weaknesses of their opponents. Then they strive to compensate for their weaknesses and the opponent's strengths, leverage their own strengths, and exploit the opponent's weaknesses. Struggling to absorb the harshly illuminated scene, Everett briefly retreated into this intellectualism as a defense against paralyzing shock and fear at the enemy's adaptations seemingly perfectly realized: *Don't attack without greatly superior numbers; neutralize American air power with bad weather; avoid detection with the cover of night, the jungle, or misdirection; neutralize American superior artillery and mortars by getting too close for them to be effective.*

Now Everett and the defenders of Fort Frog saw them in practice. Through diversion and stealth, the enemy had gained surprise, closing swiftly on the airfield and the fort with greatly superior numbers, and

270

many were already too close for artillery or mortars to help much. The enemy had not, however, anticipated everything.

Between the dying of the first flare and the igniting of the second, several hundred enemy had swarmed out of the draw, crossing the airstrip toward the tented storage bunkers and the west wall in what would prove the second phase of the attack. Although partly screened by the ground fog, there was no mistaking the scale of the attack. From his perch, Washington could see some were already disappearing from his view, too close to the wall for his gun to bear on them. Two thoughts, each more a mix of feeling and image than actual thought, fought for his attention: one that any moment they would be swarming over the wall toward him, the other that there were too many of them for everyone else to shoot, but he and only he could. He crouched, sighted along the barrels, spun them up and imagined a line running roughly from the far end of the tents diagonally to his corner of the fort, right through the heart of the swarm. He didn't wait for Newsom call out a sector or target or give an order but pressed the trigger and sliced the line with a saber of fire.

It was not just that in a matter of seconds almost one in ten of the enemy on the airstrip had become a casualty, it was the shock and confusion from the completely unexpected that was worse than the sudden carnage. Exacerbating this, Washington's fiery saber had sliced through the forward command group of the attack, breaking central control and communication with higher commanders.

Everett watched the attack stumble and all but stop, and for a moment, hope replaced shock not just in him but also in his men as intense small-arms and machine gun fire broke out along the wall. Junior leaders of enemy between the line of Arlen's fiery path and the fort soon recovered, took control of those they could, and led a rush to the west wall of the fort. It was not only their target but was also the nearest shelter from the surprise weapon that had decimated their force and split them in two.

Briefly mesmerized by the shift from stalled chaos to chaotic assault, like a riptide shoving the surf on a Carolina shore, it took Everett a moment to realize it was numbers, not organization, that now mattered. From the base of the wall, men scrambled over each other to reach the top, like ants building bridges with their bodies. Bayonets and rifle butts jammed into the earth gave leverage, and up they came.

Looking left and right, Everett realized again the limitations of the fort. The parapet of the earthen walls was not wide enough for men to dig foxholes in, so they had dug cutouts, niches, on the inside of the wall, where they could kneel or stand and fire over the top with minimal exposure; but to fire at enemy already at the wall, they had to rise up and expose their torsos. Everett shouted to his platoon leader, "Harry! Grenades! Use the grenades!" But his order was superfluous; the men were already pulling the safety pins on their hand grenades and rolling them down the face of the wall. The first wave of grenades created carnage, but after that, they had much less effect. They were falling between and under bodies before detonating. The dead and dying were shielding the living.

Everett did not see that. He felt almost cowardly leaving his lieutenant and sliding back down into the fort to rejoin his radio operator and get reports from other sectors, which were hard to understand, for now the air was full of noise.

What Sergeant Ferreia saw when the second flare burst to again briefly burn the night away from the airstrip was just as shocking. His shock was amplified by the mournful, hooting roar of the minigun, the myriad ricocheting tracers arcing above the storage tents, and the sudden, brief, shocked silence of men and weapons that followed. Moments later, through the space between the storage bunkers and the west wall of the fort, he saw what the men in the fort could not—dozens of enemy crowding at the base of the wall and swarming toward the road. Indeed, the gap between the wall and the storage bunkers that blocked much of his view was black with enemy silhouettes. He was with the crew of the gun nearest the west wall and shouted to raise the front of the camouflage net clear of the gun's muzzle and the gunner's sight. Seconds later, he clapped his hands over his ears and shouted, "Fire when ready!"

The loader checked behind the jeep, slapped the gunner on the shoulder, and shouted "Clear!" The gunner peered through the telescopic sight, traversed the gun slightly and adjusted its elevation, and pressed the trigger on the .50-caliber spotting rifle attached to the gun. A bright tracer tore through the shadows clustered at the base of the wall. Instantly, he reversed his action on the trigger, firing the main gun. Great lances of flame like rocket exhausts shot forward from the muzzle and backward from holes in the breech of the gun. The opposing blasts were exactly balanced, and the gun didn't move as it launched the four- -inch-wide and nearly foot-long shell.

It was not an antitank shell but an antipersonnel shell. It flew a short distance and broke open, releasing hundreds of flechettes—steel darts that hummed weirdly in their supersonic flight. Anyone who ever heard them pass—and survived—would never forget the sound. With the flechette round, the 106 mm antitank gun became a giant shotgun. A moment later, Ferreia's second gun, fifty yards down the road and beyond the storage bunkers, fired a second giant shotgun blast.

The surviving enemy on the far side of Arlen's sweep had begun to retreat toward the safety of the draw. Ferreia's second shotgun blast and a second sweep by Arlen turned that drift into a rout, as Arlen could and did sweep after the retreating enemy as one might sweep a walk with a hose. Those that reached the relative safety of the draw began to reorganize to focus their effort on the southwest corner of the fort, which they could approach through the cover offered by the draw and where dense brush and trees offered concealment almost to the base of the wall but also concealed from them a rugged ravine that was as much an obstacle as a screen.

To the enemy escaping the fire of the minigun by crowding toward the fort wall, the blast of Ferreia's recoilless rifle loudly announced that they had jumped from the frying pan into the fire, yet withdrawal back into the minigun's field of fire was hardly an option.

Enemy that had not quite reached the wall when Ferreia's gun fired fell back to the cover of the tented storage bunkers, which seemed to be out of the line of fire of both weapons. But they, too, were trapped.

The enemy group closest to the road and Ferreia's gun, decimated by it, realized that whatever the weapon was, it had to be quickly destroyed or neutralized. Likewise, the rest of the survivors along the wall realized that the carnage from the hand grenades could be ended only by scaling the wall and taking it.

The battlefield was now being steadily illuminated by Captain Thieu's heavy mortars and Seventh Division's artillery. Even so, it was hard to pinpoint Ferreia's guns because of their camouflage nets. The best they could do was concentrate their rifle fire on the hummock shape, which forced the gun crew to drop down beside the jeep, out of the line of enemy fire. Ferreia crawled down the line to a machine gun crew and coordinated with them to spray the enemy on his signal. He then waved to the loader, who was watching from behind the sandbags. The machine gun opened up, the enemy fire dropped off, and the gun crew leaped into action.

Of the many bullets fired at the hummock, by chance one went straight down the barrel of the gun and became wedged between the warhead of the shell loaded in it and the barrel. The designers of the recoilless rifle had carefully calculated how much propellant charge would be needed to propel the warhead out the muzzle at the desired velocity and blow enough hot gases out the back to exactly balance the recoil. But with the bullet wedged in the barrel, it was like trying to shove open a door with a wedge under it. It might be done, but only with a lot more force. In this case, more force than the gun could stand.

Ferreia saw only a little flame come out of the muzzle, a great gout of flame flare to the rear, and a third gout that shot upward, shredding the camouflage net. The gross imbalance between gases escaping forward and backward threw the gun and the jeep violently forward. Ferreia ran to the gun, and yanked the torn and burning camouflage net free, only to find the gunner and driver dead, almost torn apart, and the loader on the ground looking for his missing left forearm.

Sickened and furious, Ferreia put a tourniquet on the gunner's ruined arm, got the medics to him, and then ran to his other gun jeep. Arriving there, he could hear that the battle at the west wall of the fort was still intense, and to him it meant the bastards who'd destroyed his crew were still there.

Ferreia's view of those bastards was now blocked by the storage bunkers and the tents that covered them. He looked at his driver. "Back out of here, pull across the road but not past the tent."

"You sure, Sarge?"

"I gave you a fuckin' order, Jimmy; what do you think?"

The jeep jerked backward, bounced out from under its camouflage netting, swerved, and shot across the road. Ferreia called to the gunner, "Flechette loaded?"

"Got it here, Sarge," the loader replied, pointing to a shell gripped between his knees.

"Load!" Ferreia dismounted, peered around the corner of the bunker, and then ran back to the jeep. "The fuckers are there! And the guys in the fort are in deep shit. Pull ahead of the bunker, turn to aim at the fort, and stop. Range—call it a hundred and fifty meters. Base of the wall. Aim at the thickest bunch." The jeep surged forward, turned hard left and braked.

The gunner adjusted the elevation and traverse. "Ready, Sarge."

The loader looked behind them and shouted "Clear!" slapping the gunner on his helmet.

"Then fire!"

Flame shot out fore and aft. The crush of enemy at the wall looked like a garden of black flowers planted at its base swaying in a breeze. With the blast of flechettes, a swatch of the garden simply collapsed as if an invisible weed whacker had swept through. But along the rest of the wall, they could see surviving black figures leaping and scrambling over the wall, as much to escape the flechettes as to press the attack. Ferreia's gun has again decimated the enemy, but its main effect was to spur on a desperate assault.

At they loaded another flechette round, Ferreia and his crew came under fire from the enemy near the bunkers and from across the airstrip and were forced to withdraw before they could fire again. Worse, his loader took a bullet through his cheek that smashed several upper teeth but miraculously missed his tongue. There was no good way to bandage the wound, and Ferreia drove straight to the medic's tent.

The enemy grouped by the storage tents had realized the best they could do was to keep up a steady suppressive fire on the wall to protect their comrades at the base and give them enough respite to organize and launch an assault over the wall. And the enemy at the wall organized a party to slip down the wall to take out the gun at its southwest corner.

Soon the volume of defensive small arms and grenade fire from defenders on the west wall began to fall off.

Now mortar fire was beginning to fall on the airfield. While it could not be brought close enough to the enemy groups on the airstrip to do them real damage, it had the effect, along with the fear of Washington's and Ferreia's guns, of reducing their options, it seemed, to two: victory or death.

Even as the defense of the west wall weakened, the noise of the battle—the explosions of grenades, rifle and machine gun fire, and the shouts and cries of men—seemed not to slacken. Washington's position was too far back from the lip of the wall to see what was going on near the wall on the enemy side. Farther out, the airstrip was all but clear of enemy except for corpses and the bunch hunkering by the sandbagged storage tents. Knowing tons of ammunition was stored in some, he was afraid to shoot there, and when he saw enemy popping up over the wall, he couldn't shoot there either, for fear of hitting remaining defenders. They were too close. In the cacophony, he didn't hear—or, rather, didn't notice—the frequent pinging of bullets against the sides of the dump truck or the fainter snaps of their passage through the nearby air.

Sergeant Newsome and Ricochet began to realize that the enemy by the storage tents were a major threat to the defenders on the wall. Newsome scrambled to Washington and shouted to him to fire on the enemy by the storage tents. Washington shouted back he couldn't because there were munitions stored in them. "Hell, they're sandbagged up like four, five feet! Shoot below them!" Newsome shouted. "Those assholes are picking off our guys!"

"Sarge, I can't aim this thing that good! You know it's got no sights!"

"Shit! No! Wait. Walk your fire to them. Watch me!" He scrambled back to his M60, braced it on the tailgate of the dump truck, aimed low, and fired, watching his bullets kick up small fountains of dirt well short of the enemy. As he slowly raised his aim, by the tracers and light of the flares, Washington could track the march of Newsome's bullets toward the tents. Washington followed suit, using very short bursts, and then swept the enemy line. The minigun fire was deadly, and the surviving enemy there scattered, some moving backward, others forward, breaking their ability to put effective fire on the defenders on the west wall. Still, that relief was all but too late for the defenders.

While Washington could not see much of what was happening on the enemy side of the west wall, he could see what was going on inside. He saw the faint puffs of light from the infantry's mortar as it was fired. He saw a large group of men clustered near two of the big cannons and what looked like the lanky figure of Lieutenant Hanley and the stouter, barrel-like figure of Captain Cornwell. Looking along the west wall, though, he could see only four or five men firing. He saw one jerk upright and fall backward into the compound. He saw another—he thought it might be an officer, for he was brandishing a pistol—scramble to the where the man had been and begin firing, and then he, too, suddenly jerked backward, slipped, and slid down the bank into the compound. He saw heads begin to appear above the outside of the wall. He swung the gun in that direction and bit his lip, stifling a shout, for he still dared not fire. There were still defenders there, though pitifully few.

Arlen's hands trembled on the gun handles. A hundred yards out, he could shoot the hell out of them, but they weren't the danger. The ones he needed to shoot, he couldn't. If he fired at the enemy on the wall, he'd surely hit the very guys he needed to protect—the handful still holding the wall. It was all going to shit again. It had been his idea to put the gun where it was, and it looked as if, somehow, he'd fucked that up, and now he was watching men die for it. He felt like screaming, but he simply stared.

A flash and a deafening explosion came from just beyond the rear of the truck. A hand grenade, thrown in from the outside, had exploded between the truck and the OP on the southwest corner, killing one of the men and wounding the other. Newsome jumped out of the truck with his machine gun and sprayed the enemy on the slope nearby. As he did, a bullet glanced off the top of his helmet. He dropped below the wall, put his weapon down and turned his attention to the wounded man. "They okay?" Washington shouted.

"No! You two keep your eyes peeled!" Newsome shouted in reply.

Washington did, or tried to. The battle was getting closer to him. Fear began to grip like choking vines, but his attention kept straying, keeping the fear at bay. He knew he should be focused on the enemy, but he couldn't help alternating between looking out and looking in. Another soldier on the west wall jerked backward and fell. He didn't fall all the way, for his lower leg jammed between the sides of his narrow dugout. He flailed weakly with one arm in a vain effort to free his leg.

Arlen recognized Enrique Vasquez as he dashed out from the makeshift medical station near the northeast corner sheltered by a couple of trucks. He saw the wounded man hanging head down and raced toward him. As he did, two of Hanley's engineers burst from the group and raced after Vasquez. As Vasquez scrambled up the slope one of them grabbed his boot and jerked him back, shouting, "Goddammit, Enrique! Stay the fuck down. Can't lose you! We'll get him. We'll get him for you." The two men scrambled up to the wounded man. One grabbed the man by the shoulders; the other went a little higher. He raised his rifle over the top, turned it sideways, flipped the selector to automatic and sprayed until the magazine ran out. He put the weapon down, but it was unbalanced and slid down the slope. He grabbed the wounded man's leg and straightened up to pull it free. Just then, he jerked, fell, and slid to a stop at Vasquez's feet. It took Vasquez only seconds to confirm the man as dead, and he cried out, "Madre de Dios!" burying his face in his hands.

The other soldier pulled the wounded man down to Vasquez. He looked over at his friend. He didn't need a medical opinion. He saw the jagged hole in the back of his helmet made when the bullet had exited. His mind clamped down on all feeling. "Enrique! Come on, man! This guy needs help!" Dully crying, Vasquez helped the other get the wounded man to the relative safety of the medics' area.

Washington glanced at Ricochet. His rifle was braced on the tailgate, a little over three yards closer to the lip of the wall. He was methodically aiming and firing, the sound of his shots lost in the general cacophony.

Washington couldn't remember where he'd put his own M16. At the moment, it would be a lot more useful than his badass minigun. As he watched, helpless, it grew hard to breathe; he seemed to choke on each effort. It had to be his fault, for his hands were on the triggers, yet the gun remained silent, unable to fire where it was needed without killing his own.

He looked around, trying to find faces, forms he could recognize. Where was Shirtless? T-Shirt? Sergeant Lassky? Were they even alive? In his head, he heard Shirtless laughing again. Looking back into the compound, he saw the officer with the pistol stumble to his feet, his right hand pressed over his upper left chest. His left arm flapped when he tried to bring it up, flinging drops of blood from the fingertips. He looked around and fixed on the dead soldier. He stumbled to the body and tried to pick up the man's M16 but couldn't get his hand to grip it. He sank to his knees. Two other men ran forward, lifted the officer, and carried him off to the medics.

Wodzinski was standing beside Ricochet, rifle in hand but not firing, just looking around, especially at where the grenade that had nearly gotten into the truck had come from.

Out of sight below the wall, an enemy soldier ignited a short fuse connected to roughly five pounds of high explosive in a small canvas satchel with a canvas handle. Quickly, he swung the satchel by the handle and, with a great underhand heave, sent it flying over the wall.

Only Wodzinski saw it. As if he had a sudden seizure, his body jerked from a pair of conflicting impulses, one to duck. He followed the other and, like a baseball fan reaching for a foul tip into the stands, leaped up, hand outstretched, and caught it. He stumbled as he came back down and nearly fell back into the bed of the dump truck but dropped his rifle and with his free hand caught himself on the tailgate. Then, with an overhand swing, he threw the satchel back. As it disappeared over the lip of the wall, a deafening explosion followed. Even largely deflected by the wall, the blast wave knocked both Ricochet and Wodzinski to the floor.

The explosion was immediately followed by shouts and cries and a surge of enemy up and over the central and northern sides of the west wall, and Randy Hanley realized the defense of the west wall had collapsed. He needed no order to act. "Second Platoon! Line up! Line up!" The idea came from somewhere, some story—maybe from his father, maybe just a movie, but definitely not from a training manual. "Fix bayonets!"

That archaic command, combined with the fact that every man could see the absence of defenders along the wall, filled them with a terrible fatalism tensioned between "Oh, God, I'm gonna die" and "Those assholes are gonna pay."

Along the west wall, many defenders had been hit; worse, virtually all had run out of hand grenades. They could not rise enough to shoot down without almost certainly getting shot, and when the enemy crested the top, they would have but fractions of a second to shoot and no chance to reload. Some pulled their bayonets out, desperately bringing a knife to a gunfight. Others slipped down inside the fort, thinking to shoot up as the enemy came over.

The attack was weakest at the southern end of the wall, where, thanks to Stephan Wodzinski, the satchel charge had blown up the enemy, not the truck. It was also much weakened at the northern end of the west wall, where Ferreia's gun had done the most damage. As enemy soldiers reached the top nearest the north end, they saw only empty positions, but before they could go further they were gunned down. The surviving defenders from those positions, having run out of hand grenades, had realized they could move to alternate positions on the north wall and still sweep their part of the west wall with rifle fire. With bodies falling back on them, the remaining enemy at the northern end crowded toward the center of the west wall. Consequently, the greatest surge over the wall was in the center.

Randy's men heard the explosion of the satchel charge from beyond the wall but had no idea what it was; they knew only that almost immediately afterward, waves of enemy rushed over the center part of the west wall to tumble, slide, and stagger down the inner face. Some fired their as they came, but most were simply trying to get over the wall any way they could. As they rose from their tumbles, they were dumbfounded to see a line of Americans standing almost shoulder to shoulder like soldiers on parade, with the sight of the bayonets bringing on a brief, visceral, paralyzing reaction. For what felt like an eternal moment, both sides stood frozen in place.

As Washington watched the enemy now swarming over the central section of the west wall, it had taken a moment for the meaning of it to break through his paralysis of anguish; there was nothing but bad guys on the wall. He shouted a shout no one heard, depressed the gun to the closest section of the wall, and walked his fire along it in a three-second burst, firing roughly two bullets for every foot of wall within his reach. A dozen bodies rolled down the inner face, bumping into the legs of their comrades. Even more fell back down the outside face. At the last second, Randy, about to yell "Charge!" instead yelled, "Fire!" and twenty-odd M16s blazed.

Moments later, almost all the enemy that had made it over the wall were dead or wounded. Perhaps half a dozen had managed to slip to one side or another to hide behind a truck or other obstacle and clamber back out of the fort, some with the bad timing to be cut down by the minigun. Randy cried out, "Cease fire! Cease fire!" The firing had become compulsive, as if the men had forgotten how to stop. When it did stop, someone in Randy's platoon said loudly, "Oh, God!" but no one else could speak. It had been too easy, too quick, somehow too total—a turkey shoot, fish in a barrel. It left an almost shameful taste, and they couldn't exult. The enemy had fired back, but in their crush most of their efforts went wild. One of Randy's men had been shot through the hip and had fallen; two had minor flesh wounds but in the rush of adrenaline were still unaware of them. A third looked like a casualty but wasn't, a bullet having struck his helmet, dazing him.

Everett Rosen had not run back to the west-wall heat of the fighting. He and his radio operator had instead scrambled to the top of the east wall to join his other platoon leader so he could assess what was happening and decide what to do. It was the smart thing, the responsible thing, but it felt cowardly. He had barely gotten there when he saw Lieutenant Harris fall and the wave of enemy rush over the east wall, signaling the collapse of the defense there. Then he saw the fiery sword of Washington's minigun sweep the wall clear of life and watched the couple of dozen enemy that had made it into the fort be wiped out by the engineers, who were lined up as if on parade. For the moment, no one owned the west wall. Everett cried out as loudly as he could, "Randy! Hanley! Take the wall! Take the wall!"

For Randy, the call was a relief. He couldn't stand staring any longer at what he had just done. He turned to his men and echoed Everett's call. "We've got to get the wall! Charge!"

The neat line of men turned into a raggedy and smaller line, for the two lightly wounded men had to help the one shot in the hip to the medics, and the dazed man simply did not move. The rest rushed forward, still charged with the adrenaline from the firing, but soon stumbled and split up to avoid clambering over the men they had just killed.

Lucius, the grader operator, was at the left end of the line, and the man he'd followed to get ammunition, whom he recognized but didn't know, was beside him. He stumbled forward with the others, but as he came upon the first bodies, he stepped to the left to get around them. Now, somewhat separated from the others, they scrambled together up the wall. The other man reached the top first, fired two shots over the wall, and then realized his rifle was empty just as an enemy soldier also reached the top in front of him. Lucius saw this, and as if he were poking a stick at a barking dog, he reflexively poked his rifle at the enemy soldier in a similar reactive "Get away!" sense. Unintentionally, he bayonetted the soldier in the throat and, horrified, dropped his rifle.

The enemy soldier grabbed at his throat and slid backward, dragging Lucius's rifle with him. The other man grabbed it and jerked it free. He got his finger on the trigger and tried firing it, but nothing happened. He jacked open the bolt and nothing came out. Lucius had not chambered a round. Through all the carnage inside, Lucius had not been able to fire a shot. The other man jerked the bolt back and released it, chambering a round. The weapon fired perfectly. He looked at Lucius. Lucius had his hands over his eyes and was trembling. Just then he heard the lieutenant call for them to spread out and occupy the wall.

Lucius's companion slung his empty rifle over his shoulder, switched Lucius's rifle to his right hand, put his left arm around Lucius, and said, "Come on, buddy; we gotta move that way," pointing to the left. "Let's go. You and me, we'll be cool." Lucius felt himself being pushed to a crouch and shoved gently forward. After a few steps, his companion asked him to carry the empty rifle, which he did. His companion had seen that some of the enemy inside had slipped away to hide behind vehicles, and he switched his rifle to his left hand, telling Lucius to watch to the outside and shout if he saw something. His companion kept his eye on the inside. A few steps on, he saw an enemy scrambling up the wall to escape. He fired and missed, and the enemy vaulted over the top and disappeared. Lucius froze. "We're good; we're good, man," his companion said, and they moved on.

Lucius and his companion ended up occupying a cutout not far from the dump truck. They became the left flank of Randy's defenses on the west wall. As they spread out to occupy the wall, a couple of Randy's men moving toward the north end found two men huddled in the next-to-last cutout. They were unhurt but completely out of ammunition. They had gone through half a dozen magazines each and did not remember it. Resupplied with ammunition, they became Randy's right flank.

CHAPTER 22

MALVERN HILL

Washington had watched attackers and defenders shooting at each other within spitting distance and even at arm's length, and, one by one, men suddenly jerking and falling back into the fort. He watched the incident with Vasquez, and all the while his hands trembled agonizingly on the gun, desperate to shoot but unable to because he could not be sure of missing any defenders. He saw the flash and sound of Ferreia's gun, but it didn't register with him what it was. Then, when he saw the enemy swarming over the top of the wall, he knew there was no one left, and he fired. He saw the bodies fall right and left, and he saw the dozens that had gotten over before he fired suddenly facing the engineers lined up as if on parade and the carnage that followed.

On the west wall, faced with death from behind, death in front, and the slaughter atop the wall, the enemy broke. They fled south along the west wall into the thickets of the draw, stumbling past a still-smoking crater and dismembered bodies of the group that had tried to silence the gun. Some stumbled into the group that had been pushed back from the airstrip and had been working its way to attack the southwest corner and ended up briefly shooting at each other.

Just as the shooting faded along the west wall, Washington heard sharp explosions behind him. The third wave had arrived, achieving almost total surprise.

Two factors contributed to this. First, the third wave was late, having moved more slowly and cautiously after the brief encounter with OP Echo; and second, the attack of the second wave and the quiet along the south and east walls had drawn all attention to the west wall and the attack from the airstrip. Men on the other walls had even turned around to fire at the enemy scrambling over the west wall, and the noise of the battle more than masked any sounds of the approaching third wave.

Ricochet was the first to identify what the explosions outside the south wall meant, hearing someone shout, "Claymore!" It could only mean that the enemy was close to the south wall.

Like everyone else, Ricochet had turned his attention to the battle at the west wall and used the advantage of his scope to pick off enemy with a metronomic efficiency. Had he been using it to keep watch to the south, he might have detected the enemy a hundred or more yards out. As it was, no one noticed until the enemy tripped a claymore mine set some forty yards in front of the wall.

These mines were designed for close-in defense, composed of a rectangular sheet of plastic explosive bent in an arc with seven hundred small steel balls embedded on the convex side. As the claymore was designed to be manually detonated, a long extension cord connected it to a hand-held detonator. When a soldier detonated the mine, the seven hundred steel balls were blasted out in a sixty-degree fan. It was a very effective mine, and it didn't take soldiers long to learn how to rig it as a booby trap. As the enemy crept toward the wall, one of them bumped a taut wire that pulled a plastic C-ration spoon handle from between the jaws of a small stick, partly split, with each of the split ends wrapped with bare wires leading to a flashlight battery and the mine. When the spoon handle was pulled free, the wire-wrapped split ends snapped together, closing a circuit and detonating the mine.

Moments later, two more claymores were tripped. The three mines caused a dozen casualties and alerted the defenders, but they also triggered a rush to assault the wall now that surprise had been lost.

Washington was seeing over and over the last moments of the fight at the west wall as if his mind were stuck in a loop, wondering whether he couldn't have fired earlier, positioned the truck differently, or raised the bed higher. He couldn't get the images of those men fighting so close and then jerking and falling backward, with him unable to do anything to save them. Or maybe he could have. Maybe he should have grabbed his rifle. That he'd cleared the wall and broken the attack was lost in the images of the lives he didn't save. It was Sergeant Newsome that snapped him out of it when, alerted by Ricochet, he turned and saw what was coming. "Holy shit! Arlen! Get the gun over here!"

To aim the gun to the south, Washington had to free the strap controlling the gun's recoil, turn the gun around, and then secure the strap again. As he did this, Wodzinski finished freshening the ammunition feed. It all took less than a minute. But in the space of those few breaths, in spite of the claymores, dozens or more of enemy made it to the base of the wall. They were now firing and throwing hand grenades from where the gun couldn't reach. But dozens more were close behind, and these the gun could reach.

The sounds of battle were muted by the distance and the thickness of the woods, but the sudden increase in intensity, from sporadic sounds to an almost continuous rumble, made it clear to Major Graham that the fort had come under attack. He and Captain Thieu and his company were still waiting for the scouts he had sent out to find something. He had told Graham that the enemy would have a rear guard and that if they intended on withdrawing on the same route, there would be guides as well. After a radio call to Green Granite, Graham said to Captain Thieu, "The troops in the French fort are under attack. They report hundreds of enemy on the airstrip."

"We are still almost two kilometers from there."

"Can you go that far on your, uh, security patrol?"

Captain Thieu pressed his hands together as if praying, two fingers rubbing the bridge of his nose. After a moment, he replied, "I think we find rear guard much closer. Attack rear guard."

"What will that do?"

"Enemy!" His voice grew irate. "Enemy sneak right past my battalion, pay no attention; we gave them no worry! In his mind, we no danger to him. We attack him, he surprised, not know who. Or how many. Platoon, company, battalion? He must think battalion. Americans in front, unknown enemy in rear. He must feel in danger of being trapped, yes?"

"What will he do, do you think?"

"Think like enemy. Enemy attack American position of maybe 250 men. First on the north. De-de—"

"Deception?"

"Yes, deception, then attack with several hundred from airfield. Why airfield? They can be seen. Why a few hundred? Enemy know he need five- to ten-to-one advantage. Need maybe one thousands or more—a regiment. So attack in west to deception, on airfield, to fix, then must come a third—the leaping tiger for the kill!"

"So this may not even be the main attack?"

"Maybe. Maybe not, I think. But easy plan—overrun Americans and go straight north, short way to Cambodia safety. Fail to overrun Americans, maybe come back this way. Most jungle to conceal movement. But"—Thieu's lips twitched with a flicker of a sly smile—"if this way blocked by unknown force, must retreat north around Chu Song. Longer way, less concealment; maybe fighters and gunships catch them in morning."

"So we attack their rear guard."

"No!" The sly smile came back a bit stronger. "We patrol. Then we maybe get attacked by rear guard. Maybe they are not rear guard but advance guard coming to attack my battalion."

"Yeah. Yes. Taking advantage of the fog of war."

Captain Thieu blinked, not understanding the remark, but in moments, the company was moving forward. Graham laughed; he felt the impulse but restrained himself from slapping Captain Thieu on the back.

The outside slope of the south wall of Fort Frog was a bit steeper and higher than on the other sides, as the ground there sloped away from the fort. Everett and his men had noticed this slight advantage, but it did not change how he disposed his defenses. Enemy scouts had apparently also noticed this difference, for it did change how the third wave attacked the south wall. They had fashioned bundles of thin saplings or bamboo about twelve to fifteen feet long and about eighteen inches thick. Placed against a wall, they made ramps the attackers could run up over half the height of the wall—high enough to shoot over it and scramble or jump to the top.

The ramps were all too effective.

The third wave itself was broken into three groups. The first carried the bundles, positioned them against the wall, and threw hand grenades so that the following wave could charge up the ramps without pausing. By the time Washington could bring the gun to bear, both of these initial waves were already too close. The claymore mines that were tripped cut down a quarter of the first wave, reducing the number of ramps they could place for the second wave. Some in the second wave picked up bundles from the fallen, but still the second wave was somewhat slowed. Behind them the third and largest wave was advancing more carefully in teams that fired at the defenders while a companion team dashed forward, and then the teams reversed roles. However, as soon as the second wave hit the makeshift ramps, they stopped firing and began moving faster.

When Ricochet saw what was happening, he cried out, "Jude! Jude! I'm coming!" and leaped from the truck to scurry along the ledge and join his friend in a cutout near the center of the wall.

Jude slapped Ricochet's helmet by way of greeting. "You got grenades?"

"A few." Jude took them while he began picking off enemy soldiers in the teams that were firing at them, but he then fell victim to Chinese luck. A bullet that would have hit his head didn't. Fortunately, he had just moved his rifle to firing position after changing his magazine, so the bullet hit the starlight scope, deflecting upward to ricochet off his helmet. Unfortunately, it also slammed the eyepiece hard against his forehead, opening up a deep gash and knocking him backward out of his position. Fortunately, he rolled down the inner face of the wall, landing next to the ditch dug at the base of the wall to catch grenades thrown in from outside. Unfortunately, that knocked him unconscious, and he bounced out of the ditch. Fortunately, his bleeding head wound left him looking like a corpse.

The event distracted Jude for several seconds, and when he turned his attention to the front again, he was stunned to see heads rising above the wall—one so close he couldn't bring his rifle to bear, and he punched the enemy soldier in the face. But one right beside him swung his rifle like a club, striking Jude's helmet and knocking it off. As he struggled to bring his weapon up, the first slammed the butt of his rifle against Jude's forehead. Jude slumped unconscious into the cutout. The enemy soldier stepped onto the wall, turned his AK-47 assault rifle around, and was preparing to finish Jude off when another soldier behind him pushed him forward to give himself room to get onto the wall. After that, Jude, also looking like a corpse, was ignored as the enemy poured over the wall and into the fort. Other defenders were not so lucky.

Washington could not see the makeshift ramps and had no idea how so many got so quickly up and over the wall, but he was again paralyzed by fear of hitting his own men, even as he watched Ricochet and Jude go down. Seconds later, dark shapes were also swarming over the wall just opposite his truck, where they could jump from the wall to the truck. Without thinking, he swept the top of the wall in front of the truck and then the whole wall when Newsome, seeing the defense gone, screamed at him to shoot, at the same time opening up with his machine gun. In seconds, the wall was swept clear.

Dozens of enemy had made it over the wall, but Washington's gun had, at least temporarily, isolated the enemy inside the fort from further reinforcement. Now, because of Arlen's gun, the attack was stalling and would ultimately fail unless the gun could be quickly eliminated.

Inside the fort, the forty-odd enemy that had made it over the south wall found themselves cut off, at least for the time being. Here, too, a kind of pause occurred as each side took stock of what they were facing, the cluster of enemy on one side, and Captain Cornwell and the second reserve made up of his gun crews, Captain Rosen's mortar crew, and a couple of engineers that had been evacuating wounded from the west wall. Captain Rosen was still on the east wall, and Lieutenant Hanley was on the west wall, taking charge of the defense there, placing some of his engineers and remnants of Lieutenant Harris's platoon while Everett tried to assess his overall condition. That effort ended when firing suddenly erupted at the south wall, and almost immediately he was stunned to see enemy swarming over it.

The enemy was first to react, for they had come over the wall expecting to continue their rush but had paused, first at the terrible sound of the minigun sweeping away the comrades behind them, and then at the peculiar sight of a cluster of Americans staring at them as if they had been waiting for them. Chris Cornwell, an artilleryman, was now suddenly in the role of leading his men as infantry. Randy's cry of "Fix bayonets!" echoed in his mind briefly. There was the enemy. Most of his men had already fixed bayonets. To cry "Charge!" seemed somehow absurd. A more commonsensical command—"Take cover!"— struck him simultaneously. He was about to choose the latter, but before he could issue the command, two soldiers shouted "Grenade!"

A leader in the enemy group had taken the initiative, arming a hand grenade and throwing it at the Americans with all his strength, giving his men precious seconds to take cover and prepare to advance.

For a second or two, Chris and his men stood in a kind of jerking paralysis, their minds screaming silently, "What? Where?" Some in front who now saw the grenade simply froze; others stumbled backward or flung themselves to the ground. But the man who had seen it and had shouted the warning sensed that it was too late for everyone.

The grenade was rolling straight at him. He saw it was an American grenade, which had a wide killing radius. In that instant, it seemed it was God's purpose for him. He pulled off his helmet and ran toward the grenade, two strides and he went to his knees slamming the helmet over the grenade and his body over the helmet an instant before it detonated. The helmet split open like a flower opening and heaved the soldier into the air, and yet it shielded his abdomen from dozens of the grenade fragments that would have torn him apart. He tumbled and fell onto his back a couple of feet away. The men who'd not moved opened fire and scattered. The enemy were already scattering. Two men, however, rushed to the body of the soldier who'd saved their lives. Captain Cornwell stood where he'd been, firing his pistol until the two returned with the body and carried him to the medics, who found he was actually still alive. In the next moments, defenders and attackers all took cover behind various vehicles, shooting at each other.

In the lull outside the fort, Arlen looked inside wondering what he could do, if anything, about the enemy that had gotten inside. But there was nothing. He saw the grenade thrown, and he saw the soldier run and throw himself on it. Arlen couldn't look. He turned his face south and opened fire, screaming at Wodzinski for more ammo, who shouted back a warning: "We're running low!"

The enemy inside had split in two, most having headed toward the east side of the compound, and a smaller group for the west side. In the same way, Chris's men split in two. Both sides began trying to work their way forward. The group moving toward the west wall encountered the ramp and the dump truck. As they did, Arlen fired the gun, and the enemy at the ramp realized the dump truck held the weapon. There were only three men in a position to protect it: Hutchinson, the driver, braced on the running board nearest the wall, and Lucius and his companion in the nearest cutout on the west wall. All three had seen the surge over the south wall. Hutchinson, shielded by the truck, was the first to fire. Lucius's companion, growling, "Shit! They're comin' for us, buddy!" was the next to fire. Lucius pointed his rifle at the enemy but otherwise froze until his companion grunted and fell sideways onto Lucius's knees, gasping and moaning, and Lucius was faced with a dilemma; to stop and help his companion would kill both of them, but to not shoot was to kill both of them. He had gotten this far in both battles by not deciding—going with the flow and pantomiming what he couldn't bear to do. He didn't put his rifle to his shoulder but held it out in front of him as if he were holding a dead skunk. But it was pointed at the enemy, and he pulled the trigger so reflexively that in seconds he had emptied the magazine.

Under the hail of Lucius's fire, the enemy broke for the shelter of vehicles deeper in the compound. Lucius had no sense of actually hitting anyone, but several bodies were left behind. Lucius found his companion's wound, bandaged it, and held him, telling him softly, over and over, "You'll be okay. We're … we're cool."

On the east side, Everett's platoon leader in charge of the east wall defense did have a problem, for about a hundred or more enemy had slipped or been pressed by events around to the east wall. They didn't have the ramps and appeared to be trying to move around the east side to attack Task Force Baker's positions across the road or perhaps the fort's entrance. There had been a brief battle of hand grenades between the east-wall defenders and the enemy that the defenders won, driving the enemy into the thick brush east of the wall, several of them tripping the claymore mines that had been set out—but from the wrong side, and so suffering little hurt. The men on the east wall could more or less keep the enemy pinned in place, but the enemy's return fire also pinned the defenders in place. Worse, in their cutout defensive positions, the men on the wall had little protection from fire from inside the compound.

The enemy inside the fort could not take full advantage of the exposed positions of the defenders on the east wall, for the decisive fight inside the compound had become a cat-and-mouse battle between Chris's men and the larger enemy force. Chris, however, had an unexpected advantage in the person of Sparky, the battery mascot, who had been rescued when, a year earlier, starved and limping down a road on an injured paw, a previous commander came upon him in his jeep. The sound of guns usually kept Sparky crouched under a table in the fire control center, but now he sensed an invasion of strangers and, more, the fear and tension among his pack that this invasion brought with it. In spite of the intimidating noise, Sparky ran to find the new invaders.

It did not take long for Chris's men to realize what Sparky was doing. He was the perfect scout. Having no concept of a dog as a pet or working partner, the enemy had no idea that the nondescript barking mongrel was ratting them out of every corner. Chris's men could know exactly where to fire, and they could then quickly roll or crawl away from where their muzzle flashes had been. The enemy's superiority in numbers rapidly faded. They began retreating toward the south wall but soon realized there was no escape. Finally, some began to play dead, waiting for their comrades, who might yet overrun the Americans, or until daylight, when it would be safer to surrender.

Outside the fort, the brief lull ended. An RPG round narrowly missed Washington. A second round also missed, but both he and Newsome saw the flash of its firing. Both men swept the area with their guns. But now Washington could hear bullets snapping by and striking the truck as well. He cried out to Wodzinski for more ammunition and ducked from the incoming fire while Wodzinski reloaded. As the fire from the south side intensified, more men on the west and east sides began firing back, but the bulk of the south wall blocked any effective fire on enemy close to the base of the wall. The enemy was trying to concentrate men at the southwest corner but was having difficulty. Washington kept firing, and the enemy was paying dearly for every man he managed to get close enough to be sheltered by the wall, for Washington only had to fire a second at a time to lay waste to approaching enemy. Of those who made it, some began using the ramps to get to the top of the wall, but these were quickly shot by men on the east wall or by Newsome.

The enemy was also hampered by the terrain near the southwest corner. The ravine branching off the draw, choked with thick brush and small trees, divided the southern and western approaches, making it very hard for men approaching from the south to work their way to the western side of the corner, where the wall offered greater protection, forcing them to brave Washington's arc of fire. But as more men made it to the shelter of the wall, more hand grenades were being thrown over the wall. Newsome and Wodzinski threw their own grenades in return but soon ran out. Worse, the gun suddenly lost electrical power. Washington jumped out of the truck to trace the problem, finding the cause was Hutchinson. He had pulled the jumper cable loose when he had fallen from the running board with a bullet in his head.

Washington's heart seemed to stop. For a second it was as though all the air had been sucked out of his lungs, and he was desperate to take a breath but couldn't. All feeling shut down. He took a breath, connected the jumper cable, and was about to jump back into the truck when an enemy grenade made it into the truck. By the deafening sound and concussion, he instantly knew the explosion had been inside the truck. He found Wodzinski, dead, sprawled on the truck bed, his helmet missing, his face hidden by blood.

Arlen screamed, "Oh, fuck no!" and shouted to Newsome. Newsome had heard, but not seen, the explosion. It was no louder to him than others that had fallen between the wall and the truck. Seeing Washington's anguished expression, he forgot himself and rose to jump into the truck bed. But instead of jumping, he jerked, spun around, and fell. Crying "Fuck, no, no, no!" Arlen jumped out of the truck and fell down beside Newsome.

Newsome was conscious. "I'm hit, Arlen. Pretty bad, I … think." Blood bubbled frothily from his mouth as he tried to speak. Arlen knew then he had been shot through the lung and screamed for a medic.

He ripped Newsome's shirt open. "Shut up, Sarge; just shut up. You gonna be okay." He could see the hole, open and ragged in his chest. An exit wound. He felt around behind and found the bleeding entry wound. "Hang in here, Sarge! Stay with me!" He ripped his own shirt off, fumbled in his and Newsome's harness for wound bandages, pressed one over the entry and exit wounds, and bound them with his shirt, all the while shouting, "Vasquez! Medic! Medic!" Then he helped Newsome slide down the inner face of the wall to the shelter of the corner. But no medics arrived. The battle inside the fort was continuing, blocking the way to their corner, and there were other cries for a medic. "Hang in there, Chief! Hang in there!" Arlen looked up at the wall and then back at Newsome, who was looking at something far away. He felt he was fucking everything up, and everything seemed to be fucking him over. Now there was no one but himself left to defend this corner of the fort, and it was the key to all of it. He had to abandon Newsome. He had to look the other way. "I—I—I'll be back, Chief! Right back. Promise! But … but I gotta go." Washington turned away to scramble back to his gun just as an RPG scored a direct hit on the timber crib. The gun was not damaged, but the mount was shattered, rendering it useless.

It put Arlen was in a rage: Hutchinson, Wodzinski, Newsome, his gun. All those guys on the west wall he couldn't save, and now all of them on the south wall he couldn't save.

Arlen grabbed Wodzinski's rifle, but it had been damaged in the blast, and he tossed it aside. Newsome's machine gun lay on the wall, an almost complete belt of a hundred rounds still in it. He tossed a box of machine gun ammunition onto the wall beside it. Then he jumped to the step in the wall, picked up the machine gun, rising just high enough to aim over the edge, and expended the entire belt. He dropped back down and, taking the ammunition box and machine gun, moved a few yards. Then he dropped into a defensive cutout, loaded a fresh belt, rose up, and began firing again. After every time he fired, he moved. *Keep moving, keep moving, like being in the air, staying ahead of the assholes' bullets.* As his mind had clamped down on feelings upon seeing Hutchinson and then Wodzinski and then Newsome, it clamped down on fear and rage. Feeling vanished, he became like a metronome: tick, tock; see, react, duck, move, shoot, reload.

It was chance or dumb luck or a sixth sense that caused Arlen to glance westward just as several heads appeared over the wall. The remnant of the second wave that had been driven back to the draw and had been working toward the southwest corner had arrived. Blocked by the ravine, their lead elements had slipped up onto the plateau of the airstrip to scramble up the south end of the west wall. He sprayed them and cursed, fearing he was now being trapped between enemy to the south and to the west. It was time to run, but he couldn't. This corner, *his* corner, was key. He cursed aloud, bit his lip, and loaded another belt.

Rising to fire again and hold on to his corner, the vital corner of the fort, Arlen began to register some pain. It had taken him longer to reload. His hands felt weak. There was a rattling in his breath. His leg hurt, and his shoulder felt oddly stiff. He pushed himself erect. There was some noise in the draw. He leaned forward to fire down into it. And just then, off in the distance, from somewhere in the jungled draw, Arlen Washington heard the strangest thing—a bugle. Captain Thieu's troops had found the enemy rear guard. Stalled in front, possibly cut off in the rear, and with dawn not far off, the enemy commander had no choice.

Captain Everett Rosen climbed to the top of the east wall and gazed down the slopes toward the draw. It was literally carpeted with dead. He already felt drained of energy and feeling, but the sight left him in a complete vacuum of emotion, leaving him like a burned-out lightbulb—a fragile shell enclosing a vacuum and a broken heart. He swallowed and felt bile rise. With each breath, something seemed to block the air, and a sound somewhere between a gasp and a cough erupted. His parched lips formed the same words—"Dear God, what … what have we done?"—over and over, but no sound came out. After a long moment, he managed to tear his eyes from the sight and saw, to his left, a body curled, one arm flung over the outside of the wall—one of his men. To his right, he saw the airman sitting. Behind him he could see the raised bed of the dump truck, the shattered timber crib, and the gun, pointing skyward. Yet there was the airman, alone, sitting with an M60 machine gun in his lap. He was not wearing a shirt, and his dark skin shone in the dawn light. He seemed like a statue carved in mahogany.

He looked back at the body and walked up to it. *Dirksen.* Gently, he bent and touched Dirksen's pale face. It was cold. He was missing his helmet. He saw it a couple of yards down the outer slope, lodged against a black-clad form. "I'm sorry," he whispered. He straightened and looked back at the airman and this time noticed a pink gash in the mahogany shoulder—a reopened wound. *Good God!* he thought. *It's dawn. How long ago was he hit? He hasn't called for a medic?*

He was having trouble processing his senses, putting things in order. Avoiding the intimate sights, he looked again at the field of dead, and an image came to him from a history book—the description of a Civil War battlefield where, an observer had said, one could walk all the way to the crest of the hill without ever setting foot on the ground, so thickly had the bodies lain on Malvern Hill. An image almost overwhelmed him—an image of all the death now lying outside, lying inside instead. He rubbed his eyes to get rid of the image and walked over to the airman, who didn't move, and for a moment he thought the airman was dead too. He touched the airman's shoulder.

Arlen seemed to wake up. His eyes had been open, but he had not seen the coming of daylight. He tried to shake off the tap on his shoulder but that brought a sharp pain, and he came to himself. It was an officer. The man's identity didn't register, but he guessed he'd better stand. He managed that, a little unsteadily. He looked down and saw the gun still on the ground. He guessed he ought to pick it up but just didn't have the energy. He mouthed the words "Fuck it" and looked at the officer.

Arlen's face had no expression. To Everett, it was like looking at a death mask with wide, bloodshot eyes. It broke the last hold on his emotions, and he impulsively put his arms around Washington and sobbed, "I've lost … I've lost … My job to keep 'em safe. I didn't."

And for the first time since he'd last left Big Ma, Arlen Washington embraced another person. Except for Everett's slowly subsiding sobs, they were motionless and silent for some time. Arlen began to feel dizzy. The officer was crying. He seemed so sad, so ashamed, and Arlen felt it must mean he had also failed. He'd tried. Tears began to flow from his own eyes. "I tried, sir. I tried."

The words brought Everett back, and he regained some control. He pulled his head back and forced himself to look around again, burning the terrible scenes into his memory. Then he looked into Washington's dark, bloodshot eyes and whispered hoarsely, "Believe me. Believe me. Everyone here who's alive lives because of you."

The dizziness got stronger. "Got to sit down, Chief. Sir." He began to sag into Everett's arms. Everett pulled back, still gripping Washington's arms, and looked at him. He saw a bullet hole in his upper left chest, another just above the belt line on his left side, multiple small punctures and gashes on his arms and torso, and bloody tears in his trousers. "My God! Medic! Medic!"

Everett remained on the berm after men had come and carried Washington to the medics. They also found Newsome, still alive, and Lucius, still cradling his companion, also still barely alive. He knew he should get down and back to his men, both the whole and the wounded. There was so much to do but so little in him left to do it with.

Fifty yards away, a figure, part of a clump of motionless figures, stirred with a low moan. He had been hit and had fallen with several others and had drifted in and out of consciousness. For a while, when he came awake, he played dead, but this time he sensed the silence. It was not a real silence. The air was filled with the muttering sounds of vehicles and aircraft. But there was no firing. In that sense, the world was quiet. It was morning. He was partly propped on the backs of two of his comrades, and before him he could see the still, silent shapes of dozens more leading his eyes toward a figure standing in seeming triumph on the wall of the objective. It was not a comrade. It was wearing an American helmet. The attack had failed. All those comrades had died for naught. He managed to bring his rifle to bear and fire a burst. The figure disappeared. He pushed his rifle away, closed his eyes, and waited to die.

Everett had just gotten the attention of one of his sergeants and raised his arm to point to something when the burst of fire came. The first bullet hit something on the berm, ricocheted upward and tore a path in the meaty part of his shoulder. A second struck him in the left buttock, and a third hit his helmet at just enough of an angle to not penetrate but to daze him and knock him off balance. He stumbled, one foot slipped off the berm, and he fell, rolling into the fort.

CHAPTER 23

AFTERMATH

The first reports of fighting at Chu Song reached Corps headquarters through the Seventh Division, and when the second wave attacked the fort, the picture became confusing, as updates from the Seventh did not paint as serious a picture as reports then flowing up through Corps Artillery from Task Force Nickel. This was partly because the inexperienced commander of Task Force Baker, as inexperienced men often do, remained fixated on his preconception that a major attack would come at them from the north, directly out of Cambodia. So even as sounds of battle erupted and intensified south of them, their preconceptions caused them to interpret the diversion in front of them as a precursor to a main attack, and the main attack behind them as a diversion. But it was also partly because, given the surprise and strength of the attack on Task Force Nickel, reports they received from Task Force Nickel were very brief, cryptic, and given in tones of great stress and anxiety that could easily be interpreted as overreaction or even panic.

Both Task Force Baker and Task Force Nickel had called for gunship support, but it was not until the twilight before dawn that the low cloud cover broke enough to allow one to actually see the battlefield and provide support, and by then the battle was over. The arrival of the gunship gave Corps headquarters its first real appreciation of the battle even as reports from the Seventh Infantry Division and Corps Artillery were also beginning to paint a grimmer picture. Breaking through the lowest cloud layer at a little over one thousand feet in the dull predawn light, the pilot had wide view of the battlefield and reported an estimated two to three hundred bodies scattered around the old fort and piled against the fort walls like flotsam after a storm. Also, when the fighting had died down, Captain Cornwell had begged Task Force Baker for medics. When the task force commander heard the number of wounded the men in the fort was dealing with and realized many of his wounded were being brought in from the south side of his own perimeter, his preconceptions were finally shattered. He grabbed a dozen men and a couple of his own medics, accompanied them to the fort, and was soon reporting to his headquarters a more complete picture of the battle, whereupon Seventh Division organized air medical evacuation with a flight of medevacs escorted by gunships.

Entering the medical tent, Chris Cornwell saw Everett Rosen lying on his side, head propped on his hand, conscious and alert. "Ev, how're you doing?"

"I've got a bullet in my butt and a headache, but painkillers work wonders. What are our casualties?" Chris sat down, and they reviewed, name by name, the wounded and dead. Like Everett, Chris had seen the scale of the carnage outside the fort, but it faded to background noise against the harsh intimacy of their own losses. For Everett, an astonishing picture emerged from the painful review. The final phase of the battle had focused on the southwest corner, but during the final critical moments that broke the enemy's last effort, the southwest corner had had but one defender—the airman.

The exhausted soldiers in the fort could not rest. They had twenty-odd prisoners to guard; a dozen or more wounded prisoners to treat and guard; over seventy enemy bodies to remove from the fort—they could not even think about the bodies outside—over forty of their own wounded to tend to, not counting those with minor wounds; and over twenty dead to collect, identify, and prepare for evacuation.

It was only five-thirty in the morning when the Second Corps operations officer strode into the operations center. "What's up with Chu Song?" he asked.

"Morning, Colonel. Apparently a hell of a dustup."

"Details?"

"Some, sir." The major who was on duty for operations that night and the captain who was on duty for the intelligence side came and stood beside the colonel. The major pointed to a spot on the map and reported what he knew.

"Several hundred? No warning?"

"Don't have the details, Colonel. Just a sketch."

"Continue."

"Sir," the captain interrupted, "looks like NVA; not sure what unit, though. Might be the Eighteenth, but nothing to confirm or deny it."

"Go on."

"When the attack was discovered, apparently the enemy had already reached the fort's west wall facing the airstrip here. Not long after, another wave, of apparently equal or greater size, hit the fort's southern wall. There seems to have been fighting inside the fort. Somehow"—the major shrugged and shook his head—"they stopped the attack."

"So they reported hundreds?" the colonel asked, his tone implying doubt about the credibility of such a report.

"Yes sir. That's confirmed by a Spooky. Pilot estimated two to three hundred bodies visible outside the fort. And he arrived after the fighting."

"Jesus! What about casualties?"

"Still not firm, sir. The current count looks like thirty to forty percent, sir, for Task Force Nickel. Much lower for Task Force Baker. Kind of looks like they were a diversion."

"You say the Spooky got there after the fighting? It's over already? Three hours? Less than three hours? Hundreds of enemy KIA? Jesus!" No one spoke. There didn't seem to be anything to add. "Medevacs?"

"Seventh ID is on it, sir."

The colonel turned to the captain. "Harold, tell Colonel Butts we

301

need to get your guys out there ASAP. Get the details. Task Force Nickel was slapped together just days ago. They get surprised by what must be a regiment size attack and they—they beat them back? Extraordinary!"

Gunships circled Chu Song while medevac helicopters landed, loaded, and took off. A big CH-47 Chinook came in, landed halfway down the airstrip, powered down, and waited patiently for the dead. Off toward the north, more gunships and the Spooky cruised, searching for prey and now and then finding some. Dawn came gray and almost chilly but with a freshening breeze, and with full daylight came more helicopters carrying higher-level commanders. Among these were Lieutenant Colonels George Short, Sherman Greystone, and Hamilton Vanderpoole, the battalion commanders of Lieutenant Hanley, Captain Cornwell, and Captain Rosen, respectively. By coincidence, their helicopters arrived almost simultaneously. They couldn't land close to the fort, and no one seemed to have jeeps or drivers to pick them up.

Colonel Short was the first to land. He had also brought with him Major Gridley. He had radioed ahead, and someone had answered, but there he was, on the ground, with no one there to pick him up. His irritation grew as he endured the the rotor wash of the next two helicopters landing with colonels Greystone and Vanderpoole. After introductions, Short asked if either had a ride coming. Greystone hadn't radioed ahead. "I like surprise visits," he said.

Vanderpoole looked at both oddly and said, "My boys don't have any wheels. Not that far, gents; guess we can walk."

All three had seen the many bodies scattered around the fort as they had come in. Now they found themselves walking past some. Colonel Short asked abruptly, "When will they get to cleaning up the mess out there?"

Again Vanderpoole looked at him oddly, not noticing that Greystone had dropped behind. "Reminds me of some"—he hesitated, searching for a word—"uh, scenes from my time in Korea. They would sometimes just send in hordes."

Short gave no reply. Greystone had fallen back for a few heartbeats, for he had noticed not only the bodies in general but also a particular corpse: a body with a young, innocent-looking childlike face with a surprised expression fixed forever. This was a boy with a mother, a father, siblings, friends, comrades, and no future. All those hundreds of still, dark shapes seen from his helicopter condensed into the face of a boy. He felt a constriction in his chest and a pressure on the heart and on the mind he couldn't identify. He took a breath and caught up in time to hear Vanderpoole conclude a comment: "Looks like our boys had a hell of a challenge last night." He was about to continue when Short interrupted.

"Yes, yes. Hell of a scene. I'm worried about my lieutenant, though. Only hope he didn't prove an, uh, impediment, or anything."

Neither Vanderpoole nor Greystone replied. "He had a dustup a few days ago," Short continued. "Sent on a night mission to pick up some downed airmen. Managed to lose two armored vehicles, one just to running it into a ditch. Then another dustup—enemy attack. Got the feeling he was a bit, well, overexcited. Just concerned is all. Want the best for him, of course."

"Yeah, I had some of my boys with him. Here too. It'll all come out. Sure he did well." Vanderpoole then added, "I'm bringing in another company today. They'll help with, uh, policing the battlefield and such; then they'll take over Charlie Company's mission. After a fight like this, they need to be pulled out of action for a while, get in replacements, reorganize, integrate the new guys, you know."

They were near the entry to the fort. Vanderpoole stopped and looked at Greystone. "How about you, Colonel? Feel okay about your guys?"

Greystone felt trapped. Vanderpoole's level, expressionless gaze and his reference to experience in Korea unnerved him. "You were in the Korean War?"

Vanderpoole grinned. "A raw lieutenant, mostly pissing his pants."

"Well, sir, I have absolutely no experience to relate this to. It's … it's beyond me. The most combat-experienced officer in my battalion now is Captain Cornwell. I can't judge here," he replied, thinking of his earlier judgements. "I guess …" He didn't finish.

Vanderpoole addressed them both. "Gentlemen, our guys are

basically in a state of aftershock right now. They're running on adrenaline and are probably close to running on empty. My advice, for what it's worth? Talk to the troops. Buck 'em up. Don't ask for reports 'n' shit. Tomorrow or the next day will do. Colonel Short, if I might suggest, since some of my guys have been with your boys pretty much all through this thing, why don't we go together to talk to 'em?"

Taken aback, Colonel Short nodded, and Colonel Greystone was left alone at the entrance to the old fort.

Sherman Greystone was reluctant to enter the fort but did not want to just stand there. Abruptly, he had to step aside, and three men came out, two bearing a stretcher carrying one of the wounded, and the third holding an IV bag for him. He almost tripped over a body as he got out of the way and turned to see bodies of enemy soldiers stacked almost like cordwood and, next to them, a pile of weapons. He quickly entered the fort. Inside he immediately saw where the medical station and the fire control center were. He guessed Captain Cornwell would be in one of those places. As he was deciding that he would avoid them for the moment, Captain Cornwell suddenly appeared, having been alerted. He saluted and, biting his lip, said, "Welcome to Fort Frog—I mean Fire Base Nickel, sir. Seems we're not quite Vietnamized here yet, sir." It was a restrained but biting and angry remark.

After a moment, Colonel Greystone nodded. "That appears to be the case, Captain. And, well, I guess I'll leave it to you to let me know if and when it, uh, is."

"Sir." Chris cleared his throat. "Sorry."

After another somewhat awkward silence, Colonel Greystone said, "I ... look, I think I need to sort of absorb this. I, but I ... I would like to know, how ... how are your men? I guess I mean, how many casualties? How're the others doing?"

"I ... sir." Chris straightened. He hated speaking the numbers, because it made them real all over again. "Five KIA. Ten percent. Twelve WIA. Twenty-four percent, but half of them pretty light wounds; only four look really serious. The others? Okay, I guess, sir."

"I know you've got stuff to do, and I don't want to get in the way. I'd like to just look around. But first, is there anything I can do for you right now?"

"No sir. Things are in hand. Guys from across the road, Second of the Tenth, they weren't hit bad; they're being a great help."

"Thanks. Do carry on." Colonel Greystone turned away and shortly found himself staring at a number of enemy soldiers squatting together, their hands behind their backs and sort of resting against the side of a truck. Several GIs were guarding them.

He walked over. One noticed him and called, "'Tenshut!"

"At ease, men. Don't get up." He noticed two of the soldiers were hand-feeding prisoners C-rations. "What outfit you gents from?"

One stood, a sergeant. "We're First Squad, First Platoon, Charlie Company, Second Battalion, Tenth Infantry, Seventh Division, sir."

Greystone chuckled. "You forgot Second Corps, USARV, USARPAC, US Army." He chuckled again. "Sorry, Sergeant. That was very complete. But I thought it was a cavalry outfit providing security for my big guns here."

"We were sent over to help out, sir. We didn't get hit so bad."

"Oh." He wasn't sure how to read that. He then remembered Vanderpoole's remark about bringing in a replacement company. "I see. Where were these guys captured?"

"Right here, sir. They got into the fort, then found they couldn't get out."

"You're feeding them?"

"Look at 'em, sir. Look like they haven't eaten in a month." Greystone gazed at the stoic faces that could not quite conceal a deep, hopeless aloneness. The sergeant added, "Not feeding them much. C-rats suck, but the captain told us they're much richer than what they get. Too much'll make 'em throw up or something. Guess they're used to rice, but we ain't got any."

Greystone thanked the soldiers for their help and wandered off, still feeling confused, almost lost, as if, like Alice, he had fallen through a rabbit hole into a place too surreal to be real. He ran into a captain from Corps with an entourage of cameramen and note-takers. He talked to him a few minutes and heard a variety of vignettes picked up in interviews with soldiers and NCOs. They had yet to interview any officers. The captain explained, "We get the best picture working from the bottom up. You one of the Battalion COs, sir?"

Greystone nodded. "Artillery."

"Well, sir, looking from the bottom up, so far, you can be proud of your men. And your officers." The captain flashed a brief sardonic smile. "Not always the case. But hard to know if you haven't been in their shoes. I haven't, sir."

"Well, neither have I."

"This place is like a fucking tourist spot," Ricochet said to his friend and foxhole partner Jude as they sat on the edge of the cutout they'd nearly been killed in. They were looking at the colonels and other strangers milling around inside the fort. Technically, they were both among the wounded but had been patched and left to return to duty, which they were happy to do. Some men had been detailed to security, manning the OPs, but no one had given them a duty to perform, so the two friends had gotten away from the clutter to just sit. Jude didn't really reply but said, "I smell bacon frying. Now that's fucking normal, right? Morning? Breakfast? So why don't it feel right? Feels totally weird right now."

"What's weird?" They both looked up and saw the engineer PFC Bert McAllister, who had been assigned with Jude the night of the battle at the engineer camp.

"Hey, bud," Jude said, "You trying to attract enemy fire on me again?"

"I don't know how you put up with this asshole," Bert said, plopping down beside them. "You guys look kind of worse for wear. Doin' okay?"

"Well, we're sittin' up and not lying down. You?"

"Got a hole shot in my pants pocket."

"And they didn't medevac you?"

"I begged them to, but no dice. So what's weird?"

"Can't believe I'm sittin' here smelling bacon cooking," Jude said, almost choking. He looked over at Ricochet. "Partner, you and me ought to be dead; you know that? Why aren't we? Answer me that."

"Craps, I guess. Some roll seven or eleven, some don't; or maybe some got angels over 'em and some don't. I don't know, man."

"Craps or angels? Something more, man. It's just got to be." Jude put his head in his hands for a moment and then straightened and sighed and looked away from them, his eyes glistening. "I don't know, man. They walked right over me. Right over me. And here I am, sittin' in the exact same spot, smelling bacon frying! I just, like, feel burdened, like I stole something from someone and … and I can't give it back even if I try."

"Yeah," Bert said softly, as if in a confessional. "I got a hole in my pants. That's it. How is it all I got is a hole in my pants and … and … and Brian Cash got a hole in his head?"

A voice came from above them, clipped, nervous. "You men okay?" The three men looked up. It was an officer in crisp jungle fatigues. They started to get up. "Don't get up, men."

The soldiers relaxed. "You men with A Battery?" the officer asked.

"No sir. Charlie Company, Second of the Twenty-Second Cav, sir," Ricochet replied. "Except McAllister here's from the engineers."

"Oh. Your battalion commanders are down there." The soldiers didn't respond. The officer stared across the compound for a full minute, coughed, cleared his throat and said, "I'm Colonel Greystone. One Fifteenth Field Artillery. A Battery here is one of mine."

After a couple of breaths of silence, the three soldiers gave their names and ranks. Another silence followed before the colonel thanked them and walked off along the wall. But after a few paces, he stopped, his gaze drawn, almost reluctantly, to the bodies still littering the base of the wall outside. He looked from the bodies back to the three soldiers. This was his first experience of war, but he realized it was an experience of reports, not of the senses. Here, standing between the dead and the living, he felt he had stepped into an alien world. On impulse, he turned back to the three men. "Could I ask you gents something?"

The three looked at him. The officer's expression was almost timid. Ricochet shrugged. "Sure, sir."

"You … you don't have to answer, really. Could you tell me about it? The battle?"

"Sir, we don't know much at all, only what we seen. I mean, like, well, we were out of it for a while too."

"Out of it? How?"

"As in knocked out, sir." The colonel looked blank. Jude waved at his bandage. "Butt of an AK."

Gradually, they told what they had done and seen, including seeing Captain Cornwell in the middle of the compound, firing his pistol; hearing the roar of the minigun sweeping just over Jude's head as Arlen swept the enemy from the wall, and watching the enemy survivors surrendering near where Ricochet had fallen.

Suddenly, just at the end of the telling, Ricochet bent over, slamming his head into his hands, and cried, "Oh, man, oh shit, shit, shit, it—it's my fault! My fault!"

Jude looked at him, astonished, and grabbed his shoulder. "Your fault? What? What the hell you talkin' about, man?"

Ricochet jerked his head up and flung an arm out over the berm, pointing almost violently out toward the draw. "This was our sector! We were supposed to watch it! I'm the guy with the starlight scope! I could've seen 'em! I should've seen 'em! But no! I was busy shooting at those bastards over there!" He swept his arm toward the west wall. "I should have been watching!" He buried his face in his hands again.

Jude grabbed his shoulder again. "Partner, you was doing what you had to do! Listen to me, partner. I could've seen 'em too, but you and me, we had to be shootin' where we were! You and me, we were doing what we had to do, man! It's not on you, man!"

"I could have seen 'em," Ricochet mumbled.

Colonel Greystone was stunned, as if someone had just punched him in the chest. The stories they had told were stories—engrossing stories, but stories. Ricochet's outburst exposed something no stories did—a glimpse of war at the quantum level, where countless individual decisions are made in darkness, fear, and haste, where the fog of war is the thickest.

He wanted to comfort Ricochet in some way but felt incompetent to do so. Finally he said, "I think your friend is right." Then, realizing

McAllister hadn't spoken, he took the opportunity to deflect from Ricochet and asked him his story.

"Not much, sir. Engineers were the primary reserve. So we didn't really do anything till the gooks got inside. Over that wall." He pointed. "Lieutenant Harris's platoon caught the real shit."

"What ... what happened then?"

"Lieutenant Hanley had us fix bayonets." Bert fell silent a moment. No one spoke. Then he took a breath, blew it out harshly, and went on, and the colonel learned about the second phase of the fighting within the fort.

As the three told their stories, Greystone tried to imagine himself in their shoes, but he realized he couldn't. "If they got over the wall, how come they didn't just keep coming?"

"Washington, sir. And his gun." They pointed to the dump truck and the shattered gun mount. Greystone got up to examine it, and the three soldiers followed. After a while, he thanked them and left in search of Captain Cornwell. He found him sitting at the makeshift table in the mess tent, holding a cup of coffee and staring at some unseen thing far away. He saw the coffee urn and the cups, poured himself one, black, and sat down.

After what seemed like several minutes, Chris became aware of his CO. "Sir. Sorry, I didn't see you."

"It's okay. I've been thinking. After looking around, talking to the men, I don't have all the details ... no, by no means. But one thing seems clear: the battle last night turned on snap decisions made by young men never really trained to make exactly such decisions—privates, sergeants, young officers. Decisions that emerge from their character more than their training, but tuned—I think that's the word, yeah, tuned—by the men and leaders around them." Greystone cleared his throat and looked away from his subordinate. "Your decisions, yes, but more importantly, your ... your tuning ... yes, your tuning of this bunch—a motley crew too—looks to have been decisive, as I see it." Greystone drained his cup and rose. "I'm ..." He paused and cleared his throat again. "I was about to say I'm proud of you, but I've had nothing to do with making you who you are. More accurate to say I'm very glad to have you in my command, Captain. Anyway, I'll get out of your hair now."

Just as he turned to leave, Colonels Vanderpoole and Short came in, trailed by Major Gridley. Greystone caught the tail end of a remark from Colonel Short that sounded as if he was still negative on his lieutenant. His first, instantaneous, thought was, *How the hell can he be?* His second was that Short seemed to be echoing his own attitude of thirty-six hours earlier. His third was that a man's mind must be in a lockbox to not be opened by what he saw today. The last thought brought him up short. He'd been in his own box. He suddenly remembered a remark by the Corps Artillery commander when A battery had been given permission to make the run to Chu Song. He had taken it—erroneously, he realized—as complimentary of himself, as A Battery belonged to his battalion.

Greystone stood at the tent entrance as Captain Cornwell excused himself to escape two more colonels, and Vanderpoole and Short made themselves coffees. As they seated themselves, he went over to them and said to Colonel Short, "George, I just remembered something the Corps Artillery commander told me a couple of days ago—right after I assumed command, in fact." He paused, tapping his nose, and then went on. "Two things. First, specific to your lieutenant. Hanley, isn't it? Anyway, the commanding general received a letter from the air force praising the rescue operation and, specifically, your Lieutenant Hanley for his speed and heroism. And oh yeah, second. It seems it was Hanley who recognized a window of opportunity to get my battery to Chu Song and Hanley, and my battery CO who recommended they try for it. When Colonel Preston presented it to the CG, the general said Hanley and Cornwell were exactly the type of young officers the army needs. Thought you'd like to pass it on to your young man, especially given it looks like his conduct here was exemplary."

Short coughed, looked very taken aback, and finally replied, "Yes, of course. Of course! Thank you." Major Gridley had uttered no more than ten words since landing. He stared at his boss, and the rigid set of Short's features did not match his words. Gridley had been feeling an odd mixture of a sort of dreadful curiosity, fear, and envy: dreadful curiosity of what real combat was like, a wondering fear of what the true answer to the question "Would I hack it?" would be, and a kind of envy of those who now had been through the crucible and knew the answer. But what he saw in Short was different. That was jealousy. Envy and jealousy seem so close. But balancing Short's expression and his own feelings, he saw that jealousy is at the bottom, bitter, while envy is wishful.

Vanderpoole looked at Greystone and nodded with a flicker of a smile.

Arlen Washington awoke—or rather, he thought he did. Big Ma was looking down at him, smiling tenderly. Timmy Otis was sitting in her lap, her big melons framing his head. Timmy seemed to be sleeping, but he was smiling. Arlen wondered what the hell Timmy was doing in her lap. Timmy looked exactly like Timmy, but he was too small, like a little boy. Timmy had a spot on his forehead—not a hole, just a smudge—and so did Big Ma, in the same spot. *Ashes ... ash something. Timmy went to church with Big Ma? Man, that makes no sense at all.* Timmy had no business being in Big Ma's lap. It didn't make him feel angry, though, but kind of sad about something he couldn't identify and that didn't make any sense either.

Then a guy showed up. He was big and brawny and wore gold chains. He laughed at Arlen and handed him a set of car keys. He made a sweeping wave with his arm, and a brand-new shiny black Lincoln Town Car appeared. It was beautiful. He thought he didn't want it to be black, though. In the next moment, he was in the driver's seat, driving slowly, majestically, through his neighborhood. Big Ma and Timmy were standing on the sidewalk. He waved, but then shadowy black figures began to appear from side alleys and trash cans, ventilation grates, and manholes, crouching and running until they loomed all over the canvas of his mind. Big Ma and Timmy disappeared, swallowed up by the black figures.

He heard the distinctive sound of the minigun spinning up, and then the deafening roar of it firing from inside the car. He turned around, and the guy who'd given him the keys was smoking and laughing and firing the gun out a window. The shadowy figures were being ripped into bits of black confetti that flew away on a breeze. More and more appeared, and they were also shredded, and he saw Big Ma again, and she was shredded into colorful bits of confetti. He hit the brakes and turned to the guy, screaming for him to stop, but the guy just laughed, and the gun kept firing, and the guy's breath was hot on his face. He felt again the terrible mix of fear and anguish welling up. The guy had given him the car, but he realized he must have given the guy the gun or let him use it. Finally the gun fell silent except for the spinning of the barrels, which were smoking hot and then began to sizzle. It sounded exactly like the sizzle from a frying pan when Big Ma flung drops of water into it to test its heat.

The sizzling stopped, but the hot breath was still in his face, smelling like bacon, and something warm and wet was slapping his cheek. Arlen opened his eyes. The hot breath was coming from a small black nose. He jerked his head back, but there was nowhere to go. He was lying on a stretcher. The nose and hot breath belonged to the mutt Sparky. He'd never been this close to a dog before. His instant fear ebbed to amazement. The little mutt was licking him! Some words came back to him, "See? You're part of his pack now."

There was noise all around him, a great throbbing. It had been there all along, it seemed. Vaguely, he recognized the sounds of multiple helicopters. A face loomed over him, one he'd never seen before. He felt himself lifted. Sparky disappeared, the face moved aside and spoke. "Hang in there. You're on your way home, brother."

Arlen had been operated on and sewn back together. The anesthesia had worn off, he'd come semiconscious and moaned. His vitals had been checked and a morphine drip added. He'd drifted back to sleep and to dream. An earlier dream had terrified him. It was gone and half-forgotten, but its echoes lingered like a bad smell mixing in with different, even good, smells in a new mixed-up dream that induced both sweat and unconscious smiles. He was jawing with Shirtless and Vasquez and Stevie, and Newsome and Otis and Bert and Ricochet and others, and even officers and noncoms, them listening, asking, thanking, and

Jarvis patting him on the back. And in between these images, he saw images of Otis dead, Stevie dead, Newsome shot through, men jerking up and falling down, his hands frozen on the triggers, wanting to fire but unable to, fearing to hit the very men he wanted to protect, only to see them, again and again, jerk from the impact of bullets and fall away. In his dream, he searched for them. Where was Shirtless? T-Shirt? Ricochet? Bert? Vasquez? Where the fuck were they? Did they all die like Timmy? Like Rosie? In the darkness of his dream, it seemed he could find no one alive. He'd tried! He'd tried! he cried silently to the gods of dreams, but they ignored him.

Then it seemed he heard a familiar voice. It was almost shouting. The words became clearer: "I've got to get back to my men!"

Another voice said, "You've got to get your ass healed! Literally!"

"They're just flesh wounds!"

"Your boys are okay. They've been pulled back to An Khe. Resting and recuperating there. They're being taken care of."

"Not by me! They need me! The guys who're left, they need me. God, I need them. Got to debrief! Lessons to learn! Don't put some newbie who doesn't know shit from Shinola in charge! Just ... just give me a cane or a crutch and let me go back!"

"You've got a point, Ev. I'll make it happen, but if you don't quiet down and quit being disruptive, you'll cook your own goose. I'll get you out as soon as possible. They'll be glad to see the last of you here anyway."

"Yes sir! Promise?" the familiar voice said.

Arlen opened his eyes. There was someone standing over him, dressed in a flight suit. No, there were two of them—a white guy and a black guy. *What the hell?* he thought. *Where are the others?* He said, "You're not him."

"What's that?" Captain Eddie McLaughlin asked.

"You ain't ... boss?" The face had come into focus.

"It's me, Washington. How do you feel?" Eddie asked, chiding himself for again wishing it were Otis, not Washington.

"Shit's happening. I ... I gotta find them. All gone. They all gone! I ... Boss ... I tried!" Arlen's hand fluttered. "I told him, 'Stay down!' I couldn't shoot! Our guys still in the way. If only I could've. I tried! But they gone." Arlen raised his head, and then it fell back. "They're all over! I let 'em die! I tried!" He ran out of breath.

Eddie blinked several times, shaking his head in tiny jerks. He couldn't understand what Arlen had said and didn't know what to say. The black guy, younger, shorter, stepped closer. "Hey, Ace, man, you're okay. Man, they tell me first you MIA, then you dead, then you not dead. Man, I'm sure glad to see you. It's all cool now. You're gonna be okay. You're back, man. You're cool."

"Jaz? Jason?" Arlen asked. It was Jason, nodding and grinning. Arlen looked as if he recognized his friend but at the same time was horrified to see him. "Man, get out! Get out! The fuckers are coming. I can't shoot, man; I can't!"

"I heard you were in some deep shit, Washington," Eddie said, finding his voice. "It's over now. You're patched up. You're going to be okay, hear?"

Three beds down, Everett Rosen recognized the voice. He raised himself on his good elbow and called, "Washington? That you?"

Eddie looked over. "You know Airman Washington?"

Everett didn't reply to Eddie. He said, loudly, "Washington, you hear me?"

"Yeah. You, sir ... saw you on the wall. I stood up."

"That's right! That's right! I heard you! You didn't let 'em die, Washington. You didn't! I told you on the wall." He looked at Eddie. "Captain, you in his chain of command?"

"I guess. I was his pilot; he was my gunner. One of them."

Everett looked at the officer by his bed. "Well," he said, rising higher on his elbow with a grunt of pain from his buttock, "listen. Everyone I saw—my grunts, the redlegs, the engineers—they tried. Did their best. Did their jobs. More than that. But like I told you, Washington, everyone that lived through that lives thanks to you. You got that? Without him, we'd have been overrun. Simple as that!" He lay back. "Don't forget it. You hear me, Washington? Don't you forget it!"

Arlen heard. His body relaxed. He looked away from them. Eddie looked down and saw tears flowing. *Funny*, he thought. *Did Arlen change, or did I never really know my own men?*

Jason reached past the officer and grabbed Arlen's hand.

Arlen spoke again, softly. Eddie and Jason almost didn't catch it. "Keep the gun. I don't want it," he mumbled.

What in hell does he mean? Eddie wondered.

Jason squeezed Arlen's hand. He knew.

GLOSSARY

AC-47	Stands for "armed cargo aircraft, model 47." "C-47" was the military designation for the Douglas DC-3, manufactured from the mid-1930s through the late 1940s. When the air force turned some C-47s into gunships, they became AC-47s.
AK-47	Russian-developed rifle used worldwide by communist countries and nations and groups getting military aid from them. Like the M16, it can fire in fully automatic or semiautomatic modes. Very rugged and reliable.
air cav	Air cavalry: This group began with horse cavalry—essentially infantry mounted on horses for speed and mobility. Then came motorized cavalry—light tanks and vehicles replacing the horse. Then, in Vietnam, these were replaced with helicopters. These infantry units were necessarily more lightly armed, but they were highly maneuverable.
AN/PRC-6, 10, 25, 90	Typical portable tactical radios used in Vietnam. The PRC-6 and PRC-90 were handheld radios, the PRC-10 and PRC-25 were backpack radios.

AN/PVS-1	A first-generation night vision device, the AN/PVS-1 was a telescope that used internal electronics to amplify low ambient light, such as starlight, and was called a "starlight scope."
AO	Area of operations: Generally, an AO was a defined geographical area assigned to a unit. That unit was then responsible for the control of operations within its assigned AO.
Arc Light	A high-altitude saturation-bombing mission flown almost exclusively by B-52 strategic bombers. These raids were mainly used to target suspected enemy bunker, tunnel, and cave complexes
arty	Slang for "artillery."
ASAP	An abbreviation standing for "as soon as possible."
B-52	An eight-engined strategic jet bomber first flown in the 1950s and still in service.
battery	The principal unit of an artillery organization. A battery is typically commanded by a captain and includes four to six artillery pieces. The fictional Battery A, First Battalion, 115th Field Artillery had four guns: two eight-inch howitzers and two 175 mm guns.
C-130	A four-engine turboprop air force cargo aircraft designed in the mid-1950s and still in service. Designed to take off and land on short, unimproved runways and airstrips.
call sign	A call sign is an assigned radio identification for a unit or a particular position in a unit. "Green Granite" is the general call sign for Battery A, First Battalion, 115th Field Artillery in the story. In Vietnam, numbers were usually added to identify positions. The commander of a unit would typically be "Six"; thus, the commander of A Battery would be "Green Granite Six."

caltrop	A steel spike originally invented to cripple horses but also very effective against tires. It usually consists of four sharp steel spikes welded or twisted together so that when dropped, three of the spikes form a tripod and the fourth points upward.
CEP	Circular error probable: Any ballistic projectile, such as an arrow, bullet, shell, or missile, will deviate in flight to some degree from its theoretical trajectory owing to minute differences or inconsistencies in manufacture, variations of wind and temperature, and so forth. The CEP is a calculated maximum probable deviation from the calculated trajectory at any given distance.
CEV	Combat engineer vehicle. See "M728."
Chinook	Army CH-47 (CH for "cargo helicopter")—a medium-lift helicopter with two main rotors, one near the front of the helicopter and one near the rear. Variations of the Chinook are still in service.
claymore	The claymore mine was an antipersonnel mine used extensively in Vietnam as perimeter defense, for early warning, and in ambushes.
commo wire	A thin, black plastic-insulated two-strand steel wire originally used for telephone communications on the battlefield and for other electrical purposes requiring only a low current—such as the electrical detonation of explosives.
concentration	In this usage, a concentration is a precalculated target for artillery or mortars. The "target" is a specific map coordinate. It is given a simple designation, such as a letter and a number (e.g., Alpha One-Zero). The responsible battery precalculates the firing settings for each gun (usually four to six) so that when the concentration is fired, the shells from each gun will land in a predetermined pattern around the target point.
CP	Command post: the communications hub and the primary location for the commander of a battlefield unit.

det cord	Detonating cord: explosive rope, roughly one-fourth inch in diameter, used to link explosives one wishes to explode at the same time.
E&E	Escape and evasion: methods and tactics used to escape enemy detection and capture when caught behind enemy lines.
ETA	An abbreviation standing for "estimated time of arrival."
fire base	Since there were no front lines in Vietnam (nor are there in most counter-guerrilla or similar types of warfare), units traditionally situated behind friendly lines had to be self-defending, so they had to have dug in, fortified bases that provided a 360-degree defense. When artillery units had to build such a base, it was called a fire base, since they were sources of fire support. Usually they were reinforced with infantry to aid in defense.
fire in the hole	The cry "Fire in the hole," repeated three times, was used to warn soldiers of an impending intentional explosion.
flechette	A flechette is a small steel dart about an inch long. Hundreds can be packed into an artillery or other gun shell, effectively turning the gun into a large short- or long-range shotgun.
Gatling gun	A machine gun with a revolving cluster of barrels, each firing once per revolution. Originally designed by Richard Gatling in 1867, the barrels were rotated by a hand crank. The same concept is employed by a variety of modern machine guns and even cannons today. Small-caliber gatling guns are called miniguns.
GI	Government issue: the abbreviation was originally a slang term for a soldier first used in World War II.
grunt	A slang term for "infantryman."

gunship	Gunships came in two flavors: helicopter gunships and fixed-wing gunships. A helicopter gunship is a helicopter specifically designed or configured to provide fire support to ground troops (typically rocket, missile, and machine gun fire) as opposed to those designed to carry troops and cargo. A fixed-wing gunship is basically a cargo plane specifically configured to provide fire support to ground troops. While it is slower and more vulnerable than fast jet fighter-bombers, it can carry vastly more ammunition and stay in support of a battle much longer.
HEP	High-explosive plastic: This type of cannon shell was designed for demolition. When the shell strikes a target, the explosive content of the shell spreads (like a ball of Silly Putty might) over an area of the target surface before exploding, creating a shock wave that will tend to knock an entire wall down rather than just blow a hole in it.
hooch	A slang term in Vietnam for any kind of living quarters for troops or natives.
howitzer	Traditionally, there were three types of artillery: mortars, howitzers, and guns (or cannons). The mortar was designed to lob shells over high walls, such as castles and forts, or into defensive trenches. The modern mortar has become so light weight that it is used by infantry units and is no longer artillery. The cannon, or gun, was designed for longer range and more direct fire, such as battering a fort's walls or enemy troop formations, firing shells with a longer, flatter trajectory. The howitzer was designed to lob shells not over high walls but into trenches and over berms. So mortar fire can be thought of as being like a basketball throw, howitzer fire like an outfielder's pitch to second base, and cannon fire like a pitcher's fastball.
KIA	An abbreviation standing for "killed in action."
klick	A slang term for "kilometer" (one thousand meters, or roughly thirty-three hundred feet or 0.6 miles).

LAW	Light assault weapon: In Vietnam, the LAW was the American equivalent to the RPG, with a roughly equivalent effectiveness against tanks, bunkers, and exposed troops. The main difference from the RPG was that the LAW was a throwaway weapon. The rocket was packaged inside the launch tube. Once the rocket was fired, the tube was thrown away.
loiter box	For aircraft in a combat zone, a loiter box was a defined area that was or would be free of other aircraft and outside the trajectories of artillery, mortars, or other friendly weapons that might pose a hazard.
LT	An abbreviation for "lieutenant" used as a slang form of shorthand address to lieutenants. Pronounced "El-tee."
M16	Principal rifle used by American forces in Vietnam. The M16 can be fired in semiautomatic (one shot for each pull on the trigger) or automatic (firing roughly seven hundred rounds a minute as long as the trigger is squeezed, taking less than two seconds to empty a twenty-round magazine) modes.
M60	Principle light machine gun used by American infantry units in Vietnam. The M60 is belt-fed, meaning ammunition is not fed to it from a magazine but from belts, which can contain many more rounds than a magazine. M60s can be fired using a bipod or a tripod to steady the aim and accuracy. They fire about six hundred rounds a minute.
M79	In Vietnam, usually one or two men per rifle squad were armed with an M79 rather than a rifle. This weapon looks like a fat sawed-off single-shot shotgun and fires a 40 mm grenade accurately to almost four hundred yards. The grenades it fires are lethal to exposed troops within ten to fifteen yards of where they explode.
mad minute	The mad minute was a practice of some infantry units in which, usually early in the morning, all troops in a defensive position would fire all weapons to, presumably, surprise, kill, or intimidate any lurking enemy.

military time	Military time is based on the twenty-four-hour day. There is no a.m. or p.m. Hours and minutes are lumped together in a single number. 11:00 a.m. would be 1100 or "eleven hundred," and 11:00 p.m. would be 2300, or "twenty-three hundred." 11:25 p.m. would be 2325, or "twenty-three twenty-five hours."
minigun	A version of a gatling gun. See "Gatling gun."
napalm	A form of gasoline thickened into a jelly, usually by a kind of soap. When a napalm bomb explodes, it ignites and scatters the jellied fuel, which sticks to whatever it touches.
NCO	Noncommissioned officer. All ranks above the equivalent of private (army or marine corps) or airman (air force) that are not commissioned officers (Lieutenant through General).
NVA	North Vietnamese Army: North Vietnamese army units sent to South Vietnam, as opposed to the Vietcong, which were made up of native South Vietnamese fighting on the communist side.
OP	Observation post: OPs are typically established outside a defensive position to provide early warning of enemy approach.
out	In radio etiquette, "out" means "This conversation is ended."
over	In radio etiquette, "over" means "I have finished speaking; I am waiting on your reply."
perimeter	See "fire base." The perimeter of a fire base would be the line on the ground described by the defensive positions.
PFC	Private first class: A rank one step above the lowest army enlisted rank of private.
prick-	A slang term for the abbreviation PRC. A "prick-25" was an AN/PRC-25 model tactical radio.
punji stake	A simple, but often deadly, booby trap used by the Vietcong. It usually consisted of a sharpened bamboo spike hidden in the grass and often smeared with excrement.

push	A slang term for a radio frequency. A radio operator might say, "You can contact me on this push."
R&R	Rest and recreation: Soldiers typically were allowed a period of R&R, usually two weeks, once during their one-year tour in Vietnam. R&R could be taken anywhere from Bangkok to Hong Kong, Japan, Hawaii, or even stateside.
RDF	Radio direction finder: This technology was used before the launch of GPS. It determined the direction from an airplane to a radio station at a known location. By using two RDFs tuned to different radio stations, the navigator of an aircraft could determine its location.
redlegs	A term for soldiers in the army artillery branch, taken from the red stripes on the dress uniforms.
RJ	An abbreviation standing for "road junction."
roger	In radio etiquette, "roger" means, "I understand what you just said."
RPG-7	A Russian-designed weapon that fires a rocket-propelled antitank grenade. The launcher is lightweight, man-portable, and fired from the shoulder. It is essentially a tube with a sight and a trigger. The rocket grenade is loaded into the front of the tube. The soldier aims the tube at the target. Squeezing the triggers fires the rocket. The RPG warhead could penetrate most tanks of the day and destroy bunkers. Shrapnel from the warhead made it effective against exposed troops.
Skyraider	A single-engine propeller-driven fighter-bomber developed at the end of World War II, used extensively in the Korean and Vietnam wars.
SOP	An abbreviation standing for "standard operating procedure."
starlight scope	See "AN/PVS-1."

task force	A task force was a temporary grouping of different units or parts of units tailored for a specific and usually temporary mission and put under the temporary command of a single leader.
thunder run	A thunder run was a tactic of rapidly moving a unit down a road, banking on speed to surprise and get past any enemy before they could react, rather than moving slower and using caution and reconnaissance forces to screen and protect the movement.
UH-1 Huey	The Bell UH-1 was the principal helicopter used in the Vietnam War. It was one of the first helicopters powered by a turbine instead of a piston engine and was relatively fast, agile, and rugged.
VC	Vietcong: indigenous guerrilla forces in South Vietnam.
WIA	An abbreviation standing for "wounded in action."
wilco	In radio etiquette, "wilco" means "I understand what you're telling me to do, and I will comply."
Zulu	When "Zulu" is attached to a military time, the time refers to Greenwich Mean Time (i.e., the actual time in Greenwich, England). Thus, if it is 1200Z (i.e., noon) in Greenwich, England, it is 1900 (7:00 p.m.) local in Saigon (now Ho Chi Minh City) The military assign a letter to each time zone. Vietnam is seven hours ahead of Greenwich; thus 1200Z is equal to 1900G.